EUGENE IZZI has live

He is the accla

BY THE SAME AUTHOR

Bad Guys
The Booster
The Eighth Victim
Invasions
King of the Hustlers
The Prime Roll
Prowlers
The Take
Tony's Justice
Tribal Secrets
Safe Harbour
Players

PLAYERS

Eugene Izzi

ARROW

Published by Arrow Books in 1996

1 3 5 7 9 10 8 6 4 2

First published in the United Kingdom by
Arrow Books Limited
20 Vauxhall Bridge Road, London, SW1V 2SA

Random House Australia (Pty) Limited
20 Alfred Street, Milsons Point, Sydney,
New South Wales 2061, Australia

Random House New Zealand Limited
18 Poland Road, Glenfield
Auckland 10, New Zealand

Random House South Africa (Pty) Limited
PO Box 337, Bergvlei, South Africa

Random House UK Limited Red. No. 954009

A CIP catalogue record for this book is available from the British Library

Papers used by Random House UK Limited are natural, recyclable products made from wood grown in sustainable forests. The manufacturing process conform to the environmental regulations of the country of origin.

ISBN 0 09 920871 7

Typeset by SX Composing, Rayleigh, Essex
Printed and bound in Great Britain by
BPC Paperbacks Ltd,
A member of The British Printing Company Ltd

For Esther Newberg

The last time that Mute could remember being on his knees, it had been due to his propensity to overindulge in alcohol. He'd done a lot of that in his life and still sometimes did; Mute truly liked his beer. Outside of those times, though, he had to figure it to be fifteen, twenty years since he'd done it, been on his knees, with his hands folded in front of him and his eyes closed, Mute's lips moving near-silently, in prayer.

But he was doing it now, praying – or trying to – for help.

He didn't know if God was listening, didn't know if God even gave a shit about him anymore. As a matter of fact, Mute wasn't even sure if he himself believed in some God floating up there in heaven, but it was worth a shot, no matter how embarrassing it was. No matter how stupid he felt, talking to someone he couldn't see.

Grandma had made him do this constantly, and it had, for a time at least, always made him feel better.

'God,' Mute whispered, 'it's been a while.'

How true.

Mute decided that he had to have been in high school the last time he'd said a prayer, before he'd decided that he didn't need God, would be better off on his own without any divine intervention in his life. Some people, Mute knew – and had seen with his own two eyes – could take that religious stuff way too seriously, use it to screw things up for themselves and everyone else around them.

His grandma had been like that, had been one of those people who took their religious beliefs to extremes. She'd take Mute to church every Saturday night and force him into that little booth where he had to make his confession. He'd come out and Grandma would tell him, whispering, 'Now say your penance, and then pray that you die right now, tonight! That you get hit by a bus on the way home!' If that should happen, Mute's grandma believed, he would go straight to heaven for all eternity.

Grandma would tell him this, and her eyes would be shining, wildly. She wouldn't push him into the path of a bus, but she wouldn't go out of her way to help him out, either. Every Saturday, Mute had to listen to such shit. The first few times, it had scared him something terrible, the thought that his grandmother truly wanted him to die. But after that he'd figured out that - like everything else his grandma told him – it was just some more of her bullshit to let into one ear and out of the other, and Mute was good at that. If he'd been good at anything back in those days, with the exception of jerking off. He'd been on a professional level when it came to that.

On Sundays Grandma would take him to Mass, wake him before the sun came up. Make him dress in his one blue hand-me-down suit, and she'd tie his tie for him, push it up too tight against his Adam's apple. 'What are you going to pray for?'

'To be made handsome,' Mute would say, and he didn't blame God when it never worked out that way. Grandma would tell him that he just hadn't prayed hard enough for God to answer him, and Mute had believed that for a number of years, until he'd found out that doctors, not God, were the entities that could remove at least part of his disfigurement. He hadn't asked God for much in the intervening years, knowing from past, painful experience that he wasn't a good enough Christian, that he couldn't pray hard enough for his prayers to be answered.

He tried it now, though, tried praying hard enough.

'God, can you hear me?' Mute could feel the heels of his shoes touching the flimsy door behind him. His elbows were resting on hard plastic. He didn't think he could do this for very long if he had to bow his head. His voice was garbled; it was the way he spoke. Mush-mouth, they'd called him, back in school. Among others things. Until he'd turned sixteen and gotten his size, then nobody ever made fun of him again without having to pay for the luxury. It hadn't taken them long to learn.

'It's me, Mut – uh – Michael Buffo.'

Did God know that everyone called him Mute? He had to, shit, He was supposed to know everything. Mute opened his eyes for a second and stared toward the ceiling quizzically.

He shut them again real quick, and squeezed his hands together.

Did God know what you were *thinking*? Jesus Christ, he hoped not. Mute thought that God was only supposed to know what it was that you said. It had been so long . . .

Or then again, maybe it hadn't been. He *did* remember praying on the bus that was taking him to Stateville penitentiary. Fat lot of good prayer had done him then.

Mute forced such blasphemous thoughts out of his mind, and concentrated. He snuck a quick look at his watch, then folded his hands again, fingers now pointed heavenward. Behind him, outside the door, he could hear people moving around. Someone pulled twice at Mute's door before deciding that it had been locked from the inside. He had to make this quick. He had less than ten minutes for his prayer to reach heaven and get answered, one way or another.

'Look, God, I know that I've screwed up. I know that I've made a lot of mistakes, and I know that I ain't been praying a lot lately. But I need your help now, I'm in trouble, bad.' He paused to make sure that he hadn't been whispering too loudly. Nobody behind him could be allowed to hear what he was doing, because, Mute knew, if they did, they'd all laugh at him. And when people laughed at Mute, Mute got violent. Which put him in a situation, because if they laughed at what he was doing, he couldn't blame them, he'd have done the same thing just a couple of minutes ago, himself. But things had changed now. Now, he needed a miracle.

'Help me, God, please, I'm fuc – I'm begging you, God, help me out, just this once. I'll change my ways, I'll straighten out if you help me. No more chasing married women, no more drinking all night, no more gambling. I really mean *that* one, God, I swear to you, no more gambling.'

Outside the room, a horn began to blow. Mute knew the guy who'd be playing it, fingers flying over brass keys. His knees were really beginning to hurt. Some other son of a bitch pulled on the door again.

'What the hell are you doing in there?'

Mute made a face of displeasure and twisted his head toward his shoulder. 'I'll be out in a minute,' Mute said, in his normal tone of voice, then turned forward and hurriedly began to whisper again, before he got in trouble.

'See, God? I didn't even get mad at that asshole, I won't say nothing to him when I get out of here, either. I'm changing already, because I know I'll get your help.' Mute began to rise, then fell quickly back to his knees, almost forgetting to ask for what he'd come in here to seek.

'Please God, it's the tenth and last race coming up, and I'm already almost broke. Please let Sabi's Skipper win this race.'

Mute made a fast sign of the cross then stood, wiped at the dust on his pants.

Someone pulled on the door, hard, and a loud voice called out, not pleased.

'What the fuck are you doing in there? Come on out of there, right now!'

Mute unlocked the toilet stall, and stepped out into the bathroom proper. There was a security guard standing there in his dark blue uniform, a flashlight where the gun should be, staring at him, sternly. He looked pointedly past Mute, seemed surprised that he was alone. Looked back at Mute and tried not to let his displeasure show on his face. Behind the guard there were a dozen urinals, men standing with their backs turned at every one. There were lines to get into the three other stalls.

'What were you doing in there, buddy?' Now, having a close-up view of what Mute looked like, the guard was trying to be friendly. A lot of people did that, pretended to have a relationship with him, either that or they looked away. Mute could see people shooting fast glances at him as he stood in the stall doorway, then looking quickly away. Sometimes some ignorant bastard would openly glare at him, but such times were rare.

They didn't call him Mute for nothing. It was short for mutant. He'd picked the name up at Stateville penitentiary, before the operations, doing six years on a plea-bargain that had begun as attempted murder.

The guard said, 'What were you doing in there?' and Mute looked at him like he was stupid.

'I dropped a contact.'

It satisfied the guy. He said, 'All right. Sorry. I got a couple of complaints, guys waiting to piss, you know how it is.'

'What do you mean, I know how it is, I don't know how nothing is. What the fuck are you talking about, you get paid to hassle people?'

'Hey, pal,' the guard said, holding his hands up, palms out. 'What am I supposed to think some guy's on his knees in a racetrack toilet? All I could see was the bottom of your shoes. For all I know, someone else was sitting on the shitter.'

Mute understood then, what the guy was thinking. He tightened his muscles under his shortsleeve shirt, squared his large shoulders, rotated his neck on those shoulders, and stuck out his chin. He knew the effect it had on people when he did that, all together. When he spoke it was in the same sort of voice that he'd used when he prayed; a soft gentle whisper, but now it was filled with malice.

'You thought I was in there sucking a *dick*? Just 'cause I'm physically handicapped, you think I'm a faggot, too?'

'Hey, now, wait a minute, nobody said no such thing – '

'I got lawyers on call to take care of people like you. They get their hooks in you, this place'll be called Buffoland instead of Balmoral Park.'

The guy, he was getting his nerve back. Mute kept his muscles tight, knew how impressive they were. Large arms bulging, blue veins prominent. Grandma used to say that it was the way that God had compensated, giving her Michael a superb athlete's body in order to square the scales for His making her little boy so incredibly damned ugly.

The guard was looking past Mute's face now, though, little bald-headed bastard in his playing-cop uniform, getting his balls together and standing up for himself. Rent-a-cops loved to think that they could get away with pushing you around.

'You was on your *knees*, mister, with the stall door closed. Who could see your face?' He stood there with a tell-that-to-your-lawyer look on his face, the dolt, acting smug.

Mute said, 'I got about three minutes to post, Kojak, you gonna step aside so I can go and watch my horse?' The guard moved out of his way and Mute strutted past him, his head held high.

He had learned long ago to ignore the stares of strangers, knew that it was the only way to ensure that they couldn't hurt him, but now they thought they had a legitimate reason to stare, and they did so, looking at him openly. He looked straight ahead, as if they weren't there. If they'd seen him fifteen years ago, they'd have looked at him now as if he was Robert Redford.

The guard, trying to make up to him, said, 'Party's over, folks, let's head back to the windows,' and Mute ignored this, too, didn't even nod his head in acknowledgement.

Mute stood at the third-floor window that looked down upon the track itself, staring out at the gathering horses as the nags were called to post. He liked to stand there, at just that spot, and watch the horses run, because he could see his reflection in the glass before him. He never looked above the neck, tried not to, anyway. It spoiled the fun for him, the sight of that magnificent body. It was dark now, at the end of the afternoon card, daylight savings time in effect for a couple of weeks, and Mute couldn't get used to it. He liked standing here by the window better, though, when it was dark outside. He could see himself as big as life, look at the body that he had.

Mute wore a size fifty-two jacket, and had a thirty-eight inch waist. Wide, powerful shoulders tapered down to slim hips that carried no extra fat. He wore shortsleeve shirts until it was far too cold for them, and he always stood with his shoulders back and his chest pushed out, knowing from experience that advertising paid. His neck bulged with muscles, and he twisted his head often. A lot of times the back of him was the first thing women saw.

He'd look up and see some asshole staring at him in the glass, and Mute would hold their gaze, and they'd look away real fast. Sneaking a peek at the freak, until Godzilla caught them at it. Sometimes he'd turn and glare, or take a few steps toward the person who had offended him, but most of the time he ignored it, it wasn't worth his trouble. Most of the time, since he'd gotten past thirty and had gotten out of jail, since he'd discovered the joys of sexual release with varied women, it didn't much bother him, unless they said something.

Except when little kids broke into tears. That always bothered Mute, even to this day. Not that it happened often anymore. Today, that was a rarity.

His head had been huge before the doctors operated, and it was still overly large, about the size of a head-and-a-half, with slight bulges on the forehead that made him look like an ape. At one time, those bulges had been twice as wide as they were today. He still had extremely flat cheekbones, and a chin that stuck far out, a steamshovel jaw nearly as wide as his head itself. It had been sculpted that way, rebuilt from scratch, and Mute had been released on parole before the doctors could finish the job they'd begun. The top half of his face was nearly a perfect square, his eyes walled, his nose flat. For most of his life he had looked like a deformed deep sea fish, stuck into the neck of a professional wrestler. When he'd been a full-time thief it had been a real bitch, especially when cops were questioning witnesses, asking them for descriptions. Line-ups back then had been, as far as he was concerned, unconstitutional.

They'd worked on him in a series of operations that had freed his tongue so that people could usually understand him when he spoke, and they'd carved down the bones in his head, had removed most of the tumors, but still and all, Mute was ugly, and he was, for the most part, shunned. The scars that they'd left didn't bother him; he thought that they gave him character.

Not that his looks always worked to his disadvantage. His hair was jet black and extremely rich and thick – another sign of celestial compensation – and he wore it long, combed it straight back. With the oversized head, he thought that he looked like a lion. He carried himself with dignity, his face without expression, and when he was in the presence of strangers he almost always stayed within himself. At the gym, he would work out alone, looking away from the women, never eyeing them, never ogling them, never giving them any reason to think he was a pervert. If he had the need to speak to one of them he would always do so with his eyes cast downward, Mute looking at his feet, speaking in a tone of voice that made it clear that he knew what he was.

He was amazed at how often he scored with that attitude. They would want to mother him, or would be attracted to his body, housewives tightening up the cellulite, having a cheap affair with the partially deformed but incredibly muscular hospital afternoon-shift worker. And if there wasn't a wedding ring on the woman's left hand, Mute would leave them alone. He got off on the idea of fucking somebody else's woman almost as much as he enjoyed the sex acts themselves.

One of the housewives had even told him that their affair was like that TV show, 'Beauty and the Beast'. Mute had watched a rerun one time, just out of curiosity, and had been angry at what he'd seen. He wasn't near as ugly as the guy on that show, and the broad who'd seen them as being so romantic wasn't by any leap of imagination as fine as Linda Hamilton.

Mute now felt strange, calm, relaxed, a little spiritual. Nostalgic, too, feeling the sense of tranquility that he'd once gotten from praying in church when he was a young boy.

Was there a God? He sure hoped there was. And that he'd prayed hard enough this time, that God would hear his prayer.

Now the horses were all lined up behind the pace car, and Mute knew that they would be off in a matter of seconds. Friday had been payday, and here it was Sunday, and his last two hundred dollars had been bet on Sabi's Skipper, to win. He made a good buck at the hospital, and he was constantly hustling on the side, but still, blowing two grand in one night, as he had tonight, was more than he could afford, what with the rent on his apartment and half a dozen fake address drops and God only knew how many other bills due tomorrow. He needed the help of a higher power. Had the Lord heard his prayer?

Mute held his tickets tightly in his fist, looking past himself through the well-cleaned glass, sucked on his lower lip for a second then reached into his shirt pocket and fumbled out a cigarette. He did not realize that he was bouncing up and down on his toes, like an excited child. Muttered encouragements were coming out of his mouth even before the horses left the gate, in a rhythm of his own, Mute cheering Sabi on as he lit the filtered cigarette. It was part of his racetrack ritual; he would light a lucky smoke just before the start of every race.

He didn't see the people behind him now, elbowing each other and pointing at him furtively, smiling at their companions and making fun of him behind his back. Mute was moving his head up and down, the motion growing faster as the race progressed.

He was used to people feeling superior to him, sometimes even snickering as he passed them on the street. As long as they didn't have the balls to do it to his face, he figured that there wasn't much he could do to make them stop. He did what he could to stay away from them, though; he never ate in fancy restaurants, and he never went into a bar where the model-types hung out. He had a history of violence, and if he had too many more arrests for it, the judges might stop feeling sorry for him, and send him away again. He'd done one term in the pen, and he didn't want to go back. He'd wasted a big part of his twenties on the inside.

As the horses turned on to the stretch and began to race for the wire, Mute began to cheer for Sabi's Skipper, neither realizing nor caring that he was shouting at the top of his voice. Sabi was in fourth place but coming on strong, going wide and trotting his ass off, his jockey whipping his ass, bringing him out across and passing the third horse, the second . . .

When Sabi's Skipper crossed the finish line first, Mute jumped in the air with joy.

Ben Morer walked hurriedly toward the near South Side bar, his hands deep in the oversized pockets of his suit jacket, the collar turned up against the mid-November cold. Chicago had caught some Indian summer these last few days, but still, at night, it could get pretty nippy. He didn't mind it much; the weather matched his mood. Fall always depressed him, and this year, for good reason, that depression was worse than usual.

He'd had to park a block-and-a-half away because both sides of the street were crowded with cars, a lot of them new, most of them foreign. There were some new Cadillacs and Lincolns and Chryslers at the curb, though, the big cars bumper to bumper, some of them in there tight. Ben could see that some of the cars were parked right up against the high concrete curbs, had scrape marks on the sides, down low. In the morning, when the owners sobered up, they'd be mad, he knew, thinking someone had sideswiped them. Although the parking meters on the sidewalks were all showing red flags, there wasn't a single parking sticker on any of the car windows.

Ben drove a seven-year-old Eldorado that he wasn't proud of, but it was all that he could afford right now, and it wasn't his way to complain. He'd been on top at various times in his life, and he'd been on the bottom, too. In the middle, where he was right now, was better than being dead. Better, too, than being in jail. He'd had enough of that to last him.

The He Ain't Here bar was in the middle of the next block, and Ben spotted the three young white kids leaning against the wall of the building on the corner too late to be able to cross the street without looking like a coward. They were staring at him, half-smirking, the way they did these days, making fun of you without knowing a single thing about you.

Ben didn't care for it when people made fun of him. Plenty of serious people in Chicago didn't dare try it, even when he wasn't around. He had a reputation as a serious man, and things got back to you when people wanted to be your friend.

Ben stared at the kids, his face impassive. He knew that to look away would be weak, and they would smell it if they knew how, would jump right on it, and he didn't need that headache, he had enough of them tonight. A doctor's appointment in the morning because of the sourness in his chest; a woman at home always giving him shit; guys owing him money and him having to come looking for them; all things he didn't need, like he didn't need this now - three punks giving him the jailyard stare. Punks who weren't old enough to have seen anything heavier than the inside of more than maybe some district lock-up, acting like they were lifers leaning against the bleachers in the big yard.

One of them nodded at Ben, as he began to cross the street.

'How you doin' man?' the kid said.

Ben looked at the kid, narrowing his eyes a little. He did not bother to reply. The kid pushed himself off the wall and his buddies stood close behind him, three kids in leather jackets at night in a tough neighborhood, looking at a man they didn't know, seeing him as sport, or maybe worse.

Ben knew what they'd be looking at: a tall slender man they'd see as middle-aged or old, with a decent if baggy suit on his back, a good watch on his wrist, and money in his pocket. Ben's shoes had cost more than all three of those leather jackets combined. They thought he'd be an easy mark, now waiting for him to pass.

He had to look them over and make his decision quickly, Ben knew. If he judged them too lightly, he could die. If he judged too harshly, they could die.

There were kids this age in this city, he knew, who would be packing automatic weapons, Uzis and Aks and mini-Macs with extended clips. Twelve or thirteen thousand people a year were shot in Chicago. Only seven or eight hundred of them would die. Up this close, mere feet from each other, Ben figured that if they had firepower, he'd be a murder statistic.

Still, he hesitated. He was getting on in years. Twenty years ago he'd be doing battle with them right now, only it wasn't twenty years ago, it was today, and he might be dying. When you looked mortality in the face, your lifelong convictions often changed.

Ben stopped in the middle of the street and looked at them without much emotion, as if staring at some artwork that he couldn't figure out. His feet were slightly apart, his head down into his collar, but his eyes were blazing out at them. Even bored, Ben had the look.

He slowly took his left hand out of his pocket, the hand holding a pack of cigarettes, and he shook one out as he watched. He put the pack back in his pocket, took a lighter out and lit the smoke without taking his eyes off the punks. He dropped the lighter back in his pocket and left the hand inside, too, Ben turning his head so that the smoke wouldn't get in his eyes. He nodded, slowly, three times, as if he had them figured out. He sure hoped that he did. For their sakes as well as his own.

'I said, how you doing, man!' the lead punk said. His face was twisted in anger, either real or feigned. Ben couldn't tell.

They were young, none of them looked to be out of his teens. Too young to have learned many tricks, but old enough to have killed, maybe more than once. The kid with the big mouth stood right on the corner, and his two partners stood on either side of him, slightly behind him, their hands out by their sides. Ben saw six hands balled into fists, which told him that they were amateurs, that they weren't carrying weapons. If they had them, they'd be showing them. Bad complexions and bad attitudes, ugly punks with distorted world views. They'd hung around with each other long enough and had mugged enough people to develop the mistaken impression that they were real tough guys.

They stood like that for a second, in the center of the soft glow of the street light. Sizing each other up, Ben taking drags off the cigarette while the kid at the head of the pack began to smile widely. There were no headlights coming up the dark streets, no lights shone in any of the windows. No one would be coming out of the single tavern on the block; Ben knew the crowd inside, they'd be in there now until closing.

'You deaf or just stupid?' The kid stepped off the curb, down into the street. He stopped there, though, did not move toward Ben. Ben decided that it was time to answer his question.

'You've seen what was in my left pocket. If I pull out what's in my right, I'm gonna use it, three times.' His voice was soft and low, Ben trying to appear amused. They didn't have to know that his heart was madly pounding. He'd had experience in hiding his feelings, though, Ben doing it and doing it well since before any of them were born.

The kid's smile faltered, and Ben spoke before he could collect himself.

'I'm not gonna count to three, I'm not gonna play any fucking games with you punks. I'm gonna turn my back so you can have a sporting chance. If I don't hear feet running away from me, real fast, I'm gonna draw and turn and I'm going to blow your fucking heads off.' Without hesitation, Ben turned his back on the punks. It was a sign of his disdain for them as well as their opportunity to run. He would never have turned his back on a man, or anyone he respected.

He heard feet, moving fast, moving away from him, and he turned. Saw the three of them racing toward the alley, glancing over their shoulders. He shook his head as they turned into the alley, eased the hammer down on the .32 automatic he was holding in his right hand, inside his pocket. He flicked the safety back on with his thumb, took his hand out and flexed his shaking fingers, trying to control his breathing before he headed into the bar.

It hurt when he breathed in deeply; a yawn, to Ben, was agony. He'd been spitting up spots of blood along with his usual morning garbage, and he'd gone in and taken the tests, would get the results tomorrow.

'Bring your wife, Mr Morer,' the doctor had said to him, over the telephone, last Friday. And he'd had to live with that all weekend, wondering what that meant.

In the frame of mind he was in, he hadn't been bluffing the kids, although he was relieved that they'd taken the smart way out. If he'd shot them he would have had to run away, and there were two guys in the He Ain't Here who owed Ben a sum of money that he believed he'd soon be needing.

He waited, in the middle of the street, until he was sure that the punks weren't coming back, then Ben put his head down once again and stepped up on to the curb, heading for the bar, where it would at least be warm.

Mute bought a drink for the woman who'd approached him at the track in some weird tavern in one of the South suburbs, near Balmoral racetrack, a place that she said she knew and said was pretty quiet. It was that and more; Mute was used to biker bars. In here, soft lights shone down from tracks, casting the joint in shadows. Dance music from the forties played on the jukebox. Sunday night and the place was jumping, if you could describe anything that people this age did to be jumping.

It was mostly middle-aged folks, people in their forties and fifties, who barely glanced at them when they walked in, some of them even nodding at them, smiling as they walked to the two empty seats over in the corner, next to the waitress's station. A lot of them were on the dance floor, and all of them were well dressed. Plenty of nice new cars were sitting out in the parking lot. He could enjoy himself in here today, but ten years ago, it would have been different. Mute would have been very careful about what he said and did in a place like this. This sort of tavern would have had a lot of possibilities; if he were ten years younger, he might even be coming back to see if he could run a score on any of them. There was money to be made off polite, older people, the type he used to scam when he'd been a runaway kid.

He told MaryAnn about that now, sitting in the old-timers' bar in some town called Steger, appreciating her more and more, her body language and the way she held her skinny white cigarettes when she spoke; between the very tips of her fingers, real feminine-like, as women used to hold them before someone wrote in some magazine that they were men and they believed it.

'I'd stand on the street corners, staring up into their eyes, too ugly for the perverted ones to want to take me home and screw me, stand there with my hand out, begging for enough money for the operation.'

'That's *terrible*,' MaryAnn said, in a voice that told Mute that she didn't really think it was. She was smiling at him, too, one hand on his arm. The other was on his knee. Mute liked the possibilities in this place more and more.

'I couldn't do that shit no more, now, mind you. I learned not to hurt older people. Generally only play with the horses.' Mute smiled at her, looked her up and down. 'Among other things.' His smile grew wider.

'But I'm still ugly enough to pull it off, I'd bet. Like that black guy that hangs around the sports stadiums, the guy that's all burned up real bad, all the time begging? You know about him? I hear he pulls in a ton of money every year. And you know what?' Mute leaned forward, and when he spoke, his tone was filled with awe.

'There's doctors want to fix that son of a bitch for *free*! He keeps walking out of the hospital every time they try to help him. He don't want their help, he don't want to look normal.

'Me, when I got the chance, man, I *jumped* at those operations. And I was a lot uglier than he ever dreamed about being.'

MaryAnn said, 'Come *on*, it's not like you're de*form*ed.'

'I had a whole bunch of operations, I still talk funny, in case you didn't notice. The scars, the lumps, they're a part of me, what I am. You should have seen me before I got fixed up, though, Jee-zus, but I was ugly.' Mute said this proudly, as if his looks set him apart from the pack. 'It's what's inside that counts, that's my philosophy today.'

'So what do you do when you're not winning millions at the racetrack?'

'Millions, don't I wish.' Mute took a drink of his Bourbon and Coke, twirled the glass as he held the liquor in his mouth. He swallowed it, felt it blast into his belly like a blowtorch. The first one of the day was always the best for Mute, and he hadn't even had a beer all day long. He knew he'd be going to the track, and he never drank when he was working. He put the glass back down on the coaster, and lit a filter cigarette. The alcohol had dulled the guilt he felt about breaking his promise to God so soon. Besides, he wasn't getting laid yet, just having a drink; he wasn't even drunk. God would forgive Mute; He always had before.

'It was only a couple of bucks,' he said modestly, Mute being coy.

'More like a couple *thousand*.' MaryAnn seemed impressed, even though the engagement ring on her finger had to be worth two or three times more than the six grand he'd won on Balmoral's tenth race. The engagement ring that was right behind the thick gold wedding band.

'I work at South Chicago Community, in the lab on afternoons,' he told her. 'Three to eleven, leaves my days and nights open, that's the way I like it.'

'My husband hates it when he has time off. Even when he's home, he brings it with him, tons of work in a briefcase, so he can go in his den and hide all night.'

MaryAnn put more than a hint of deprecation in her tone.

'He's a lawyer, but now he's stuck his nose into *my* work, like he's going to straighten everything out and the place'll make millions. He never does anything in that house at night, if you catch my drift, Michael.'

Women never spoke to him unless they were hitting on him. Mute had known she was coming on to him as soon as she'd opened her mouth, back at the racetrack, the pretty woman who looked to be in her early thirties, a little younger than Mute. MaryAnn had been standing next to the payout window, standing there smiling widely at him, wearing a pair of extremely tight blue jeans and a leather jacket.

She'd told him she liked his style, how he didn't care what anyone thought. She could tell that by the way he'd been jumping around and howling when he won the last race on the afternoon card.

'A lot of guys, you know, they'd be standing there trying to act cool.'

'How could I ever look cool?' Mute had told her, smiling, though, so she'd know that he was only kidding and wasn't feeling sorry for himself.

She was wearing those tight jeans, which were tucked into cowboy boots, and now that the jacket was hanging over the barstool, he could see that she was wearing a shirt that showed that she had a pretty solid rack. She had blond hair that didn't match her eyebrows and a pouty mouth that was set the way a drunk's mouth always was. From that, and the glassy stare, he figured out that MaryAnn had had a few drinks before she'd run into him.

'I do some hustling, too, here and there, pick up a few bucks now and then,' Mute said. 'But I don't hurt nobody, it's not the way I operate. I can't stand those tough guys, mugging old people and doing mean shit. They got no imagination.'

'My husband thinks he's a hustler, but he couldn't hustle his way into a hooker's bedroom.' The hand on Mute's knee slid up a few inches, and MaryAnn squeezed his thigh, rubbed the back of her hand across it. They'd been sitting there probably a total of five minutes, and she'd already finished her first drink. She lifted the glass and waved it at the bartender, MaryAnn's elbow on the bar, holding the glass with her fingertips around the rim.

'Buy me another one, Mr Lucky,' MaryAnn said, and Mute decided that it was time to press his luck.

'How lucky do you think one man can get in a single night?'

MaryAnn waited until the bartender took her glass and walked away, then she leaned forward, biting her lower lip, smiling, and licked at his neck, one time, her tongue flicking over him as quickly as a snake's. She made Mute forget all about his serenity, about his promise to God. God could wait, at least a little while more. Until the night was over. Then Mute would change.

'I don't think,' MaryAnn said, 'that you'll ever get this lucky again. This might well be the luckiest night of your entire life.'

Ben walked into the bar, not paying attention to the cable football game being played over the two large-screen television sets standing against opposite walls of the place. He seemed to be one of the few guys in the bar who wasn't at all interested in what was going on at the Meadowlands. New York and Philadelphia, and New York was favored by seven. Philly was winning by three, and there were two minutes left in the half. Joe Theisman's excited voice told Ben these things, Ben hearing the words in stereo, as soon as he walked through the door.

The joint was ostensibly a sports bar, but there was a lot more than that going on inside. Along with the usual crowd that such places catered to, there were people in here who gambled for a living, who stood to lose or win plenty on the outcome of this game. You could tell who had bets on what team by the looks on the bettors' faces. The bookies that hung out here didn't care either way. Ben knew them all and was now seeking a couple of them out, and saw a couple of others talking to their girlfriends, seeming as bored by what was happening on the screen as Ben himself was. These weren't people with anything to lose.

Ben heard snatches of conversation, not paying much attention to them, letting them go in one ear and out the other. People were talking about Magic Johnson, what had happened to him, about the virus he'd caught. Strangers kissing strangers, hanging all over one another in a seedy sports and gambling bar. Maybe they'd stop at a drug store for some rubbers on their way to a sleazy motel.

He didn't think about them much, though, he had other things on his mind tonight.

He found one of the men he was looking for leaning

against the bar, his back to it, elbows resting on the hardwood. Fat Tony talking to some young redhead who looked almost old enough to be there.

Tony's shirt was opened nearly to the waist, one of those silk shirts with a lot of funny designs, the type that had been popular back when disco had been hot. Obviously making a comeback now, Tony was always in fashion. Except when it came to his body; he'd never gotten into the fitness trend.

Tony was about Ben's height, but outweighed him by seventy pounds, most of it fat, most in the belly. He seemed proud of that extra weight though, of the way it stretched out his pants. Look at him, sticking his gray-haired gut out toward the broad. Tony had been losing his hair for some time now, and there was only a little left, and what there was was gray and greased back, shining at the sides. Even from across the room Ben could see that the man was drunk. He did not like dealing with Fat Tony one bit. The guy reminded him of a snake, of a lizard with some hair. He didn't believe that Tony worried much about practicing safe sex, either.

Ben elbowed his way past a bunch of young executive types who were slumming, out for a night of football and beer and illegal gambling, and, if they got lucky, maybe some strange pussy. Away from the strains of their marriages and jobs. He kept his face impassive as a couple of them threw high-fives, their soft guts jiggling under official gray NFL New York Giants sweatshirts.

'Ben, how you doing.' Tony said it without any feeling, as if he didn't much give a shit one way or the other as to how Ben was feeling, was only being polite because his girlfriend was right there.

Ben resented that, right up front, this piece of shit bookie and loanshark talking down to him so he could look big in front of some small-time hooker. Up close, he could see that she was a working girl. Probably with a gambling jones, working off her debt to Tony, slowly, in increments.

'Good,' Ben said, hiding his feelings, at least for the

moment. He leaned against the bar himself, facing forward, though, away from the crowd and the game.

The bartender was sweating, or else the mousse that he'd generously applied to his hair was dripping off his fancy hairdo and down on to his forehead. He was a skinny guy, young and cocky, wearing a referee's shirt with a whistle around his neck. The type who didn't understand that it was no longer cool to take drugs.

'Help you?'

'Royal Salute,' Ben said, 'no ice, and water back.'

The bartender moved away, searching for the bottle, and Ben heard Tony say, 'Take it outta here.'

The place had once had a reputation as a gangster hangout, and there was mob money behind it, as there was wherever there was money to be made and suckers to be taken. But no heavyweights ever hung out here, not anymore. They couldn't stand the noise, couldn't put up with the bullshit. These days it was mostly a place for small-time outfit wannabes, guys like Tony and his partner, Lino, who owned the place and paid the mob for their protection, middle-aged men who made a good dishonest buck and still thought that you had to party all night in order to enjoy yourself.

Above the bar, on a board nailed to the wall above the mirror, there hung what was called the Wall of Fame. Round little brass coins were nailed into plywood. There always seemed to be more of those coins up there every time that Ben stopped in. What had happened was, the manager had once had three years sober, had gone to AA and had lived for a time without booze. He hadn't made it, though, and the Wall of Fame was for him and other losers. If you dropped out of AA and brought in your time coin to prove it, you drank free of charge that night, and your coin was pounded in the Wall in a little ceremony that everybody participated in. The manager and the bartenders and the patrons saw that as cute. It was the kind of place that the He Ain't Here was.

In the mirror behind the bar Ben could see Tony's partner Lino, making his way across the room. He would have seen

Ben walk in, was hurrying to back up his partner. Lino's action and Tony's ignoring him answered the questions that Ben was here to ask. Lino was glaring, but not at Ben, staring instead at his associate, Tony. Lino was heavy, but in better shape than Tony, and he didn't dress as well, had on a shortsleeve white cotton shirt with the first three buttons undone. Lino was the type of man who thought it was classy to sprinkle Aramis cologne under the seat of his brand-new Lincoln.

Ben looked away from the mirror, not wanting Lino to know he was wise. He wanted them to think that he was relaxed and being casual, wanted to give them the impression that he thought they were still his friends.

'Salute,' he said to Tony, and raised his glass, then drank.

'Good health,' Tony said, sarcastically, wishing Ben anything but.

There were basketball hoops set up on either end of the bar, the types you saw at amusement parks, with mesh nets running high along the backboards and underneath them, there to catch the missed shots. For a dollar you got two shots at the basket, and if you sunk both balls, you got a free drink. There was a line forming now at both baskets, young guys waiting for the chance to shoot oversized balls into undersized rims while the half-time bullshit ran. Their laughter and shouted encouragements to each other, mixed with the shouts of the football fans, along with the sound of Joe Theisman's voice coming out of the oversized speakers on the TVs, were beginning to get on Ben's already frayed nerves.

He said, 'Tony, talk to me, where's my money?' To hell with the girl. Tony should have sent her away.

'Benny, please, not in front of my immorata.' The girl giggled, as if what Tony had said had been romantic.

Ben decided that it was time to stop playing around. He looked right at her, gave the same look that he'd just given the punks outside on the corner.

'Take a walk,' he said. 'Come back when you see me leave.'

'Stay right there,' Ton said to his girlfriend. 'He's leaving now.'

'As soon as I get my money.'

Lino said, 'You get your money every month, what's your problem, Benny? Shit, what's wrong with you lately?'

As Tony and the girl laughed at the statement, Ben pushed off the bar and reached slowly into his left pocket, came out with his cigarettes and lit one before he spoke. After he lit it he stuffed the pack down into his right pocket.

'I come in here, to get what's mine, and I gotta talk my business in front of a teenage broad young enough to be the daughter of either one of you. And you want to know what's wrong with me? What's wrong with *you*? Way you act, you'll both be in the pen before New Year's Eve. And you ain't going away with my money in your pocket.'

Tony said, 'Ben, calm down, not in here, all right?'

Lino said, 'How about talking in the bathroom, Ben, you and me, we can talk this over.' He was trying to sound friendly, as if his goal was to calm Ben down. But Ben had known him long enough to hear the violence under his tone of voice.

Ben lifted his glass casually and poured the booze down his throat, but still managed to catch the look that passed between Lino and Tony. Even though Tony was bigger and fatter, it was Lino who spoke to the slow-paying clients, got them alone somewhere and then shattered the bones in their ankles. Tony was the front man, the flamboyant one who gave the impression that gambling was a victimless crime. It was Lino who proved differently, after it was too late to change your opinions.

Ben, acting mollified, said, 'Come on, Jesus, that's a good idea, we'll go in the can where nobody can hear us.'

The motel room was tiny, with a cheap landscape painting bolted on a cracked wall. It was a one-storey business set in the middle of Route 30, with fifteen rooms and a neon sign outside that announced: CABLE TV! TRUCKERS! WELCOME! Mute wondered aloud how much it would cost to have a trucker sent into the room with you, asked MaryAnn how many lonely women she figured to have misread the sign and stopped in, looking for some long-haul love. There were battered old American cars in the cracked pavement parking lot, but just a few. There were plenty of vacancies this evening at the Twilight Motel.

Although it was still early, they'd awakened the woman who was running the front desk. She'd come out to the hallway in a flannel nightgown, with pink curlers in her hair. She pushed a registration card out to them, and MaryAnn took the pen and signed them in. When she asked she told the woman No, they did not have any luggage tonight. In a bored tone that she'd probably used a thousand times in her life, the woman told them that in that case, they would have to pay in cash.

Now Mute lay, sated for the moment and racked with guilt, on the squeaky narrow bed in room 13. He could hear the television set running in the room next door, and decided that whoever had been in there had turned it up just to drown out the noises that were coming from this room, which was a good thing; it showed they weren't renting a room next to some pervert.

She was a screamer, MaryAnn was, and Mute liked them best of all, loved to hear them moan and groan, shout his name as they came around his pecker. He knew that she'd probably done the same thing with a million other guys, but still, it made him feel special, as if he alone had ever been man enough to elicit such a response.

And to top it all off, she was the best piece of ass that he had ever had in his life, and that was saying something indeed; Mute prided himself on getting around these days. He'd never tell this to MaryAnn, nor to any other woman that he'd had sex with, but he had never had sex in his life until he was thirty years old; four years ago, after getting out of the pen.

Now Mute wondered how any man in his right mind would not keep this filly at home. She was a wild Mare, was what she was, in fact, that's what he'd call her, his Mare, as in MaryAnn. Bucking under him, trying to throw him off at the same time that she drove her heels into his asscheeks, forcing him into her harder. Christ. That husband of hers had to be some kind of retard not to keep a woman like that happy and loyal.

His hands were behind his head now, Mute looking at a cracked ceiling with water marks around the edges. He felt relaxed, at ease, would be ready for more in just a few short minutes. She'd been one hell of a lot more than he'd expected, firmer than most women her age. And she screamed. Screaming covered a lot of other sins, as far as Mute was concerned, but when it came to his Mare there were no sins to cover; the woman was a virtuoso, a one-woman whorehouse, and tonight, she was all his.

But now, after it was over, his earlier prayers to God were right there in the front of his mind. He'd last seriously considered them as he'd leaped in the air after winning the race, Mute shouting 'Thank you!' to the heavens above. Now, though, his problem had been solved, and not only had he won the race, he'd gotten laid to boot. Mute played some games and he ran some scams, and he lied to any woman who was wearing a wedding ring. But he saw himself as a man of his word, and he'd made a deal, a deal with God. And God could not be put back on the shelf for another fifteen years.

If it hadn't been for the guilt, he would be feeling almost elated, with money in his pocket and a married woman beside him, Mute able to see his bulging biceps from the way that he was lying, proud that they were so large.

'How did you ever come to bet so much on a thirty-to-one shot,' MaryAnn wanted to know. 'Do you know somebody out there?'

Mute almost laughed, flirted with telling her the truth, relieved that he had something to think about beside his broken promise.

Mute said, 'I know *every*body out there. Trainers and drivers and the guy who sweeps up the shit after everybody's gone. Everyone but the idiot who works third-floor security, he's got to be new.'

He said, 'See, I been betting on Sabi for over a year now, he was always a good horse, but he'd get in the lead and he'd break. You want to know why?'

'Why's that, Mute?' Her tone of voice made it clear that MaryAnn was losing interest. He hurried to tell her why, believing she'd enjoy the story.

'His *balls* are too big, can you believe that? The son of a bitch, he'd get going good, then he'd bust a knee into one of his balls, they were hanging too low down for him to be able to avoid them.'

'Balls too big? Sounds like somebody I know!' MaryAnn licked at his neck again, flicking that tongue out, shit, real fast. The things she could do with that tongue.

'They made him a special harness for them, kind of a horse jockstrap made outta leather. Holds them in good, and he's blazing fractions at the workouts. This was the first race he ran since they'd had the diaper on him. See the way he came out of the stretch? Damn, he looked like a bolt of black lightning.'

'You've got an excellent body.' Was she changing the subject, or did she really mean it? Mute took a quick look at her, decided that she meant it. She was looking at him the way his grandma used to look up at the cross above the altar at St Columba's.

'God compensated, Mare,' Mute said, 'for making me so ugly.' There wasn't even a hint of self-pity in his voice, Mute was merely stating a cruel, believed fact.

'Ugly?' She traced the course of a vein in Mute's forearm, MaryAnn on her side, breasts up there firm, holding herself up with her elbow on the bed and one palm on the side of her head. 'I think you're kind of cute, I think you look like a lion.'

She wasn't making fun of him, it seemed an honest appraisal. He felt her finger run up his bicep, and he tightened it, trapping the finger in the underside of his elbow when it roamed back down.

'I don't believe I've ever seen a man with a body like yours before, not outside of the movies.'

'It's only partly from working out,' Mute admitted, nearly embarrassed by the obvious awe in her voice. 'I was born with the gene, Mare, only got to work out about fifteen hours a week or so.'

'Fifteen hours? That's more than most people in my company work at their *jobs*!'

'Ain't my fault they're lazy. What is it that you do?'

'I'm a real estate broker, I have my own office, with my *hus*band now, the lawyer, sitting right there most of the day, looking over my shoulder.' MaryAnn laughed. 'Over on South Chicago Avenue. Right in your neck of the woods.'

'Good luck.' Mute said it sarcastically. 'A lot of them have sure popped up out there recently, since the airport's going up in Hegewisch, since the city sold them all out.'

MaryAnn laughed softly, in a way that made Mute feel awkward and disturbed. It was the laugh of someone who knew your secrets, and was waiting for the right time to humiliate you with them.

'They don't have what I've got.'

'What's that?'

'Well, there's a number of things.' She was looking at him strangely, and he felt a shiver of fear. Was she some psycho? Was she going to cut his balls off while he slept? The look she was giving him, the smile on her mouth, it was the sort of look he thought serial killers might have, right before they started working on you.

Her eyebrows were raised innocently, but the look in her eyes was cunning. MaryAnn was about to give him information, but playing it cute.

She said, 'I've got a few lawyers who work for me. I think *you* might even know some of them. I've got friends in your line of business, and I've got a computer wizard working for me, who can find out anything about anyone. Do a Dunne & Bradstreet on you while the rest of the world sleeps. But there's one thing I have that none of the others have.' MaryAnn glared at him now, that innocent smile gone. Now, she was the predator, coming in for the attack.

'I've got *you*, Mute, and they *don't* have you,' MaryAnn

said, then before he could ask what the hell she meant by that MaryAnn quit playing around and got down to business. She lowered her arm, shot out that killer tongue and began licking Mute's left nipple, pausing there for a while on a journey further south.

Ben knew that he had to stay within himself, could not allow his fear of who and what Lino was to counteract his plan. Lino had connections? Ben had them too. Lino was a legbreaker; Ben had murdered, twice. Lino paid people to bust somebody's head; Ben knew the same guys, and had won their respect and loyalty without having to reach into his wallet.

He was thinking these things as he led the way into the bathroom. The last of the guys who had raced into there during half-time was walking out the door just as Ben pushed it open. He stepped through, patting his pockets: 'Where the hell are my smokes . . .?' reaching into his right-hand pocket and pulling out the pistol just as Lino turned his back on him, locking the door behind himself.

Lino was turning, half-smiling, the smile transposing into a rictus of pain and terror as Ben hit him, hard, high on the forehead, with the butt of the pistol. Ben hit him again and again, all over his face, smashing his jaw and his nose and cutting both of his ears, following Lino to the ground, one hand holding Lino's shirtfront, the other swinging the gun, Lino falling to the dirty tiled floor in a heap, making terrified noises as he realized what was happening.

Ben, too, was doing some talking, speaking in fragments of sentences, emphasizing portions of them with hard swings of the pistol.

'*Bastard!* . . . *My* fucking money . . . Kill *both* of you son of a bitches, now I'll kill you *both*!'

Ben stopped when his arm got tired, when he found that he couldn't draw a breath without gasping. There went his heart again, too, racing like a Wisconsin greyhound who'd spotted the mechanical rabbit at the start of a race. Ben was shaking as he fell away from Lino, breathing in short gasps, his face red, veins bulging in his neck as he fought desperately for air. Lino tried to get to his knees and fell over, on to his side, blood dripping from his nose, his ears, his face.

Ben leaned shakily against the wall and shook his head, trying to clear it. The red rage was being overpowered by a terrifying thought: I'm dying. He knew it, felt it, his body had betrayed him.

After a couple of minutes Ben could move away from the wall. He ignored the pounding on the outside door, removed some paper from the dispenser and wiped the butt of the gun. There was blood on the front of his shirt, on his suit jacket and his hands. Ben dropped the pistol carefully back into his pocket and washed his hands, breathing through his mouth, inhaling as deeply as he dared, stopping when the pain grew too intense for him to continue. When he was finished he stepped away from the sink, wiping his hands with rough brown towels. The pounding on the bathroom door had stopped. Ben didn't care either way; no one around the He Ain't Here would be calling the police department anytime soon.

Lino had worked his way to his knees, was holding on to the sink that was farthest away from Ben, trying to pull himself to his feet. His face was unrecognizable, bloody, puffed, swollen, cut. Good for him; he'd been warned. What happened just now had been his choice.

Ben said, 'I've got an even fifty grand out there on the street with you two assholes.'

Lino grunted, in fear.

'I told you Friday, I wanted it tonight. But the two of you, you and the child molester out there, you're gonna do what you want, you're gonna forget where you came from and who helped you get there.' Ben allowed all of the hatred he felt into his voice, and as he spoke he felt a flash of deep, intense anger. He walked over to where Lino was struggling and lifted his foot, pushed the man away from the sink. Lino fell back to the floor, and covered his face with his hands. Ben saw that Lino's fingers were shaking terribly, covering a face that was not only smeared with blood, but with tears.

'You know me thirty years and you're going to insult me in front of some teenage *hook*er?' Ben's voice was near-awed, as if he could not believe the extent of their disrespect. 'Gonna bring me in here and do what, break my toes?' He reached into his jacket pocket and took out a cigarette, lit it and took a slight, tentative drag. His chest felt okay, the rot inside his lungs under control, at least for the moment.

'I ought to blow your head off right here in this toilet. I will, too, if I don't get paid tomorrow. You, Tony, and all of your goddamn workers. I got fifty grand coming, and I better have it by tomorrow night, or there ain't nowhere on this earth that you can hide from me.'

'I'll get it, I'll get your money.' Lino's voice was shaking as badly as his hands. Ben could see the whites of his eyes through the webs of Lino's fingers. The man had finally learned how tough he was, and had come up a lot shorter than he ever figured to. Ben squatted down, folded his hands between his thighs.

'You ignorant piece of shit, you knew I wanted it Friday!'

Lino whimpered at the sound of Ben's voice.

Ben said calmly, 'You're not planning to pay me, not even now; what you'll do is you'll go to the Man. I talked to him last Thursday, before I ever came to you and Tony, told him what happened and what I wanted, and he told me my money is mine, it was between just the three of us. So you go to him, cry about what a good earner you are. See what he says. Then get tough again, forget about what happened tonight. Come looking for me, but remember one thing if you do.'

Ben reached out and slapped Lino's hands away from his face, held them down on the man's chest, glaring into Lino's eyes. He pushed down a little, not enough to crack any ribs, but it got Lino's notice, he was paying strict attention. A line of blood and saliva was stuck to the floor, one end still in Lino's mouth. Ben was careful, he did not want to touch any of this man's secretions; he had enough health problems right now to last him the rest of his life.

He said, 'If you don't settle this tomorrow like a man, like the way I came to you Friday, if you come looking for me and I got to kill you, then I go after your family. I'll get the fifty from them, one way or another. Do we understand each other, Lino? Are you gonna have my money tomorrow night?'

As Lino opened his mouth Ben saw that his front teeth were cracked in half. Air hit the stubs and Lino winced, cried out in pain. He shut his mouth and nodded rapidly.

'That ain't good enough, Lino, give me your word.'

'I pwomise,' Lino managed to say, then shut his mouth tight again. He'd never even opened his eyes.

'Tell your partner.' Ben stood up and moved back, nodded his head in satisfaction. 'I gave you fifty grand a year ago, and now I want it back. What I got between then and now is gravy; I get it all tomorrow or I swear to God, I'll kill the both of you.'

Ben backed away, knowing that Lino was capable of grabbing his feet if he turned his back on him. He might even have a knife in his pocket or his shoe. Ben got to the door and turned the lock, pushed it open and stepped out into the hallway.

Tony was there with a bunch of men who couldn't have done him any good if he'd handed them loaded pistols, males whose concept of strength and manhood came from watching science fiction movies that starred musclebound freaks. Heart? There were five men there, including Tony, and Ben didn't think that there was one heart between them.

He said, 'Tony, go get your partner, he's got something to say to you.'

Tony backed up against the wall, looking wide-eyed at Ben as Ben walked past him. As with the children outside, Ben turned his back on him without a second's worry or hesitation. He'd taken care of the fighter, the tough one. Now Tony would fall in line. And if he didn't, Ben had no doubt in his mind that tomorrow he would kill them both.

She'd kept the name Morer, and at first she wasn't sure why.

It had taken Diane three years of therapy after her divorce from Ben finally to understand her reasoning, and when she did comprehend it she didn't much care for what she'd learned. But she hadn't changed the name, either.

She'd kept it because it opened doors, and because the name itself carried weight in this city; it even instilled fear in certain segments of society. Everyone seemed to know who Ben was, especially the types she had to deal with, day in and day out, men who thought that because they were male they had some God-given right to touch women they didn't know, or else to give them bullshit, talk dirty and make insinuations that couldn't just be laughed off as boys being boys. These men would hear the name Morer, and it would give them pause.

One of the rules she lived by in her business was that she'd always do the initial calls herself, in order to show that her business believed in that special, personal touch. She could have hired people to do that for her, had people on the payroll who were more than capable of performing that task, but her name was on the cleaning vans, and the checks were made out to her, so even though the business was successful, she still felt the need to go out herself, to win the contract personally. Besides, she was superstitious; getting the contracts personally was the way she had begun, and she feared, in some recess of her mind, that if she stopped doing the initial work herself, her business would fail.

She'd sat in countless offices of local Chicago plant executives, looking cooly at a guy who probably cleared thirty-five a year and, if he was lucky, another five in expenses, and he'd eye her when she came in, look her up and down as if he were Dale Carnegie and she'd walked into the offices of US Steel. They would hold her hand a beat too long, sometimes rub their other hand over the back of hers, and invariably they'd call her Mrs Morer, pronouncing it 'More-er', that or Miss Morer, never Ms.

It was then that she'd correct them.

'It's *Moy-ray*,' Diane would tell them, and she'd watch their faces fall.

It worked with policemen, too, but sometimes not to her advantage. She'd be stopped for speeding or for only making a Hollywood stop at a stop sign when there wasn't any other traffic present, and they'd either give her a fast, respectful break or they'd nail her to the wall, make her get out of the car and then they'd search it, even going so far as to take out her back seat. It was a new car that belonged to a Morer, and that was all that some of them needed to know to believe that it was dirty.

The executives would fawn over her, once they understood that the woman before them was related to the man that they used to see so often on the nightly news. Or read about the next day in the papers, about his escapades, years ago.

There'd been a time when her ex had been seen as flamboyant, as a renegade in the limelight who was charming, if bent. Long ago, when she'd first met him, she herself had been wildly attracted to that side of him, to the kiss-my-ass attitude that he wore so proudly and with such cavalier daring. It hadn't taken long before she saw the other side of him, though, and by then she'd been too far involved to walk away from him and live.

How many contracts had she gotten over the years, simply because of her name? Diane did not know, and wasn't sure that she ever wanted to find out. She was certain, though, that there had been more than a couple, men who'd signed on with her agency because they thought that it gave them connections. She could see them, in Bennigan's or some other trendy bar, after working an eight-hour shift, hoisting a cold one and whispering her name when someone asked them what agency cleaned their plant. 'I'm with Morer.' *Moy-ray*. The thief, the fighter, the wildman, the killer.

She thought about him a lot, even five years after she'd last seen his face. If she really wanted to see him, all she would have to do was walk upstairs to the bedrooms of her sons. Look in at them as the eldest, fifteen-year old Benny, did his homework, or in the room next door to see fourteen-year old John, who as usual had waited until Sunday night before studying for a test that would decide a fourth of his grade. She could knock on their doors and wait for them to tell her it was all right to come in, then turn the knob and enter, look at inquiring young faces and know what Ben must have looked like when he'd been just a teenager.

Lean and limber, with tight, ropy muscles that didn't look anywhere near as strong as they actually were. Dark brown hair that was thick and full and shiny, combed back, straight, hair that needed bi-monthly cutting. Their chins were strong and their cheeks were full, high cheekbones under eyes that were dark and somewhat menacing. She could look at Benny from a distance and see her husband when she'd first met him. Ben didn't have any pictures of himself as a child, the foster homes in which he'd been raised didn't run to photography equipment. And although his mother was living, Ben had been taken away from her at an early age, and besides, she wasn't the type who'd look to preserve his childhood memories. But this was what he must have looked like, the way his sons looked now.

Ben's face wouldn't have been so unlined, though, so free of worry, such a stranger to fear. Although her sons had seen enough fear in their lives, Diane wouldn't sugarcoat them. Seen his tantrums, seen him punch his fists through hardwood doors. Cowered under beds as their mother shrieked at a madman. Ben had loved them, she believed that, but he had never learned how to show it, and that was, when she thought about it, maybe the saddest thing about him, and the thing she couldn't forgive.

Well, *one* of the things that she couldn't forgive; when it came to Ben, there were a lot of unresolved issues.

He'd never hit her, although he'd come close, he'd turn at the last minute and attack the wall or the door. Punch at them without regard for his safety, breaking bones and skin and whatever got in the way.

She'd once seen him hold a man up against the side of a van and swing at him, and when the man ducked Ben had punched his fist right through the steel part of the door, getting his hand stuck in there good, all the way up to the wrist. The fire department had to be called to come and carefully pry his hand out. After it was stuck, though, Ben didn't seem to notice the blood or even any of what must have been considerable pain. He'd kicked at the man he'd shoved up against the van, his tongue out, his eyes wild, his face set in that mask of rage that always terrified any human being who'd ever seen it. The man he'd swung at had turned and run away, choosing not to swing at Ben, even trapped and near-helpless as her husband had been at the time.

The mistake that the man had made in that parking lot was in looking at Diane and smiling as they passed.

He had been like that, long ago, could be laughing and joking and suddenly go crazy. Some imagined insult would send him into a rage, and somebody would get hurt, always somebody else.

Why did she think of him so often, why was he always on her mind?

Dear God in heaven, why did she still love him?

If they'd still been married it would be eighteen years this Tuesday, but still, four other anniversaries had passed, and she hadn't gotten like this, grown so sad, staring into a dead fireplace, remembering him, loving him, even for some reason missing him.

Diane was forty-one years old and had married at twenty-three, college educated with a future in front of her and look what she'd done with her life. By the time she had finally gotten him to leave she'd weighed almost two hundred pounds and had a serious drug problem, speed mostly, and downers to level her out, sleeping pills that she got in large quantities, Ben getting her a discount.

She wasn't that woman anymore, though. The fact was that these days, she wasn't even close. She'd lost seventy pounds through abstinence and hard work, had given up the pills and suffered through that, alone. The boys had taken care of themselves – at the time they'd been ten and nine – making their own meals and cleaning the house while Mom crashed in the bedroom. They'd done that for five whole days while Diane had slept through most of them, getting up only when she had to drag herself to the bathroom. They'd taken care of the house, and gotten themselves off to school. Now she could only imagine the torment those days must have cost them, how they'd suffered as they'd wondered if Mommy would ever be normal again. As for their father, she was sure that they'd missed him terribly. Even though Ben could never have been considered normal by any rational person, he'd always done what he could to be there for them, a constant in their lives until that terrible day, a rock. And then, suddenly, he was gone.

On the sixth day, when she finally felt good enough to get out of the bed without passing out from exhaustion, she'd called them to her, and the three of them had sat down, in the kitchen, and talked about things for several long hours.

That night all three of them had cried themselves weak, and the decision had been made: they would live far more happily if they never saw Ben again.

He'd been angry, on the phone, accused her of poisoning their minds, he'd thought that it had been a set-up from the start, a plan to drive him out of all of their lives. She'd told him that they'd made their own decisions, and he'd hung up on her, and she hadn't heard from him since.

Except for the envelopes, which came every week. Certified mail, for Saturday afternoon delivery; she'd sign for the envelope and take it to her bedroom. Every week, without fail, five crisp hundred dollar bills were delivered to the house from Ben. For The Kids, the note always said. These days, the message was scrawled on a Post-it.

It was the sort of thing she could see him doing, no matter how he felt about her. Taking care of his flesh, his blood, the sons he never saw. Doing something for them that his father had never done for him. Anything he'd done for them would have been more than his own father had ever done; Ben had never known who or where his father was.

'Ben,' Diane Morer said, sitting on her living-room couch, thinking about the man. God, how she'd loved him, and still would be loving him, if he hadn't pushed her as far as she would go without breaking in two. He'd pushed her right to the edge, and when she'd looked over, she knew that it wasn't yet time for her to travel that route. At the time she'd thought that there were only two options for her; she could either jump, or she'd be pushed. Somewhere, somehow, she'd found the strength to see a third. Back away from it, get out of it while she could. Step back from the edge of madness or death and find a way to get her life in order.

It was getting late now, and she knew that she should get up and go into the kitchen and unload the dinner dishes from the dishwasher. This week it was Benny's turn to cook dinner, John's turn to clean the kitchen, and Diane's turn to unload the dishwasher and get up early enough to make breakfast. Next year, when he was fifteen, John would be old enough to take his turn cooking their dinner. She'd seen it as a sign of good rearing when he'd become impatient, waiting for that day to come.

They all did their own laundry, had specific days where the washer and dryer were their personal property. They had different cleaning duties, their bedrooms, of course, being their own responsibilities; the upstairs and downstairs and basement chores were rotated. It had been difficult, at first, training these boys to take accountability for chores that had always been hers, but now they had accepted their duties, and she usually didn't have to point their frequent lapses out more than a couple of times.

She should unload the washer and then take a relaxing bath, then come back downstairs, play a game of Parcheesi with the boys before they went to sleep.

Had they been damaged by Ben's actions, by being raised by such a man? He hadn't been there much, and when he was, it had been volatile. And when he went to prison they'd been ostracized, had lost all of their friends for a time. If not for the girlfriends that she'd had since she'd been a child, Diane would have been alone herself, she and her boys pariahs.

Their grades had slipped, after he'd left, as if they'd been testing their new boundaries, seeing how far they could go with her. Ben had always been strict yet fair, had never hit the children, but the threat had always been there. He'd want to know what the hell was wrong with them, why did they settle for Bs. Would ask them straight out: 'Do you want to grow up like me? Hustling all the time? If I'd had an education I'd be a millionaire today!' He'd never wanted his life to be theirs, had always seen them as better than he, even when they'd been tiny.

She could remember the look on his face, as he pushed their carriages down the street. He'd tell her that his sons would go to Harvard and be doctors, would give her the glare when she'd mention that they might grow up to be lawyers.

'No kid of mine will ever be a fucking lawyer,' he'd growl. 'I'd kill them first.' She never knew if he truly meant that.

The proud papa had gone to jail, and their lives had fallen apart. She'd had to sell the Cadillac and nearly everything else to pay his lawyer, and his 'friends' in the mob had abandoned him. For three long years, she and the boys had been on welfare.

When he'd been in jail it had been difficult for the boys to build any new friendships, but now that they were both in high school, and their father had been out of the papers for a while, they seemed to have adapted pretty well. The house was usually swarming with kids that she hardly even knew. And both of them had girlfriends, that was an encouraging sign.

They never asked about him, or how he was, didn't seem to care if he was living or dead. They were like war veterans who never discussed their experiences, and she often wondered if they had truly forgotten about Ben, or if their fear of him was still there, hiding in a corner of their minds.

She herself had a different point of view; she saw them as survivors. People who had been on that edge and had seen what was beyond it, who'd come through that and had grown better for the experience. What could happen to her now, to give her a nervous breakdown or to make her act like a neurotic? Her employees marveled at how well she faced adversity, and she felt that her ability to spit in adversity's eye was because she'd had so much of it; her problems today were unimportant, when she thought of what they might be. In fact, when she thought about it, she didn't have any real problems. Just things she didn't like about her life, things that she could change.

She had well-adjusted children, who loved her, deeply. So far there'd been no problems with drugs or alcohol, no acting out violently when things happened that they didn't like. There didn't seem to be any genetic problems with either of them. They didn't smoke, as their father did, nor fight or drink the way he always did. In fact, since Ben had been gone, they'd made out just fine, the three of them against the world.

Now, though, it seemed that outside forces were once again trying to destroy their happiness.

They were going to tear her house down, to build a new airport; the mayor said it was because it would generate a lot of jobs. The mayor of Chicago had legally betrayed them, and just as badly as Ben ever had. They would have to start all over again, somewhere else, wipe the slate clean and give up their community roots. Which was nothing short of a crying shame; she'd been born and raised right here in Hegewisch.

She couldn't think about that now, though. She was already too upset; just thinking about Ben had hurt her, even after all this time. So she thought about the boys, and about her life, about *any*thing other than the fact that she was in mid-life and alone.

She must be doing something right; they were the words that Diane lived by.

She had a new car and some money in the bank, owned some property and her own booming industrial cleaning business and home maid service. Had built it all up from the ground, too, using Ben's weekly payment for seed money. Every dime of which had been replaced as the years passed, going into tax-free municipals for the boys' college tuition.

The houses she owned were all paid off, and three of them were rented out to families that took care of them. The other house, that Diane lived in, with Benny and John, was the largest and the homiest of the four, the house that Ben had paid for in cash, and had been forced by necessity to put in her name alone.

The others, she had bought for investment purposes, and she'd invested in property for a reason. Her father had always told her that land was the one thing in the world of which there was a finite supply, and that it never went down, that real estate always went up.

How wrong the man had been, but Diane hadn't known that then, had thought that every word her father spoke was the word of the Bible itself.

What would they give her for her four homes, a couple of hundred thousand? It would be robbing her blind through public domain, if that was all that they offered.

Stop it!

Diane forced her mind off the imminent sale of her homes, pushed herself back into the here and now, where it was safer, where she was secure.

It had been one of her downfalls back then, thinking into the future too much and dwelling on her past. When she'd been married to Ben, she would regret that she'd hadn't paid off on the promise of her childhood. That or she'd ponder the future, how she'd live if she ever escaped. She'd disciplined herself these past five years, and today she could drag herself out of the blues at will. Sit down and think about what she had, compare it to what she *would* have today, if she hadn't gotten away.

There was no contest, self-pity could never win out. If she'd stayed with him she'd be dead by now, either from a drug overdose, or by her own hand, no matter how much she loved him. No matter how much she missed him. In any event, it was a sure bet that he wasn't sitting around thinking about her tonight.

Diane jumped as the telephone rang, and she looked at it, then at her watch. Who could be calling her on Sunday night? There was only one way to find out.

Ben walked into his apartment and collapsed into a chair, took short and grateful breaths of air until his nerves calmed down. Forty-eight years old and look at him, breathing like an old man. He looked around the apartment, at the mess that Sunny had left, shook his head in despair, wondering what he'd done with his life, how he'd come to destroy it.

Tony and Lino were dangerous men. He would have to keep himself right, in his heart and in his head, if he was ever going to see the money that he'd invested with the two of them. They'd make one more move on him, Ben was sure of that. The beating he'd given Lino had been the first shot across their bow; war had just been declared, and they'd probably try him again, he knew.

Simply because he hadn't killed them, he'd made himself more vulnerable.

Still, that would come later. They'd make their move and if they failed, he'd kill Lino. If he had to kill one of them, it would be Lino who'd have to go. Tony wasn't really much of a threat, but Lino would never forget the way that Ben had forced humility upon him, had shown him what he was truly made of.

Ben had seen it before, too many times for his liking, men who thought they were tough guys finding out how wrong they'd been. Raped in the penitentiary, or humiliated on the street; those who had any balls at all had only one thing on their minds, later, after they'd had a little time to contemplate their prospects. Revenge, was what they'd think about. They'd have to get even or die in the attempt. The punks, those who gave in, seeing it as their only means to survival, were not people that men like Ben would ever consider a threat. But those with some balls, particularly when those balls were mixed with a little imagination, could be a threat to your health. Even worse than cancer.

There were guns in the apartment, and he kept two more hidden in the car. He'd have to keep all his senses alert, because tomorrow would be tough. They wouldn't come tonight, he knew; tonight they would talk and plan. Tomorrow they would go and see the Man, and Ben knew what he'd tell them. It was their problem, not his, the thing was between Tony, Lino and Ben. None of them was made, none of them had a button. The Man would sit back and watch, and make a deal with the survivor, and Ben knew without doubt that he would have to be that survivor. There was fifty grand involved here, and that would pay for his kids' education.

He'd have to leave them something, after he was gone, as he'd given them nothing in life but a bad name to live down.

There were four rooms in the South Chicago apartment, on the fifth-floor rear of an old and once-proud building. He was on 92nd St – a block away from the church of Our Lady of Guadalupe – a street that still had the original red cobblestone out there in front, laid during the early part of the century, the trolley rails still imbedded in the cobblestone. Most nights, after dark, he could hear gunfire through his windows.

He could hear the neighbors fighting, too, screaming at each other in Spanish through the paper-thin walls, and he'd often hear the sound of a slap and then a woman's cry. It was one of the few things that he prided himself on; he had never hurt a woman. At least not physically.

Sunny might be the first one though, if she didn't clean up her act.

Sunny, twenty-one years old and thinking she knew it all. Raised by an animal who'd taken liberties with what he considered to be his property, she'd escaped at thirteen, had come to the city to make her fortune.

She spoke funny sometimes, with her own little language, lapsing into a dialect that only she understood. At other times, though, the way she acted could scare him. At those times Ben could only wish that he didn't understand what she was saying.

She had a little handpuppet that she kept hidden under her side of the mattress, a Sherry doll, she called it, with a young child's face, that face now torn and faded, the button eyes having to be resewn into the head of the thing almost weekly. Sunny'd put Sherry on her hand and would have conversations with it, Sunny being the adult, the puppet being the child.

The things that the two of them talked about would sometimes chill his blood.

At other times, though, Sherry was far less shocking. Sunny would wear the puppet and let Sherry do the talking, mouthing off about a TV show, or how much she liked pizza or beer.

'You like football?' Sunny would ask the doll, and then make Sherry answer, in a high-pitched little girl's voice.

'Oh, yes, Sunny, me like football. I like to see the big tight asses in those snuggly football pants!'

When she wasn't being Sherry, the woman was a pig and had a mouth on her like a truck driver, but he kept her because he was afraid of growing old and being alone. Yet sometimes he thought that the alternative would be better, no matter how good Sunny was in the sack.

She worked nights dancing topless in a biker-owned joint in Lyons, sometimes until midnight, sometimes until two. She never worked past then, even if the boss wanted her to stay until four. The boss knew Ben, and he never pushed the point.

She never went in early because Ben wanted her there when he woke up each afternoon, wanted her beside him, someone real he could feel there. In the joint there had only been a smelly pig lying in the bunk above him, and after that there'd been no one, at least since his wife had kicked him out.

It was the way he thought of Diane, even after five years divorced. His wife, possessive, the only woman he'd ever loved. Sunny was twenty years younger than Diane, and she knew tricks in bed that Diane would never have heard of, but it was Diane that Ben thought about, at nights when he was alone. He never thought about Sunny, or about what might happen to her as she walked to her car after her shift had ended. As far as Ben was concerned, Sunny wasn't his problem.

Diane, though, that was another story; he worried about her all the time, about her and the boys.

They were getting big now, strong and good-looking kids. He'd seen them every other week or so, would go over to Washington High School and watch them as they came out. They'd stand on the corner of Avenue O and wait for the bus to take them to Hegewisch, and Ben would sit in his car, anonymous among all the Driver's Ed vehicles that filled the parking lot, and look at them, missing them, and his heart would fill with pride. Benny the sophomore would be playing it cool, straight hair blowing in the wind, one arm around his girlfriend, the other holding his books. John the freshman seemed a little less secure, his eyes roaming the street, as if on the lookout for gangbangers doing drive-bys.

Their mother had done a fine job with them, even with him as a father.

How many times had he wanted to drive up, beep the horn and wave them over into the car? What stopped him was the one thing that he had never admitted to, the one emotion that everyone who knew him thought that he didn't possess.

Fear. Fear had stopped him, fear and the unshakeable belief that he'd be rejected by his sons.

Ben had never shown his fear to anyone, not since he'd been a very little boy. He'd never shown it to the junkie that was his mother, or to the series of brutal foster parents. He'd never shown it to the Marine Corps DIs, and he had never even shown it to the Viet Cong. He'd done so well over there, in fact, that the officers had begged him to sign up for another term.

But he'd learned other things over there in Asia, too, things that, like his fears, he never openly discussed. He learned that he enjoyed violence, when he knew that he could get away with it, that it was even valued in some quarters, and officially condoned. And he'd come home to search for people who would appreciate such talent. Had found them easily enough, and his work had been well rewarded.

Growing up, his violent tendencies had caused him nothing but trouble. How often had he been sent to the reformatory as a kid? Christ, he'd lost count. But often, he'd go away. Some kiddy judge would look down on him and tell him that he had to learn to fit in, that someone had to teach him that you couldn't live life with your fists, then sentence him to a place where the adults kept order by beating you. As far as Ben was concerned, those places were still better than the foster homes he'd lived in. At least in the reformatories, they didn't tell you how much you owed them at the same time that they were kicking your ass.

Growing up Ben had learned that if you hid inside yourself they couldn't hurt you, and if they tried, you could kick their asses, make them afraid of you, and then they would leave you alone.

In Nam, he'd learned, there were people who treasured your talents if you could convince them that you loved what you were doing and if you never showed them fear.

Fearless Ben Morer, who was feared by all, frightened of his own two sons.

Should he ask his wife to come to the doctor's office with him tomorrow morning? The thought had never entered his mind to take Sunny along with him. He hadn't even told her that he'd been feeling poorly lately. Didn't explain about the blood in his spit, the pain in his chest when he exerted himself. What would he say to her, that his lungs felt the way a banana probably did when it started to go black? She'd laugh in his face, not understanding that it was the only thing he could compare it to. No, that was wrong, Sunny would laugh behind his back. Nobody laughed at Ben Morer. They could put that statement on his gravestone.

There was no doubt in his mind that what he had was fatal. If it hadn't been, if it was just stress or a blocked artery or something, the doctor wouldn't have asked him to bring along his wife. And what kind of doctor was this guy in the first place? It said right on Ben's papers that he was divorced and lived alone. Hadn't the guy even looked at that? Young enough to be Ben's son, if Ben had had a kid before he'd entered the Marines, and looking down at Ben because he paid in cash, because he said 'ain't' and didn't have a fancy checkbook. Calling him 'Ben', instead of Mr Morer. If Ben had what he thought he might, he should maybe kick the doctor in the ass, teach him a little something about showing men respect. If Ben had what he thought he might, he'd have nothing to lose by doing so. As if he had anything now, who did he think he was kidding.

Forty-eight years, and this is what he had: a rat-trap apartment in a gang-infested neighborhood, listening to gunshots at night and church bells Sunday morning. Cash in his pocket, but no bank account, anywhere. A few grand in cash crossed his palms every week, and he blew that almost as fast as he got it. How? He wasn't quite sure.

He sent five bills a week back home to the kids, wrapped it inside a couple sheets of paper and sent it by certified mail. He ate all his meals in restaurants, usually with someone else, and he always picked up the tab; Ben was known through the city as a sport. He liked to cabaret, to hit the bars a couple of nights each week. He never used to be much of a drinker, but he found it helped the pain. And he kicked back ten points of whatever he hustled, over to the Man, to the guy who took care of the heat and gave him the license to steal. The cops, too, got a piece of his action so they'd leave him alone and not pinch him every other week. He hated the cops, but he liked the Man, had known him a long time, but he'd never discussed his fear with him, would never tell the Man of his pain.

The pain in his heart as well as the one in his chest, the pain that had been there, killing him these past five years.

He was a man who never thought that he'd ever need anyone else, one who laughed at other men when they told him that they were in love. Ben Morer, in love? Even the thought of it was a joke.

But he'd loved his wife more than he'd ever told her, in fact he'd never told her at all. He'd known that before he'd left the house, he'd known it since he'd met her, how much he'd loved her, how much he'd needed her.

Which was really the reason that he'd finally left. He'd seen what was happening, how he was hurting them, and knew that he couldn't change. In one of his rare bursts of personal insight, Ben had left so that Diane and the boys would have a shot at a real life, one where they wouldn't have to wonder if the head of the household would call one night, in jail, again, needing someone to throw his bond. That, or worse – the coroner would call, or some reporter to break the news to them that their father and husband was dead.

He wondered if she'd maybe gotten married again. To some guy who liked women who were pretty overweight. He'd married a skinny young wasp with looks and he'd wound up with an Italian grandmother.

Still, he'd loved her, and he'd tried to overlook her weight.

Why had she eaten so much, what had driven her to it? He hadn't been around much, he'd grant her that, but still, she couldn't blame him for what she'd turned into.

Even fat, though, even taking the pills to sleep, and the other ones that she told him she took to help her lose all the weight, still and all, with all her faults, she was better to him than any of the women of the men he'd known in his life. Even now, five years later, he'd never seen a woman who'd loved a man the way that she'd loved him.

What could he have done, was there anything at all? Something he could have said or done to make her want him to stay? She'd told him that when love dies, it's the same as a human death. It could never be brought back, nothing could resurrect it.

And for most of their marriage, he thought that she'd been happy, that he'd given her the world. She'd waited for him when he'd served some time and she'd never fooled around on him; he'd had guys watching and would have known if she had. So what had caused it? Diane had never told him, but he'd seen it, felt the anger there, seething just under her skin. Seen the unhappiness in his children's eyes, and knew that he had caused it.

Maybe it was time to ask for forgiveness. It would be nice to have them grant it to him, before it was too late.

Ben looked at the eight-thousand dollar wristwatch that he'd gotten for less than a grand. It was only a little after nine, she'd be awake, still, maybe watching television with the kids, some movie of the week. He reached for the phone before he could change his mind, and punched in a number he hadn't called in five years.

'Hello?' Diane said, and the voice on the other end of the line stopped her cold.

'Diane?' Ben sounded tentative, my God, he even seemed nervous.

'Have you been drinking?' He sounded somehow different, his voice terribly hoarse, as if he had a horrible cold or the world's worst sore throat. She felt a tenderness try to descend down over her, and she stopped it cold in its tracks. She couldn't want to mother a man like Ben Morer.

Even though the boys were both upstairs, with the doors to their bedrooms closed, she found that she was whispering, and that she'd begun to breathe quite fast.

'No, I haven't been drinking.'

'Ben, you shouldn't have called here, it's been too long, the boys, they'd be hurt – '

'I didn't call to hurt anyone. I won't bother the kids if you don't want me to.'

'Want you to? *Want* you to? Since when do you care about what I want? Since when do you care about what anyone wants but yourself?' Diane found herself half-shouting, and made a conscious effort to lower her voice, to control it. This was still Ben Morer she was speaking to, still a man of violence. The man who'd forced her to live in terror.

She caught herself then, and took a deep breath. Who the hell was he that she had to worry about what he'd do? She didn't live that way anymore, wouldn't allow him to control her emotions. She wouldn't get angry anymore, either. That anger, like Ben himself, was just a part of her past.

In a crisp, cool, businesslike voice, Diane said, 'Ben, I'm going to hang up, now.'

'Thirty seconds, just give me thirty seconds.'

The pleading in his voice made her look at the phone in wonder. Had he gotten religion or something? Was she even sure this was him? She put the receiver back to her ear, and said, calmly, 'Go ahead.'

'Look, Diane, I'm, uh, sick . . .'

'Another hangover? That happens when you stay out all weekend, drinking.' She stopped herself again, his problems were none of her business. Recriminations would do no good, either, it was way too late for that. She had no ties to him, other than the money he sent for the kids. If that's what he was calling about, if he was in a bind for cash, she could give it all back, every dime of it, with interest.

'No, I'm not hungover.'

Diane was still in shock, he hadn't responded to any of her insults.

'The fact is, I'm *sick*, I mean, I think I'm really sick.'

'Ben, what is it?'

'I think I've got some cancer.'

'Think?'

'I got to go to the doctor tomorrow, Diane, gotta meet Doctor Evan in his office at eleven at the South Chicago Community Hospital. He asked me to bring my wife.'

'Then take her with you, what do you want from me? It's been five years, Ben. You really shouldn't have called here.'

'I want you to go with me. Please.' The last word had seemed garbled.

'*Me*? You want *me* to go with you? My God, Ben, you can't be serious.'

'I'm dead serious, Diane, I need you to go with me.'

'Tomorrow, Ben, I've got work to do. I'll put in ten hours at work and then come home and spend some time with the kids, then I'll go upstairs while they eat and do my paperwork for another hour or two. Then I'll spend some time with my sons, help them with their homework, or maybe play a game. I took them to the Bears game this afternoon, Ben. We had a great time, the three of us.'

'Don't do this to me, Diane.'

'You've done it to yourself.'

Diane felt strong now, the fear hadn't lasted too long. She'd just been taken off guard, that was all. She told herself this, and believed it without question. He had no claims to her emotions, he could not hurt her, not anymore.

Strongly, with dignity, Diane said, 'Goodbye, Ben,' and hung up the phone, cutting him out of her life.

So he was sick, so what? What the hell was he to her? He had no claims to her, nor any claims to the children. He'd given that up in the divorce decree, where she'd sued him for desertion and he hadn't contested the claim.

So who the hell did he think he was, coming back into her life after all this time, seeking help from her? If he was sick, it was due to his antisocial lifestyle, to his heavy drinking and his constant smoking, his gambling and chasing whores. She'd been married to a man who'd truly believed that drinking only a fifth of Scotch on any given day was taking it pretty easy. He chainsmoked non-filtered cigarettes, drank like a fish, ate as if he'd never heard of heart disease or the dangers of red meat. And now he was sick and was coming around, sniffing for sympathy from a woman he'd once terrorized.

She should go with him.

The thought passed through her mind and then was gone as fast as it came. Go to the doctor's office with him? *Why*? Diane had to sit back and think about that.

He hadn't terrorized her on purpose, he would never see himself as having been cruel to her. He had only been himself, and he was a violent man, hadn't even understood it when she'd finally worked up the nerve to beg him to leave them alone.

When they'd first gotten married she'd worn jewels on every finger and had fur coats draped over her shoulders well into spring. There'd been cash, a lot of it, filling her purse, and new furniture in their apartment. She'd walk down the street with him and crowds of teenagers would gather, knowing who he was and respecting him, wanting to be like him, to win his favor.

There had been a time when Diane could not walk into the corner grocery store, she'd been so embarrassed by the treatment she'd receive. Like royalty, they'd treated her, bowing and scraping, coming around the counter and taking her purchases out of her hand, moving her to the front of the line, no matter how many people had been waiting there before her. Shopkeepers desperately trying to curry her husband's blessing, hoping that their largesse would be repeated to him, so that he'd look upon them with kindness, so that he wouldn't hurt them.

He was a man who knew everyone of any kind of importance, and knew how to get things done, for himself and for his friends. One who did favours for everyone; a man you either loved or hated, depending on whether he'd beaten you silly.

There had been other times, too, when she'd sat in booths in nightclubs and seen the respect that he'd been given firsthand, people showing it through her. Strangers had come up to her in lounges when she'd been pregnant, trying to hand her envelopes that had been stuffed with sheaths of cash.

'For the baby, for the christening,' these strange men would say. Her husband would see what was going on and would kindly refuse the offering, pat the man's shoulder and thank him profusely, tell him that he would not forget how he'd tried to show his respect.

She'd wondered, back then, if that was what the men had been doing. She'd often thought that they'd been paying protection, their dollars keeping them out of the path of the tornado to whom she'd been married.

He'd been, in his way, good to her. The problem was that he had two outstanding emotions: smoldering anger that could on a dime be turned into violent rage.

But then again, that wasn't quite true, either. Time and hours of thought had given her a slightly kinder perspective.

She could remember him laughing, a lot when they'd first gotten married. Ben marveling at the wonder of her body, worshipping it, at first. Before she'd taken to eating to hide her own rage, the fear of him that had such a tight and deadly grip on her. He would always show her respect out in the world, and she believed that he'd been true to her, as true as a man like Ben Morer could be with anyone, ever.

She'd come to believe, as the years passed her by, that Ben had truly loved her.

But if he had, wouldn't he have found a job, wouldn't he have changed his ways in order to keep her love? She couldn't ever see that happening, though, without years of intensive therapy, and the thought of that was laughable, Ben on a leather couch, getting in touch with his feelings.

And now he thought he was dying. Did what he'd once given her outweigh all the things that he'd taken away? He'd robbed her of her self-esteem, of any sense of worth. Had put her in an emotional prison where she'd been afraid even to look through the bars. He'd been so strong, so violent and mean, that she'd subsumed her own will, had molded it to conform with his own. There had been times in her life when Diane would have died, gladly given her life in order to make him happy. So what did she owe him now, if anything? He'd nearly destroyed her, it had been more than close. Did she have any obligation to him, after all this time? After what he'd put her through?

Only that she loved him, but she couldn't think of that now.

Something her analyst had once said to her now popped into her mind, the thought filling her with guilt.

'He didn't do anything to you that you didn't allow him to do.'

She'd hated the therapist when she'd spoken those words, had sat up on the couch and had glared at the woman. But now, she could see, the therapist had been right. No one manipulates anyone else without that person's permission.

Ben had been powerful, physically and in other ways, could pick up the telephone and take care of something in a minute that other men would have to work for months in order to achieve. He'd carried his power on his sleeve all the time, never tried to hide the fact that he had it, or tried to convey the message that he was anything but what he was.

He'd told her that, too, pointed it out to her when she'd

finally screwed up the courage to confront him and ask for a divorce: 'You knew what I was when you married me,' he'd told her, and the fact was that that was the truth.

He was never a hypocrite, had never pretended to be legitimate. Her inner fight for years had been over her belief that she was weak; that she simply couldn't stand up next to him, because he was so incredibly strong.

And he sent the five hundred, every week, for his kids. Didn't that count for something?

As time passed, she could even think of him as sensitive. She could remember times when he'd been on his knees before her, as she lay on the bed, crying.

'What's wrong?' he'd demand to know, his face and voice betraying his concern, and she couldn't tell him, could never tell him the truth. That what was wrong was not something he could fix by picking up a telephone, nor was it something that he could beat into submission. He'd always wanted to protect her, always was watchful of her, trying to solve all her problems.

What she couldn't tell him was that he was wrong, their marriage, their *lives* were wrong. It was something she'd fully understood during the three years that he'd been in prison, when his letters would come to the boys, or when they'd visit him in jail, where strange black women would search Diane's body, looking for illegal contraband. It was over, she'd known it then, even though she could never bring herself to tell him while he was gone.

She wondered now how he'd have taken it, if it would have been easier for them both if she'd just divorced him then.

None of his letters was ever filled with self-pity; pity was something he never asked anyone for or would ever give. In fact, his letters went mostly to the boys, short, printed letters with many spelling errors, their father telling them what it was like in there, how important it was that they didn't follow in his footsteps.

He'd probably have accepted it, would have seen her as a gold-digger who'd bailed out when things got tough. Maybe that would have been better, it most certainly would have been better for the sake of the children's mental health.

But she hadn't, she'd hung on, had stood by her man and hoped that jail would make him see the error of his ways. Which it hadn't. All that he could think about, after he got out, was how quickly he could make up all the time that he had lost.

Finally, even though she'd never stopped loving him, she had asked him for a divorce, and had cut him out of their lives. And he'd accepted that, too, hadn't come storming around, as she'd half-expected. Hadn't made any scenes in front of the kids or the neighbors, hadn't tried any emotional blackmail or terrorism to try and get her back. He'd simply upped and left, and after one phone call, he'd left them alone.

Except for the weekly mail delivery, except for the money, For The Kids.

Did she owe him some obligation because he was living up to one of his? Should she stand by him now, when he would need someone to love him? Maybe not, maybe she owed him nothing. But if she didn't owe him anything, then why was she so upset?

For all she knew, he was married again, living in luxury with some ex-hooker he'd met. Maybe he had other children, maybe he even had five of them. But somehow, she didn't believe that.

He'd only had a little love inside him, it was all that God and life had allotted him, and she believed that he'd given it all to her, to her, and to the kids. His love was all used up.

Dear sweet Jesus, why hadn't he left her alone?

She heard footsteps on the stairway, and she rapidly wiped at her eyes, reflexively knowing that she'd been sitting there crying. She looked over at the wall, trying to compose her face, felt weight fall upon the other side of the couch as John flopped down next to her, put his arms around her.

'All done, Ma,' her youngest said, kissing her on the cheek. 'I'll ace this test, or I'll eat the history book.' He looked at her sincerely.

'I apologize, Ma, I should have told you Friday. I'm sorry I didn't mention the test until tonight.'

'You know that I would have made you miss the Bears game.'

'Well . . .'

'John . . .'

'It was in my mind, I gotta admit.'

She looked at her boy, at her miniature Ben Morer, and knew full well that he'd never be like his dad. She smiled at him, wiped at her eye, felt a wetness on her finger.

'You been crying?'

'Me? Don't hold your breath.'

'Really, Ma, is something wrong? Did I do something? Did Benny?'

'You two, how many times have I told you? It's not your fault when someone else gets upset. You tried to blame yourselves for the divorce, my God, when you had nothing to do with it.'

'The di*vorce*?'

'Yes, when I divorced your father.'

'What's up, Ma?' He was looking at her, strangely. 'You haven't mentioned the divorce around here in years.'

'Just sitting here thinking about it, that's all.'

'Thank God he's gone.' Her son's voice was bitter. She looked at him and saw rage in his eyes, burning, the way his father's used to, and she was afraid.

'Thank *God* he's gone,' Diane said, and smiled. 'Now go upstairs and see if Benny's through with his homework. See if he wants to play some Parcheesi with us before bed.'

Ben sat at his kitchen table, looking around at the pig sty that he now called home. The pain in both sides of his chest was back now, strong, and he twisted his lips in disgust at the thought that his body was forsaking him. He was getting paranoid in his old age, he knew. It was probably just something that had to do with nearly forty years of smoking, not cancer, nothing deadly. Cancer wouldn't come and go like this, would cause him pain all the time. Tomorrow he'd find out, tomorrow was D-Day.

For now, he'd been embarrassed enough, had lived like

an animal for too long. Speaking to his wife had made him feel dirty, made him think about what might have been, if he'd gotten a job and settled down fifteen, ten, even five years ago.

There was a bottle of Royal Salute on top of the icebox, and he'd get his strength back and go take it down, wash out a glass and have a little taste. It would taste good right now, would wash away some of the pain. And it would help him later on tonight, too, when he planned on telling Sunny that he wanted her out of his life by tomorrow.

Mute came half-awake at the sound of the shower running, shaking his head and scared until he remembered where he was. Once, as a teenager, he'd awakened in a jail cell, hungover, and he didn't know what he was doing there, had no idea as to what he might have done. When Mute had wondered aloud about it the older Irish guy in the cell with him had said, 'Man, the kid you hit just died a little while ago,' and Mute had spent three hours in complete and total terror, knowing that he was going to the joint again, for an extended stay this time. By the time they came to get him and let him go on an I-Bond, he was so relieved to learn that the charge was only drunk driving that he didn't even want to go back in the cell and kill that son of a bitch who'd lied to him just to scare his ass.

Now he lowered himself further into the bed, pulled the covers up to his chin, curled his huge body into the fetal position and sighed, Mute satisfied, feeling content, his guilt gone for the moment, hell, he hadn't done that much wrong.

He was used to women who'd been hurt, wives of power-trippers, wounded, looking for salvation in the arms of a man whom they thought would understand them. Sensitive enough to see past his looks, they'd get their fantasies going, Mute being their knight in shining armor, and roll with them, thinking what they wanted, until it came time for him to drop them, and when that time came he didn't much care how they responded to the news. He *wasn't* used to women who laughed and joked and grabbed his leg in bars.

Sometimes it took him a while to score, and that was all right with him, the chase was sometimes half the fun. Talking some emotionally injured woman into jumping between the sheets was his challenge and a way to get back at them, for all the laughs that had come his way from their species, due to his appearance.

But this one, dear Lord, she was something else altogether.

MaryAnn seemed secure and strong, not the type of woman who had ever before found him attractive in any way. She was aggressive, where most of the women he knew were meek. Most of the women he slept with were shy and bashful, submissive before the force of his personality and physical strength. MaryAnn, now, she was none of those things.

Where he had to cajole most women out of their panties, she had torn hers off with abandon, had leaped upon him the second the motel door had closed behind them. He was used to taking a lot of time and effort in getting a woman down there with her mouth, and here he was, in some shabby hotel room, with a woman who climbed down there with something approaching joy and seemed to enjoy every second of what she'd been doing. She'd climbed astride him a couple of times, too, held him down with arms that were a lot stronger than they appeared, MaryAnn enjoying the dominant role, staring down at him with a look in her eye that told him who was boss.

She was so damned different from every woman he'd ever had that he had to stop himself and ask the question: was he falling in love here? Had God sent her to him to help him straighten out his life? It was something to think on, He worked in mysterious ways, His wonders to perform.

She came out of the shower with a towel around her middle, her titties holding it up on top, the towel barely covering her thing down below. She had long, shapely legs; his Mare really was put together.

'Come on back in here with me, babe, I got something I want to show you.'

'Not tonight, I've got to go.'

'Come on, shit, it's the middle of the night.'

She was wiping herself dry with the towel now, Mare unashamed of her body, swiping at it without even looking at him. She dropped the towel on the floor and began to pull on her clothes and he watched her, growing excited at the sight of her private, intimate moments, Mare ignoring him as she clasped her bra from the front, then turned it so the clasp would be in the back where it belonged. He watched her stuff herself into the front of the bra, then adjusting it, Mute groaning as she pulled her shirt on over it and buttoned it deftly, seeing her in the light coming from the bathroom, along with a lot of steam.

'Come on, Mare, we hardly got to know each other.'

'I'll be walking funny all day, Mute, are you kidding me? How much can one man handle?'

'Me, I'm insatiable. Like the name of that porn film with Marilyn Chambers. Nothing can stop me, I just drink a glass of milk and *bam*, I'm ready for action again.'

She was pulling her jeans on now, going through contortions to get her shirt into them. Even unbuttoned, the jeans were hard for her to pull up. The lines on her belly from the waistband of the pants had turned him on when he'd first seen them. MaryAnn now had to lie down on the floor in order to zip them up. She was too smart to come and try it on the bed. She sat up and pulled her cowboy boots on to her feet.

Straining, she said, 'Another time, maybe . . .' as if she didn't really think that she'd ever see him again.

Mute sat up in bed, stared down at her, on the floor.

'Mare, come on, you've got to be kidding, what do you *mean*, maybe?'

'Come on, I'm married, you've got your life. It was a fun night, okay? I'm glad we got together.'

'Listen, I don't want you to go like this, I want to see you again.' Mute experienced a moment of panic; she seemed to be looking at him as a one-night stand.

She laughed.

'*All* men want to see me again when they're lying in bed, naked.' She got up and grabbed her purse from the ratty chair she'd tossed it on. She dug around in there, found a pen and a card, and sat down on the chair and flicked on the reading light.

'Give me a number where I can reach you.'

'Well, I don't exactly have a phone over at my apartment . . .'

'How about at work?'

'They don't like us to take personal calls, how about if I call you?'

She stuffed the card and the pen back into her purse.

'Why don't we just forget it, all right?'

'What's the matter, what's wrong? Shit, what did I do?'

Mute felt growing hysteria at the thought of never seeing her again; this was the sort of woman who rarely ever crossed his path. One with stamina and ability, and that tongue, sweet Jesus, that tongue.

And besides, women usually fell for him, in a big way, once he'd bedded them. Had to romanticize it and imagine themselves in love, Beauty and the Beast, in his dreams, with Linda Hamilton. When it came time to cut it off, it was always Mute who walked, leaving a trail of crying women from South Chicago up to the North Side missing that powerful body, that protective, physical safety he'd given them. And the sense of danger, there was always that. Mute had enough shrewdness to know that it wasn't his good looks alone or his body that aroused them.

But this one wasn't like that. She'd seen what they'd done as a night's fun and nothing more. But if that was true, then why the scam earlier? What was that shit about having *him* when no one else did? He didn't have time to think about that now, not with MaryAnn ready to walk out of his life. God was punishing him, he figured that out now, giving him love and then taking it away.

'I'll see you, Mute,' his Mare said, and started walking to the door.

Mute leapt out of bed and stood in front of the door, holding both hands out, blocking her exit. She looked him up and down, amused, and when she spoke her voice was wistful.

'God, what a body. I'm going to miss that.'

'You don't have to miss anything, you don't have to miss *shit*. Take that pen out, I'll give you my number at work, and I want a way to reach you, too, Mare, this ain't over yet. Hell, it ain't even really started.'

She studied him for a little while, looking at him appraisingly, then nodded her head and went back to the chair and – thank God – took out her pen and the card. Mute went back to the bed and sat on the edge, flexing his muscles. He wanted her to notice them, to miss those arms around her body.

'What is it?'

Mute gave her the number, and then asked for hers in return.

'Not yet,' she told him, 'not until I know I can trust you not to call me and make a scene in front of my husband. He works with me, too, you know, and I don't want him knowing about you.'

'Shit, I don't *want* him knowing about me, I don't want him even knowing I ex*ist*.'

She looked at him in a way that made him think that she might never call.

'It was fun, wasn't it, Mute?'

'More than fun, Mare, it was downright goddamned in*cred*ible.'

'See you, honey,' Mare said, blew him a kiss and walked to the door, then pulled it open and stepped out without even looking back at him once.

Mute lay there, smoking, thinking, wondering what her game was. An incredible piece of ass – he hadn't been lying when he'd told her that she was – but he believed that she mistook his ugliness for stupidity. A lot of people did.

Mute wasn't dumb, he was nobody's fool. The only time

he'd ever gone to jail was for an act of violence he'd committed while he'd been drunk and therefore, not responsible. Been young, too, not that he was old now. Still, they'd never caught him for even one of the many burglaries or other acts of theft that he'd committed, and they didn't have a bead on him now, while he dealt with insurance companies, ripped them off, did the occasional marijuana deal. He wouldn't deal in violence, and he never robbed anyone who couldn't afford to lose what he'd taken.

He was careful and he paid attention, and he didn't think with his dick, although it was tempting to do so now, with Mare, was she ever something. The thought that he might be in love with her, that God had sent her down to straighten him out, kept playing around in his brain.

Still, he wasn't dumb, no matter what anyone thought. So he had to lie here and figure things out, what she knew about him, why she'd approached him.

It was some kind of set-up, he knew, he'd figured that out in the bar.

He'd taken down her little vanity license plate number as he'd followed her to the motel. He'd seen her talking on her car phone, and at the time he'd thought that she was calling her husband, making excuses for being late or for not coming home at all. Now, he wasn't so sure.

Because she'd called him Mute. He'd introduced himself as Michael, the way he always did. His married girlfriends would call him Mike until he got to know them. Then he'd tell them about his nickname, and usually it scored him pity and attention, which was the reason that he told them about it in the first place. He'd gotten the panties off of more than one of them who'd wanted to be just friends by telling her how they'd christened him in the pen, about the name they'd laid upon him.

The name didn't bother him, in fact, he kind of liked it. It was better than Michael any day, there were millions of Michaels, but how many people had he ever met named Mute?

Still, he knew damn well that he hadn't told her about it.

She'd been looking for him at the racetrack, their meeting had been no accident.

Now there were a couple of ways that he could play this, ways that it could work itself out. She might have heard about him from a girlfriend, heard how well hung he was, how good he was between the sheets, and she wanted to find out for herself, wanted to meet him without making a big thing out of it or getting an awkward formal introduction. Or maybe her girlfriend had just bragged about him and pointed him out in a restaurant or something. There were more than a couple of nurses at the hospital that he'd once had something going with, and she'd said she worked in South Chicago. She might have been having lunch with one of her pals and he'd walked right in and hadn't noticed them together.

He could picture it, what the girlfriend would have said to MaryAnn.

'That's him, over there. Isn't he *ugly*?' Then she'd go on to tell MaryAnn what a stud he was in bed, how muscular he was.

That's probably how it had happened.

Still, it never hurt to be careful. He'd check her out. It would cost him a few bucks –

Mute jumped out of the bed and stormed around the room, found his pants where he'd dropped them behind the chair and searched through them quickly, found the wad of money in his pocket. He took it out and looked at it, did a fast count to make sure that it all was there. Jee-*zus*. Thinking about buying her address from a cop had scared him, got him to thinking that maybe she'd rolled him as he'd slept. But the money was all there, she hadn't ripped him off.

So what was her game? Did she want him for more than his body? For ten bucks Mute could find out, give a cop he knew her license plate number and have him get her address. He could sure afford it now, and he had his own plan forming in his mind as he thought of her, of that body, tight and strong, that tongue she had on her . . .

But for now he wanted to get some sleep, so he could do

what he had to do tomorrow without being all fuzzy-headed and tired. He had to work tomorrow afternoon, and if he was going to look her up, he would have to do it in the morning, as he had something else he wanted to do tomorrow that would have the potential to sweeten his bankroll further. And the big lab boss frowned on it when Mute came in late, and when his boss frowned on something, his probation officer did too. It was one and the same thing; the two men had what they liked to call a good working re*lat*ionship. Mute just figured that they were hot for each other.

There was one more thing Mute wanted to do before sleeping. He got down on his knees at the side of the bed, rested his elbows on the lumpy mattress, folded his hands and looked up toward the ceiling, saw the cracks, the water stains . . . He looked down at the bed and saw a stain on it, his own sperm, part of it still wet. There were brown spots on the mattress, and other assorted blotches that he couldn't even begin to grasp the origins of.

Mute looked up again, squinting.

'God?' he said. 'You there?' The Twilight Motel might not be the best place to try and establish an affinity with the Lord. Mute said, 'I'm sorry, God,' thinking of his grandma, thinking of his childhood. 'Let me know the way?' Would He? Was He there?

Mute got up off his knees and rolled on to the bed, got comfy under the covers.

He had money in his pocket, a good job, and a few other things going for him that brought him in some dough. For the time being, at least until tomorrow, God could stay on the back burner. It would give Mute that much more time to have some fun in his life.

They started pounding on Ben's door at five in the morning. He leaped out of bed, panicked, dreading he'd made a mistake in thinking that Lino and Tony would go to the Man first before they made their move on him. In his sleeping state he'd been sure that they were kicking the door in, coming to kill him. He fell to the side of the bed, forgetting his physical pain, dragged the gun out from underneath the bed and lay there, panting, waiting for them to make their move.

Nobody came into the bedroom; he could hear nothing out in the living room, no footsteps entering the apartment through the front and only door. It hadn't been kicked in; at least not yet.

Ben peeked over the bed, trying to adjust his eyes, shook his head, trying to clear it, as the pounding began again.

"Ey, Benny,' Ben heard the voice, seductive and low, the guy making fun of him, and realized who it was.

It was the cops.

He immediately dropped the gun and pushed it back under the bed, looking around in panic for a place to stash it. There were too many weapons, and too little time. It was a roust or they wouldn't be coming this late, and they'd catch him holding weapons, would have enough to bust him, if that was what they were looking for.

'You gonna be an asshole about this, or are you gonna invite us in?'

It would be useless to ask them if he could see a warrant first; that stuff was great for television, and that was about it. As it was, they'd have been all over him by now, if they thought that he wasn't packing. Their reluctance to enter wasn't out of respect, or the fact that they wouldn't have a warrant. As arrogant as they were, they were still afraid of Ben, and Ben knew that they'd compensate for that fear by being ready to shoot him the first time he made a move that they decided they didn't care for.

Ben got to his feet and walked over to the door, unlocked it and pulled it open.

'Come on,' he said, fighting to keep his voice level.

Two of them came in, dressed well, big men whose guns and badges made them even more formidable than their size already dictated. He knew them, had been paying them off for years – Midler and Slinski, two dicks from the Fourth, looking for more money.

They sauntered into the apartment with their weapons

drawn and ready, Midler staying there in the kitchen with him as Slinski passed by, making a beeline for the bedroom. Slinski blew Ben a kiss over his shoulder as he entered the bedroom and began to search it. Ben sat down at the kitchen table, feeling exposed and angry, fighting both feelings. Any sign of anger would be greeted with a violent response.

'So,' Midler said, 'how you doin', buddy boy?'

Ben looked at him, wanting to knock the smirk right off his face. He said nothing, though, needing to stay within himself if he was going to avoid a pinch.

'What's the matter, we catch you in the middle of a sweet dream?'

From the bedroom, Slinski's voice rang out. 'Wet dream, probably, ain't no bitches hanging around you anymore, Ben?' Then Slinski said, 'Bingo.'

He came out of the room holding the .357 that had been under Ben's bed in two fingers, preserving any prints that Ben might have left on the butt or barrel.

'Convicted felon in possession of a firearm. You're gonna do some federal time on this one, Benny.'

Midler said, 'You think that scares him? Federal penitentiary gotta be better than living in *this* dump.' He turned to Ben, one foot on top of a chair, elbow leaning on his knee. Midler's gun was dangling from his fingers, pointing downward.

'Now you *know* it ain't right for a guy like you to have a gun.'

Ben stared at him, trying to appear emotionless. They'd tell him what they had come to say as soon as they were through fucking around. Still, it wasn't easy. He wanted to smash them both, destroy them, and he could do it without a lot of effort, too, even as sick as he was. But he couldn't and he knew it; their badges gave them immunity. If he touched them, they would shoot him. They had him and they were well aware of the fact.

Midler now blew him a kiss.

'Lookin' good for a guy your age, ain't he, Slin?'

Ben heard Slinski grunt. Although both men were big,

they both had bellies, extra beef hanging off them. Ben had always been tight and strong but slender, and, recently, he'd been losing some weight. He sat there in his shorts, unembarrassed, in control of himself. He'd had experience over the years in being undressed before other males.

'How you figure the niggers at Stateville gonna take to this boy, with that tight white butt?'

They were going to start with clichés now? They were fishing. Still, they should have known better than to try to scare him with tactics that only worked on seventeen-year-old punks who were facing their first pinch. Twenty years ago, he would have told them: I don't worry about that, see, I'll sell them naked pictures of your wife and daughters. Say it and take a beating, and then they could do whatever they wanted. But twenty years ago his entire life had been in front of him. Today, he wasn't sure if he even had another year.

Ben remained silent, turned his gaze to the wall.

'We heard you come into a little money tonight, Benny.'

'Somebody lied to you.' Ben's first words.

'Nah, I don't think so, these guys, they lie to us, they know what kind of response they'd get. We help them out, see, the same as we help you.'

Ben couldn't listen to this anymore.

'When'd either one of you ever do anything for me? The way I see it, it was the other way around.'

'Hey, Benny, good to see you back. For a minute there I thought you'd lost your famous sense of humor.'

Midler said, '*Sure*, you've helped us out. And we've been grateful. So much that we didn't lock you up a hundred times when we had you dirty. And the deal is, we get ten points of everything you bring in.'

'I ever hold out on you?'

'Not that we know of, but a guy like you, with all the fingers you've got into other people's pies, who knows what you really make, how much comes in that you don't tell us about? Things you decide not to *share* with us.'

'There's something supposed to happen tonight. That's

all I can say. There's money in it for me, if the guys comes through.'

'How *much* money?' Slinski asked.

'Fifty grand.'

He saw the look that passed between them as soon as he said the words; Lino and Tony would have told them the amount, there would have been no use in lying to them, pretending that it was lower. And if Lino and Tony had tried to tell the cops that the amount was a lot more, then these two parasites would have wanted to know why they hadn't been getting more from the sharks. No, Lino and Tony would have told the truth, for once in their miserable lives.

'So, you saying you ain't got it yet?'

'I'm saying I might not get it at all.'

'Yeah, you did a real number on one of the guys who owed it to you. Outsmarted yourself by doing it, too. Where do you think this son of a bitch Lino shows up? South Chicago Hospital.' Midler performed an elaborate shrug.

'Instead of staying downtown, he comes home to roost, to lick his wounds. Now, Benny, there ain't much that goes on at South Chicago Community Hospital that we don't know about. Hell, our station house ain't but a few blocks away. Whenever certain things happen, such as tough guys getting the shit kicked out of them, we hear about it, you know what I'm saying? A lot of them take care of us, and we got to protect our investment, even if they got too much pride to come over and tell us what happened, to ask for help in getting things straight.'

'He didn't pay me shit.'

'Okay, so he's a liar. We'll talk to him.'

'Later,' Slinski said. '*After* they give you your money.'

'And Benny,' Midler said, 'you'd better have five grand sitting in an envelope here on this table by this time tomorrow night. 'Cause if there ain't, we're just going to have to turn this pistol over to the state's attorney.'

'That ain't evidence,' Benny said, before he could stop himself.

'*Oh*, now he's a *lawyer*.' Midler raised his pistol, pointed it right at Ben Morer's face. Ben looked at it as if it were a toy; he would die before he'd ever show an enemy his fear.

'What are you thinking, fruit of the poison tree? Illegal entry? I got news for you: when we come back, we're gonna *have* a search warrant, all signed and everything by our friend, the judge.'

Slinski laughed. 'You see the look on his face, partner? This son of a bitch, he's slipping.'

Midler said, 'You heard me right. All the judges, all the crooked lawyers always been your friends, suddenly, they ain't gonna be so friendly towards you no more. The Man for some reason made a few phone calls.'

Ben desperately wanted to ask them *when* the Man had made his calls, but he didn't, and for two reasons. For one thing, they wouldn't know, and might, in fact, even have the wrong information. The second reason was that they thought they were only confirming what Ben would have to know already; they assumed that any falling out he'd had with the Man would already be a well-known fact of life to Ben. He sat there, thinking, inside himself, but deflated.

'We'll be back tonight, and you'd better have our money.'

Ben watched them walk away, swaggering out his door. He waited until he heard their footsteps on the wooden stairway before he got up and went over and locked the door.

He went and got out a different gun, sat at the kitchen table with the pistol pointing toward the door, and thought for a time, wondering about what had just happened.

They had a gun that undoubtedly had his fingerprints on it. Tomorrow, if he didn't come through in a hurry, they would at the very least pinch him for having it, and then he'd do a couple of years with Uncle Sam. He didn't think that he had two years left, and did not want to die in the federal penitentiary hospital in Springfield, Missouri. And he knew that it was only politicians who'd been busted who ever got out of the federal system because they'd gotten ill.

What had been his options? If he hadn't opened the door they'd have kicked it down, and come in blasting. Ben could get away with a lot, and had in his life even gotten away with murder. But you didn't kill a cop in Chicago, you couldn't do that and walk away. And they had his gun now, one of them, that they could give to the state's attorney.

He could see another scenario, though, one that would be more appealing to men such as these. They'd kill one of their enemies with his pistol – someone who hadn't paid adequately or often enough, or someone they'd been trying to bust who'd been just too slick for them. Then they'd run a ballistics test on the .357 while Ben was being processed for possession of a weapon. Then they'd have him for life, in a state penitentiary, and he'd die in some filthy medical ward, alone, being used for unspeakable acts by jailhouse orderlies after he'd grown too weak to fight them off, or by anyone who'd paid the orderlies off.

Christ, some choices he had.

But would they do him like that? Or was it just an empty threat?

He'd paid them enough over the years to retire, paying them since most of the guys who now ran the Fourth District had been rookies working out of a squad car. You'd think that they'd be grateful. How many times had he sent Christmas presents to their parents, taken care of things for them when they had a problem with the mob? These cops would get in trouble, over their heads with bookies or sharks, and he'd go to bat for them, help them out whenever he could. Some of them respected that, and knew how to show their gratitude. Others, like these two pricks tonight, they took it as their due.

He used to pay them for looking the other way when he had a tavern over in Hegewisch, and he'd want to stay open late or wanted them to ignore the gambling action in the back room. And he'd been paying them regularly ever since then, whenever they came around, sniffing, as he always had something going, and paying the cops was part of the overheads.

Still, he hadn't expected any loyalty from these two. He'd known them for many years, and when he thought of them as pricks it wasn't a figure of speech. They were paid to perform a service, and he hadn't assumed that hard greenbacks could ever purchase personal devotion. They'd done what they'd been paid to do, and now they would be looking at a man that they'd see as washed up, and would want to squeeze every last dime he had out of him before he burned out or wound up in the trunk of his car.

The thing that bothered him most today was what they'd said about the Man, how the Man had made some phone calls. He'd talked to the Man just last Thursday, and the Man hadn't shown any sign of disapproval. Then again, he wouldn't have; if he was angry at Ben, he would have acted even more friendly than usual. Then after Ben had left, he would have given orders to have him killed. It was why he was the Man, instead of a guy like Ben.

It could make him crazy, thinking about that, after all the money he'd paid out to that bastard. The Man was supposed to take care of things for him, protection from certain cops came as a part of the package.

So what he had to figure out was, was their information wrong, or had the Man really made the calls?

On the one hand, the two of them had been dead wrong about Ben's having come into some money, but that could be put down to Lino's stupidity. He'd have lied to them just to anger Ben, knowing that they'd roust him if they thought that he had come into a windfall.

Which was the smart move to make, from their point of view. The fact was that Ben had made thousands of deals in his lifetime for which the law did not get their share. The Man now, Ben had never cheated, nor the outfit bosses before him, but the cops, he'd beat them out of anything that he thought he could get away with. So they'd thought that he had money, and that had been wrong.

On the other hand, why would they bluff about the Man? Telling Ben they knew about the fifty grand was all that they'd need to do in order to see a piece of it. With Ben's record and reputation, he could be shaken down by any two-bit punk in the department and he'd have to eat it, take what they handed out and hand over what they wanted. Who would a judge believe, the cops, or a man like Ben? He would get the chance to explain himself, sure, but then the judge would laugh at him. Judges and cops could get away with laughing at him.

So he had to assume that they were telling the truth, that the Man had sold him out. All right, then there was only one thing he could do. He could move.

But where in the hell could he go that would be far enough away that such men couldn't find him? He'd been born a couple of miles from here, over on the East side. Had gone to school in the area, had been expelled from Washington high. He'd lived with a dozen different families on the East Side or over in Hegewisch, people who'd take him in for the pittance that the State would pay them, money that was supposed to go to his support but which wound up sitting on the bar at the South Shore Inn, or over at Blondies.

Everyone he knew was in Chicago, everyone he'd ever worked for or with. It looked as if he could get out of his trouble with the law for five grand, which was the going rate, but what about the Man?

He had to think about that, and he had to think rationally. It was no time to go off and get emotional over what he'd been told.

If the Man had wanted him dead, then he'd already be gone. The Man would not have risked losing Lino and Tony, and he knew from his own experiences that Ben was capable of murder. So, he didn't want Ben dead. Didn't much care if Ben killed Lino and Tony. What was it that the Man wanted, and why was he abandoning Ben now, after all these years?

Deep thoughts before dawn, when he had an appointment with fate that morning.

Ben couldn't go to the Man, that would be the same as putting a noose around his own neck. If the Man was turning his back on him, he wouldn't want Ben to know about it, until after it was already too late for Ben to take revenge, the way everyone who knew him would expect him to.

The Man was *it* in Chicago these days. He instilled so

much fear, garnered so much respect, that no one ever even called him by his name, even in his presence. He carried all the weight, and he owned the politicians. For a time things had been run by a committee of twelve, but that hadn't worked out; there had been too much infighting, too much jockeying for position and power and glory. After Sal Luchessa's death, everything had fallen apart, and the Man, one of the twelve, had pulled it back together. Blood had run in the streets, and most of the men who had survived had gone to federal prison, and after it was all over, the Man ruled supreme.

And ruled with an iron fist; he was the most feared man in Chicago. Everyone was terrified of him.

Everyone but Ben.

Ben was the last of the old-time hustlers, the type who lived by words that these two-bit punks and killers on the streets today would scoff at: honor, he was big on that; and respect, too, self-respect most of all. No favor was ever left without repayment and no slight was ever ignored. Death would be welcomed before humiliation, before he would allow an insult to pass without immediate retaliation.

The Man knew that, and it seemed that there were other things he might know, too. Ben would have to think about those things and would, later, after he saw the doctor.

But for now he had to think about one thing and one thing only: if the Man had truly abandoned him, how could he get even? There was only one way to do that with someone as powerful as the Man.

Ben would have to kill him. And he could too, if he had no other choice. It would even be easy, he'd be doing the world a favor. And if what he suspected about his health was true, what the hell would he have to lose?

MaryAnn Ceterra had a tough time getting up, but once she dragged herself into the shower, she knew that she'd be all right. She was like that still, at thirty-two she could still bounce back from a night of little sleep, lots of booze, and hours of rough sex without too much trouble. The thought never entered her mind that this would be harder for her to do as she grew older; she still was naive enough to believe that the ability would stay with her forever, and dumb enough to think that her sins would never be called in for payment – through her good looks.

Which she had in abundance. The breasts had been bought and paid for by Walter, after hers had begun to sag a little after her second abortion. But the rest of it was all her, and no surgeon's scalpel had ever touched her face. The deep blue eyes were all hers, too, she wore no contact lenses, she had her father's eyes. Eyes that were shot through with red right now, she'd have to drop some Murine in them before she left the house. She'd found ways around the small failings, the modest treacheries of her body. Getting up every morning at an ungodly hour would send you in search of them, the little cures that healed slight physical transgressions.

She got up early every day of the week, was in the office every Sunday, and didn't plan to take a holiday off until she'd made her fortune. Given a choice, though, she'd have stayed in bed every day until noon. And she would be able to, someday, too, after she'd gotten what she'd worked so hard for, after she was a legitimate millionaire. But today she had a business to run, by God, and nobody was going to stop her from reaching her goals, not even her husband, Walter, who seemed bent on trying, or on taking the credit for all of her hard work and effort. She was lecturing the trainees this morning, and Walter would be at the office, doing the work that was rightfully hers, looking over her shoulder for any small inaccuracies in MaryAnn's paperwork.

So she'd have to be very careful; he was an asshole, but, like a lot of lawyers she'd known, he was an extremely smart asshole.

She stepped out of the shower with only a slight headache, and dropped a couple of Nuprin to take care of that. MaryAnn dressed hurriedly, although she had plenty of time. She liked to linger over coffee before she did her make-up, drink three cups and smoke a couple of cigarettes before she even brushed her teeth.

The silk blouse she'd chosen to wear today now hung clinging to her wet skin, and she liked the way it clung to her because her husband Walter would be downstairs, having eaten his two-minute egg. He'd now be having a cup of tea, would look up at her, see her nipples sticking up at him, right through her flimsy bra. See what he couldn't have right now, what MaryAnn was withholding from him, the cheap son of a bitch.

She entered the kitchen, aware of the fact that even without make-up she was something to see. Her hair would dry while she drank her coffee, but now it clung in ringlets around her cheekbones, natural, carefree. Walter, a product of the sixties, would eat his heart out. MaryAnn had been born in 1960; she'd missed the entire thing, the days that Walter craved so terribly were ancient history to her. But she knew that he loved a natural woman, without make-up; the sight of her as she looked right now always made him get a wistful look on his face.

There he was, poor thing, looking at her with longing.

'Morning, Walter,' she said civilly, the voice she used when she first met clients and didn't know if they could afford any of the houses she was trying to sell.

'MaryAnn,' Walter said.

His bald head shone under the chandelier light above his head. Already, it was sweating, droplets beading up. He was dressed in his usual three-piece suit, white shirt, and thick patterned tie with a Windsor knot that he always kept pushed all the way up. His shoes would be shining under the table, without a spot of dirt on them. She'd seen them down there close up, MaryAnn under the table as Walter sipped his tea, slipping under there to add some spice to their relationship, her head bobbing in his lap, seeing those fucking shoes gleam.

Well, there'd be none of that anymore, not without a little attitude adjustment on his part.

'So, what time did you come rolling in last night?' Walter said, from behind his paper.

'Are you my father now?' MaryAnn was sifting coffee into

a white drip filter, pissed because he hadn't thought of doing it for her this morning, the way he usually did. Walter punishing her, for staying out late.

'No, but I *am* your husband.'

MaryAnn only grunted.

'Giving your lecture this morning?'

'Yes,' MaryAnn said. She carefully measured the water into the pouring jug, mineral free water out of a cooler next to the counter. 'I'm speaking to the trainees, I'll give them the usual, then be in the office after lunch.'

'No hurry, I'll have it under control.'

'I'm sure you will.'

Walter was holding the *Tribune* up, reading it creased, folded over precisely. When he was finished he'd wash the ink off his fingers before he even rinsed out his teacup. MaryAnn sat down with the *Sun-Times*, spread it out on the table before her. The edge of the paper touched Walter's saucer, and she had to fight the urge to give it a push, see if that broke his in-control facade, hot tea all over his nether region.

He shook the paper, Walter grunting.

'MaryAnn . . .' Oh, Jesus, here it came. His reprimand voice, turning up on the 'Ann' in her name, dragging it out.

'I believe we should discuss our problems like civilized adults.' He folded the paper over and set it down beside his tea.

'All you want to know is if I'm fucking somebody else.'

'Since you put it that way. I mean, this is a frightening time for anyone to live promiscuously, and you do owe me that much, I should know if you're having an affair.'

'*What* do I owe you, Walter, you tell me that. What have you given me that I haven't paid for over and over again?'

'This house, for one thing, the car you drive. I paid over a quarter of a million dollars for this house, you know – '

'Yeah, and by the end of next year I'll be able to give it all back to you and not miss it too much. We've been in this house for three years out of seven we've been married, and not a single day goes by where I don't have to fucking hear about the quarter million dollars you put out to buy it. That's a thousand *times*, Walter, that I've heard about your sacrifice.'

'If I hadn't encouraged you, you'd not be selling real estate.'

'Are we making lists, now, Walter, of the things we've done for each other? Who else ever polished your knob for you the way I do?'

'*Used* to.'

'You're goddamn right, used to. I killed myself going to real estate school, then working for assholes who kept half the money I earned, only to finally become a broker myself and having *you* looking over my shoulder every goddamn day of my life. I busted my ass to get away from that, and now there *you* are, like my daddy, watching over his little girl so she doesn't screw things up.'

'I invested quite a bit of money in that business.'

'*Bull*shit. You lost your clients, you couldn't pull it off in court anymore. You're in my goddamn business because there's nowhere else for you to go.'

Walter, who prided himself on never losing his temper, on always being in control, was beginning to lose it. She could tell because his skull was turning red. His face, though, never gave him away, he had the same look that he'd had on his face when she'd walked through the kitchen door. She hoped that he went berserk, that for once in his life, he would blow up. Of course, if he hit her, she would beat him into the ground, and he knew it, so it would never come to that.

Walter took a second to make sure that he was composed before he spoke.

'MaryAnn, your fantasies must be fun to discuss over lunch with your gossipy friends, but I assure you, the decision to not re-enter the courtroom was mine. I was reinstated by the bar, and I had a client list just *wait*ing for the day that I decided to step into a courtroom. But I'd made my fortune, and now I'm retired from the practice of defending the sort of people who used to sell you heroin when you were prowling the streets before you met me.'

'I never took heroin.' MaryAnn's voice was small.

'Whatever,' Walter said, knowing that he'd scored. 'I've made millions. One would think that a *wife* would enjoy sharing a career with her husband.'

'Walter?' MaryAnn rose and went over to the coffee maker, poured herself a cup and opened the fridge, hunting the milk. She wanted to pull herself together before she spoke to him again. His reminding her of what she'd been had cut her, and she hadn't thought that it would, seeing as it wasn't the first time that Walter had reminded her of where she'd come from. She stirred in cream and sugar, carefully carried the cup back to the table, put it down and lit a Virginia Slim, blew smoke across the table.

'You've been holding my past over my head like a sword for seven years, Walter. Even when you got in trouble and they kicked you out of the bar, I stood behind you, and I never said a word to you about it, never jumped on it when I was mad at you.'

She saw him lift his cup to his lips and sip at his tea, Walter eyeing her indulgently, the typical trial lawyer, thinking he was smarter than everybody else in the world.

She said, 'You won't stay away from the business, and you won't give me a divorce.'

'That's not true,' Walter said. 'I told you I'd give you a divorce.'

'Right, and leave me with nothing.'

'You earned nothing.'

'I earned every goddamn cent that my real estate company had made! Who else earned it, you? Sitting on your ass, looking at my paperwork all day!'

'You can divorce me and force me to give you half of what I've acquired during the relationship.'

'And have my past in every newspaper gossip column the day I file. And lose my broker's license before the ink's dry on the papers.'

'Well . . .'

'As I was saying, Walter,' MaryAnn took a drag on her cigarette and smiled, and when she spoke, it was in the syrupy voice she always used when she knew that she had a sale and there was no further use in being cold and professional.

'You won't stay away from the business, and you won't give me a divorce.' She paused, to give the idiot a chance to argue with her again, but he didn't. Walter just sat there, half-smiling at her, thinking he was humoring her.

'But I'll tell you this, and I won't say it again: what I was, I was a long time ago. If you ever throw it up in my face again, I swear to God, Walter, I'll take a knife and cut your balls off while you're sleeping, then stick them in your mouth.'

'That doesn't shock me, actually. You've been trying to castrate me since the day you graduated from real estate school.' He pronounced the words 'real estate school' as if they were beneath him, a law school graduate who could look down his nose at everyone else's lesser accomplishments.

MaryAnn grabbed the paper and stood, folded it under her arm and picked up her cup of coffee. He was staring at her; he wasn't good enough to keep his eyes off what she'd been keeping away from him. It must be driving him crazy. He hadn't been the first man to tell her that she was the best they'd ever had.

'Actually, there *is* someone else, Walter, but there's no need for you to worry about disease. You'll never get any of *this* again, not in this fucking life.' MaryAnn walked out of the room and she could feel his eyes on her, so she threw the wiggle in for all she was worth, kept it up until she turned the corner, out of Walter's sight.

It was a nice house, but not that nice. It surely wasn't the Scottish castle Walter tried to make it out to be. In the south suburbs a quarter million could buy you a lot of house, but you still had to kick in about twice that much if you were looking to buy a mansion.

MaryAnn sat at the make-up table in her bedroom, thinking about this, with the door to the hall and the adjoining door to Walter's bedroom locked. He'd tried three times this past week to sneak into her bedroom at night, thinking that all she'd have to do was to see his little shriveled dick and she'd succumb to his manly charms. Not even in his dreams, little man that he was.

Walter had served his purpose, and he'd served it a long time ago. Which didn't mean that she hadn't loved him once; you could love a man and still use him, MaryAnn truly believed that. Long ago, eight years ago, he'd been a saviour, when she'd been working. With his nice car and his flashy clothes and his diamond pinky ring. She'd give him a date and she'd sit in awe at some of the names he'd drop, people he knew personally, from the mayor to mob chiefs, friends of his, he'd tell her, they were all his buddies.

Walter had fallen in love with what she could do, more than he had with her. Had taken her off the street at a time that had been perfect for her, because in another year or two it would have been too late.

She'd realized that after he'd married her. In retrospect, she knew that her days had been numbered, that before long she would have burned out or got herself killed. It wasn't the sort of thing you thought about on the street, you just sort of played it by ear and took it a day at a time.

When she'd been out there MaryAnn had never used a pimp, and this caused her grief from them, the pimps wanting to recruit her, threatening to cut her every now and then. Mark her face up so bad that no man would ever want her. She'd known that to be bullshit; some of the women out there had been beaten with the ugly stick, and they could still sell it without a lot of difficulty. The sort of man who left a wife at home and hit the street looking for it wasn't looking for Hollywood glamor, he was looking for someone that he could control. No, MaryAnn hadn't been particularly worried about the pimps ever hurting her. Not as long as she was fucking cops for free, for their protection. Some pimp killing her, however, that was one thing she worried about.

If they had, who would have cared? Another dead hooker for the coroner's boys to make jokes about as she lay on the slab, beyond caring. Death and drugs, they went hand in hand, and the drugs had a better chance of getting to her than the pimps had.

She liked her cocaine, MaryAnn had truly loved it.

But that was a long time ago, and she didn't appreciate this hippie reject she was married to throwing that shit up into her face every time he got something in his uptight, funky ass.

There were ways around guys like Walter. Things she could do that could hurt him. She had not planned to set him up, the way she'd set up Mute last night, but Jesus, what choice was he leaving her? He just wouldn't leave her alone. She would never use his name, would not allow it to be placed on the papers that were legally filed after each of her secret cash transactions – the sales that he didn't know about, of which Mute would soon be a part.

But if the authorities ever investigated what she was doing, if anyone ever complained, she'd blame it all on Walter and she knew that he'd take the fall. And the cops, the judge, the jury, they'd believe her. They'd certainly take her word over the word of a man like him. One who'd already been arrested and disbarred for not keeping his clients' money in escrow, for using it for his own personal gain, in his own account.

He'd nearly gone to jail for that, but prison hadn't been his major concern. What he'd worried about was getting killed; the money had belonged to heavyweights. It had taken all the goodwill he'd built up over the years to stay out of prison and the cemetery, and he'd taken his disgrace and hidden it somewhere, he surely didn't act any differently after his public humiliation. No, what he'd done was he'd paid his fine and looked at his life, found that he'd spent the bulk of it making sure that he was rich, and now he was making investments. And, bastard that he was, everything he'd touched since then had turned into solid gold.

Especially her real estate agency. Bankrolling it had been his smartest investment. Ceterra real estate had sold over eleven million dollars' worth of property this year already, and that was *before* the government had decided to put the airport in Hegewisch.

The airport, the airport. She loved that word: airport. Nobody wanted to live near an airport. The people that were dispossessed would need places to live after the government threw them out; others, from the East Side, South Chicago and Calumet City, would want to move, getting out before the noise from the jets taking off and landing made them nuts. And they'd want to sell their houses, too, before they moved into something else.

She'd be there for them, had already dealt with some. There were those who needed cash money fast, and who could not wait around for an official closing or sale. Legally, there were ways to help them out, and MaryAnn could buy the houses dirt cheap, and sell them to veterans at a good profit for herself. Those dealings were all above board, unlike some others that she was doing, more and more of them every day now, as the date for the beginning of construction drew ever closer.

But old dipshit Walter, he had to sit at the office all day, reading everything that came in and demanding explanations for every sale. MaryAnn had been forced to keep separate books, separate contracts for such deals, and she made them undercover, and so far no one had complained. The type of people she bought from were not in a position to beef. Still, though, it was a pain in the ass, having a separate office, separate files, a private telephone number so that Walter couldn't learn about what she was doing and cash in on it along with her. She already had enough partners to worry about, Alfredo and that damned genius partner of his, James. Those two would be her partners until they dissolved a certain trust fund. MaryAnn would get sixty percent of all the profits, and Alfredo and James would divide what was left. The profits from their secret deals, the deals that Walter could never find out about.

Old people who'd been there all their lives, in the neighborhood and now frightened, listening to her horror stories about how the government would steal their property.

They'd gratefully accept her kind offer to buy, to help them out of their troubles. She'd get them cash and buy their houses, and then put the papers through, set everything in motion, and at the closing everything went smoothly – hell, they'd already been paid, who was to complain?

The second someone said that they wanted to consult their lawyer, she walked. Told them that she didn't deal with lawyers, that lawyers got too expensive and they always muddied the waters. That lawyers never looked out for anyone but themselves, and they certainly wouldn't look out for the poor clients, not unless there was monetary compensation in it for them.

There were others, too, who MaryAnn could talk into doing things they wouldn't ordinarily do. People with things on their minds, laid off mill workers who'd owned their houses forever and who would never even have thought about selling unless tragedy had struck them. They were even easier than the old folks, wanting to take care of their families.

Which was where Mute came in. She'd had designs on him for a while, since her connection at St Margaret's Hospital in Hammond had lost his job. She'd heard about him through James, who'd used the man to help in one of his insurance scams. Now, with her, Mute could earn a good buck and all the erotic benefits that went into her personal employment plan, if he decided to play along. If he didn't, well, what had she lost? A night of wild sex with a man who was built like a Mack truck. What a shame.

But she'd bet that he'd play along, would be dying to hear from her. She'd wait until half his shift was over, when the bosses would be gone and he'd be anxious, awaiting her call. He hadn't fooled her for a second last night, he'd fallen for her charms as badly as Walter had, eight years ago. An ugly mutt like him, how much could he be scoring?

He was kind of cute, after his own fashion, and she *did* think that he looked like a lion. Things could get interesting if Mute decided to play along. She'd know before the day was out, one way or another.

For now; though, she had to comb out her hair, put on her make-up, brush her teeth, and get ready to face the day. It was fun, something to look forward to, her life as it was today.

Now if she could only get rid of Walter, everything would be perfect.

Mute awoke early and got out of the motel before eight, heading home to his two-room apartment, which was really nothing more than a single bedroom that had once been huge and had a wall put up and a door hung to cut it in half so it could be rented out as what the landlady called a two-room apartment. The bathroom was down the hall, and he shared it with four other people, old men who never cleaned the tub and who most of the time didn't even bother to flush the damn toilet after their pig selves. Mute seemed to spend half his time in there, with a can of Ajax and a sponge. There was no cooking allowed in Mute's 'apartment' house, which was the upstairs portion of what had once been a large single-family home.

Still, no matter what he did or how hard he scrubbed things, washing the tile floor of the hallway and cleaning the bathroom until it sparkled, the place always smelled. He could always smell wine and the unwashed bodies of elderly males, the stinks merging with the cleaning agents he used, Lysol, Ajax, and wino mingled together. And cats, the place always smelled of cats. The sweet little old woman who owned the place just loved them. And they seemed to take to him, didn't back away from him, the way most people did. Cats couldn't understand ugly. Mute thought that was because all humans looked alike to them.

Mute would clean the bathroom mirror the same way that he combed his hair, looking away from it, peeking at his reflection out of the corner of his eye. Shaving was the most painful part of his daily ritual. Mute had trained himself not to look himself in the eye, but still he couldn't avoid it, seeing what he was.

He knew what he looked like, and did not like to be

reminded. When he was living his life these days, he could even think of himself as being somewhat attractive. He was downright gorgeous, compared to how he'd looked for the first twenty years of his life.

God wasn't the only one who compensated; Mute did, too. He might have some physical drawbacks, but by God, he was clean. Always smelled good, used powder as well as his scented deodorant and foreign cologne. He never even let his car get stale-smelling, would wash it once a week and spray it with some shit they had over at the Spot-Not car wash. Came out of a little spray gun, and you got your choice of smells. Mute always used pina collada, he loved the scent of the stuff, the fragrance that would linger in his car until the following Saturday.

There were only two things that he ever spent any money on, and those two things were horses and married women. Between the two of them, he always managed to keep himself broke, no matter how hard he worked, no matter how much he hustled. There were various ongoing scams that brought in thousands of extra dollars every single year, money he should have kept in the bank somewhere, money he fully intended to bank, but every time he got a check, he wound up cashing it and blowing every dime. On married women or ponies, he didn't know exactly why. Then again, there were other expenses, that came up every month.

Mute had over a dozen phony addresses set up around the city, where mail sent to him was forwarded, and this service didn't come cheap. There was also the fleet of junk cars that he kept in various rented garages. He got the cars for next to nothing, but they all had to be insured and have stickers and license plates on them. It was his latest money-making brainstorm, the cars, and he was really milking it; hardly a week went by where some insurance company didn't send him a settlement check. He paid his bills, usually on time, but still, where did all the money go? Shit, he didn't even have a telephone, and his landlady, Mrs Calloway, paid for his electric and heat; they came along with the rent, along with the smell of cats.

The horses he could deal with, winning was fun and losing was normal. He always figured, on a losing day, that he'd get them next time. As for the married women, he sometimes felt guilty about them, when he looked back at the way he'd hurt them, the way he'd cut them loose.

Nobody had sent them to him, though, it wasn't like he was forcing anybody to do anything they didn't want to do in the first place. Cheating on their husbands, hell, what kind of women could they be? It never dawned on Mute that the problem lay within his character, that he couldn't establish a lasting relationship with a single woman due to his terrible insecurity over the face that he'd been born with. The fact of the matter was, at the beginning of a relationship with some married woman or another, was the only time that Mute ever felt handsome, did not feel like some sort of freak inside. He had no concept of this, did not understand that he'd been doing it for so long now that it had become second nature to him. All he knew for sure was that he was searching for it constantly, for that feeling of goodness that came over him after sex.

All that he had the insight to understand was that something was wrong with him, but he figured that he was too young to settle down, and still too full of awe at the idea of women wanting him to give up chasing them around. He had, strangely enough, grown that confidence in the penitentiary, and he'd come out cocky, figuring that if he could survive and prosper in there, the outside world belonged to him.

As he pulled to the curb outside his rooming house, Mute automatically checked the curbs on either side, looking for strange cars, wondering if the cops had gotten on to him, if they were waiting for him again, as they had been once before.

It was how they'd gotten him, caught him after he'd beaten a man near to death in a bar for saying something about his looks. He'd been heading home that time, too, going over to Grandma's with a half a bag on, staggering to the sidewalk when the cops had come at him from all sides. Jesus, how he'd fought, torn into them with everything he had, and it had seemed to be a point of honor with them not to pull their weapons; he was an unarmed man, why the hell would they need them?

The deal was, though, they had no concept of his strength. Wooden clubs broke in two over his head and still he fought on, Mute enraged, trying to kill them all, trying to murder them for what they were doing to him with his grandma watching from her living-room picture window.

She'd up and had a heart attack, had died that very night, and ever since then Mute had always looked around when he'd come home, expecting some cops to jump his ass, and some old lady – probably his landlady, Mrs Calloway – to have a heart attack and die. History, Mute knew, had a habit of repeating itself if you weren't careful about the way that you lived your life.

Grandma had left her house and her money to the Roman Catholic Church, not a dime had come Mute's way, but he didn't hold that against her. Maybe she'd even been at his side last night at Balmoral, a little miniature angel Grandma with wings, sitting on his shoulder and whispering Sabi's Skipper's name into his ear, telling him that after all this time, the big-balled son of a bitch was about to pay off big. He'd like to think that was the way it had happened. As long as she'd packed up her harp and flown off before he'd hooked up with MaryAnn.

Get off it, shit. He made himself stop thinking about it. Only a pervert could even want to imagine his own grandmother watching while he did the dirty with a girl like MaryAnn, particularly in light of the fact that his grandma had been so religious.

Mute walked up the stairway to his room, heard the downstairs door pull open, his landlady's voice calling up at him.

'Michael, is that you?' He stopped.

'It's me all right, Mrs Calloway.' As if she didn't know; he'd seen her watching from her window, the way that Grandma had when he'd come home on that long ago night. He waited for her to come up.

She was a big woman, in her fifties, and her husband had been dead for years. She liked to tell him stories about when her kids were small, how the oldest son had lived in the room Mute now rented, before she'd partitioned the upstairs off and begun renting out the space. Her kids never came to see her anymore, poor old woman, all alone. He'd listen to her, though, the same stories over and over, and she'd cook for him on Sundays, big meals that made him believe that he got the better part of the deal. He figured that he'd replaced her kids in her life, and he had a pretty good idea of whose place she'd taken in his. He looked forward to Sundays, to being with Mrs Calloway. It was the closest he ever came anymore to being a part of a family.

She huffed and puffed her way up the stairs, and Mute turned to her, smiling.

'Rent's due, you know, today,' she said. 'I'll tell *you*, those stairs are starting to get to me.'

'Should have said something, I'd'a come on down to you.'

'No reason to,' she said, with a gleam in her eye. 'All the roast's gone, you ate most of it yesterday afternoon.'

That he had, before heading off to the track. Mrs Calloway liked to have her big Sunday meal at noon, right after she got home from Mass, as she'd fasted since midnight in order to take communion. Mute would awaken Sunday morning to the smell of meat cooking right below him. The rummies and winos she rented the other rooms to would have to sit up there all day with their mouths watering, wandering down to the 505 for burgers if they had enough money left over after Saturday night's libations. He was the only one she ever invited to join her for Sunday dinner. She liked Mute pretty good, had gotten on with Mute's grandma before the poor old woman had passed on, the two of them going to Mass most mornings, cleaning the rectory for the priests on Saturday afternoons.

'You been staying out all night on me again, Michael?'

Mute said, 'Mrs Calloway . . .' but not in a threatening manner, more or less kidding with her, but telling her to mind her own business.

'Had another renter did that some time back, and he came to no good end, Michael. A boy named Thom Geere, boy damned near killed me – '

'Yes'm, I believe you told me that story.' Mute reached into his pants pocket and pulled out the wad of hundreds, peeled off three and handed them to the woman. 'Here's for two months' rent.' He watched her eyes widen as she spotted the roll.

'Michael!'

'There's things you don't want to ask me about, ma'am.' He hoped that he could give her the impression that he worked for the CIA.

'I'll tell *you*, I guess you're right.' She took the money and turned and hurried down the stairs, and Mute waited until he heard the door to her downstairs apartment close before he squatted down next to the door to his room.

There was a piece of white thread still stuck between the door and frame, still right there where he'd left it; she hadn't been in there snooping around. He stood and put his key in the lock, walked into his room and locked the door behind him.

A ratty couch and a black and white TV sat in what he called his parlor. A single bed, a dresser – out of which he had carefully removed the smoky mirror – was about all there was to his bedroom. An aluminium frame with a bar across it served as Mute's closet. His clothes were hung there neatly, still in the plastic bags that had come from the laundry. He had the woman down at the laundromat wash and iron his underwear and blue jeans, everything else went out to the cleaners. There was a bottle of Seagram's VO atop the dresser, and a toilet kit made of vinyl. His cleaning equipment – a can of Ajax cleanser and a sponge – sat next to a stack of *Soldier of Fortune* magazines.

Mute learned a lot from that magazine, had profited well from the things he had learned. For instance: there were a heap of different drivers' licenses he kept stashed in a safety deposit box, Mute keeping only two spares alongside his own in his wallet, with his picture on them and everything.

Different names and social security numbers, separate license numbers on every one, but with Mute's smiling face staring out from the picture part. The addresses on the licenses displayed Mute's various phony drops.

He'd learned how to get them from a book he'd ordered from *Soldier of Fortune*, his favorite magazine. He had a couple of pistols and a rifle too, that he'd ordered from a mail order company that advertised in *Soldier of Fortune*, and they too were locked in the box; the knives he'd ordered – with the razor-sharp blades and the brass knuckle handles – he kept in the car, one under the seat and one in the trunk, in case of an emergency. He couldn't take a knife with him into the track or into a bar, as he was partial to wearing skin-tight, shortsleeve shirts, and the knives tended to bulge, so he could only carry them in the winter, when even he had to break down and wear a heavy coat.

Mute had never gotten any passports, although the books he'd ordered had taught him how to do that. He didn't fall for their standard line that in order to be a man you had to be ready to go out there and fight in Algeria or some fucking place. Mute stood firm in the belief that the only thing worth fighting for in this life was himself. He used what he needed from *Soldier of Fortune* and disregarded the rest, and he got it every month because he never knew what would be inside it, what he might learn.

The magazine and the books he'd gotten through its ads had opened up entire doors for him that he never even knew existed, let alone had ever owned a key to. Well, he owned plenty of keys now, would even be using one in just a little while.

Mute took his toilet kit and his can of Ajax cleanser and the sponge and went down the hall to shower. He had a busy morning lined up, and he had to take care of a lot of business after he saw a cop he knew, if he was going to find MaryAnn today. MaryAnn, who'd told him that the edge she had over other realtors was him, Mute. She'd said that she had *him*.

He wondered what she'd meant by that. He'd find out, he'd bet, soon enough.

MaryAnn stood before the class, thirty-two new agents who were raring to go to work for her. Some of them were even angry about having to take this course, tailor-made by MaryAnn, to extend her agents' training. They thought that they'd learned enough in real estate school to hop right into the office and become millionaires, get on those phones and hustle up clients. Some of them would have relatives that they'd already talked into selling their homes.

She could see it in some of the faces, the desire to get up and leave, but they knew that if they did that they'd lose their jobs, and they didn't want to go to another agency; they knew that with Ceterra Realty, they were coming to work for one of the newest agencies, but one with a rapidly growing reputation for being the best and most aggressive.

She lit a cigarette as the trainer introduced her, smiled at the class's polite applause. Waited until they finished and then started with a little humor to break the ice and lessen the intimidation factor; she was the boss and they knew it, she could see awe in some of their faces.

She waved her Virginia Slim in the air.

'One of the many pitfalls of this business; I'm up to four packs a day.'

There was scattered laughter and from the back of the room, a female voice spoke up.

'It's funny, if you don't mind dying young.'

MaryAnn looked back at the woman who had spoken up. An overweight young woman with a complexion that was as bad as her attitude. How the hell had she snuck through the employee screening? MaryAnn smiled at her, sweetly, one of the girls.

'I've learned, over the years, to not hold anything against non-smokers.'

The woman didn't know how to quit when she was ahead. She said, 'How about non-smokers with asthma? These people have been smoking in this room for the entire two weeks!'

'Yes, well,' MaryAnn said. The bitch, she'd be gone in a week, maybe less. MaryAnn took a deep drag to show the woman who was in charge. 'It's a good thing you're sitting in the back. If the rest of the class doesn't mind, perhaps you could open a window.'

There was a collective groan, the class now turned against the complainer. She'd sat through and passed the real estate course, and she'd paid her fifteen hundred to get her license. She'd been hired on at the firm and she'd gone through two weeks of training. MaryAnn wondered how long she could take the peer pressure, now that she'd effectively turned the class against the fatass.

MaryAnn smiled again, and nodded at her trainees, almost three dozen bright faces, some old, some very young, all wanting to make their fortunes in real estate, all staring up at her now. It was time to lay some ground rules, to show the steel fist inside the velvet glove.

'There're two things that I'll speak to you about today, and then I'll take your questions. When I do, I expect that you'll stick to the topics that I have chosen to discuss. I have neither the time nor the inclination to talk about the past two weeks of your lives.' She turned to her trainer.

'That's why I hired Mal, here. If you have questions about what he's taught you, you should ask them of him.

'Now, first thing, right off the bat, I want you to know that most of you just won't make it.' She waited while they groaned, she'd given the spiel before and knew how they always reacted.

'No, it's true, most of you won't work for the company very long. Some of you will get an attack of conscience, feel morally superior to the work you have to do. Some of you will not be able to handle the long hours and the constant, round-the-clock phone calls from clients.' She took a drag on her cigarette.

'And *some* of you, well, some of you will just not be up to Ceterra's standards, in spite of the rigorous screening. Some of you will be let go within the first month of employment.'

She looked at them, trying to make eye contact with each of them, seeing the belief in those faces, in those eyes: *they'd* be good enough to hang in there and get rich. Good. It was what she expected, no, de*mand*ed from them. Because as they got rich, she got richer.

'Now, first off, what I want to address is a common problem that a lot of you have when you first start out. *None* of you is Mother Teresa,' she bowed her head at a male who was leering at her in the second row, 'or the Pope.' She listened to giggles for a second.

'None of you has a responsibility to your clients other than the ones set down by Illinois statute. I bring this up because without fail, every single class has a few people who argue ethics with Mal, wanting to know where your obligations started and stopped.' She saw a couple of them bow their heads, the ones who had probably given Mal a ration of shit.

'If you want to make money in this business, you have to be hardhearted. If someone wants you to list their house at twenty thou more than the market will bear, you have to pass them by; it does no good to have a listing if no one can find a sale.

'A veteran now, looking to buy a house, you must remember at all times that such men and women are golden. In my years in this business, I have never seen a breathing, working veteran lose a mortgage qualification. The government guarantees the loan, and they *want* the veteran to get that loan, to show their gratitude for their service and sacrifice. So, you have a veteran who works in a factory and makes twenty-five a year. This vet qualifies for a fifty-thou shack in Robbins or South Chicago, and you do a work-up, the financial statement, and find out that the vet's payments will be five-fifty-eight a month. Now, after taxes, and with other bills, you know damn *well* that this vet won't be able to make the nut for long; what do you do?' Hands shot up and MaryAnn smiled; the bitch who had the problem with smokers had her hand up there, high.

'Yes, you,' MaryAnn said, pointing at the woman, who stood up before she answered. Catholic schooling, it always showed.

'I'm sorry, MaryAnn, but I'd have to point out to him that he couldn't handle the loan, that he should save some more for a down payment, that within a year or two of his buying the house he'd be out on the street, bankrupt.'

Oh, dear God, did her voice ring with moral indignation. MaryAnn would get rid of her right now, cut her off at the knees before anyone else decided to jump up on her high-minded, holier-than-thou bandwagon.

'In the first place, my name is Ms Ceterra, I'm not MaryAnn to you. In the second place, why do you insist on referring to the veteran as "he"? Don't you realize that more and more *women* are in the military these days?' The woman had remained standing, and now she slowly sunk back into her seat. She obviously wasn't used to rebuke. Her pudgy little face was as red as Walter's skull when he got angry, and she bit her lower lip. She stared straight ahead, refusing to look at MaryAnn. The girl was at most in her mid-twenties, and already looking like the Church Lady.

MaryAnn said, 'If you want to steal the American dream away from this veteran, miss, if you want to break his heart and that of his family, you go right on ahead and do it. But you're going to have to do it at Century Twenty-one or Santefort Cowing, because your asthmatic ass just won't cut it at Ceterra's.'

The woman shot a filthy look MaryAnn's way.

'How *dare* you?'

'It's easy,' MaryAnn said, and smiled.

The woman was trembling with rage, and MaryAnn was relaxed, showing all the composure of a veteran stand-up comic looking down at a heckler in the crowd. The woman jumped to her feet, grabbed her belongings and strode haughtily out of the room, and the rest of the class began to applaud. She slammed the door behind her, hard.

'Anyone else?' MaryAnn said, and the thirty-one remaining trainees in the room all laughed. 'No, I'm serious, is there anyone else in this room who thinks that we're in the business of charity? Because if there is, I want them to go on out the door now, join Miss Emphysema of nineteen-ninety-three, catch up with her out in the parking lot and commiserate with her right now, because there is no way on earth that anyone with such an attitude can work for me for very long; I'm not running the Little Sisters of the Poor. I'd rather say goodbye and good luck right here and now than spend all the time and trouble and money involved in setting you up with an office, only to find out later that you were working against the best interest of the company.'

The faces before her were blank and silent, no one left was a wimp. She smiled at them, lit another cigarette.

She didn't pity Mal his job. How many of these people had wasted time in the last two weeks, asking him foolish questions just to get themselves noticed? As if winning his respect would get them up the ladder any quicker. She could picture them thinking that Mal would come to her, tell her about the kid in the front row, with the long hair and paisley tie: 'Keep your eye on *that* one, MaryAnn, he's a pisser! Asks all the right questions!'

MaryAnn said, 'Now, what I'd like to discuss is something that Mal has spent three entire days going over with you, but something that still cannot be emphasized enough. Control. Control. You *must* control the client. They don't know what the hell they want before you *tell* them what they want. They don't know how much their property is worth until *you* tell them what it is worth.' MaryAnn had been sermonizing, but now she stopped and smiled.

'I know, I know what you're thinking – *control again*. Well, you're right. In fact, I'm going to spend the rest of the morning discussing it, and by the time you report for work tomorrow you'll know it backward and forward, have control coming out of your *ears*.

'But first, before I begin, I'd just like to say that for the rest of the morning, and after you come to the company, you may all call me MaryAnn. I only insist on Ms Ceterra from assholes.'

She paused while they applauded wildly, MaryAnn basking in their adoration. Sharks, she'd produced, joining in the feeding frenzy, chewing on the corpse of the outsider, the woman with asthma.

She had them in the palm of her hand and they'd stay that

way for a time. And a time was all she'd need them for; they would be there to satisfy Walter more than her, while she herself set to the task of making the real money. By the time they put that airport in, MaryAnn wanted to own, through various machinations, at least a full tenth of the Hegewisch neighborhood. She'd come out of it a millionaire, and then Walter, Chicago, and her past could kiss her ass.

She stood at the front of the room and began to tell the trainees her feelings about the importance of control, a master speaking to well-heeding pupils, wanting to get it over with so she could go home and get something to eat. She'd missed breakfast, and she didn't want to eat in a restaurant today. She had too much to think over, without any outside distractions. She had to decide on what she was going to do about Mute, about how soon she would be able to bring him into the fold.

Lino sat in the Man's living room, looking at Oprah on the television set, seeing two of her through the one eye that still opened. That bastard Morer had done him in good.

There was a thick surgical bandage around the entire top of his head, they'd had to shave his hair off to stitch the cuts in his scalp. His nose was broken, his jaw ached, and three of his teeth had been destroyed. When he spoke, he now had a pronounced lisp.

He had stormed out of the hospital, even though they'd wanted him to spend a couple of days under observation. Observation, his ass. The only thing he wanted to observe was Ben Morer's body, in the street, filled with bullets, and he was here to seek permission from the Man to do just that.

For some reason, Ben had an in with this guy.

It wasn't like Ben was made, or even was on the short list for future consideration. Ben wasn't like the rest of them, like himself and Tony and all the other crooks in the city. Ben didn't *want* a button, he liked being a free agent, even though he didn't have the protection he would have if he worked directly for one of the guys who ran the Man's crews. Still, Lino knew, the guy, he was an earner. And he paid the

Man the same as everyone else, and you didn't take food off the Man's table without permission, not if you wanted to last for long in this city.

Lino was chewing painkillers like candy, mostly to kill the pain from his busted teeth, but also for the way they took him away on a magic carpet ride. He didn't feel too humiliated when he had about eight Tylenol #4s floating around in his system.

Still, even high, he was terrified. A sit-down with the Man made strong men weak. One look, one wrong word, and you might wind up going for a late night swim with steam irons chained around your belly to keep you from floating to the surface before the fish ate off your fingerprints.

A guy Lino had never seen before came into the room, out of the Man's office, looking at him blankly. He did not look the carefree type. He was a young guy, about half of Lino's fifty-one years, tall and muscular, and Lino resented him. He'd spent his entire life hustling around this city, always giving his share up without question to the mob. If the Man was looking for confidants, he could do a lot better than this pistolero standing there, now crooking his finger at Lino like he was some kind of a boss.

Lino stood, pulled his suit jacket down and squared his shoulders, trying to glare at the punk but knowing that he wasn't pulling it off. It was a hard thing to do with one eye and about forty pounds of bandages covering the stitches in your head.

'He'll see you now,' the kid said, in a deep voice, filled with his own self-importance.

Lino nodded, took a deep breath, and walked through the door with the kid right behind him.

Lino looked at him, looked at the Man, who was sitting behind a big wooden desk, staring at him with black, dead eyes.

The Man had to be in his sixties now, and a life of excess showed on his face and on his body. Wrinkly skin hung off his neck, wattles shook even when he was sitting still, coming off a neck like Alfred Hitchcock's, the Man having many chins that jiggled but which didn't give the impression of any sense of joviality. If he'd had any hair left, it would have been gray. His belly hung over a belt that was cinched tight, the Man wearing altogether, including his watch, about forty dollars, total. He didn't believe in pretention, the Man didn't. What he did believe in was power, and he had more of that than the mayor of Chicago.

Lino was scared shitless.

Still, he said, 'Sir?' You always called the Man sir; it was what he told you to call him the first time you met him. He didn't want you saying his name, didn't want you even *think*ing it. The Man looked at Lino, looked right through him, and didn't ask him to sit down, or give any indication that he'd even heard Lino speaking.

'I got to talk to you alone.' The Man didn't blink an eye.

'What the hell do you want.'

The Man never spoke in questions, he was a guy who knew everything, who had all the answers. He didn't waste his time and he never gave explanations. Back before people were too terrified to speak his name, the word had been that he had a thing for really young girls.

Lino decided that it would be prudent not to mention the young guy again.

'Look at me, I want permission to extract revenge on the guy who did this to me.'

'Ben Morer.'

'Yes, sir.' Lino couldn't hide his surprise.

'You owe Morer money.'

'He gave us fifty grand to put out on the street for him. Every month, we give him five grand, every month, he gets his piece. That was our deal, and it was understood, the principal stayed the same for him; he never lost the fifty but it never got paid back, not in a lump sum like he wants it. He'd just collect the five grand every month, for the rest of his life.'

'You explained that to him?'

You didn't lie to the Man, although Lino was now tempted. Instead, he told the truth, looking away from his eyes, in spite of himself.

'No, but it's understood on the street.'

'Like some fucking law, is that what you're telling me?' The Man didn't raise his voice, but it cut through Lino, in there deep.

'Like some shit everybody's supposed to know about, because *you* happen to think that they should? I want to tell you something, Lino, and you better hear me good.' The Man waved a hand and the kid came around the desk, stood standing there until the Man fished into his shirt pocket and pulled out a cigarette, then the kid, Jesus, he leaned down and lit it for him, like the guy was some kind of king.

The Man blew out smoke and said, 'I don't need this shit, this referee bullshit. You say you're coming here for permission, but what you're looking for is my help, you want me to do it for you, because Ben kicked the shit out of you last night. You want me to kill him for you, or at least, you want me to call him and tell him to lay off.

'Well,' the Man said, 'I ain't gonna do that. You guys out there gotta learn how to handle this shit yourselves. All you get from me for your percentages is your life. You don't pay, I kill you. You do pay and get out of line, I kill you. You pay and *don't* get out of line, and maybe I kill you anyway, 'cause I don't like the way you look. And let me tell you something, Lino, I don't like what I see today.'

Lino stood mute before the tongue-lashing, too scared to talk. If the Man wanted to hear from him, he'd ask a direct question. The kid stood behind the Man as if he were a statue, unmoving, his face giving away nothing. Not approval, not disapproval, not anger, not humor, not one flicker of emotion passed over the guy's face.

'Ben Morer pays me, he's an earner, and you want to kill him because he beat the shit out of you. Or to save yourself from having to pay him the fifty grand you owe him. You come in here all pissed off, like we're in some Hollywood movie and you're at the wedding of my daughter, but you gotta understand something, you and your partner, that Fat Tony asshole. Real life ain't like that. Never was, Lino. Now let me ask you a question: before you came in here, did you spend one second thinking of what I'd lose if Morer dies?'

'And if he kills me, sir, what then? Me and Tony, we *got* to pay you more than that broken-down chump.'

'Don't you count on it, he might pay twice what you do.'

'All right, you give me permission to whack him out, I'll pay you more.'

The Man didn't even have to think about it.

He said, 'Here's how it is. Neither one of you is with me, but I run you both. All right, you got a beef, you settle it. Whoever comes out ahead comes out ahead, it don't make no difference to me; guys like you are a dime a dozen, and Morer's getting old. Ten years ago, he'd have killed your ass last night, and Tony would have fallen into line and paid him off. He wouldn't waste time playing any games with you. So, you come here for permission, I grant it, fine, it's yours. But I don't want to hear another word out of you, or from him. You either pay him what's his or you kill him and give me a tenth of the money you owe him. Then you cough up ten extra points a month for me; instead of the ten points off the top you pay me now, you give me twenty, you got that? So, you either pay Morer or you pay me. With me, you get protection. I'm not telling you what to do, mind you, but if you pay him, what can he give you? Still, either way, I don't want to see you in here again until the situation has been resolved, one way or the other, you got me?'

'Thank you,' Lino said, and didn't need to be shown the door.

He had permission, which was all he'd wanted, no matter what the Man might think. It had been worth it, worth the shit he'd been forced to eat. He'd kill Morer now, and no one would say a word.

It would even enhance his reputation on the street. The Man might think that Morer was over the hill, but Lino knew better, he'd acted pretty young last night.

Still, was he a cold son of a bitch, or what? He'd written Morer off as if he was a car that had broken down, was throwing away a guy who'd paid him tens of thousands of dollars over the years. Not that he was complaining. It could have gone the other way, and still could: Morer could kill him, instead of his killing Morer. But he didn't think that would happen; he thought he knew the way to get Ben Morer out into the open, with that famous temper of his blazing. Guys with hot heads, Lino knew, usually never lasted anywhere near as long as Morer already had.

Maybe that was why the Man had given in so easily. Easy, shit, the bastard was taking another ten points. Still and all, it wouldn't be so bad; Lino and Tony paid him five and told him it was ten. They had a lot more money out there than the Man would ever know about.

Lino pulled his car to the curb, got out and walked over to a pay phone and dropped a quarter into the slot. Jesus, the weather had changed overnight, all of a sudden it had to be below freezing out here. He squinted at a number that he'd written down on the back of a matchbook cover, after calling information that morning, as soon as he'd gotten out of the hospital. That son of a bitch Morer had threatened Lino's family last night. Lino couldn't let that pass. He would have to give Ben a little taste of his own medicine. Then, tonight, he'd kill the son of a bitch.

He wasn't worried about Morer coming after him; Ben was more concerned with money than he was about anything else. But still, it would teach him a little lesson, let the man know that Lino was a player, too. It would get Ben all worked up, get his thinking all worked up, too. And when a man was mad, he made mistakes. Lino would capitalize on that anger, would use Ben's famous temper against him.

Lino punched the number in slowly. His fingers were numb with cold and he had to hang up twice and start all over again. Under his leather jacket, down in his waistband, was a pistol, a revolver that he could get to quickly, that had no slides to play with and no safeties to take off. The gun that had all that garbage, the little .380, was in a holster clipped to the back of his pants, in case he needed more firepower than the revolver had to offer. With Ben Morer, you couldn't take a lot of chances. All he had to do in order to be reminded of that fact was to look into a mirror, he'd see how dangerous the man could be.

What did Morer have, what kind of kids, boys or girls? There were two of them, he remembered that. One of them, Lino was sure, was named Diane.

The phone rang only twice before a woman with a tinkle of laughter in her voice picked it up, telling him that he'd called the right number, and he asked for Mrs Morer. When she asked him who was calling, he told her none of her goddamned business. She dropped the friendly voice and asked in a bitchy way what the matter referred to. He said, smiling. 'Tell her it's about her kid, tell her she had an accident at school.'

Diane was going over an insurance problem, her lawyer sitting across from her, wondering what to do about the women in the crew who used to work at the building where some rolls of copper were suddenly missing. The lawyer's name was Melissa, and she was as angry as Diane was, knew what an accusation of theft could do to a small businesswoman.

'You'll take a loss on it, for the quarter, your premiums are high already and they'll go up even higher after this. There's a slight tax advantage, I think, but still, what you made there won't be worth the bad will you'll get if the word gets around.'

Diane appreciated the special attention, the things Melissa was telling her that could save her face in the business community. Still, it irked her, stuck in her craw; she knew all of her women, she couldn't see any of them as a thief.

'They'll agree to pay the claim without a problem?'

'We have the police report, and the company's agents have already investigated. *They* came to the conclusion that it was one of *your* people who managed to steal the copper. The company hadn't thought of it until the insurance adjustor pointed his damn finger. Then they filed suit against us. Diane, it's easier to settle than to fight.'

'But the insurance company will pay, right?'

'They won't like it, but it's easier to settle, they know it and I know it. All I have to do is call them and relieve their minds; a lawsuit would get expensive, and they don't know yet that they're not liable for the fees.'

'Shit,' Diane said, and looked down at her buzzer as it rang on her telephone. She depressed a button and said, 'Yes, Marie.'

'There's some man on the phone who won't give his name to anyone but you – '

'Then get a number and tell him I'll call him back.'

'Wait, Diane? He said one of your kids has been hurt at school – '

Diane had been half-daydreaming, wondering if one of the women who worked for her was actually stupid enough to steal from one of the plants that they cleaned. Now, though, she was all business, her heart beginning to pound as her mind raced over the implications of what Marie had told her. She cut her off before Marie could give her the rest of the message.

'Put him through,' Diane said immediately, not even trying to disguise the sudden terror that gripped at her, seeing Ben or John dead.

'Mrs Morer?'

'Yes, yes, sir, what happened?'

'Calm down.'

The guy had a gravelly, wiseass voice, the type she'd heard a thousand times during her marriage when someone would call the house, looking for her husband. The only difference being, this guy had a lisp.

'What?' Diane said.

'I said calm down, ain't nothing happened, yet.'

'What do you *mean*, yet?'

'I mean your old man stepped on the wrong toes. I mean he fucked around with the wrong guy. I mean I know where you live and where your daughter goes to school. What I *mean*, lady, is if your old man don't make things right like a man, I'm gonna grab that little girl and start sending her home to you through the mail, piece by piece.'

'You son of a *bitch*!' Diane shouted. 'You won't have to worry about *him*, you motherfucker. You call here and threaten my child? Are you crazy? Forget about Ben! *I'll* kill you, you filthy bastard, with my own two hands, if you ever threaten my kid again.'

'Listen – ' He was trying to be belligerent, but she'd shaken him, she could tell by the sound of his voice. Good.

'Listen, my ass. And thanks for the warning. That kid will be guarded before school lets out today, and I hope to hell I see your cowardly ass hanging around my house, I hope you have the balls to come near me or my kid. I'll blow your head off first and tell the cops later that you tried to rape me.' She slammed the phone down, hard, then sat there shaken, staring down at the phone.

The good news was that the bastard had threatened a daughter, did not even know that Diane had two sons. But he *had* mentioned Ben, or words to that effect. What had the guy said – 'Your old man'. That meant the same thing. But she couldn't let Melissa know, Melissa had to think that it was just an obscene call.

'Di*ane*?' Melissa's voice broke through her fear, her rage, and she looked up, saw her friend, as if she'd just walked into the room.

'Some man just threatened me over that phone.' She looked at the telephone as if it were a strange creature that might bite her at any second, looked back up at Melissa, who was businesslike now, herself.

'I *heard*. You have to call the police. And right now, Diane.'

'No. The police don't get called. My God, it was a crank call.'

'Yeah? Then why did you say that he wouldn't have to worry about *him*? Whoever it was mentioned Ben, and from what I heard of your side of the conversation, he threatened one of your children. That's more than a crank call. If you won't call the police, I will.'

Melissa reached for the phone and Diane put her hand over Melissa's on the receiver, held it down firmly.

'Melissa, I haven't spent the last five years coming back from what I did to let the newspapers have a field day, trying to mix me up in Ben's business. And I didn't spend thirteen years living with him without picking up a few of his tricks.'

'*Ob*viously.'

Diane turned Melissa's hand over, held it in her own. When she spoke her voice was pleading, and she stared at Melissa with a strong desire for understanding.

'One thing I do know, if people like my ex-husband are going to do something, they don't warn you about it in advance, that's only in the movies. They do it and *then* call you, bargain from a position of strength.'

'You sound as if you've had experience.'

'Thirteen years' worth, dying every time the phone rang. This is a cheap thrill, an obscene call, someone who knew Ben and who's trying to be cute. I can smell assholes a mile away. I handled it, Melissa, and now it's over.' Diane could see that Melissa didn't seem convinced. She squeezed Melissa's hand for reassurance.

'Come on, don't you see? Anyone can see through it. Even if it was a serious threat, okay, let's say it was: would the man call me *here*? No, he'd call late at night, at my home, call an unlisted number that you can't get by calling information. That would prove he at least had connections, that he knew how to get something done. All *this* proves is that he knows how to dial four-one-one. And Melissa, he threatened my *daughter*, he didn't even know that I don't have one.'

Melissa still didn't seem convinced, but she finally at least squeezed Diane's hand. She pulled it away and sat back in her chair, looking as shaken as Diane felt inside.

Diane said, 'All the police will do is file a report. They'll say the same things to me that I just said to you, then they'll go back to the station and one of them will call the newspapers. You know how cops are, they have to think that they've got these tight connections with everybody in the media, and that they know everything about you, why you're doing what you do. They'll tell Sneed what they figure to be my motivations, and she'll print that this place is a front for a gangster, and the city will believe her, and I'm out of business in a week.'

'You'd increase business a thousand percent, every small-time idiot in the city would be calling for a contract.'

'All right, maybe so, but still, it would put a taint on my good name. The name I built *after* Ben was gone.'

'All right, you win for now, but you'll at least get the kids out of school today?'

'They'll be fine in class, and there's no need to worry them. They haven't had any contact with their father since the day he walked out of the door. I don't want to put them through any more of this, who knows how they'd respond? I'll pick them up after school and take them out for a pizza, and keep an eye on them close tonight and drive them to school in the morning.'

'I don't know . . .'

'Melissa, you've been my friend since the day that I started, when I was scrubbing floors on my hands and knees and had three other women working for me. Today I've got forty-five on the payroll and eighteen major industrial contracts. You haven't learned yet that I know what I'm doing?'

'I have to admit, you handled it pretty well.' Melissa had a small smile on her lips, thinking of how Diane had chewed the man out.

'It takes more than some anonymous fiber optic terrorist to shake me up. Or to make me run to the cops for help because I'm *scared*.'

'All right, I'll stay out of it. I promise not to call the police, at least not yet. And I'll tell you before I do. But you have to promise to beep me if he calls again, no matter where or what time, all right?'

Diane lied without hesitation. 'You've got my word.'

Melissa rose to her feet, shaking her head. 'My God, it's a strange world we live in. Shall I tell the insurance company that you don't want to fight?'

'Please. And in the meantime I'll try and figure out if any of my women are capable of doing this.'

'You can have them take a polygraph, it was a condition of employment.'

'There were eight women on that crew, and a minimum of seven of them who would see that as an insult. Maybe eight, if they're all innocent. Let me think about it, I'll let you know later in the week.'

'Good.' Melissa looked at her, as if wanting to say something more. Diane put on a brave front, smiling at her, her shaking hands in her lap.

'I'll see you then.'

'Thanks, Melissa.' Diane rose to see her out, and put her hands behind her back.

Marie wanted to know what the guy on the phone had been talking about, and Diane told her that it was a wrong number, that the man hadn't known what he was talking about. Marie looked at her strangely, but seemed to accept the explanation. At least she didn't make any further comments. It hurt Diane to lie to her, but some things were best kept secret, were none of anyone else's business. She asked Marie not to put any calls through until she told her it was all right, then went into her office, closed the door and locked it, then sat down behind her desk, determined to get to the bottom of the phone call.

Who was the man, and what had he wanted? It was obvious that Ben had angered someone, but someone without the courage to confront him face to face; someone stupid enough and weak enough to think that he could get Ben to change his ways by threatening a woman he thought was still married to him; by threatening a child, a daughter that Ben didn't have.

So, she could figure him to be a coward, and stupid. At the very least, he knew nothing about women, or at least about women like her, people with their own identities, their own strength. She didn't need to hide behind Ben's name and identity anymore. And she didn't need him to fight her battles; she'd come through hell, without Ben, she and the boys standing together for strength these past five years.

He knew where she worked, but did he know where she lived? She wasn't listed, but the house was in her name. If he was smart enough to check the County Recorder's office he'd find out that she held deeds on four properties in Hegewisch, properties that were all occupied by various families. Would he mail letters to any of them, throw a firebomb through the window of her house, or just as bad, through the window of an innocent family whose only crime had been renting a house from Diane? No, she didn't believe that he would. If he were that type of person, he'd have done the arson first, and *then* made a threatening call, after he'd already proved that he could cause them serious damage.

What it had to be was just some ignorant bastard, trying to get Ben to change his ways, and not knowing enough about him to find a way that he could do it.

Most of the considerable amount of anger seething inside Diane was focused toward the anonymous man who'd called, but some of it was directed at her ex-husband, Ben.

If he hadn't done whatever he had, the man wouldn't have called. If he'd only been straight, had only gotten a job and worked regular hours, people wouldn't be calling her, threatening her and her kids. If he had changed, gotten that job, and renounced the mistakes of his past, they'd still be married, Diane would have been the most faithful and loving wife any man could ever have prayed for.

The problem was, he hadn't.

This wasn't the first time that something like this or worse had happened because of him. The Morer family had dodged bullets shot through the front door, fifteen years ago, long before Ben went to jail. At the time she'd been pregnant with John. She cringed as she remembered her infant Benny screaming and crying in terror, tears and snot running down his tiny face. A strangely silent Ben had called a man to come and stay with them, and had then gone out for a while, had come back and dismissed the bodyguard. After an hour of demands he had finally and quietly explained to Diane that the man who'd shot through their door had gone home and committed suicide.

She'd been so fully owned by him back then that she'd half-believed what he'd said, but now she had a pretty good idea of what had really happened.

Diane looked up at the clock, saw that it was already ten-thirty. Ben had a doctor's appointment at eleven, he'd told her, with a doctor named Evan, at South Chicago Hospital. The doctor had told him to bring his wife.

Well, she'd show up, but she wouldn't be there in the capacity that the doctor had expected, nor would she scream and rage at Ben, because she knew the effect such tactics had upon him. His general reaction, when Diane had begun to scream at him, was to pick up the refrigerator and throw it across the kitchen.

This was his responsibility, the man who'd called had threatened her and her kids because of Ben. She wouldn't be running to him for help, or to have him solve her problems. This was *his* problem as much as it was hers, and one that she'd gladly hand over to him. Out of strength, though, pragmatically solving the problem in the best way that she knew. She wouldn't be going to him out of weakness, she was no longer a weak person.

No, she was different today, stronger, more in control of her emotions. She knew what she'd do, and how she'd go about it. And there was no doubt in her mind that Ben would know the identity of the man who'd called. He generally was on good terms with most of the people he knew, he wouldn't have a problem identifying whomever was that angry at him at any given moment. So she'd drop the bug in his car and be honest, tell her ex-husband exactly, word for word, what the man had said over the phone. And then, if she was lucky, the caller would commit 'suicide'.

It was what she had to do, and she felt no guilt about doing it. No one could be allowed to threaten her children, even if he happened to get the sex wrong this time. No one could ever even have the slightest opportunity to destroy the happiness that they had today, the life that she'd worked so hard to give them. So she'd tell Ben and he'd take care of it; it was the least that he could do for them, he owed them that and would know it. He'd always been protective of them, overly so, when they'd lived together. And he was the type of man who'd know what to do about the phone call without having to be told.

Mute drove slowly down Route 30 in the village of Matteson, choosing the suburbs for this type of work because intersections near malls had the kinds of stoplights that he needed and, after all, there were only seventy-seven Chicago neighborhoods, and he'd already hit more than a dozen of them over the years that he'd been doing this.

He cruised to the light at the intersection of 30 and Governor's Highway, timing it perfectly, stopping on the yellow and ignoring the honk of the dolt behind him who wanted him to race through the light so that he himself could get through. Mute waited patiently, sitting in a 1979 Ford Torino, a Starsky & Hutch car that was more a hunk of rust than the hot number it had been some fifteen years ago.

He'd paid a hundred dollars for the car, and it had already paid for itself fifty times over. Would do a lot more paying, too, before he put it out to pasture.

He was heading west, toward the expressway, in the farthest left lane that he could get into without being in the turning lane, which would get the arrow before Mute got the green, the same as the growing line of cars on the other side of the street would. He'd need, he knew, about twenty cars to line up over there, heading east, wanting to turn north, waiting for the arrow now, the sun bouncing into Mute's eyes off their shiny grilles and windshields. The line was getting longer; he should be able to score on this light.

The arrow came, and several cars travelling north and south went through on the red, before any of his potential pigeons could turn. Mute, first car in line, sat there waiting patiently. He was by law mandated to wait until the arrow faded away, and he got a green light, before he could proceed. He would wait that long, it was what he was counting on.

The arrow turned yellow, and in front of him, heading his

way, a bunch of cars sped up, wanting to make it through the light, planning on racing through into their turn right in front of him after they'd lost the legal right to do so.

The second the light turned green, Mute gunned the Torino, and it tore ahead. He could see the panic in the eyes of the white guy driving the new Buick, the guy who had driven that car illegally into the middle of the intersection, making his unlawful turn and being completely totally in the wrong when Mute crashed his car right into the dolt's side.

Mute hit the brakes, and the car behind him managed to avoid hitting him, which was too bad. It was the asshole who had honked at him; Mute would have liked for him to be a part of this. He could hear the guy now, telling the cops that Mute had stopped at the light as it was turning yellow. The guy would think that he was turning Mute in, but the cops would see Mute as cautious, he'd obeyed the law to the letter.

The man Mute had hit got out of his car and slammed the door hard, staring at Mute, screaming already.

Mute slowly got out of the car, lifted both hands to the back of his neck, as if he had an injury. He was not wearing a coat, even though the weather had taken a turn for the worse. He tightened his muscles, knowing what the guy would be seeing, and had to fight not to smile as the little shit immediately stopped his screaming, looked at Mute, saw the size of him, and shut his mouth up tight, suddenly losing all his anger.

Cars were pulling around them and honking at them, pissed off because the accident inconvenienced them, then rubbernecking as they passed and causing a bigger traffic jam than the accident itself already had, but a couple of them had pulled into the sandwich shop at the corner; people were getting out of their cars and heading this way, witnesses. If you did it on a busy suburban intersection during mid-morning, there were always such witnesses; people out here were bigger busybodies than they were in the city itself.

Mute groaned.

'Jesus, mister,' Mute whined, 'I had the right of way.'

Mute could see that his front end was dented some, but the Buick's passenger door, Christ, it was a total loss. It had folded in like an accordion, and what had once been a shiny new door was now just a hunk of twisted metal that was pushing into the front leather seat. If anyone had been sitting in the passenger seat, there might even have been a fatality. Mute always tried to be careful when he banged them, but every car he drove was different, its response to his foot on the accelerator distinctly separate from all of the others. That happened when every car you drove was almost as old as you were.

The guy was looking at him, his mouth hanging open. He finally pulled himself together well enough to speak.

'Are you all right?'

'I don't know, my neck hurts and I'm kind of dizzy.'

'I've got insurance, this whole thing is covered, you don't have to worry about that.'

'Shit, mister, you ran the fucking *light*.'

'The arrow was still green when I started to make my turn.'

'Bull*shit*!' It was a woman's voice, irate and filled with anger. 'You cut *me* off back there by Lincoln Mall, buddy, the way you were driving, it's a good thing nobody was killed.' She said, 'Are you okay, sir? Don't you worry, I saw it all. *I* know that he ran the light, and I'll tell the cops everything, too.'

God bless her heart, Mute was counting on her. When she spoke now it was as if they were conspirators, her voice low and her words vicious, the two of them working against the rotten lawbreaker who was standing a few feet away, looking at what was left of his Buick and knowing that he'd fucked up.

'He pulled out of the Mall as if he owned the goddamned street! If I hadn't stomped on my brakes, *I'd* have been the one in the accident instead of you.'

'Ma'am, thank you for stopping,' Mute said. 'I really appreciate it, otherwise it might have been just my word against his.'

'We have to work together to get people like this off the street. They shouldn't have licenses, the way they drive.'

And she wasn't the only one who felt that way. Three others had stopped, had seen the entire thing and would make statements to the cops and to Mute's insurance agency. To his lawyer, too, if it got that far and they wanted him to, if he decided that he wanted to sue, which was always a possibility.

Maybe he would, he'd done it before, when the driver he'd run into wasn't the type who was willing to negotiate. It all depended on how much trouble the other guy wanted to avoid. Those who already had a lot of traffic tickets in their past would rather pay off quick than have him appear in court. Three times, since he'd been doing this, Mute had even lucked into drunk drivers; he'd scored the best off of them. It would be up to them, though, up to the driver, if they wanted to pay him off.

If they didn't, Mute would appear in court, with fake hospital and doctor bills and a shark-ass lawyer, who'd sue the man for what he'd done, for the damages he'd caused poor, lawful Mute.

For now, though, all he did was hold his neck and moan, Mute's smile entirely inward, right next to his spreading sense of joy; this would be a good one, he had the guy dead to rights and four or five witnesses standing around, ready to swear that Mute had been in the right. He thanked the witnesses again as the flashing blue, red and white strobes of a squad car came into the corner of his vision, and he knew that he'd have the report done up and be out of the hospital down the street well before it was time for him to report to his job back in the city.

Driving back into Chicago, Mute was pleased. The other guy had gotten two tickets, and that automatically made things easier for him. He put the Torino's heater on high, and knew that he'd have to drop it off, get another car that was registered in his legal name before he went to work at the hospital. One of the headlights was busted out, and he could get nabbed for it, take a pinch and one of the South Chicago cops would run his name and number and he could get in real trouble, as a lot of those fuckers knew him by name.

But that wouldn't be a problem. At the moment, he didn't have any problems.

The scam had demanded some trial and error from him before he got it down to a science, before he knew what the hell he was doing. There were some definite rules that applied to this sort of work.

He'd never hit a car that looked to be in worse condition than his own. They generally weren't insured, even though all vehicles were supposed to be, in accordance with Illinois State law, but a lot of people didn't have the money. Unless he was desperate, he wouldn't hit a car with a young black male driver at the wheel, and if they were driving rental cars, he'd even swerve to avoid them, no matter how broke he was. Middle-aged women were the best to hit, that and old men who got shook up real easy. Black people you tried to avoid; a lot of them didn't even have driver's licenses.

The gangbangers would rent Cadillacs and Town Cars from Hertz or Avis, using stolen credit cards, luxury cars that they'd drive for a week and then abandon or sell to a chop shop. They'd use them to do their drug deals, to commute from the inner city into the south suburbs, where they were making inroads, gaining ground there because the Gang Crimes pork in the city had them all figured out, and the suburban cops, what with all their sensitivity training, didn't know what these guys were up to, were afraid that they'd get in trouble if they hassled them too much. Whenever Mute saw one of them driving, he gave them a wide berth. They wouldn't be carrying loads of dope without carrying some kind of firearm to protect it.

He didn't consider himself a racist, even though he'd had his share of trouble with the black guys in the pen. He thought of himself as a realist, as someone who saw things as they were, and he did all that he could to avoid black people, not understanding them at all.

When he'd been doing a lot of drug deals, Mute had worked with some of them, and could never understand the way they lived. One guy he knew back then drove a brand-new Mercedes Benz, a sixty-thousand dollar car, and he lived in a public housing project, used a large steel bucket for a toilet, too, as his plumbing was out of order and there was a long waiting list to have such things repaired.

If Mute ever made that kind of money, man, he wouldn't live like that. Smelling his own shit and piss, the bucket right out there, next to the large-screen color TV. The closest he'd ever come to committing suicide was in the pen, and not because of the general atmosphere of violence, but due to the constant filth and the total lack of privacy, having to shit in front of anyone who was passing by, having to take communal showers with guys who'd stand there and glare at his body, standing in filth, muck and dirty foam.

He would never have to do that again, though. He still had fifty-one hundred dollars left in his pocket, what was left of last night's winnings, all that money left even after paying all his bills off today. This accident today would be good for a couple of thousand, at least, but he couldn't count on that money, at least not for a little while. If the guy didn't jump on it right away when Mute called him, looking for a deal, or if he got cocky and asked if Mute was trying to blackmail him, then Mute would let one of the ambulance-chasing lawyers he knew handle it, and the scumbag would take a third after the settlement, but he'd make up for that by getting Mute more than he would have held the guy up for in the first place.

Settlements usually took about six months, if the lawyer had to handle things, and the insurance companies liked to settle, because if they didn't Mute would show up in court with a neck brace and a cane. Claim that he hadn't been able to work since the day of the accident. Guys like Mute knew enough people who'd testify on his behalf, claim that Mute worked for them, had worked for them for years. And seeing as it was a civil matter, Mute's criminal record would never make it into the courtroom.

It was the best of all possible worlds that Mute lived in today. He'd gotten his oil changed last night, he suspected that he might be in love. He had money in his pocket and more on the way. He had a good job and he would keep it until he met the terms of his probation.

And he had the address of his new married girlfriend, right there in his pocket, on a piece of computer paper that had come out of the police department's machine, knew where she lived, what her social security number was, the color of her eyes and hair and the date that she'd been born.

Good old MaryAnn, his Mare, who'd told him in so many words that she had a plan for him. Didn't live too far from here, either, maybe he'd even look her up before he went on in to work.

Mute began looking for an exit, driving carefully so as to avoid an accident. You could get hurt in them, if you didn't see them coming, and he was feeling too good to have to spend the rest of the day in the hospital.

It took Diane a while to find the doctor's office, working her way through the maze of corridors and nurses' stations, knowing she'd found the right place when she turned a corner and spotted Ben.

She saw him and wanted to turn back, to go somewhere else, anywhere else, as long as it was away from him, away from this place. Down the corridor, she could hear someone calling out to the Heavenly Father, in a voice filled with terror, hopelessness and agony, in complete and utter desperation.

'May God have mercy on me . . .' chanted loudly in a voice filled with pain, over and over, again and again. Diane shivered, hearing the words for what they were, from the failing voice of a man who was dying and who knew it. The voice faded out as the man was pushed off somewhere, she couldn't see if he was on a gurney or sitting in a wheelchair. She looked back at her ex-husband, saw that he didn't seem to have heard the voice, was looking at a door in front of him, staring at it in that terrible way that he had, with a glare that seemed powerful enough to break the door down if he wished.

Ben was standing, and she'd bet it was because someone had told him to take a seat and wait. It was the sort of thing he'd do, the way he responded to the orders or even the requests of authority. Diane stopped when she saw him, surprised at how his presence made her feel; even in profile, half-turned away from her, he still had it, the charisma, the power that was uniquely his. It made her legs a little weak with fear when she felt that old, strong attraction, and her reaction angered her, she shook it off, dispassionately; this was no time to revert, she was here for a reason, and it wasn't to swoon over an ex-husband who didn't have a single redeeming quality.

She wondered if what he had would somehow transfer to film, wondered what he might have been if he'd gone out to Hollywood and tried to find out. Ben could enter a room and not say a word, and within a few seconds the conversation level in the room would conspicuously drop, the people would be looking at him, feeling his intensity.

And was he ever intense.

Ben was a man who never truly slept, he was always moving, some part of him was always shaking. Even in his deepest state of what passed in his life for sleep, his foot would be jiggling or his teeth would be grinding, something always seemed to be causing him pain, whether he was awake, asleep, drunk or sober.

She used to catch him when he was alone and unaware that she was looking, see the pain in his face, the depth of his anguish. At those times he would turn to look at her, and before he caught himself she'd see the eyes of a man who had no doubt that he'd burn in hell forever. Then he'd see her, and slip his mask back on, the tough facade that was so much a part of him.

He was the only man she ever knew who seemed to carry five yards of space along with him, extending out in a circle. Even now, standing over there by a row of molded plastic chairs, doctors and nurses and patients were slipping by him, giving him a wide berth, the look on Ben's face, the way he carried himself, telling anyone who looked at him that he wasn't to be approached without the most gracious of intentions.

Tough men would cringe when Ben turned his glare their way; his look had stopped drunken criminal types dead, right in their tracks. She'd seen thcm bow their heads and scurry out of a bar, Ben watching the door until long after they'd left the place, in case they decided for some reason to return. Those who were stupid enough to try him wound up bent over a bar or a pool table, Ben pounding his fists into the man's face, over and over, until enough men gathered up the nerve to pull him off his enemy. He didn't care if there were one, five or fifty, Ben was always ready to fight if he had to, and he didn't know how to back down.

What made him like that? She always wondered and never knew, and she'd been too afraid of him to ask. But she understood the same thing that the men in the bars – the ones with enough life experience and imagination – had perceived: he simply didn't care as to whether he lived or died.

It was what made him what he was, and to earn it he had been forced to cauterize most of his human emotions. Ben would probably think that it was a more than equitable exchange.

She stood there, wondering how to confront him. He looked so angry, so damned unapproachable, with his hands deep in the pocket of his overcoat, his collar turned up halfway.

Once Diane got over her initial fear at seeing him, she was able to observe the things about him that had changed.

He was very gray now, but his hair was still thick. What could he be, forty-eight, forty-nine at the most? From a distance, he looked sixty. A lot of miles on a hard road, her father would say if he was still alive. His face was lined, the creases in it deeper. He had lost weight, a lot of it, although he'd never been fat. Diane looked at him and her fear expired, replaced by an ineffable sadness for him, at the way he'd wasted his life.

Ben would always be alone. She didn't care if he was married, she didn't care if he had five kids. In a crowded football stadium, this man would be alone. Not necessarily lonely, though; he enjoyed his solitude, the time he could get by himself. She thought it was because it was the only time that he didn't have to worry about being strong, or about someone hurting him; when Ben was alone, he could for once feel safe.

It was his loss, the way he'd lived, the life he'd chosen for himself. Other people had overcome worse childhoods, far more pain and suffering than Ben had ever seen. They hadn't succumbed, hadn't taken the easy way out, hadn't fallen into the pit of crime and despair. He had the strength of three men, it was something that had to be genetic. He was a freak when it came to physical prowess, working on a construction crew, or even as a boxer. But he hadn't, he'd chosen a life of crime, and this was the way that men such as he wound up, old before their time and utterly alone.

She told herself these things while inside her heart was breaking, wanting to run up to him and throw her arms around his neck. She wanted to tell him he wasn't alone, that she was there with him. Ben standing there so stoically, so tragically accepting his fate, by himself.

She caught herself, that sort of thinking could lead her into hell. She'd been there once, and that guy over there she was standing here feeling sorry for had taken her by the hand and had shown her in by way of the front door.

He seemed to notice that someone was watching him, and he turned, his lips curling into an unconscious snarl. She could see his right hand come halfway out of his pocket, and then he saw that it was her, and his face lost its tough guy mask.

Broke into a smile so innocent and gentle that Diane didn't trust herself to begin walking toward him. He was looking at her as if he'd spotted his salvation. He didn't know why she'd come here, wasn't yet aware that she'd only come here today to tell him about a phone call someone had made to her office.

Now, looking at him, she knew that she didn't have the heart to tell him about that call just yet.

He came toward her, quickly, the heels of his shoes making clicking sounds on the tiles.

'Diane, thank you for coming.' He seemed a gentleman, almost gallant, Ben the host of a charity ball, accepting a large check from a society matron. He took her hand and shook it, let it go with reluctance. 'I didn't think I'd see you, I didn't think you'd show up.'

'I came,' Diane said, looking into his eyes. They seemed so joyful, so happy to see her. 'So, what's wrong? You look healthy as ever to me.'

Ben shrugged. 'It's probably nothing, I was scared last night, that's all.' Ben Morer, admitting to fear? 'I'm sorry I bothered you, I should have left it alone.'

'Ben, what's wrong?'

'You want to sit down? There's some chairs over there.'

And he led her to them, gently taking her arm and guiding her, Diane allowing it because she knew that there was more wrong with him than he was letting on. She wouldn't mention it to him, but up close, she'd noticed that he looked terrible. Pale and drawn, his face waxy and colorless. He'd once been a human heat radiator, a man whose body was warm in the dead of winter; she'd put her hands on his back to warm them up when she was freezing. Now he gave off a coldness, an emptiness that was in his eyes, stamped into his face.

'They ran these tests on me, and there seems to be a problem. The guy, this doctor, he told me to bring my wife with me today, called me Friday afternoon and said that he wanted to talk to me today.' Ben shrugged again. 'No matter what, I can't complain, I had a good ride.'

I can complain!

The words popped into her head unbidden, Diane having to hold herself back from speaking them. Was he honestly sitting there saying that he had no complaints, no regrets, after the sort of life he'd led? She knew that he was lying, she'd stood there and watched him, had seen the sadness on his face before he'd known that she was there. But she wouldn't call him on it. It was his life, and he was losing it, he could do it any way he wanted, deny until he breathed his last.

'The only thing I'm sorry about, honest to Christ, Diane, is how I hurt you and the kids, I've always regretted that.'

Diane was stunned. She sat there and stared at him. Was this Ben Morer talking? Actually a*pol*ogizing? He'd lowered his voice and was speaking intimately, taking her hand and she let him. He looked her straight in the eye, turned on the force of that personality, and she knew right then that now he was telling the truth, that he wasn't looking for an easy out, or to get back into her good graces. Nor was he speaking out of guilt; he didn't know how to feel that. But he did know how to do the right thing; he'd proven that five years ago, when he'd walked out of the door and out of their lives.

And suddenly she didn't want to hear it, absolutely did not want him pleading his case. She feared that if he did, she might grant him vindication.

'I spent my whole life bad, I wrecked it, Diane. But I shouldn't have dragged you down with me. The only reason you married me was because you were so young.' Ben half-smiled then got serious again. 'I thought about this a lot over the last five years, a *whole* lot just recently, since I been – sick.'

'Ben, don't, please, this isn't the place.'

'Where is? It's not like you're going to go out with me, or invite me over, and I couldn't let you into the place I'm living, I don't ever want you to see me doing this bad. It's now or never, and this is something I got to tell you.' He flashed that half-smile again, it was enough to break your heart.

'Thank God you came. I was gonna try and write a letter to you. Can you imagine that, trying to read my handwriting?'

'Ben, please, I'll have lunch with you, I promise, and you can tell me whatever you want if you just don't try and do it here.'

'May God have mercy on my soul . . .' the words rang in her mind, the dying man's mantra. She couldn't hear Ben's confession here, not here, with the ill, dead and dying surrounding them.

'All right, I'll buy you lunch, and we can – '

'I said I'd go to lunch with you, but only if *I'm* buying.'

'So you're doing all right? I see you got your own business.'

'Yes.'

'And the boys, they're okay?'

'They're fine.'

There was an awkward silence and Diane took back her hand.

'Everyone's fine, Ben, it's *you* I'm worried about right now.'

'Don't worry about me, Diane,' Ben said, and smiled. 'The devil takes care of his own.' And it sounded to Diane's ears as if he truly believed his words.

She settled back in her chair, not knowing what to say.

'I wish I could have a cigarette in here.' Another first; Ben Morer, nervous. She'd seen him hours after an arrest, after being brutalized and beaten by police officers seeking a confession, and he had been far more calm than he appeared to be right now.

'You'd think, shit, cancer's their number one money-making deal, you'd think they'd have ashtrays everywhere, that they'd en*cour*age you to smoke.'

'Ben, if you think you have lung cancer, why would you keep on smoking?'

'If I have lung cancer, Diane, why in the hell would I quit?'

She couldn't argue with that logic, it was typical Ben reasoning. She wanted to tell him about the phone call, was turning her head to speak, when she saw the look on his face, that hate-filled, vicious glare in his eye, and she almost gasped before she realized that it wasn't directed at her.

He was staring so malevolently at a muscular young man in a white doctor's smock, who was walking briskly toward them with his hands in his pockets, his face grim and determined.

Lino walked into the He Ain't Here, and, as usual, was stunned by the way the joint looked in the harsh light of day. At night, with dim lights on, the glare and blare of the TV or the jukebox, with the place filled with happy half-drunk broads and punks who were trying to screw them, it was different. A lot different. In the daytime it looked like a fucking morgue, a parody of what it was after nightfall.

The hardwood floors that had basketball keys spray-painted on them were now filled with cigarette butts, broken glass and ashes. The sticky residue of spilled beer and peanuts. The basketball nets hung there like flags hung at half-staff after somebody dies, their orange rims joyless, the string lifeless and dull, stained yellow by the nicotine that filled the stale air. The joint smelled of stale whiskey, beer and puke. Of bad plumbing, and, today it had the coppery smell of blood. His blood, spilled at the hands of a walking dead man.

He could see his partner Tony in his usual booth in the back, a cellular phone stuck to his ear, Tony writing something down in a notebook on the table. Lino walked around the bar and got himself a short draft, grabbed a bag of potato chips and then went over to the booth and slid in across from Tony.

'All right, good, that's two dimes on the Bulls. Right, they're giving seventeen and a half points. Whattaya mean? What the fuck are you telling me, that's straight outta Vegas, Spiler.' Tony stuck his tongue out a fraction of an inch, smiled wide and winked at Lino.

'I know, you don't want your name mentioned over the phone. You want me to show you respect at the same time you're calling me a 'teef.' He listened, rocking his head back and forth, moving his lips mockingly, making fun of the guy on the other end of the line.

'Listen, hey, Spiler, how you gonna take your action anywheres else? You're into me for forty-two dimes already, and I swear to God, I don't care *what* you make, I'm cutting you off at fifty. Introduce you to my partner then, see how much lip you throw *his* way.'

Lino could hear the outraged howl coming over the connection, the guy incensed that Tony would dare to imply that he was a deadbeat. Tony's face hardened and Lino knew that he'd had enough fucking around.

'Listen, Mikey Spiler, the hotshot lawyer from Madison Street – you got that, Uncle Sam, if you're listening? – you want the fucking bet or not, I ain't got all day to fool with you.' He listened for a second, then took the phone away from his ear, pressed a button to cut it off, and laid it down on the table.

'Fuckin' lawyers,' Lino mumbled. 'They're all a pain in the ass.'

Tony said, 'They're using a new catch-phrase now, all of them, it's going around like the plague. They take me out to lunch, kissing my ass, wanting to feel connected. Sometime during the conversation, without fucking fail, they got to tell me that they're sharks, that they got sharp teeth, killer instinct, and can smell blood from five miles away. You know what I tell them? I smile at them, like they ain't shit, and I tell them, "You're only a fucking jellyfish: no spine, a big head, and I can see right through you." That shuts 'em up, they don't know what to say to that.'

'They had to make a real living, they'd starve.'

'So how you feeling, how'd it go? Jeez, you look like shit.'

'You would, too, if you'd'a backed me up instead of being out here, playing with your granddaughter.'

'Hey, rather you than me, I ain't never been the tough guy. So come on, what'd the Man say?'

'He's ours.'

'Good. That prick, Ben. He called here already this morning, said he'd be here at eleven. Didn't ask how you was or nothing, just said he'd be here at eleven to get his money.'

'We'll be waiting for him, too. He might walk out, depends on how he acts, but he won't never cheap-shot any other motherfucker with his pistol again in his life.'

'You want to give him the money, right?'

'Got to make it look good. He knows a lot of people, and they don't all tremble at the thought of the Man.'

'You think he'll bring them with him?'

'Maybe one or two, but I doubt it, it could make him lose face. That guy, he's worse than a Jap when it comes to how things look. If he don't bring someone, he'll tell some of them, though, where he's at and who he's seeing, and why. We'll let him get out of here, and then we take him at his house.'

'Who you got lined up to do it?'

'Are you shitting me? Ben Morer? Who's dumb enough to take that hit? The Man didn't even make any recommendations. Me, I'm gonna do it myself. After what he done to me, it's gonna be a pleasure.'

'Be careful, Lino, the guy, he ain't human.'

'He's human, all right, I'll cut out his heart and bring it to you to prove it. You want to talk about not being human? The Man, now, *he* ain't a human being, the way that creep looks at you, *Jesus*, like you ain't even there.'

'Watch it, would you? What if he got the place bugged?'

'We bring in too much for him to kill us.' Lino looked at Tony, and when he spoke, bitterness dripped off his words.

'And we're gonna be bringing in even more. We got to cover Morer's piece to the Man if we kill him. He wants another ten points off the top.'

'Ten *points*, is he fuckin' *crazy*? What'd *you* do when he told you that, did you tell him how bad things are?'

'You don't say shit like that to him, you want to, go ahead, but I don't ever want to do nothin' when I'm with him but get out of his place alive. I ain't never argued with him, he ain't the type of guy you argue with.'

'Wait a minute, wait a second, here. He said ten points, right? What're we paying him now?'

'Forty-two, forty-three a month. He knows we got this, the two gay bars, the S&M place up on Belmont, and the horse and loan service. He's mean but he ain't dumb, he expects to get ripped off. But now we got to pay him eight, eighty-five, just to keep operating.'

'Eight-five? In six months, we'll pay him more than we'd have had to pay Morer! And in the year we've had his money, we've *already* paid more than the fifty back to him, at five grand a month.' Tony was outraged, forgetting that they'd taken Ben's money and were getting thirty percent off it, every week. Paying Ben less than a quarter back on their profits, the principal still out there, to be collected at any time.

Pissed at Lino's lack of response, Tony added, 'And every month after that, it's eighty-five hundred out of our pocket.'

'Yeah, and still and all, it won't be the whole ten points we were supposed to be paying him all this time. And remember, we get to keep the five grand every month that we been giving to Morer.'

'Fuck that, it ain't worth it. Go see him again, tell him we changed our minds. Tell him we're going to pay Morer.'

'No, uh-uh, bullshit to that. You want to tell him that, you go to the Man and tell him yourself. See, we don't negotiate with him, Tony. What we do is, we go in there, and he tells us how it's going to be, and we do what he says. I ain't in a crew, you ain't in a crew. I go back now, he says to me "Fine, you ain't got the balls to take out Morer, you do what you want, but you *still* gotta pay me twenty points a month." See, we'll look like pussies, he'll know he can get the twenty right off the bat, the twenty that ain't really the ten we was supposed to pay him in the first place.'

'So we got no choice, is that what you're saying?'

'No matter what we do, we got to pay the Man. We take out Morer, we at least save the fifty.'

'Jesus. The way this shit is, we'd be better off going straight.'

'Yeah, fat chance. Then the Man'd be there every month, too, wanting twenty-*five* points 'cause we was stupid enough to try and walk away from him.'

'Fuck it, we kill Morer. So you got the money or what?'

'I'll pick it up on the way home, take it outta my box. You

ain't got to cover half; it'll be back there before lunchtime tomorrow, anyway. We do what we got to do, and if anyone asks, someone who was close to him, we got fifty guys owe us money, legit working stiffs, who'll tell them that Ben was in here with a bag full of money, bragging about how he took us for fifty large. Anyone could have followed him home and killed him, we'll be fine.'

'Just you be careful with that fifty grand. You lose that, we ain't gonna be so fucking fine, especially if I got to come up with half of it.'

'You ain't got that kind of money left? All the money we make?'

Lino had been suspicious as soon as the words had left Tony's mouth, but seeing his reaction now, he knew that his suspicions had a good foundation. Tony looked sheepish, shy, then got tough again.

'You my fuckin' mother, or what? Don't worry about what I got or ain't got, you just be careful with that fifty.'

Lino drank his beer and put his hand in his lap. When he pulled it back he had a pistol on it, the revolver, a silver .44 short-barrel, and he pointed it right at Tony.

'Goddamnit, that shit ain't funny, point that thing somewhere else.' Tony slapped at the barrel, irritated, and Lino put the gun away, chuckling.

'Just like Mike Hammer, ain't it? You think anyone's man enough to stop a couple of these? They can, they can *have* the fifty grand, that and I'll throw in a blow job, if they'll only leave me alive.'

'You crazy prick, you'd blow 'em anyway, I heard the stories about you.'

'Yeah, from your mother.'

'Get the fuck out of here,' Tony said, smiling, as the phone on the table rang and he began to reach for it.

'And I'm serious, keep an eye on that money. You lose that, and we'll *both* be handing out blow jobs, to that 'teef the Man, for Christ sake, 'cause he ain't gonna want to hear about our financial losses. All he wants is his money, and every month, until he says we don't have to pay it to him no more, and you and I both know that day ain't never gonna come.'

Mute did not know the village of Glenwood very well at all. As he drove around the neighborhood all the streets seemed to go around and around in circles, on and on forever. Even when he eventually located her street, he couldn't find her house.

There were some pretty nice houses out here, though, he had to admit that, but way too many black faces for his taste. He didn't like driving around here lost in neighborhoods like this; these people, they might piss in their bathtubs and be on welfare and pretend that they were the oppressed ones, but he knew damn well that they wouldn't think twice about putting a bullet through his skull if they knew that he had over five grand in his jeans.

He spotted her car before he saw her street number, that red Mustang convertible with the REAL 1 license plate, the car phone antenna stuck in the middle of the back window. The car was sitting in the driveway of a house that Mute figured had to cost a million dollars. It was bigger than Mrs Calloway's house, twice as large, at least, and a lot newer, with that pipe shit on top of it instead of a roof. It made the house look like a giant Taco Bell.

Mute pulled to the curb three houses down, wondering what he should do now. He wanted to see her, right now, let her know that he knew where she lived, that he was slicker than she'd given him credit for, but he didn't have enough information to just barge in on her.

On the other hand, he didn't want to run into her husband, and even if he wasn't home, he didn't know how *she'd* take to his barging in on her. She might get mad and threaten never to see him again. She might even shoot him as a trespasser, rather than take the chance that he'd destroy her happy home. Some women could get like that, would kill to keep what they had at home, no matter how much they hated it; it was still better than what might be out there for them if they had to strike out on their own.

Even with a real estate business in South Chicago, her old man had to have some bucks for them to be able to live in this house. Either that, or she sold more houses than he'd given her credit for. She looked to be way too young to have been in the business for long, at the most, Mare could only have been in the real estate business for maybe four or five years. Could you make a million dollars in that amount of time? Then again, you didn't need to pay for a house all at one time, did you? You only had to put some money down on it. It was like buying a car, only bigger.

He himself had never felt the desire to own a home. To have to cut the grass, wash the windows, paint the place every few years, take care of the plumbing yourself and all that other shit, it wasn't the way he wanted to live. Rented apartments, that was the way to do it. Eat your meals out and get your pussy in motels, drinks in bars and once every week go downstairs and eat a home-cooked meal and listen to a lot of shit you'd heard a million times before. That way, when it was time to move on, you just packed your stuff and hit the road. It was the way Mute liked it, the sense of freedom that came from having absolutely no responsibilities.

He saw her come out of the house and he put his car in gear and jumped away from the curb, too fast, just as he'd done at the stop and go light a while back. The car pulled away with a screech of tires and Mare looked up, angry, wondering who was doing that in this quiet suburban neighborhood.

He pulled to the curb in front of her house, seeing the angry glare turn into a look of growing surprise, then shock as she recognized him. If her husband was home, he'd pretend that he was looking for directions. If he wasn't home, well, that could be interesting. Sex was always better in another man's bed, with the other man's woman, taking for free what the other son of a bitch was paying through the nose to get. And Mare's husband, he was laying out some dough. Just look at that house, at the new red Mustang. Shit, Mare couldn't be any older than Mute was, she was probably even younger.

As he got out of the car, he said, loudly, 'Scuse me, ma'am, could you help me out here?' Mute looking slyly toward the front window, seeing no one looking out at them. Noticing too, as he looked that way, that there were no other cars in the driveway, either.

'Scuse me, ma'am, could you help me out here?' the big dumb idiot said, and MaryAnn had to wait a minute before she could respond: she was too angry to speak, afraid of what she might say to him. At last she felt calm enough to handle the situation.

She walked up to him as if she'd never seen him before, a half-smile on her face, a woman who knew her place in the world, helping out a stranger. She spoke low and in a voice that she knew only he could hear.

'Mute, what in the *fuck* are you doing here?' Her smile never faltered.

He liked the way that she caught on right away and played the same game that he'd been playing, it showed that they were on the same page. He began talking to her and waving his arms around, looking up and down the street, as if he were merely lost.

'Worried about the neighbors, are we? No problem, Mare, all you got to do is invite me in, shit, they won't notice me inside your house.'

'Mute, you don't know what you're doing, what you're getting yourself into. Get out of here, and I'll call you later at your job, I promise.'

'I know ex*act*ly what I'm doing here, and what I'm getting into, if you get my drift.' She had expected him to elbow her, from the look on his ugly face. Then he changed, the look became almost bashful, the big dumb bastard was about to impart his secrets to her, as if she gave a shit.

'I come to tell you that I think I'm falling in love with you.'

Who the hell did he think he was, Richard Gere coming to rescue Debra Winger from the factory? Look at this idiot, grinning at her, as if he were doing her some kind of favor. Getting him to fall for her had been part of her plan, but having him show up at her home wasn't in the script.

'Mute, you have to leave, right now.'

'Not until you tell me how you learned my name was Mute. And until you tell me what the game is, Mare. Don't want to? Tell you what, I'll just stand right here, telling you that I love you, *real* loud, until you decide that you want to tell the truth, how you found out my nickname.'

'Mute, you can blow everything for us.'

'Be delighted to. Then it'll be your turn. You want to do that right here, all that blowing, or are you going to invite me inside?'

She poured his coffee and put the cup in front of him. MaryAnn was deep in thought as she cleaned out the coffee maker and wiped it dry with paper towels. She'd have to remember to wash both cups, and the spoons, by hand, then dry them and put them back in the cupboard. That anal maniac she was married to would surely notice that there were two more cups in the dishwasher than there'd been when he'd placed his teacup in there before he'd gone to the office.

She took her coffee over to the table and sat down, looked at the grinning fool sitting across from her, his bulk straining the chairs. That's all she'd need, his making one of her kitchen chairs into kindling. Did he think this was all some sort of joke? He must, the way he was acting. Well, she'd have to straighten him out on that right away.

'My husband might come home at any minute.'

'Good, he can join us. I like threesomes better than anything.'

'You don't want to meet him any more than I want you to meet him. And he doesn't want to meet you.'

'What's he gonna do, Mare, kick my ass for me?'

How could she respond? If she tried to play weak and appealed to his machismo he'd have an answer for that too, and then she'd lose the upper hand that she'd had with him since the beginning. She was already struggling to keep it, fighting to stay strong and dignified in the face of his bold confrontation. She had to admit, she hadn't expected this from him. He was smarter than he looked. Which wasn't saying much; her houseplants were smarter than this guy looked.

Still, she'd misjudged him, he was more than some stiff dick who worked at the right hospital.

'No, he won't do that.'

'So, aren't you gonna ask? Don't you want to know?'

'Know *what*?'

'How I ran you down.'

'Why would I care? You're here, aren't you?'

'Yeah, and I got two hours before I got to report to work. Now how about you and me going on back into the bedroom? You can show me how much the old man spent furnishing the place.'

What was he up to, was this a power play? Did he think he could just waltz in here and take charge, and she'd be too afraid to challenge him? She knew now that he was capable of it, that she'd misjudged his little boy act at the racetrack last night. All his jumping around and squealing hadn't been a sign of stupidity, just immaturity. He was far more shrewd than she'd judged, even after fucking him. In fact, as she'd left the motel she'd been singing, thinking that she had him right where she wanted him.

But now it didn't look as if that were true. In fact, it looked as if the exact opposite were more the case.

He could in fact come in here and demand sex from her. He knew where she lived and she didn't for a minute fall for that line about his thinking that he was falling in love with her. She'd known too many others like him before; he'd use her until he was tired of her, and then he'd discard her, maybe even ruin her life while he was at it, just for the fun of doing it.

He would do that for certain if she allowed him to bed her in this house. Walter, she knew, searched her bedroom when she wasn't home, looking for evidence of infidelity so he could divorce her and it wouldn't cost him a cent. If he should find a stray male pubic hair, see the toilet seat up, or evidence of sex in the bed that he'd paid for, he'd hire private investigators to dog her every step, and she couldn't have that, not when she was so close finally to realizing her life's dream. Not when she was so close to independence for all time.

Walter had thought that she'd just been going out for cigarettes last night, or he might have followed her, or had her followed by someone who owed him a favor. There were plenty of people around who did, Walter had been big on doing favors for important people.

Which was why she'd made her move at the racetrack. She knew of several places where Mute hung out, taverns and bars in his neighborhood, over in the Hegewisch community. But that was where her business was, on the Southeast Side of the city. Where Walter's legal offices had been, before he'd gotten in trouble. There were too many people out there who knew who she was for her to be able to pick up Mute anywhere in the area without taking the chance that they'd be caught.

She thought she'd been so careful, and she'd misjudged him, and now it looked as if he was slick enough to destroy her.

But many men had tried that over her life, and very few had accomplished it. After the first few times, you grew a thick skin. Walter, even, had been trying for years, and he hadn't succeeded, and he was a hell of a lot smarter than this zeek sitting at her table.

She'd play along for the moment, until she found his weakness. Then she'd use it against him. They all had a weakness, every man she'd ever met. But for now, she'd have to manage to stay strong, to appear as if she didn't mind Mute's machinations too much. She couldn't show him any weakness, if she did she knew he'd jump on it, the way all men did when they saw it in a woman. And there was one good thing that might come of this, if he thought that he was in charge.

She might not have to pay him for the information that he got for her, the way she'd been planning to all along.

Maybe she'd found a weakness already, maybe his being an ex-con and a hustler and a small-time petty punk could be put to her immediate advantage. She had to think about it and quick, before he got overwhelmed by his power, threw her down on the floor and raped her in her own goddamned kitchen.

What did she have here, what did she know about him? Very little, except that there was larceny in his heart and he liked to gamble, liked to bed married women and didn't have much of an imagination. Well, that last one, she'd been wrong on, but the rest of it was verifiable. How could she use those things against him? How could she turn what he was to her benefit? She would have to, and quick, because she had too much to lose to be submissive to him for long. She already had too many things to worry about, too many plates to juggle. All she'd have to do was to pick up one thing too many, and all the plates would come crashing down, and she'd be back on the streets, looking for another Walter. MaryAnn was shrewd enough to know that miracles rarely happened to the same person twice, particularly after they'd blown the first opportunity. Besides, she thought that she might well rather die than have her future placed in the hands of a man again. Neither Walter, nor anyone like him, and certainly not this creature in front of her, could ever be allowed to have control over her life again.

A thought hit her, MaryAnn's shrewd mind working overtime, and as she sat there she figured out a way that she might get it even right now, to put the relationship back where it had been, with her having the upper hand. She might be able to pull it off, and if she didn't, well, she hadn't lost anything. He'd just know that she was a liar. Big deal. He already knew that she was an adulteress. The best ammunition that she had right now was his belief that she was a dummy. That might well be the rope that she would put around his neck.

MaryAnn smiled coyly, in control, and bit her lower lip. She lowered her head and looked up at him with her eyes opened wide, seductively.

'You're a smart man, Mute. You know how to get things done, but you don't know what you're getting into. If you could find out where I lived, then you must have found out who my husband is. Ceterra, does the name ring a bell?'

'Can't say that it does.' He sipped his coffee loudly and flexed his right bicep muscle at her. He put the cup down. 'Why, is it supposed to?'

'You don't read the papers, watch a lot of TV?'

'Can't say that I do. The paper depresses me, and there ain't much sense in watching the television unless I got a bet on a football game or something.'

'Ceterra, think hard, Mute. Try to remember where you've heard the name before. I'll give you a clue: his first name's Walter.'

'Listen, you could give me his middle initial and social security number, and his name wouldn't mean shit to me.'

Thank God. She believed she could pull it off.

MaryAnn lowered her voice, as if afraid to say what she was about to aloud, even in the privacy of her own home.

'Mute, he's outfit. He runs the outfit in Chicago.'

He knew what *that* meant, all right.

He'd been sitting back with his arms behind his neck, feeling in charge here, probably anticipating an imminent orgasm, and when she laid it on him he shot forward, dropped both hands to the table and stared at her, hard, his eyes panicked, not posing for the first time since she'd known him.

'Mare, come on, you're *shitting* me.'

'Mute, I tried to tell you outside, you didn't know what you were doing. Remember earlier when I said he wouldn't beat you up? That was the truth, he *wouldn't* beat you up. He'd *kill* you, but he wouldn't beat you up. He'd have a bunch of his friends take you down in the basement and hold you down while he sticks an icepick into your balls, sticks it in them again and again, until the shock kills you, or until he gets bored and just sticks the thing through your eye.' MaryAnn shrugged. 'It wouldn't be the first time. He's the jealous type.'

She felt more lies pop into her head, even as she spoke, embellishments she could use to get him to do what she wanted.

She said, 'Even though he sent me to find you, fucking you wasn't part of the deal. He finds out about that, he'll kill you, Mute. Believe me, I know from past experience.'

She'd never seen such horror on a man's face before. She had him, owned him, and the knowledge of that excited her. If she wasn't running him, she'd take him out to a motel and tear his clothes off and fuck him silly.

Still, this was even better than sex. Having total control over a man who was big enough to pick her up and break her in two over his knee, having him eating out of her hand . . .

'What? Come on, you ain't serious, you're smiling.'

'Because he'd make me watch, it wouldn't be the first time. He'd want me in on it, to see if it turned me on.'

'*Jee*-zus Christ, are you in-*sane*!'

'No, but he is. And you must be, too, to come here like this, into his house when he's not there, wanting to screw his wife in his bed.' She stood up, ran her hands suggestively down the sides of her skirt, the gesture pulling that silk blouse tight against her bra. MaryAnn ran her tongue around her lips and looked at him, turned it on for all she was worth.

'You will want to go up to the bedroom and do it, Mute? I'm wet, thinking about it. About Walter coming home and finding us.'

'Listen lady, I got to go.'

He rose to his feet, his muscles not doing him a lot of good now; two minutes just talking, and a slender young woman had reduced this steroid mutant into a terrified, trembling sissy. MaryAnn was in the moment of her greatest personal glory. This, she knew, was something she could get used to.

'Mute, sit down,' MaryAnn said, winging it, thinking on her feet, taking it all the way downtown while she had him in her control.

She said, 'We've got some time, and it's about time I told

you why my husband sent me after you last night – what he wants from you. What you better do, if you know what's good for you.' MaryAnn smiled, convincingly.

'Go on, now, sit down.' Mute shakily followed her direction, the way that she knew he would. MaryAnn sat down across from him and dropped the smile and glared, then told him just exactly what she expected him to do.

She could see why Ben didn't care for this Doctor Evan much, the guy was an arrogant, sanctimonious little prick. Diane listened to him talking to Ben, as if Ben were a child, looking at her ex-husband as if he were nothing more than an interesting specimen floating around in a petri dish. He'd lift his head back in the middle of a sentence, tightening the cords in his neck as he spoke, showing them what a man he was. She wondered if Ben had considered reaching over and strangling him when he did that. He must have, the thought had even crossed her mind, and she was a far less violent person than her ex-husband was.

'I can smell the smoke on you all the way across the room. You *knew* you were having problems breathing, and you still continue to smoke cigarettes.'

This man was lecturing Ben, and Diane resented it. If Ben did he was hiding it, sitting there all stony-faced, leaning to one side in the chair – toward her – his legs crossed and the fingers of his right hand softly stroking his chin.

'My God, Ben,' the sanctimonious bastard said, 'don't you realize that it might have taken twenty years from the time that the first cell began to go bad in your lungs until today? You've been destroying yourself for over thirty years, haven't you? Smoking those miserable weeds, even after the AMA *told* you that they caused lung cancer.' He smiled, almost sheepishly.

The doctor said, 'I apologize,' and Ben opened his hand, which could be taken as an acceptance, then went back to stroking his chin, but he didn't say a word. Maybe he was afraid of what he might say if he opened his mouth. Or, rather, afraid of what he might do if he got going.

Diane had never seen him like this, introverted and thoughtful. He'd always shown his emotions, never held them in check. The past five years must have been tough on him, he must have learned a lot.

The doctor said, 'I didn't mean to jump on your ass, it's just that this is always so rough for me.'

'How do you think it is for *him*?' Diane said, and immediately regretted it.

Ben looked at her, with those icy eyes, no warmth on his face at all.

'Excuse me, Diane,' he said, without moving his hand from his chin, then he turned back to the doctor.

'Lay it on me, Doc, you seem to have some information I ain't got.'

She saw the doctor wince when Ben said 'ain't'.

'Yes, well, it's as I suspected, what we call oat-cell carcinoma. Surgery isn't used in the treatment plan. It's too fast growing, but, it's sensitive to chemotherapy and radiation.'

'That's the good news?'

This man had just given Ben what amounted to a death sentence, and listen to him, sitting there joking around. His face hadn't changed its expression one iota. Diane wanted to gasp, wanted to cry, but she couldn't do that, it would embarrass Ben. She had come here for one reason, but was here now for another. Now she was here to back him up, and he'd be humiliated if she showed her emotion, her pain, in front of a stranger. Especially when the stranger was as big an asshole as Doctor Evan was.

Doctor Evan, who now seemed in his element, talking about cancer as if it was his personal foe. His nemesis. She thought she had his number. Doctor Evan saw himself as Batman, and cancer as the Joker, and the people who caught cancer were just pawns in the game, to be used up in his battle, fallen soldiers in his personal war.

'You hit the jackpot, Ben. Over a dozen types of cancers start in the lungs, and almost every other one is slow-growing except for oat-cell. Surgery responds on most of the others, it's not like it used to be, when being diagnosed with lung cancer meant you had to die.'

'Unless it's this oat-cell type, right? This type kills you.'

'Chemotherapy and radiation can help, can cause up to two years' remission if begun immediately.' Doctor Evan flashed a smile, and when he spoke now, it was the way a kindergarten teacher did to a student he was trying to help learn a simple fact of life that the teacher took for granted.

'See, Ben, it's not like a chart in an office, the inside of your body is really very sloppy. The lungs are wrapped around your heart, your esophagus, the blood vessels that go to and from your heart. All bunched in there in a very messy way. The lungs, you see, are divided into what are called lobes. The right lung has three lobes, the left lung, only two.' The doctor cleared his throat and stared at Ben in a way that he probably thought was filled with grave concern.

'All five lobes of your lungs have been invaded, Ben. Which means that it might well have spread to the lymph system and to other vital organs: your heart; your brain; your blood; your liver. Maybe even your bones. I don't have all the lab word in yet, I'll know about your blood later this afternoon, as soon as the work-ups are finished, and we'll need to do some biopsies to see how far it's spread.'

'All right.' Ben's voice was hoarse, but not shaking. He sounded calm, relaxed, but Diane knew that could well be an act. Yet she could tell nothing by the way he was looking at the doctor, whether he hated the man, if he wanted to hit him. It was as if they were discussing someone else's imminent extinction.

The doctor cleared his throat again, it must be what he did before he spoke about things that made him feel uncomfortable.

He said, 'I understand that you have no health insurance, and Ben, I have to tell you, treatment's going to get expensive. But you *are* a veteran, and I can call my colleagues at the VA hospital, get you in there tonight – '

'No,' Ben said.

'Ben, treatment has to be started immediately.'

'Say I do nothing, don't take any treatment. How long would I have.'

'Ben, you can't do that, you have to – '

'How long would I *have*.'

There was a soft steel in Ben's voice that Diane had never heard before, a quiet way of telling the man that he had better answer the question. He hadn't raised his voice an octave, but still, the threat was real, hanging in the air between them, and the doctor seemed to sense it, even seemed a little afraid.

Diane, however, wasn't afraid. She reached over and took Ben's hand, and he let her, wrapped his fingers around hers and squeezed them once, then lightened his grip.

'Ben,' the doctor said quietly, 'if you refuse all treatment, you've got, at the most, six months. And the last two will be so incredibly painful that you'll wish that you *were* dead.'

Ben rose to his feet and pulled his suit jacket shut, buttoned it and tossed his topcoat over his arm. He looked over at Diane and smiled, said, 'You ready?' as if he wanted to know if she were inclined to leave a restaurant after a meal.

Diane rose, holding her coat over one arm, now once again holding Ben's hand in hers. It was dry. She squeezed it, felt his answering squeeze, so gentle.

Without a word Ben turned his back and began to lead her out of the office. Behind them she could hear the doctor, clearing his throat as if he himself had something deadly stuck down in his windpipe.

'Ben, please, you have to listen to me.'

'I've heard enough,' Ben said softly, over his shoulder, then opened the door and led Diane away from that terrible place.

They sat in the restaurant, neither of them eating, Ben with a cup of coffee, his forearms wrapped around it as if protecting it from a thief, his cigarettes on the table in front of him. He was smoking one now, taking deep drags as he spoke. Diane sipped a Pepsi and listened to him, wondering if this was the same man she'd known for most of her life.

He didn't seem like the same Ben, didn't even really look like him anymore. This man sat with his shoulders hunched, carrying a burden that the other Ben would have thought that he'd never have to lift.

'You know what I thought of first when he started talking?' She didn't answer him, he wasn't really asking a question.

'He started going on about lung cancer taking twenty years to get you, and the first thing that popped into my head was you and Benny and John. Did my smoking fuck you up? Were there cells going bad in your lungs because of me? You hear all that shit now, about second-hand smoke.'

'We'll be all right.'

'No, please, you'll all go in for physicals. I'll cover it, I'll pay for it, I got some money coming to me.'

'Ben, I have insurance.'

'Please.'

'All right.'

He'd said please a half a dozen times to her today, more times than he had in all the years that they'd been married. Suddenly, those years didn't seem so terrible anymore. She could remember them even more kindly after he was gone, knowing that he was no longer capable of ever again causing her pain. Her, or her children.

And her children carried his name.

She'd sat there last night in her living room, wondering if he'd ever given her anything, being selfish in her thoughts, remembering only the things that she'd allowed Ben to take away: her self-esteem, her self-respect, her desire to be attractive. She'd sat there last night and thought about how he had killed her ability to trust, to love. Now, though, she knew that he had indeed given her something. Two somethings, in fact, and their names were Benny and John.

There was no way on earth she could ever hate him again, not when she knew that without him she would have never borne those children.

She was looking at him with compassion, making sure to cover her pity. He'd strike out at that, he hated pity. She'd never known him to utter a word of pity for anyone or anything.

But she'd seen him act on it, more than one time.

In bars he would slip twenty dollar bills into the pockets of the kids who'd come in and shine his shoes, more if he thought that the kid would use the money to buy himself what he needed; a coat in the winter, new gym shoes in the summer. She'd been with Ben on more than one occasion when he'd pulled the car to the curb with a shriek of rubber, jumped out and stopped some drunken or just plain violent male from beating on a woman or a child, Ben slapping the man senseless and then talking to him, telling him what he'd do to him if he ever hit anyone weaker than he was again.

It was the way he was. There was so much of a sense of what was fair, of what was right and wrong, that Diane had often marveled that he was, by trade, a criminal.

He squeezed her hand a little bit, and she looked up, saw him laughing at her.

'You didn't hear a word I said.'

'I'm sorry, what?'

'I said that I wanted to know if it was all right with you, if you'd think it was a good idea . . .'

'What, Ben?'

'I'd like to see the kids again, before – you know.'

'Ben, what about treatment? That doctor was a miserable son of a bitch, but he was right, you at least have to *try*.'

'Why?'

And she couldn't think of a reply.

'I seen my buddy Eddie, how he went out. Same shit, Diane, same exact thing, as if I caught it from him two years ago when he died. They told him he could have two or three years with the chemo, and I go to see him in the VA hospital, he's got big red Xs painted on him, where they aim the radiation, and he's got some radioactive shit going into his veins from a needle, coming down out of one of those bottles that hang on hooks. His hair and teeth are gone, he didn't even know who I was. He was crying, wanting to die but scared to, begging God to forgive him. Eddie had five weeks, from diagnosis to death. So much for treatment at the VA hospital. If I stay out of there, I got four months, if I play my cards straight.'

'He said six months.'

'I ain't gonna suffer, I won't be like Eddie.'

'Ben . . .'

He shook his head, and she knew that it would do no good to try and talk him out of whatever he might be planning. She had a pretty good idea of what he would do, even without him telling her.

'Would you try it if you had regular insurance, if you had Blue Cross and could get into a hospital that specialized in cancer treatment?'

'With the best doctors in the country, instead of some butchers trying to pay the government back for medical school? Sure I would. That's a good gamble. But I ain't Donald Trump. The fact is, I don't have Blue Cross, or any other insurance, and I ain't gonna die alone in some VA hospital.

'Listen . . .' Ben seemed uncomfortable for the first time since they'd sat down. He got a brief reprieve as the waitress came by with the coffee pot. The woman obviously knew him, she'd called him by name when they'd entered the place. He waited until she'd poured him another cup, Diane refusing when the woman asked her if she'd like another Pepsi.

'You change your mind about something to eat?'

'No, thank you,' Diane said. Ben didn't even bother to answer, was busy lighting another cigarette. Diane had to fight the urge to slap it out of his mouth. He looked up and seemed almost disappointed that the waitress had left the table.

'Look, I wanted to tell you.' He sat back and made a face, searching for words that he might have thought of often, but now was unable to articulate. He sat forward, determinedly, and tried again.

'Back there, you didn't want me to talk about it, and I

don't blame you. I always feel out of place in those joints. I know I don't belong, that everyone in there is looking down on me. I can't explain what it is, but it's the same way I feel in a courtroom or in jail, when hacks look at you or tell you what to do.'

'But now you want to discuss it.'

'Now I *got* to discuss it.'

She sat back, still holding his hand, preparing herself for what she knew he was about to say. He'd apologize and she'd absolve him, she could forgive him now, she knew.

And suddenly the entire world lifted off Diane's shoulders, she felt a hundred pounds lighter, the world seemed brighter outside the window to her right. Losing her resentment of him had lifted a terrible load from her. God, she felt good, and she cursed herself as she thought it. She was glorifying in the fact that the man she had once loved was dying.

She sat forward again, and smiled to give him a sign of encouragement.

'Go ahead, you can tell me now.'

'You know, I figured out what I had a while back, I've been sick a while. Knew I probably had this cancer in my lungs. I thought I was ready for it, thought I was prepared, and when that guy told me I was dying, all of a sudden it was all I could do not to break down.'

'It didn't show.'

'Thank God,' Ben said. She knew what he meant. To his way of thinking, there were plenty of things a lot worse than dying, and showing your own weaknesses in front of a man as weak as that doctor, would, Diane knew, be one of them.

'I ain't scared, I'm not saying that. I'm just saying that it rocked me.'

'I understand.'

Ben took a drag on the cigarette, and looked at her, straight in the eye, his gaze unblinking, intense, so powerful that she had to fight the urge to look away.

'And I didn't want to break down because of what he said. I was hurting because I have so much unfinished business, there's so many things I wanted to do yet, for the kids, for you.'

Diane sat locked in his gaze, mesmerized by his eyes, by his words.

'Diane, I never told you that I loved you. Thirteen years that we were married, I don't remember ever having told you that I loved you. What the hell was wrong with me, I don't know. I ain't scared to die, but I'm scared now, looking at you. I done a lot of things wrong, and I don't regret most of them. But if I could take that back I would, Diane, I swear to you, I would. If I could change things, make them different, go back twenty years and meet you all over again, I'd be different.'

'But you can't.'

'But I can't.'

'So don't talk about it.'

'I got to talk about it, I been carrying it around inside me for *five fucking years.*' He looked at her as if he'd reached out and slapped her, looked away and shook his head.

'I'm sorry, I didn't mean that, I shouldn't have cussed. I'm trying to, I'm trying to, shit, I don't know *what* I'm trying to do.'

'You're trying to make amends.'

'Is that what it's called?'

Were those tears in his eyes? Tears of honest emotion, or from anger and frustration? In all the years she'd known him, he'd never opened up like this.

She wanted him to keep on going, she was feeling better and better with every word he spoke.

He took another drag off the cigarette and immediately seized up for a second, his face contorting in pain, then it relaxed as whatever had hit him passed. He smashed the cigarette out in the ashtray.

'Damn things, I never should have started.' Ben shrugged. 'I still had twenty years longer than I ever thought I would.'

'Don't talk like that, it isn't true.'

'I know what I'm trying to say, but the words won't come

out. Diane, I love you, and the boys, too, and I know I never showed it.' He sat back and stared at the ashtray, at the wispy plume of smoke coming up out of it, shaking his head.

'I never been good with words,' he said, and Diane squeezed his hand.

'You're doing pretty good right now, Ben,' she said softly, and he looked at her and smiled.

'Can I see the kids, Diane, can I come over and see the boys just one more time before I die?' he asked, and she didn't even have to think about it, she spoke without a thought.

'Of course you can, Ben. Of course you can.'

The look in his eyes now was of gratitude and love, and he nodded his head then lowered it, and she'd be damned if he didn't reach up with one hand and wipe at his eyes, as if swiping away tears.

Ben looked up at her, surprising Diane again, he could tell, because he felt so serene and calm – rarities for him, but particularly strange now, after what he'd just learned from the little prick of a doctor – and he could see that it was translating to her mood. What she didn't know was that his good feelings were entirely predicated on the fact that she was right there, sitting across from him, smiling. And because she had come to be with him, had come to the doctor's office.

He could see that she was taken aback by the way that he'd been acting, the things he'd been saying, and for a time it even took away the cloud that was hanging over his head. It felt *good*, and she felt good with him, he could tell that she enjoyed being with him, and she hadn't made fun of him when he'd told her what he was feeling, when he'd told her that he loved her.

What *was* love, did he have any idea? He'd certainly never known it, until he'd met Diane. Then he'd overdosed on it real quick, suspicious of it, of how much of it she had to give. There was a feeling he'd had back then, something he'd believed in; if she'd loved a miserable bastard such as him, then there had to be something wrong with her.

Ben had once been forced to work for his foster mother's boyfriend, pumping gas all summer at the man's station, from seven in the morning until nine at night, six days a week. On Sunday he only had to work from eight until six. The man paid him forty bucks a week, and he gave it to Ben's foster mother, and she gave Ben five bucks for himself, told him that he needed to learn the value of a dollar. That was his first humiliation, her thinking that he was that stupid.

The second humiliation he'd faced while living in that home had come from the gas station owner himself, Tommy, who'd sit in his fucking wooden chair, his pals who worked in construction all around him in the evening, drinking beer and smoking non-filtered cigarettes and telling lies about hunting and women while Ben knocked himself out pumping gas. When he wasn't busy doing that, he was expected to sweep the place, or, if the work was there, to fix flat tires and to change the oil in cars, to grease them up from down in the pit.

Tommy's place didn't have any hydraulic lifts; there was a concrete pit that Ben had had to work in. Whenever a car ran over the hose outside, the little double bell that it was attached to would chime, and Ben would have to stop what he was doing and jump up the stairs. Tommy and his partners would laugh at him when, after racing up the stairs and wiping the oil from his hands, Ben would find that all that had happened was some kids had driven their bicycles over the hose.

He'd been twelve years old that summer, and what had happened, the things that he'd learned while working for Tommy, had changed his life forever.

How he'd suffered there, that summer, in that station mostly, but also at the house. When he was there he would have to listen to the men talking about hunting, all of them making fun of him, because he wasn't as big as they were. Tommy would talk loud enough to make sure that Ben could hear him, bragging about the broad he was fucking, telling his buddies stories about her, the things she'd do for him.

How he'd get his nut then roll over and tell her to go make him something to eat.

Ben would burn up with shame, grateful that he was down in the pit and not up there where they could see him. He'd throw himself into what he was doing and try to ignore what Tommy was saying about the woman whom he was supposed to look at as his mother.

But he couldn't, the words got through to him, and he felt ashamed, as if he himself were somehow being used and mistreated sexually, instead of just being forced into slave labor.

He'd started stealing from the man, a dollar here and there, and taking the money from Tommy had made him feel good, as if he were getting back at him, was finding a way to hurt Tommy. He'd fix a tire and pocket the money when the guy came to pick it up; change the oil and keep that money, too. It was the only way to do it, the gas money was inventoried, and a record was kept of every gallon of gas that the station sold.

So Ben had grown sly, had learned how to do it where he couldn't get caught, only in the end of course he did get caught. He was only twelve years old - still a year or two away from learning how to steal and for the most part get away with it.

Tommy didn't catch him until the beginning of September, when Ben was back in school and only working six hours a day. Caught him red-handed, too, Ben putting the money from a fixed flat tire into his pocket while Tommy was supposedly down the corner at Blondies, having a couple of drinks. Ben looking up and seeing Tommy standing in the doorway, half-drunk and watching him, angrily.

Tommy had beaten the shit out of him, had fired him and sent him home, and Ben had walked home slowly, knowing what would be on the other side of the family door.

Another asswhipping, which he was used to, but he wasn't planning on taking this one, he'd had enough of being used.

Ben walked toward the house with trepidation, his head

swimming, in physical and mental anguish, and he inventoried his life.

His mother had given him up when he was still in diapers, and he'd been shunted off into one foster family after another. He'd tried, at every one of them, to be a good boy, so that they'd keep him, want him to stay, would adopt him and make him a part of their families forever. Nothing he had ever done had been able to make that come true, however. They'd always send him back, or his caseworker would visit and for some reason take him away. He'd never caught on anywhere, never stayed more than a few months at any single place, not until this one, with the woman who was dating Tommy. Here, he'd lasted the summer. And only because he was willing to bust his ass for her boyfriend, Tommy.

She had a husband somewhere, but Ben had never seen him. When the caseworker would come around, the woman would always say that her husband was off working shift-work at Republic. Ben did everything that was asked of him, reported for work every day, busted his ass for Tommy, and even that hadn't been good enough, even giving the woman his money didn't seem to make her happy.

She'd tell him the things he already knew, how he was stupid and clumsy, how he couldn't do anything right. He'd eat his dinner and take a bath and then go right to bed, vowing to do better the next day, to work hard enough to make her proud.

But somehow during that summer, he'd figured out the truth. After repeated rejection by the woman, and the direct and indirect insults from Tommy, Ben had begun to form the philosophy that he'd stayed true to throughout his life: the strong preyed on the weak, and everyone used everybody else. If they thought that they were stronger than you, they'd hurt you, every time.

What he had to do was find a way to fight back, to make sure that nobody ever saw him being weak.

It began when he walked in the door. The woman who'd been mandated to care for him was drunk, and had obviously been alerted over the phone as to what Ben had done. There was a belt in her hand when he entered her house, and her two little brats – who never had to work for anyone, who'd spent the summer playing while Ben busted his ass for peanuts – were standing there, waiting for the fun to begin.

'Come here, you little bastard,' the woman said, and Ben had put his new philosophy into genuine practice. He'd assaulted her, thrown himself at her, and although he wasn't big enough to beat all three of them up, he'd taken him a ham sandwich while they'd eaten him for dinner.

The police came and he was taken to a juvenile shelter until the next day, when the woman filed assault charges against him with his caseworker.

It was the first time that Ben had ever been sent away to what had still been called the reformatory, to the Center, but not the last, because he'd learned his lesson well. No one would ever lay their hands on him again without having to pay the price, one way or the other.

Even Tommy, who'd learned the hard way, after Ben got out of the Center. He'd poured gas on the outside wall of the man's gas station, dropped a match and run away to watch the explosion from an alley three blocks down. The woman he hadn't had to take care of, she'd died of a heart attack while Ben had been in the Center. Within a couple of years he couldn't even remember her name.

From that day forward anyone who hurt him had always paid, and he never looked for anything from anybody he ever met, did not even believe that such a thing as love even truly existed.

Until he'd met this woman across from him, who'd wanted so much to love him. And what had he done? He'd blown it. He'd pushed her away consistently, but somehow she'd managed to stay for thirteen years. He owed her for that, owed her big, and he knew that he'd have to pay. The way everyone always paid, one way or another.

So now he said to Diane, 'I've got something for the kids, something that I can give them that can help them out in the future. I'll have it tonight, Diane, and I'll bring it with me when I come to see them.'

'You won't be able to buy them, Ben, if it's money you're talking about.'

'No, but they'll need it to help with college. I never even thought about going, finishing high school had been too much for me. How about this, I'll give the money to you, and you take care of it for them.

'All right.' He could see that she felt proud, knowing that he trusted her.

Did she still have feelings for him? God knew, he had no idea what to expect from her. After she'd hung up on him last night, he didn't think that he'd ever see her again. He'd planned on mailing the money to her, certified and insured, next-day express so some slob wouldn't try and grab it and open it up, see what was inside and keep it all for himself. Once he was in the grave, he wouldn't be able to protect his investments.

For once, the slithering pit of rattlesnakes that was his brain seemed to be under control. He could not remember the last time he'd felt so at ease, so sure of what was going on in his life. Death was four months away, maybe more, because he could take a lot of pain; it was Ben Morer's natural state. A good day was when the pain was slight enough where he could laugh, sit in his apartment and not think that he was missing out on what was going on out there, out in the street.

He had a few months to live, and was shocked to find himself seeing that as a relief. When he was dead, this would all be over. When he was dead, there would be no misery. There wouldn't even be people who would mourn him or suffer. One day he'd be here and the next day he'd be gone. He didn't believe in God, and he knew that his entire life had been spent in a personal hell. He believed that personality and strength, force of character were all you had, and when you died, these things died with you, forever.

He hoped that the snakes stayed sleeping in his skull, hoped that he could maybe visit his kids a few times, get to know them a little bit before he walked out into a forest preserve and blew his brains all over some tree. He wouldn't have to hustle much, how much did he need to get through four months? He could do that with the money that he had in his pocket. Although he'd like to put some more in their hands, for Diane, for the kids. Maybe if he took some more risks, he could do them proud, leave them something substantial. He hoped that he could, and if he got caught, what did he have to lose? The cops had nothing to use against him now. What were they going to take away, four months? Maybe he could get lucky, make one big score and do right by the people who had once been his family.

He was considering these hopes when Diane leaned forward tentatively, began to tell him about a call she'd gotten that morning, and with every word that she spoke, one of the snakes in his head came awake, hissing.

What had she said? Had telling him about the call been such a terrible thing? Diane didn't know, all she knew was that the man she'd felt so comfortable with had disappeared as she'd told him the story, about the call, and the Ben she'd known before had come back. His face had grown hard, his eyes dead little rocks in the middle of his skull, giving away nothing as he listened. The only sign of what was going on inside him were those big fists on the table, the knuckles white from his constant squeezing.

'Ben, do you know who might have done this?' she asked, and he didn't answer her right away. He didn't look away from her either, as he might if he were trying to think up a lie she would fall for. He kept staring into her eyes, that blank face twisting up as if it was made out of rubber, Ben giving her the glare, that look that turned her blood to ice. When he smiled, looking like that, Diane couldn't help herself, she automatically recoiled.

'I'll take care of it,' Ben said, but not as he once would have. He didn't scream or yell or jump to his feet making threats, just sat there calmly, speaking as he had to the doctor a while back, squeezing his fists, that terrible smile on his lips.

Ben said, 'I'll call you later, all right?' and Diane didn't know what to say.

She nodded dumbly, said, 'Okay.'

'Tonight, if you don't mind. Maybe late though. We can talk about the kids, about what we're going to tell them.'

'Yes.'

Ben stood and dropped a five on the table, nodded and walked out of the restaurant, leaving Diane, as he had many times before, totally alone, depressed, and not understanding what she'd done. She looked out the window at him as he stormed to his car, the breath from his mouth being caught in the wind and torn away as he breathed heavy, hard.

She'd done what she'd come to do, and she knew where Ben would be going. But she'd wanted him to do it before she knew that he was dying. Diane believed in a hereafter, and in sin and what it could cost you. Although not religious, she considered herself to be spiritual.

And now she felt sinful, as if she'd committed a murder herself. Because as sure as he was sitting in that booth, she knew, without a second's doubt, that Ben was on his way out into the world to commit a cold and brutal act of murder.

He could change his style, but the man inside was the same. He'd known who'd called her and that man would soon be dead, and there was nothing she could do about it because she'd set the juggernaut in motion.

Lino had driven through the freezing streets, wondering if the hole in the ozone layer was causing this shitty weather. All summer, there'd been nothing but heat, intense heat and a drought that had killed crops and human beings, and then in October they'd gotten a record amount of rain. Now here it was November, and they were having a cold snap that rivaled anything he'd seen in the middle of January, and he'd lived here for all of his fifty-one years.

Last week, at this time, it had been sixty-two degrees. Go figure it out.

He got the money out of his bank lockbox and carried it in a zippered vinyl bank bag, under his coat, stuck down the waistband of his pants, down in there good. Fifty grand in hundreds, how light it felt, so much money taking up such a small amount of space. He kept his hand on the weapon in his coat pocket, willing to shoot right through it if anyone approached him who wasn't smiling. He made it to his car and hit the button that locked the doors right away, driving away with one eye on the rearview mirror, not about to be taken off. No one would ever get away with mugging Lino.

The ozone layer, he knew, wasn't responsible for the crime wave in Chicago.

Between himself and his partner Tony, it had become an inside joke; the escalating murder rate and the way the media played it. Going for the murder record, the two of them went so far as to give odds on whether the record would be broken by the end of the year. Not a day went by where the papers didn't do the body count, tell the city how many had been murdered the night before, and add these dead ones to the ever-growing list. The papers even put that number in headlines sometimes, as if it was something for which they should feel civic pride.

Drugs and gangs, the papers said, it was what the cops told them was wrong with Chicago. Lino knew better. He knew that it was the summer heat wave, coupled with armed niggers.

They had no respect for themselves, they were like wild animals, tearing at each other all the time. No discipline, no order to their lives. Lino had done time with them, and Christ, they made him sick. Ignorant? He'd never met anyone that ignorant before, and disrespectful, they had no respect for anyone or for their position in life.

When a nigger came into one of the joints that Lino owned with Tony, they'd watch him, tell the bouncers to keep an eye on him in case it was a stick-up. They could joke about it all they wanted, but there was no way on earth that Lino was going to allow himself to become one of those numbers in Chicago's record year of murder. Shit, 127 in August, wasn't it? Gangs and drugs, his ass.

It would be a safe bet, too, that the record would not be

broken. If the weather had stayed nice, the city might have had a shot, but when it was cold like this, those people didn't even leave their houses except to pick up their welfare checks. Now that it had gotten cold again, Tony would take all the action he could get his hands on that the record would be broken. It was a sure bet that it wouldn't be, not unless it got warm again.

Thinking of Tony reminded Lino of what the guy had said, back in the He Ain't Here. Was he hard up for cash? What could he possibly be doing with all his money? He hadn't gotten too upset about that extra monthly payout that they would have to give the Man, then again, he wouldn't; they'd both been through it before, it was the price they had to pay for staying in business, for being allowed to stay alive.

Between them, they took in a small fortune every month, split it right down the middle the way they'd planned to from the very beginning. Tony took care of the book and the bars, and Lino kept the records on the loanshark operation. Lino kept a couple of bucks back that Tony and the Man didn't have to know about, and assumed that Tony was doing the same with the bar dough and with the action from the book.

It was the way business was done; no matter how tight you were with someone, you had to look out for yourself, first, and it was all right, it was simply a matter of business. The bartenders would pour a few drinks that never got rung up, the bouncers would sweep tips off of tables and stick them into their pockets, and Tony would count up the days' receipts and take ten or twenty percent for himself in cash.

So how could Tony be hurting for money, what was he doing to blow it? Young broads, maybe, Tony had a thing for them, and they could burn up the money fast. Diamonds and cars and a fancy place to live, Lino knew from his own experiences, they could eat you up, if you weren't careful. Still, how much could one broad have taken Tony for?

Lino had a sudden worry, that his partner was doing drugs. Cocaine, now, it could destroy a fortune in a very small amount of time. Lino knew lawyers and doctors, and plenty of other guys with college degrees, guys who'd once been players, who now waited outside the Christian Industrial League over at 123 S. Green on days like this, trying to get into the homeless shelter because it was too cold to sleep out on the street. They'd been doing pretty good in their careers, until they ran into coke. The bitch that cocaine was had destroyed better men than Tony, and every single one of them had figured they had it under control.

Was Tony doing drugs? It wouldn't be easy to tell. He was hyper anyway, had a lot of nervous energy for a fat guy. Still, there should be signs, wiping at the nose, licking his lips.

If Lino decided that Tony was doing drugs, he would have to kill the man. Not for some moral reason, but because he'd eventually have to start really ripping Lino off in order to feed his habit, if he wasn't doing it already. It was something he would have to look out for, and something to pay attention to.

He prided himself on being a man who knew how to see things coming, knew how to stay away from the hurricanes of his business that hit with regularity, striking selectively at people in his chosen line of work. How many coups had he seen since he'd been on the street? Had to be a dozen, at least, before the Man took over here a couple of years ago. Turf battles that blew up between competitors, some son of a bitch wanting what another guy had and not having the balls to work for it himself.

Lino and Tony had faced their share of hostile takeover bids, and had survived every one of them, and after every one of the mob takeovers, they had even managed to come out ahead. The new people would send their people around, and they'd tell them what they were making, show them papers from last month's action, some of the papers, anyway, and then they'd set their monthly street tax from what Lino and Tony showed them, and the two of them had learned that these guys weren't all that smart, just organized.

You couldn't rob them in front of their face, or they'd kill you as an example to other self-employed small businessmen. But there were ways around them, and the stealing was expected. You could tell them that you had a bad month, and they'd let you pass with less, but you had to be very careful with that; if you had too many bad months in a row, they'd want to know why, what it was that you were doing wrong. They might even want to take things over from you, give you a wad of cash and have you run your own joints for them.

It was just as bad to pay the same nut every month, without complaint, because then they'd know that you were doing good, and would start hanging around trying to see if you were doing even better than you had said.

It could get to be a pain in the ass sometimes, remembering what you said to which guy. And it was best to be diversified, as Lino and Tony now were. Into more than one thing so that the mob couldn't just sit in your bar and see what your action was. When your money was on the street, no one knew how much was out there but you. It had been Lino's idea, to get into loansharking, so they'd have a cottage industry. The bookmaking and the loan business, all under one roof, and it had turned out to be a gold mine.

A year ago at this time, they'd been soliciting donors to get things going out there in a big way, and now, all of a sudden, they were flush, doing great. Six guys had given them money – all of them street hustlers, none of them was outfit – and now one of them wanted it back. It might not be a good idea to let that word get around. If the other five decided to cash in their chips, too, then they *would* be in trouble, especially when Lino wasn't sure if Tony had any money left out of his end.

This fifty grand was about it for Lino, although he'd never let Tony know it. There had been a few more bills lying around inside the box, maybe a couple of grand altogether, which he'd stuffed in his pocket, but this was most of his savings, all that he had in the world. He could proudly say that he'd made and blown millions, that there wouldn't be a lot left to pass on to the State after his time was up.

Lino bought new cars every year, and he was no slouch with the ladies, himself. He didn't blow cash on them the way that Tony did, but his women weren't cheap, either;

class cost money these days, what with AIDS tests and all that other shit that you never used to have to worry about. He never bet on the horses or on sports, knew from his work what a sucker game that was, but he liked going to Vegas and Atlantic City, liked the way they treated him there, called him sir all the time and sent broads up to his suite. If he lost a wad there four or five times a year, so what? He saw that as the price of being a sport, and he got treated with respect in every casino on either coast.

And the hospital bills were going through the roof, too, Jesus. If he ever got really sick, he knew, he'd have to go on welfare.

It had cost Lino fifteen hundred last night, just for two hours in the emergency room over at South Chicago Hospital. What with X-rays and stitches, doctors' and dentists' fees, bandages and medicine, and it hadn't even been a regular doctor who'd stitched his head together for him. It had been some broad from India, for God's sake, in this country, acting better than him. Who knew what the world was coming to.

Yeah, the cash came and it went out, and the man who died with the most toys won. Lino planned on coming in at least in the top ten.

He drove this new Lincoln, and he had a snazzy high-rise apartment, over on the North Side where the streets were filled with young women looking for an entree into the world of the big money, an entree Lino could give them with the right introduction. How many women who'd started out banging him were now married to commodity traders or high-profile lawyers who liked to play the ponies or bet a few bucks on the Bulls or the Bears? Lino couldn't count them.

The huge apartment he lived in was filled with gadgets, two big-screen TVs, one in the living room and one in the bedroom, Sony VCRs, expensive kitchen gadgets that he never used but still felt the need to have. He had one of the world's ugliest fucking dogs, a wrinkly son of a bitch from China, that some broad had given him for a birthday present last year, after borrowing the two grand the mutt had cost from him, money that he'd never see again. He threw a fag who hung around one of his bars fifty a week to take it out so it could shit. It was what the guy did for a living, he was bonded and everything, as he needed to have keys to everyone's apartment.

Lino was doing pretty good these days, and look what had happened last night, just because he hadn't jumped when that bastard Morer had told him to. He'd been good to the son of a bitch, too, gave him a good monthly return on his money, never lied to him and robbed him the way he did with the other five investors. And look how he'd done him, how Morer had paid back Lino's respect. Taken a gun to his head and cheap-shotted him when his back was turned. Lino was the one who was used to doing that, breaking parts of people's bodies with blunt metal weapons. It wasn't supposed to happen to him.

Lino lived in an area and in a building where people just didn't get into fistfights, and everyone in the building who knew him respected him because they knew that he was heavily connected to some pretty important people, as they could only wish that they themselves were.

What would he tell them when they asked him what had happened to his head? He'd blame it on the niggers, say that he was mugged. They'd believe that, hell, it had happened to some of them. Tell them, too, that the niggers had been taken care of, they'd become part of the near-record murder rates the papers liked to go on about.

Lino was thinking about this, what he'd say to his neighbors, as he pressed the button on the transmitter clipped to his visor that would open the rolling corrugated metal security door that led to his garage. Thought about it as he parked his car in his assigned space, the one that had his apartment number stenciled on the concrete wall.

He was thinking about how much he'd enjoy killing Morer as he walked over to the elevator and pressed the button that would bring it to him, Lino feeling the slight weight of the bag pressing into his belly, his hand on the pistol again, looking around the basement as he waited for the elevator.

He'd enjoy his work tonight, no matter how dangerous it was. He usually only went out on a hit when some outfit guy needed something heavy done, and for his own reasons did not want to use any of his own people. They would call fringe freelance legbreakers like Lino, who were always on the lookout for a way to make some extra cash, and Lino did it even though the thought of doing life in prison scared the living shit out of him.

He'd never enjoyed any of the other ones, but this one would be special, this would be one for the books, something to remember.

Morer, who'd done this to him, who'd made him look like some kind of freak.

Lino got on the elevator and didn't relax until it let him out on his own floor. He got out and walked quickly down the hall, taking his hand out of his pocket long enough to find his house key, inserted it in the lock, turned it and then did the same with the deadlock, then pushed the door open wide.

There was no beep from the burglar alarm warning bell. The keypad beside the door was showing a green light, though, which meant that no one had breached his security; that dumbass Raphael had just forgotten to set the alarm on his way out of the door again.

Still, there was no use in taking chances, not when you were carrying fifty grand around in your pants.

Lino dropped the keys to the floor, slammed the door shut and twisted the bolts home. He took the gun out of his pocket, saw his dog come running toward him, something red and thick hanging off his wrinkled muzzle, the dog leaving tracks on the carpet.

'Good dog,' Lino said, although he was greatly pissed. 'How you doing, boy?'

He spoke the words in a normal tone of voice, but he wasn't paying a lot of attention to the mutt, he was looking around his apartment, looking for an intruder.

He knew he wouldn't find one. A burglar would have had

to shoot the dog, and here Albie was, running around Lino's feet, jumping up at him. Lino couldn't count the times the bastard had leaped up and slapped him in the balls with his front paws. He thought about shooting the dog now, one in the head, putting it out of its misery. What had the dummy done, gotten into the refrigerator? It would be like dumbass Albie to pass up the good shit in there, leave the beer and drink the ketchup then track it all over the fucking apartment.

'Raphael?' Lino called out. There was no reply.

"Ey, Ralphy boy!' Doing Ed Norton. The prick, he'd left without turning the alarm back on behind himself, had let the dog track shit all over the carpets . . .

Lino put the gun back in his pocket, took his coat off, and hung it up in the closet. He looked at it a second, then took the gun out, took the money bag out of his waistband and stuck the weapon in there, a bullet for cash trade. He liked the feel of the gun down in there better than he had the money. Money wasn't for hiding away, the way a gun was.

Lino walked into his kitchen, preparing himself for whatever mess the dog had made. What had been in the garbage that the dog had gotten into? He walked into his kitchen and looked at the floor, saw nothing, no mess, nothing out of place.

'Ralphy, you faggot son of a bitch.' The dog had gotten into something on the street, and Raphael hadn't bothered to wipe it off his muzzle or his paws, probably hadn't even noticed the stuff, Ralphy distracted by some young boy's ass. Well, Lino would kick *his* ass for him, tomorrow, as soon as this business with Morer was taken care of.

He walked into his living room, looking out at Lake Michigan, seeing tiny cars on Lake Shore Drive, way below him, straight ahead. Lake Michigan was blowing water on to the cars, high waves that splashed on to the rocks, sent water all the way on to the Drive. Lino looked at this for a moment. It never failed to relax him, that lake the size of the ocean he'd seen and ignored so many times in Atlantic City, out there gambling.

When he was calmed down Lino walked toward his bedroom, wanting to get the pail and sponge, wipe as much of this shit off his rug as he could. Then he would lie down and rest for a time, he'd been in too much pain to sleep much last night.

He pushed the door halfway open and it hit something and stopped, something large, but soft and yielding.

'What the fuck?' Lino said.

He put his shoulder to the door and shoved, and whatever was inside gave a little bit. He pushed harder and it gave even more, enough for him to step in.

Raphael was lying on the floor, his head busted open, blood all over the carpet. Dog prints were in it too, Albie had been in here, bouncing around Raphael.

The dog had been licking Ralphy's blood, that's what was on his muzzle and paws.

Lino turned Raphael over and looked down at him, saw that he was breathing raggedly. What had the stupid bastard done, hit his head on something? He was dressed, or Lino would have thought that he'd done one of those perverted sex things he'd heard about, lain down on the bed and had someone choke him while he jerked off.

Had someone done this to him? Lino looked at the now opened door, jumped in fear and gasped as he pulled the gun out of his belt. Somebody could be hiding behind it, waiting for him, to kill him. The money bag was still in his other hand, and now he dropped it, held the gun in both hands.

The door had been closed, and the dog had been outside. That meant that whoever had done this to Raphael was in the bedroom with him, had closed the door when he'd heard Lino's key in the outside lock.

Lino took one hand off the gun and pulled the door away from the wall.

No one.

He turned quickly, crouching, and ducked down, got down on his knees, looked under the bed. Nothing. Thank God. That left the bathroom and the closet. He'd check the closet first.

Lino half-ran to the closet door, hyperventilating, believing that he was about to get into a shooting match with someone, probably someone that the Man had sent. Had that bastard junkie Tony called the Man after Lino had left the bar? If he had, Lino would kill him.

He reached a trembling hand out and threw the door open wide. Looked in at his row of suits, at his starched shirts hanging at attention.

He jumped around and held the gun as steadily as he could, pointed it at the bathroom door. He had him now, it was the only place that the guy could be hiding.

Lino ran to it, stood to one side, got down on his knees and put his hand on the knob. He pushed the door open and flopped over and inside, both hands on the gun, hitting the floor with a thud that knocked the wind right out of him. Nothing. He could see all through the room, the shower curtain was pulled back, the door to the connecting bathroom over there next to the shitter.

Lino got cautiously to his feet and checked out the tub, in case his assassin was lying down in there. He went over to the connecting door that led to the second bathroom. Tried it, and found it locked, the way that he always kept it.

Lino cursed himself for being paranoid. He shoved the gun into his pants and shook his head, half laughing at himself. Raphael had probably cold-cocked himself somehow, performing some sex act on the fucking dog. Lino chuckled.

He began to step out of the bathroom when the sound of running footsteps filled him once again with terror, and he reached for the gun but it was way too late. Morer came tearing through the doorway with his gun out, held way back and above his head, brought it toward Lino's face before Lino could will his hand to move.

Lino felt a numbness in his head and didn't even realize that he was falling. He panicked as he saw the bathroom wall fall past him, saw the tub rise up to him and felt it jump up to meet him, smacking its bottom into Lino's head. He gasped and tried to cry out as a hand gripped him and spun him around.

A big hole was looking him in the eye. Lino squinted, confused, and realized that he was looking down the barrel of a gun. Morer was holding it a fraction of an inch away from his eyeball. Lino looked up into Ben Morer's face and knew that death had come calling.

'You called my *wife*!' Morer was breathing as if he'd just finished running a marathon, spitting the words out through clenched teeth. This was Satan himself in front of him, holding on to Lino's shirt, sticking a gun into his eyeball.

'You filthy cocksucker, you called and threatened my *kids*!'

Lino managed to say, 'I got your money, I ain't called no one, what's the matter with you, are you crazy?'

The last thing Lino heard was Ben Morer's voice saying, 'Yeah', before Ben pulled the trigger and blew Lino's brains all over his bathroom.

Mute sat in his chair against the wall in the lab, waiting for one of the workers to tell him what to do, staring at the wall, ignoring the workers around him, worried about his future and wondering if he had one. Doctors and assistants and technicians filled the place, and would, until five, when they all got to go home. That would leave Mute alone with this month's boss, a lab tech who would spend the rest of the night ordering Mute around, in a bad mood because he didn't have enough seniority to get out of the rotating shift work.

Mute had worked for most of the less senior techs during the time that he'd been in the lab, and for the most part, they were all right, but this guy Smithers was a major pain in his ass. Smithers didn't give one damn about Mute's size, how strong he was. Smithers had graduated from college, and thought that made him better than Mute.

Someday Mute would run into this guy somewhere on the street, and then he'd show Smithers what his college degree was good for. Then again, maybe their paths would never cross. Smithers might like to have a drink or two, but Mute didn't frequent gay bars, which was where Smithers could probably be found, dressed in woman's clothing, sipping a Shirley Temple. Smithers was a lazy prick, too, sitting out in front of the lab now, not doing any of the day work, with his arms crossed, showing them that if he had to work nights he wouldn't help any of them out for the two hours that their shifts overlapped.

'Mike, you want to run this up to Doctor Evan? He needs the report, like yesterday.'

A new female tech was asking him to do what he got paid for. Mute was lower on the hospital pecking order than an orderly, just what the hospital called a runner, a delivery boy who knew where all the offices were. She was pretty, with long brown hair, an upturned nose, and a slight overbite. She would talk with her head down, sometimes with her hand covering her mouth, the girl shy about petty deformity. She would be the type that would be easy to get into the sack, but she didn't wear a wedding ring, so she wasn't for Mute. He might even swear off the married ones, too. He had enough problems with that cunt from Glenwood, whom he'd thought until a couple of hours ago that he might even be falling in love with.

'Sure,' Mute said, took the report and turned away.

'Mike?'

Mute turned, hearing the concern in her voice. He raised his eyebrows at her, saw the look of apprehension on her face, the woman appearing worried about him.

'Are you all right?' She lowered her head, shyly. 'I mean,' – there the hand went, to cover her mouth, in front of a guy who'd had operations done that hadn't made him even come close to appearing normal – 'you seem so depressed today.' She began to turn red in the cheeks.

'Is everything all right?'

'I'm okay,' Mute said, then turned his back on her, walked away.

Stupid move, that. He knew it as soon as he'd done it. She would sooner or later be his afternoon supervisor, telling him where to take what samples, Mute running to deliver all the work that had been done during the day and afternoon to whichever doctors would need them first thing in the morning. Alienating her was not a good idea.

But he had no choice, he was depressed. The mob were aware of him and expected him to work for them.

He knew what the mob did to you when you'd served their purpose. They'd gotten paranoid, since the government was putting so many of them away for the rest of their lives, men who were used to living like kings having to spend what was left of their days behind brick walls, some of them being turned into princesses and queens. No, you did what they told you to, and then they killed you when you'd fulfilled their objective. That way you couldn't rat them out later, turn into a government witness against them in court.

Why did he have to think with his dick? Why did he always have to rush into things with these bitches. Mute hated himself, hated MaryAnn Ceterra, hated the husband that he'd never even met. Hated the lab tech, too, with her education and her phony sense of concern as to how he was feeling. He could die tomorrow and someone else would take his place, and nobody would give a shit. Except maybe MaryAnn and her husband, who wouldn't have gotten their information from him yet. They'd mourn his ass until they found his replacement, and it wouldn't take them long, what with MaryAnn's unique recruitment pitch. And he'd thought that he'd been falling for her. So many things had run through his mind outside her house, and later, in it, wanting to take her in his arms and hold her.

For the first time since he'd been seeing married women, he'd met one that he'd seriously considered having feelings for. Wanted to get to know her better, his mind playing around with the idea that maybe they might have been fated for each other, that perhaps he had found the woman of his dreams. And what had she done? She'd broken his heart in her home, told him what she really wanted, told him that she'd been using him from the very beginning.

Mute was not a man to shed tears easily, but he'd come close, back at her house. He'd been playing around with her before she'd dropped the bomb, talking trash to see how she'd take it, having seen the disgusted look on her face outside, when he'd openly expressed his feelings. It made him feel less guilty about the things he'd been doing with married women – showed what happened to you when you started to take them seriously.

Still, he had to do what she'd told him to, or else they'd kill him right away. Icepicks to the balls, Jee-zus. Those dagos could be cruel. How many times had he walked away from people and deals that could have made him good money, because he'd suspected the mob to be involved? Too many to count. He had two strict rules that he never allowed himself to break: Mute would not do any crime that would hurt another human being, and he stayed away from the mob, no matter how much money there might be for him in one of their deals.

As Mute waited for the employee and freight elevator that would take him to the oncology wing, he looked at the report, opened it and read about this guy, Benjamin Morer, who was doing even worse than Mute. He had cancer in his blood, the guy was *all* fucked up.

This was the sort of thing that the mob wanted from him, wanted him to find them dying patients who had no hope for a cure. As simple as that, they wanted all the names of such patients from the South Chicago area, including the East Side and Hegewisch. People who were on the way out, they wanted copies of their entire files.

He could do that, and he would. A hundred apiece, she'd told him, if the people panned out as she'd hoped.

Yet, how would he know? For all Mute knew, every single file he gave her could somehow be worth a fortune to her. Her husband might even be out drumming up business, approaching them or their relatives, working an insurance scam. Her old man could be killing them and making it look like an accident, collecting a piece of the accident money, that double indemnity insurance shit that he'd seen in movies when he was a kid, her old man getting paid for assisting them in their suicides. Mute couldn't live with that, with dying people getting ripped off.

But Mute had to sit back and take it, listen to her bullshit and just hope that they didn't kill him after he had gotten them enough files.

He'd make a copy of this, and the rest of this guy's file, later, after Evan had gone home for the night. It would be easy for him to do. One file a day, she expected from him, five each week, and if he got caught, he'd get canned. Then his probation would be violated and he'd go back to the penitentiary.

All because he'd thought with his dick; all because of a simple piece of ass.

Mute hated to be backed into a corner by anyone, hated it when some dolt could get away with telling him what to do. It happened all the time here, with doctors and techs always ordering him around. Now MaryAnn had him by the balls worse than his PO did.

And what if MaryAnn decided that stud service came with the program? He didn't know if he could even get it up for her anymore, knew on some level that it was power that got him going good. He might not be able to perform when someone else had that power over him, instead of the other way around.

My God, he'd done himself royally on this one.

Mute stepped into what they called the employee and freight elevator, but everyone knew they just called it that to keep visitors and patients out of the thing. What it really was was the elevator they used to bring dead bodies back and forth between their rooms and the basement pathology lab.

He ignored the greeting of the orderly who was standing next to the stiff on the gurney, the dead person covered with a sheet. Mute would rather die than have a job like that, having to be in an elevator all the time, alone with a fresh corpse. He knew that some of the orderlies paid people off to get that assignment. The nurses had their instructions, but some of them forgot the hospital policy, did not take the valuables from the stiff, to be kept for the family, before sending it downstairs. A ring and a watch from time to time was worth the hassle, to some of these guys. A gold tooth that would never be missed. All you had to do was to carry a pair of pliers in your pocket, and you were in. Mute never acted too friendly to these orderlies. Anyone who'd rob the dead had to be some kind of pervert.

Then again, if he could get transferred to that duty, if he could somehow pull that off, maybe MaryAnn would let him off the hook, for old time's sake. Then again, he doubted it. She was as heartless as they came.

Mute got off the elevator and walked down to Evan's office, not happy because like most of the doctors here, Evan was a miserable little bastard who liked to throw his weight around with people who couldn't hurt him. If Evan suspected that Mute was copying his patient files, he'd not only get Mute fired, but would probably file criminal charges as well.

Jesus. And all because of MaryAnn, all because of one night in a motel with a married woman. And all this had to happen just when he thought his luck was turning around.

Well, maybe he could figure a way out of this, maybe he could outslick her. He'd think on it while he worked tonight. There wouldn't be much else for him to think about, what with that lazy dolt Smithers in charge of the night lab for the entire month of November.

Diane was on the phone in her office, finally getting the call back from the doctor at a few minutes before five, the time of day when she was always her most busy. Still, she couldn't complain, at least the man had called her back. After the problem they'd had in his office, she had thought that maybe he wouldn't.

They were talking about her ex-husband, about Ben, what he was going through.

'You can get books on it, a woman named Elisabeth Kubler-Ross – *you* probably haven't heard of her – has written the definitive work on the subject, how they act when they're told that they're going to die.'

Diane had to bite her tongue to keep herself from lashing out at him. How arrogant could this man be? '*You* probably haven't heard of her', as if she were totally ignorant. She got herself back under control. She needed information from this man, and no matter what she said, there was nobody in the world who could make him less of an asshole.

'Thank you, doctor, but I was looking for something a bit more immediate. If Ben were to go to Sloan-Kettering – '

'He has no insurance, Mrs Morer.'

'Let's just say that he came into some money. How much would he need for first-rate care in a hospital that specialized in cancer?'

'I'm not used to dealing in assumptions, Mrs Morer.'

'Let's try, just this once,' Diane said, and listened as he cleared his throat, half-expecting him to hang up.

'Put it right there, Orderly,' she heard the doctor say.

'Excuse me?'

'Nothing, one of the lab orderlies brought me Be – a file.'

'You were saying?'

'That's one of the best. Sloan-Kettering. He'd want to be there, or at Bethesda or Mayo, most likely, if he could afford it. There are special lung cancer departments there, study groups, that have experimental therapies as well as all the traditional programs.'

'How – how much would it cost, altogether, the best doctors, the best help he could get?'

'Oh, Mrs Morer, *please*! There's no *way* I could answer that question. Do you understand the different variables involved? One specialist that might be able to help him might be in Europe, my God, anything is possible.'

'Say a ballpark figure, if everything he needed was at Mayo.'

'I couldn't begin to speculate.'

She was losing him, she could tell. In a second he would have to go, take another call or maybe not bother with such sophistry, a man with his lack of sensitivity would simply cut her off.

She said, 'Couple hundred thousand, is that about right?'

'I'd say that's a reasonable projection, for traditional treatment, yes. But what we have to look at here is quality of life, how long Ben can hang on, and if you even *want* him hanging on. Do you want to take desperate measures? You don't want to hang on waiting for a medical miracle, you don't want to fall into that trap.'

He suddenly didn't seem about to hang up now. In fact he was getting into his stride now that he had an audience that didn't make him feel threatened or intimidated. She heard pages turning over the phone, as if he were reading something as he spoke.

'What you should really look for is good hospice care for your husband, if you can even afford that. That's far, far less expensive, and they'll prepare you both for the inevitable.'

'Doctor, say he had the best treatment, say he went to Mayo and got every possible bit of help that they had to offer. How long could he live then?'

'Outside? Two, maybe three years. You do understand that I'm not speaking to be quoted, you asked me a general question, and all I can give you is a general answer.'

'I understand. And in those three years, what about the quality of life you were discussing? Ben wouldn't be trapped in a hospital bed, would he?'

'Well, some treatments mandate that, and others, he can go home after each five-day session of radiation. Today, they drip it right into the blood in cases such as his. But after that, he's free to go for as long as two weeks. There are hotels nearby just for that purpose . . .'

'Thank you, doctor.'

'Let me know how Ben makes out.'

Diane clicked off without making any promises that she knew she wouldn't keep.

Two years. Maybe three. What would it feel like, Diane wondered, to go into the doctor's office and have him tell you that you were dying? She couldn't speak for Ben or anyone else, but two or three years would seem a lot easier to handle than four to six months. Or, like Eddie, five weeks from diagnosis to death. It wasn't so immediate, there were things you could do, amends to make and affairs that could be gotten into order.

Such as establishing a relationship with two young men who hated you.

Diane wondered about how the boys would take it, when they learned that their father was dying. There was no way on earth that she would try to keep it from them.

John, she decided, would try to act macho and tough. He'd probably pretend to be glad, and then go into his room and cry. Benny she wasn't so sure about; he'd seemed close to his father, although he never asked about him anymore. They were all right, her sons, home now with the doors locked and strict instructions not to open the door to anyone, not even to the police. Ben would take care of the man on the phone, would kill him at Diane's subtle suggestion.

She could imagine what a therapist might say about her sons' hopes for leading normal adult lives. Would it be good for them to establish something with him now, now that Ben was calmer, older and dying and aware of the mistakes he'd made? And what if they did? What good could it possibly do them, even if they could forgive him and learn to love their father, only to lose him in four to six months, or however long it took Ben to die?

Diane pushed her chair back and stared at the ceiling. She paid six hundred and fifty dollars a month for full medical and dental coverage for herself and her children. The company workers weren't covered at all. They had absolutely no health insurance, other than whatever their husbands might have. Some of the women who worked for her did have husbands, but most of them didn't, most of them were like her, single mothers, trying to get ahead.

Her six-fifty bought her a $250,000 deductible policy on each of them, calendar year through calendar year, and each policy had medical coverage up to half a million dollars.

One catastrophic disease, and they'd be wiped out.

Ben had no coverage whatsoever, and she knew that the reason he'd turned down the VA hospital had nothing to do with his friend Eddie, but was because he wasn't covered at the VA, either. He might have forgotten telling her about it, but she knew that he'd been kicked out of the Marines with a dishonorable discharge for beating up some lieutenant who hadn't liked the way that Ben had saluted him, had called him on it at the Camp and had insulted Ben in front of other Marines. She could see Ben pulling that off, after fighting a damn war for thirteen months, having only a few months to go until his discharge, and then getting into trouble because his pride had been hurt.

His pride would keep him from accepting her help, too, but she thought that she might have to find a way to give it, or she could never live with herself. She knew that Ben would kill today, due to what she'd told him about a telephone call. A man would die, and right after she'd gotten the call, that had been what she'd wanted to happen, but now she wasn't so sure, now she didn't think that that was such a good idea.

She'd be the killer, responsible, as much as Ben was. She didn't know what the legal ramifications would be, nor was she worried about them. It was the moral responsibility that bothered her, that, and the spiritual one, the way that her actions would have offended God.

Thou Shalt Not Kill.

Diane had broken a lot of the Commandments in her life. She'd dishonored her parents, she hadn't been inside a church in years. She'd had lewd thoughts and she'd coveted her neighbors' property. She'd done those things and more, but she'd never committed murder.

Would it be the same as killing someone, if you'd set the wheels in motion? Would God blame her the same as she'd blame the person who actually pulled the trigger? Deep philosophical and theological questions. Not Diane's strong suit. But she had to think about them, because if she'd learned one thing in the past twenty-four hours, it was that life was even shorter than she'd known; you never really knew when your time would be up.

Ben was the type of man you always thought would live forever. Strong, vital, he'd been through so much and had come out virtually unscathed. She'd seen him as a survivor, as someone who couldn't be defeated. Not even jail had broken him, he'd come out after his time was up, stronger and meaner than ever.

Then this, dropped in her lap after five years without any contact with the man. Ben dying, having only a number of months unless he got immediate and adequate treatment that would cost well into six figures. The man who'd seemed indestructible was being eaten alive, his own body turning on him. And a couple of hundred thousand dollars could put that off for two or three years.

She didn't have that kind of cash, nowhere near that kind of liquidity. If she had it, she would offer it to him, sit him down and try to talk him into taking what she could give. Yesterday, if you'd asked her about that, she would have laughed in your face for being stupid enough to bring it up. Yesterday, she hadn't seen Ben. Yesterday, there was only bitterness.

That was before she'd seen him face to face, heard how much he'd loved her. Before she'd heard his apology, and before she knew that he was really and truly dying.

Before she realized that she was still so very in love with him.

She didn't love him the way she used to, and never would love another man that way again. The emotion she'd felt then had been as much need as it had been love, Diane having compulsions back then that needed to be filled.

Now, five years older, and far wiser than she'd ever been while married, she could see why she'd fallen in love with him, and knew that it wasn't for the reasons she had thought when she was just a young girl with fancy dreams and a desire to be paid attention to. Now, she could see that behind that facade was a gentle man who didn't know how to show that gentleness, a troubled man who needed help if he was to be led out of the darkness. A man who needed someone, as Diane had once felt the pressure to be needed.

In five years Diane had bought three houses and paid them all off. She'd put together college trusts for her children, and had eleven thousand cash money in the bank in case of emergencies. She had a business that showed a good profit every year, though not as much this year as last. Still, they'd be holding no smokers for her, no benefits to get the money to pay for any illness that might come up in her life. Could she afford to risk throwing that all away, for a man she hadn't lived with for over five years.

What would Ben do, if she ever got truly sick? If she found herself with cancer and did not have health insurance? Diane didn't even have to think about it twice.

Ben would rob every bank from here to Los Angeles in order to get the money to help her. She'd seen him give away all the money they had in the world in order to help some friend of his who had legal or health problems. She'd been married to him for thirteen years, he would go to the wall to help her. He'd see that as her due, what Diane had coming. Because he knew that he owed her.

But what did she owe him?

She had to look at that in light of what it was, instead of only thinking kindly of him because he'd fathered her children. She had to sit back rationally and ponder what she owed Ben, what he had coming from her, if anything at all.

He'd taken good care of her, for the time they'd been together.

Until he'd gotten arrested, then she'd gone on welfare.

He'd protected her, most of the time, had tried to keep what he did away from her.

Until that wildman came to their house and shot through the top window part of the front door.

He'd loved her, she'd known that, although he'd never said the words. For the first year of their marriage, he was constantly touching her, gently kissing her. And not only as a prelude to sex, although there'd been plenty of that.

Diane was looking a tragedy in the face and did not know how to respond to it. Maybe, instead of looking at what she might possibly owe him, she should think more about what she owed herself, what she owed her sons.

If she dumped the houses and took out a loan, Ben might live two or three years longer, but then he'd still die. And she and the boys might be out in the cold, alone and broke, without him around to help them in any way.

In the back of Diane's mind, there'd always been one constant, one thing she never doubted for a minute, even at the times when she'd hated Ben the most: if she ever really needed him, he was a phone call away. If one of the kids ever got hurt, or if some maniac ever harmed one of them, he'd come and help, he'd bail them out, and she had proof of that – look how he'd acted when she'd told him about the phone call. It was a fact that sometimes caused her tremendous resentment, and one that calmed her at other times, but still a fact, no matter how she might feel about it. If she or the kids ever needed him, he'd be right there.

Ben had stayed away from them when he could have made their lives miserable. He had enough class and compassion to know that further contact with them could only harm his sons. And he'd stayed away, done what he would have called the right thing by them, as right as a man like Ben could ever be. Sending money every week, that would be his hug. Make up for missing graduations and birthday parties. She'd raised those kids alone; he'd been gone most of the time, even when they'd been married. She'd gone to the Halloween parties with them, gone to their schools for the Christmas celebrations. She'd healed their scrapes and stayed up all night, sitting at their bedside, when they had the flu. His five hundred a week could never buy any of that away.

She had to apply his standards to her own life, just this once. What was the right thing for her to do? If she helped him, saw to it that he got all the help that money could buy, she might be jeopardizing her future, even the futures of her sons. In four years, they'd both be in college, and she'd need every dime she could get to see to it that they graduated. If she did nothing, however, he would die in four months, and she knew how, too, knew that the cancer would not kill him; his death would be by his own hand and would be brutal and violent and ugly.

There'd been a time, five years ago, when Diane had been

at her lowest. She'd lain in her bed and suffered for five days as the drugs ran their course in her body. She knew now that no matter what happened in her life she would never be that low, not ever again. She'd come back from that in five short years, had property that belonged to her free and clear, and she was relatively successful.

Nothing could destroy her, she could bounce back from almost anything. As long as those boys of hers were healthy, she could conquer anything at all.

So, should she help him? Yes or no.

'God help me,' Diane said, hoping for a sign. Wishing that it could be that simple. You put your trust and your faith in the God you believed in and he took care of you, showed you the way.

Ben would call, and soon, probably tonight. She could never sleep with him again, could never live with him under the same roof, but he was the man she loved, the first and, from the way things had gone these past five years, the last man she would ever really, truly love.

She had some time to think about what to do, she didn't have to make a decision before maybe ten tonight. Some choice. Help him live for a little while or just sit and watch him die.

She'd never been a selfish person, but the urge to be so was there inside her now: a voice in her head was telling her that Ben could kiss her ass, to keep what she had for the kids and herself, she wasn't getting any younger.

But her heart was telling her differently, her heart went out to Ben. Seeing him had rekindled old feelings and brought new ones down upon her. She'd looked at him and wondered, about what might have been. Looked again and had to fight the urge to think about what might still be. Money came and went, and although it was important, it wasn't the world itself.

Love, on the other hand, was supposed never to die.

Diane pushed her chair back and gathered the papers on her desk, shoved them into her briefcase and snapped the thing shut. She'd go home now and spend some time with her sons, do the rest of her work there after dinner and try to concentrate on what she was doing, and keep Ben off her mind until he called her later tonight.

Ben had found some pills in Lino's coat as he'd searched the man's house, looking for any more money. On top of the fifty, he'd found more cash in Lino's pocket, two grand in hundreds, and he'd taken that, too, the kids would need that money; they could surely put it to better use than Lino could, now. He thought for a time that the guy who walked Lino's dog would awaken to find two bodies in the apartment, Lino dead from a gunshot to the head, and Ben dead of a heart attack.

He had been unable to control his breathing, had begun to see dark spots, had raced into the bathroom and attacked Lino before he planned to because he was afraid that if he didn't, he'd pass out. He'd been hiding in the bathroom until he heard Lino come into the bedroom, then he'd snuck out, locking the door behind himself, gone around to the other bedroom door and waited for Lino to go into the john. His plan was to coldcock him when he came out of the bedroom, then question him, make sure that it was he who had called Diane at work, be sure of that in his mind before he took the man's life.

But things hadn't worked out that way, Ben's body had failed him. The one thing he'd always counted on was beginning to let him down – the strength that had always seen him through was now being sapped, depleted by the cancer.

He'd grabbed the pills gratefully and had immediately taken two, sat down on Lino's couch and looked at the dog, who'd sat right in front of him, begging to be petted, sticking its head up under Ben's hand and whining until Ben finally gave in and rubbed it behind the ears. When he thought that he could move again without passing out from exhaustion, he'd searched the apartment thoroughly, looking for money.

Did it happen that quickly? He'd had trouble attacking Lino last night, but that had been nothing like this. He'd finished his search and then left, had headed home. Although he hated to do it, the money and Lino's .44 had been left in the car, hidden under the spare tire in the trunk, parked on the East Side in the bank's guarded parking lot. It would be safe there until eight - the old retired mill worker who manned the station at night would keep a close eye on Ben's Eldorado, he'd tipped the guy well. Ben had taken a cab home, had it drop him off at Our Lady of Guadalupe's, then waited for it to leave before he'd walked across the street. As soon as the cops found out about Lino, a couple of them would be paying him a call. He couldn't afford to let them find the money, couldn't let them take it. The money was for his kids, it was all that he could give them.

As for himself, he didn't care anymore. He sat in his apartment now and wondered why he didn't. Was there something wrong with him, something lacking in his character? Shouldn't he be filled with fear at the thought of his approaching death? He'd lived a life of total corruption, and now saw the end of it approaching, coming on fast, and all he could feel was relief. Relief, and some sadness, at what had passed him by. Well, there was guilt, too, but a lot of that would be wiped out when he got things right with the kids.

Ben could not feel as other men did, though he did not realize that fact. Indeed, he thought that all people felt as he himself did, elementally, primitively, with survival the major goal. He had no concept of charity or compassion – though he was capable of both – and he had spent most of his adult life believing that love was something that other men lied about, pretended to have; at least, he couldn't feel it, the way other men seemed to.

Maybe he could, though. He felt something powerful toward Diane, had nearly broken down in front of her that afternoon. And what he felt for those kids, it had to be love, or else it wouldn't hurt like this to be away from them.

What had Diane's agenda been? He'd been so glad to see her, to have her show up at the doctor's. He'd looked at her and felt his heart fill with something. Love? Relief? All he knew was that after seeing her he'd been happy.

Then, later, she had told him about that phone call. Had the call been the only reason that she'd bothered to meet him? Diane couldn't be that cold, or maybe she could, he didn't really know her these days. She wasn't wearing a wedding ring, but he would have heard if she'd gotten married. Somebody would have told him. Was she having an affair? Were there other men in her life? There had to be, she was young and very attractive, far more so than she'd been as a girl. She had character now, something in her attitude that had always been lacking before. She'd probably gained that character from having survived living with him. Ben knew how he'd hurt her, how his temper had destroyed her pride, any sense of self that she'd had before they'd met.

There had been a time before he'd gotten sick when he'd thought that things would work out between them, that enough time apart from them all would heal the painful wounds, that they would wind up together, after Ben had put enough money together to retire from the Life. He had pictured himself doing it at times, making up to them, getting back with Diane, the two of them growing old together, babysitting their grandkids. Those thoughts had kept him sane at times, when he would look at what he was.

A middle-aged man towards whom the years had not been kind, alone in a shitty apartment with a woman whose best friend was a handpuppet.

Sunny had taken it hard, had stormed around and slammed clothing into paper bags, although she hadn't cursed him as she packed; she was goofy, but she wasn't crazy. She'd taken everything down to her car and had then come back for Sherry, and it was Sherry who'd had the last word, who'd had the courage to call Ben an asshole before Sunny had slammed the door for the last time, on her way out of his life forever.

He'd sat in the same chair that he was in right now, sat there late last night, drinking, and thought about his family, although this time his fantasies did not include his getting old.

Last night Ben had thought about making things up to

them, dropping the money in their laps and watching their faces glow. The kids would then be assured that they could go on to college, start lives for themselves afterward, have the start in life that Ben himself had never been offered, courtesy of their father.

Then he'd sat with Diane this afternoon, and knew that money alone wouldn't be enough. They'd need more than that, and even if he knew what those things were, could somehow figure it out, he would not have enough time to give it to them. An 'I'm sorry' would not be enough, not after all this time.

What was he looking for, did he want them to love him? He'd killed a man less than two hours ago, and felt no guilt about it, only relief over the fact that he'd gotten away with the murder. Was that the sort of man that any decent person could love?

Maybe it was immortality, maybe that was what he wanted. People to love him and talk well about him after his death, spread the word to their children - Grandpa Ben had been a good man.

And yet he hadn't been, and he knew it. He'd been a miserable human being, a failure as a husband, even more of a failure as a father to his sons.

He'd taken one look at Diane today and he couldn't believe his eyes. She must have lost a hundred pounds, and what could he say to that? Some normal guy, a working stiff, he'd have found a way to compliment her. But everything that Ben had thought of to say would have, he thought, been an insult. So he'd kept his mouth shut, had let his attitude speak for him, and the happiness he'd felt at seeing her in the hospital corridor had translated itself to her, they'd had a good time together. She'd held his hand and pretended to be his wife in front of that idiot doctor, she had sat with him through one of the darkest days of his life, and hadn't walked away from him later, had gone to the restaurant with him and stayed there, being his friend.

Did she know how much he needed one? And did she know that he'd die before he'd reach out, before he'd go searching for a friend to comfort him? She hadn't acted the way a woman who hated you would.

She'd listened to his apology, and he'd seen her eyes glow as he'd told her that he loved her. Loved her and the boys. Maybe that had been the only thing that she'd ever really wanted from him. He'd tried to give her the world, tried to buy her everything that any square John's wife could ever desire, but that hadn't been enough, he knew now, that hadn't even been in the ballpark.

Ben had killed three men in his lifetime. Had stolen well over a million dollars, and had served eleven years of his forty-eight in the state penitentiary. Eight years of his twenties had been spent behind the walls, it was the reason that he'd waited until the age of thirty to marry.

He'd tried going straight right after the wedding; for a short time, he'd worked at various jobs. He'd driven a cab and he'd worked construction, loaded trucks with a forklift and even made it through an entire eight-hour shift at the Republic Steel plant, working in the 16-inch mill. But it wasn't for him, working for some stranger, not the life he could lead and ever have any hope of future happiness.

He'd see the despair in the faces of the men who'd spent their lives working in such places, see the arrogance in the attitudes of the punks who wore the white hard hats, the foremen and the other bosses. Guys Ben could crush with a single punch, talking down at him and chewing him out if he didn't do what they wanted him to fast enough to suit them.

How many of them had he punched out, beaten the living shit out of then stalked off the job? Christ, too many to count. He didn't worry about them now, didn't give them, or the men he'd killed, or the places and people he'd robbed, a second's thought this evening.

But he did think about Diane, about how she'd deserved better than he'd ever been able to give. Ben lit a cigarette and thought about that, while the pills eased his pain and made him feel pretty mellow.

Men like him had no right ever to get married. It had been a mistake, unfair to a woman whose own mistake had been to have innocently fallen in love with a man she'd seen as strong and powerful. What right did he have to father children, to bring them into a world, with him as a role model? He had sat in prison cells and listened to older married men talk about their sons, talking about how when they got out, they'd have to straighten the punks out. Because the kids were smoking cigarettes and getting into trouble at school, some of them into drugs before they got into their teens, stealing and beating on their mothers when the women tried to stop the kids from acting like their fathers.

Those men never figured out that their kids were just doing what they'd been taught, and Ben never felt the urge to tell those men the truth. They were the type of people who would not understand, who would take it as an insult and shank him in the back when Ben wasn't looking, paybacks for insulting their kids, for putting them down when they hadn't asked for any advice.

He'd heard the stories and understood about the kids, long before he'd gotten married and had two kids of his own. Still, he'd done it, married Diane, and gotten her pregnant. Why? Was he that stupid? Did he think that he'd somehow be different?

When she asked him to leave, when she'd finally, tearfully, begged him to get out, Ben had come as close as he ever had to crying since he'd been ten years old. He'd looked down at his wife, Diane on her knees, the children around her trying to comfort her, their little arms around her, staring hatred up at Ben, and he'd known, right then, that he had to get out, that he had to leave, that if he cared about them at all, he'd have to go, for the sake of his children. He was always out of control, always yelling, always breaking something. He hated himself when he did it, but he couldn't bring himself to stop.

'Please,' Diane had begged him, in a voice that was little more than an impassioned, desperate whisper. Her hands had been together, as if in prayer, Diane squeezing them together as the tears rolled down her cheeks. She'd been trembling, he remembered that now, spit dribbling out of her mouth and dripping in a connecting line to the tile on the kitchen floor. Her face had been contorted into a mask that made him afraid, because he'd seen such anguish before, on the faces of young kids in the joint who'd suddenly discovered and understood that they truly wanted to die, after being raped repeatedly by guys who would now see them as their women. The kid who in the outside world had seen themselves as tough, had suddenly seen what they were truly made of, had been shown what the future held for them, and Ben could not remember ever having seen a face like that where the guy who'd owned it hadn't then committed suicide.

He'd known then, standing over Diane and looking down at her – Diane pleading with him to leave – that if he didn't go, she'd kill herself.

'*You're killing me*,' she'd said, in that voice . . . And Ben had packed his stuff and left.

He'd done the right thing, the honorable thing, and the only time he'd ever gotten mad at her after that was when she'd told him that they'd decided amongst them that he couldn't come around anymore. He'd wanted to see his kids, try to explain things to them. Let them know that he'd be there for them, that it wasn't all his fault. That they'd never want for anything, that he'd take care of them until he died. But he hadn't told them any of those things, because the kids had told their mother that they didn't want to see him anymore. At least that's what she'd told him.

He wondered how many times over the years they'd wanted to see him, wanted to look him up. When bullies were picking on them, or when they had problems with girls. They'd have wanted to come to their father but hadn't, probably thinking that he wouldn't understand, would see them as weak because they had problems. After all, he'd never let them know that anything had ever bothered him – he'd been just as bad a father as the guys back in the pen.

Although he'd never touched them, there were other ways to beat your kids, to keep them down and hateful. Ben understood that now.

Would they hate him now, even knowing that he was dying? Maybe he should just forget about it, forget about even trying. Take out his .38 and kill himself right now, while he was still strong and feeling pretty good. No, he couldn't, because if he did, they'd never get the money. Somebody would eventually steal the car and find the dough, or the city would come and tow it, compact it into a little square, and all that money that Lino had died for would never do anyone any good again, not Ben, not his kids, not anyone.

He had to live long enough to get it to them, but after that, it didn't much matter what happened. And he'd take it over to them tonight, after he got a little rest. It had been a long night and he'd hardly slept, what with throwing Sunny out, then having to go to the doctor in the morning. Even the booze he'd drunk had not done the job, had not stopped his mind from racing or caused the anxiety to cease. He'd go to sleep now, get two or three hours, then go and see his kids when the effects of the pills were entirely out of his system. He wanted to see them without any false courage, wanted to face them like a man, with honor. Either way they went, no matter how they acted, he would stand before them like a man and take whatever they handed out. Love or punches, Ben could handle it either way.

He'd have to go before it got too late, before the cops came to shake him down, because the kids would need that money, and there were two things he was sure of: those two miserable thieves with detective badges would not get a dime of that money, the money he'd killed for; and he wasn't, under any circumstances, going to be taken in to jail. Not for questioning, and not to face charges on the gun they'd stolen from him last night. He'd die first, and he probably would, but he'd go out his way, not theirs.

Because he knew that his body was failing, and he couldn't take the beating, could not sit in a chair and put up with what they'd give him; he was too frail inside for that. He'd start shaking and trembling, his heart would start working overtime and his hands would start shaking, and the cops wouldn't know that he was sick, that he was dying. They'd just see him as a coward, and he couldn't let that ever happen. So if they were going to kill him, they'd have to do it here in his home, because he would never let them see him weak. He'd die, one way or the other, and soon, but he'd go out the same way as he'd lived; like a motherfucking man.

Ben stood and stretched slowly, breathing as deeply as his diseased lungs would allow, and he had a thought, standing there with his arms over his head, an idea for a scam that no one would ever suspect him of pulling.

The Man had already put the word out on him, for some reason Ben was no longer under his protection. And, Ben was dying. He couldn't ever forget that. He had an appointment set up at eleven that night, with Tony and Lino, at the He Ain't Here.

Maybe he should keep it. Maybe he should go and look Fat Tony in the eye and tell him straight out how things were going to be. What would the guy do, go to the Man and complain? Let him. Ben didn't need the Man anymore, and a dying man couldn't get too worked up about someone whose only leverage over you was his willingness to kill you.

Maybe he'd keep his appointment. Maybe he would.

MaryAnn sat in the parking lot of the South Chicago Community Hospital, her red Mustang idling, talking on the cellular phone, putting her foot down to that lamebrain, Mute.

'You think I care if your boss is watching you? Do you think my *hus*band cares? You get a coffee break, don't you? You get a lunch hour? Fine, take it now and come on down here, I want that file *tonight*!'

She hit the End button before Mute could whine anymore. God, what a baby, didn't he know that everyone had problems? MaryAnn lit a cigarette and sat staring out of the windshield, watching as the smoke hit the glass and curled away, gracefully.

She was tired and she was beginning to smell, and she felt sour, had a headache, and she knew she was getting an ulcer.

She'd put in seven hours at the company, managing, mostly, helping the agents with sales, scamming with them, sitting in her glass-enclosed office while the agent appeared to be arguing with her, for the benefit of the buyer, who'd be sitting outside the office, in the agent's little cubicle. Watching with growing respect for their agent as he or she battled with the boss of the entire company.

The idea was to get the buyer to congratulate themselves on their wise choice of agent, never allowing them to realize that it was usually blind luck or good advertising which led them into any individual real estate office. And once they were inside, it was the pick of the draw; whoever was next up for a cold call would be their agent, whether they liked it or not.

It was one of the things Mal taught over and over in her training class, something she wanted every agent to be accomplished at before they ever left the classroom and got into practical sales. She'd told Mal straight out, she wanted them not only trained, but role-played until the act was coming out of their ears, until they knew it in their sleep. It was nearly as important to her as the issue of control. It was perhaps their strongest sales technique, one that won them tons of good will from the gullible people who'd come into the office, looking to buy a home.

The agent would tell the buyer that the seller wouldn't come down in price, that it was the boss's listing, that MaryAnn would never allow her own client to accept lesser money because she'd felt that it was her duty to get them what she thought their house was worth.

Then the game would begin, the agent coming in anyway, working on behalf of his own client, the buyer. The agents would wave their arms around and even pretend to be shouting, pointing out toward their clients who were sitting outside, telling MaryAnn, in Oscar-worthy performances, how these were good, hardworking people, how they deserved a break.

They weren't allowed to kid around in the office, were under the strictest orders to play their roles right to the hilt.

They had to *believe* that they were fighting for their client, had to be thoroughly self-righteous and worked up into a moral rage, because the client would be too embarrassed not to sign on the dotted line after they went back out to them and told them how they'd battled for them.

MaryAnn would know the second that the deal was set, before the buyers, even before her agents. She would send the agent out of her office and watch how they acted with their clients, telling them that MaryAnn was calling the seller, to try and convince them that they should lower their price. MaryAnn would further the charade by picking up her telephone and pretending to be talking to her seller.

The buyer would not know that, by law, MaryAnn and her agents were mandated to bring every legitimate offer before the seller, no matter how low. The buyers almost always sat there with a look of bewilderment on their faces, in awe over the fact that a total stranger would fight for them, would risk their job so that they could buy their dream home.

MaryAnn would see it, that look that would pass between them, the wife and husband exchanging a glance that told her that there was nothing she could do, no number she could come up with, that would stop them from buying that house, to repay this agent's kindness. She would see that look and would lower the price accordingly, judging only on the basis of how they looked how low that she'd have to go in order to win them over.

Twice, she had even tested her theory to the max, at personal risk to her own monetary profit. MaryAnn had walked out of her office and shaken the hands of the people looking to buy, had told them that she was sorry, but the seller was not coming down. Once they had told her that it had been worth a shot, but they understood, and they still wanted to buy. The second time they had thanked her profusely for calling her personal clients and trying to get them to lower their price. These buyers had then gone on for several minutes about what a great person MaryAnn's saleswoman was, how much they respected her, how they couldn't imagine going anywhere else and trusting any other agent, what with what you heard about people in the real estate business. My God, you were better off trusting a used car salesman.

They'd told her these things before telling the agent to go ahead and get the contract, they still wanted the house, even at the higher price.

Both of these examples had become in-house legends, spoken about in awed tones wherever her agents gathered after hours to drink away their stress.

She'd spent most of the afternoon doing that, listening to salespeople, making notes as they talked as to how they could improve their performances. By the end of the seven hours that she'd been there, her agents had signed up over two hundred thou in sales, and others, out on the streets, had racked up nearly as much in new listings to be put on the market and sold.

The way things were going, she might even be able to give up her sideline. She discarded the thought as soon as it came into her head. In the legitimate business, Walter got half. Walter, the one constant in her life that she couldn't totally control, and wouldn't be able to, up until the day she left. But then it wouldn't matter, all that would matter would be what she was carrying in the suitcases that would be stuffed in the trunk of the little red Mustang.

Control was everything, everything and the only thing. When you were in control, nobody could stop you or hurt you.

MaryAnn saw Mute walking toward her car, coming out through the Emergency Room exit, lighting a cigarette the second he came out of the door and then walking quickly, furtively, his head on a swivel as he searched the parking lot for undercover spies. It had to be ten below out there with the wind chill factor, and this bonehead was wearing only his white sleeveless hospital top. She shook her head at his stupidity; he had been so easy to control.

Mute slid into the passenger seat and shoved the papers in his hand underneath the seat.

'I got one, a guy, dying of more shit than I ever heard of.'

'Does he own a house?'

'How the fuck would I know? I ain't his accountant.'

'Mute . . .'

Mute turned his head to look out the windshield, and when he spoke, his voice was calmer.

'All right, I'm sorry, but I could go to jail if I get caught doing this shit.

'Then don't get caught.' MaryAnn told him, then said, 'Who's his insurance company?'

'Ain't got none.'

'He has no in*sur*ance?'

'Says so on the form, None written in there. Says the guy's self-employed, too.'

'Oh, my God,' MaryAnn couldn't hide her excitement. 'How old is he?'

'Forty-eight.'

'Outpatient or in?'

'He just got the news today, went home after seeing the doctor.'

'Perfect!'

'I get paid now?' His tone of voice told her that he had no desire to get paid for what he'd done, that he felt like he was nothing more than a whore.

MaryAnn leaned over and kissed him, once on the cheek, a peck without any passion. She said, 'I won't know until tomorrow, I mean, *Walter* won't know until tomorrow or the next day. We have to check a few things out, have some of our business associates go and talk to these people, but if they sell their house, if they even *have* a house, then sure, you get paid. Right up front in cash, you don't even have to wait until the closing.'

'What's a closing?' Mute said, and MaryAnn cursed herself silently.

In her excitement, she'd said too much, had given too much away. She was tired and she'd had a long night with this man, and she'd acted as if she could trust him, for a second, she'd lost control.

She couldn't allow that to happen to her, not ever again.

My God, what if she had slipped in front of Walter? He could destroy her life, have her imprisoned, if he knew about what she was doing. Being tired was no excuse; there *were* no excuses for failure.

MaryAnn said, 'Don't worry about it, if things work out, you get paid.' She thought for a second, wondered if she could cover her tracks.

Mute said, 'MaryAnn, this shit is *wrong*. The guy's *dying* for kee-rist sake. You can't go and take his house away from him.'

'Oh, we have a *conscience* now.'

MaryAnn reached into her purse and fumbled around until she found a single bill, took it out and turned on the dome light to make sure she had the proper denomination. She did. She left the dome light on so that Mute could see the picture of Benjamin Franklin, the one and the two zeros at the corners of the bill. If he thought that he was a whore, she'd treat him like one, show him who was in charge here.

'Here, here's payment for this one, whether it works out or not. Just to keep you happy. And remember one thing, Mute. If you decide to get all morally outraged here, it was *you* that gave me this man's name.'

Mute stared at her, and without looking at the bill, took it out of her hand with his fingers. He then reached into the pocket of his thin white uniform pants, took out a large wad, his winnings from last night. He slipped a rubber band off the roll, put the one she'd given him on top, then put the rubber band back on the wad and snapped it once, for effect.

'You see any appreciative difference in the size of that wad?'

Oh, was he a cute one, telling her he didn't need her money. But what he was really doing was showing her how much she owned him, how much in her control he really was. He didn't need her money, but he'd still do what he was told. At least for a while, and a while was all that she needed.

'Those are racetrack winnings, Mute, found money, you lucked into it. What I'll give you, you'll earn, and that's always more important.'

'You gonna keep coming here at night, when I'm working? Can't I meet you somewhere else, where my boss can't walk out and catch me? You don't know this guy, believe me, MaryAnn, he's an asshole and a half. He comes walking over to me, his face all sour, like he just sucked his first dick and got the cum still in his mouth, he says to me, "You have a *personal* phone call, some *woman*", like I ain't got a right to do nothin' but bust my ass all night. I tell him I'm taking my dinner and he nods his head at me, and I *know* he don't believe me. He's probably in the window up there right now, watching us with binoculars.'

'Then let's give him something worth seeing.'

MaryAnn leaped across the seat and grabbed Mute's head in her arms, shoved her tongue into his mouth and lowered her arm and rubbed his nipple with one hand. He pushed her away, disgusted.

'What's wrong with you?'

MaryAnn smiled.

'We've got to make it look good, for the boss, if he's watching. Don't act like you don't like it, you liked it well enough all night.'

'That was then.'

'And you're going to do what I tell you now, whether you like it or not. If the boss is watching, he's got to think that you're out here necking with me. Now kiss me, Mute, or do I have to tell Walter that you won't do your job, that you balked at my instructions?'

That did it. Mute took her face in both hands and kissed her hard, smashed her lips to his. MaryAnn fumbled with his pants, rubbed his crotch, realized with a shock that he was soft, unresponsive. After a second, that turned her on more than if he'd been as stiff as a fencepost. He was totally in her control now, kissing her even though he was completely turned off by her, by what she was making him do.

It was the ultimate act of control, making a musclebound male bend his will and his body to suit her wants. She became aroused, MaryAnn wanting him, but not tonight, not here. In a motel somewhere, maybe this weekend, with

Mute subdued and vanquished, completely subordinate to her will, to MaryAnn's personal desires. And he'd do whatever she told him to.

It was something to look forward to. It sure beat thinking about Walter.

MaryAnn pulled away from the kiss and pushed Mute with the palms of both hands. 'Go ahead now, get out of here, I'll see you tomorrow, Mute.'

She watched him get out of the car, watched him swagger back to the electric door of the Emergency Room entrance, watched him go inside, the power she had over him ready to explode inside her.

Her own personal slave. She owned a human being. If she wanted to, she could even probably talk him into getting a tattoo, with words to that effect: *PROPERTY OF MARYANN* stenciled on that tight little ass.

MaryAnn reached under the seat and took out the papers Mute had shoved under there, looked them over quickly, liking what she saw. If the dying man was indeed self-employed, then he'd want to cover his family, come up with the cash that he could give to them in his estate, tax-free after his death. The paper had a mark next to the word divorced, in the box where it asked you about your marital status. So what? He was divorced. It didn't mean that he had no kids. A man his age, he'd surely have had one or two.

The thing about not having insurance, though, bothered her. This guy could be homeless and too proud to put that down in the box.

She had another long night ahead of her, she knew. She'd have to go to the office that nobody knew about, do a work-up on this guy, find out about him and then maybe even take a ride to where he lived. If he owned any property on the Southeast Side, she wanted it, and would have to take a look at it before showing up at his door with her offer.

MaryAnn bit her lower lip and put the car into reverse, carefully backed out of her parking space, then drove out of the lot. She was still smiling over what had happened with Mute as she reached for the phone, calling her computer wizard to check out the financial status of this Ben Morer guy.

Mute sat in his chair, looking across the room at his night supervisor, wondering if the man knew anything, if he'd report Mute to the head man, even if he did. Sure he would. The guy, Smithers, he was a ladder-climbing, networking, useless piece of shit. He had no friends in the lab except those who could do him some good. He looked down his nose at the newly hired techs, even those who hired in at positions higher than his own. He was always trying to suck up to the doctors, too, but they had nothing to do with him, they had their own political pecking order, and lab techs weren't even allowed in their stratosphere.

If Smithers reported him for kissing MaryAnn in the parking lot, what would be the worst thing that could happen to him? The head man of the lab, Doctor Raimas, would report what he'd learned to Mute's PO, and they'd both probably be happy that he'd found a steady girlfriend. Maybe he'd catch a little hell for taking personal calls on the job, but then again, maybe he wouldn't. Mute knew for a fact that one of the orderlies was running a bookie service out of the hospital, and at least two others that he knew of were running a pretty large-scale drug operation out of the place. A personal call to Mute wouldn't even merit the attention of the bosses.

So at least for now, he was covered. Until somebody caught him making copies in the administration offices after all the bosses had gone home, and wanted to know what he was doing. Then he'd be out on his ass. On his way back to the pen. There weren't any married women in Stateville, he'd be engaged to his hand for around three years.

He'd been to prison before, and it had been tough, but he'd made it. What he was doing now, though, felt like robbing the dead, and that, Mute knew, was worse than almost anything.

He hated to do it, but he had to ask Smithers a question.

Mute said, 'Billy?' and Smithers looked up from the

report he was typing up, still wearing the rubber gloves that he'd had on while he was working on the blood samples for one of the doctors.

'*Billy*?' Smithers said. 'Did I just hear you call me *Billy*?'

'What the hell am I supposed to call you?'

'Either sir or Mr Smithers.'

Well, kiss my ass. Mute felt the urge to hit him, to grab this arrogant little dolt and bang his head against the concrete wall. Sir or Mr Smithers? Mute would cut his tongue out first, before he'd show this guy that kind of respect. Everybody in the lab called him Billy or Smitty, and the guy wanted Mute to speak to him differently.

He sat there, stunned, staring knives at the little guy. Smithers shook his head and grunted in disgust, turned his back to Mute, then said, 'Buffo, take this blood work up to Doctor Farmington, he needs it right away.'

'Scuse me? You talking to me? If you are, you better call me sir, that or *Mr* Buffo.'

Smithers spun on him, fat jiggling at his waist, Mute could see it right through the starched thin fabric of his lab coat. This would be fun, he'd had enough shit to last him for one night from MaryAnn.

'That's insubordination, Buffo. Do you want me to report you?'

Suddenly Mute wasn't concerned about his job, about his freedom, about the doctor who ran the place or the doctor's relationship with his probation officer. He stared at Smithers, and started to laugh. A high-pitched snicker that would cut Smithers worse than anything that Mute might say. Still, he'd already set the ball rolling, he had to say *something*.

So he said, 'Smitty, you stupid little bastard, you go on ahead and report me for calling you by your first name, I want you to. Ain't no sense in beating your ass yet, you ain't done enough worth losing the job over. But going to the boss, *that'd* be enough incentive to beat you from one end of the lab to the other.'

'Are you threatening me? I won't be threatened! Is that what you're doing, threatening me?'

Mute got out of the chair and swaggered over to where Smithers was sitting, saw his sissy-boy face crumple all up, watched as Smithers tried to push himself back into the chair, become part of the damned thing. Mute kept his face straight, although he wanted to laugh right in the man's face. He lifted his hand and Smithers cowered in the chair, throwing his hands into the air and covering his face with his forearms.

'Don't!'

Mute grabbed the papers out of Smither's rubber-gloved hand. Maybe later, he'd spill some blood from one of the lab test tubes on to the guy, pour it over the top of his head, if he didn't fall into line. Let the blood flow into Smitty's eyes and he could hold his breath until he got his AIDS test. But for now, humiliating the little porker would do just fine.

'Don't *what*?' Mute said, and sauntered away, toward the door. He banged the report against his leg, casually. 'Didn't you say that you wanted me to take this report to Doctor Farmington right away?' Mute made it to the door, and even from all the way over there he could hear the sound of the man's breathing, fast and furious, like a little baby before it broke down into wailing tears.

He found out what he wanted to know at the nurses' station on three, shooting the shit with one of the girls who hadn't been around long enough to get the lowdown on him. Or maybe she didn't engage in gossip. Or, maybe – and this was the best scenario, as far as Mute was concerned – she had heard about him, about what he was known to do, and she wanted a piece of that action for herself. She was wearing a teeny little diamond ring on he finger, and a slim wedding band in front of it that looked to be about 24 karat. He'd file her away for future reference, once he got out of the trouble he was in. Even though Denise was batting those big eyes at him. He told himself that he had to be strong, that he could not give in, that he'd have to put it on hold.

But man, it wasn't easy.

'So tell me, Denise,' Mute said, leaning on the nurses' counter and acting casual, trying to give the appearance that he was just making conversation, 'what's a closing, like when you buy a house.'

She was a big one, well-proportioned, although a little homely for his personal tastes. They could sometimes be the best kind, though, the ones who thought they were ugly, thought you were doing them a favor. You could get them to do all sorts of things for you. She had long dark hair that she parted down the middle, kept back in a ponytail while she was working the floor. Nice tits, sticking out of her uniform. She wore the thin white pantyhose that most nurses had given up. He wondered if they were stockings that were attached to one of them garter deals. Man, how he loved those things. Shit, listen to him, acting as if everything was all right, when in fact he was in serious trouble.

Even as he thought of her naked, Mute was suddenly feeling guilty. What the hell was wrong with him? He'd never felt that before. It took two to tango, and if her old man wasn't man enough to handle her, then why the hell shouldn't Mute take a shot? He surely had enough lost time to make up for, not having ever had a woman until he was nearly thirty. He had to clear his mind, keep it on the topic at hand. Had to stop seeing every woman he ran across as some challenge that had to be met.

Denise was half-smiling at him, like she thought he was pulling her leg.

'Closing? You want to know what a *clo*sing is?'

'Yeah, like when you buy a house, what's the closing mean?'

'Are you serious?'

'Denise . . .'

'All right, fine, don't make fun of me later, though.'

'With a face like this, would *I* make fun of anybody?'

'You're not so bad,' Denise said, flirtatiously. Hmm.

'The closing is where both the people buying and the people selling the house sit down with the real estate agents, the mortgage people, and – if they're smart – with their lawyers, and settle everything up. It's where the property changes hands.'

'It means like closing the deal?'

'I knew you were putting me on.'

'Was not.'

'Mr Delacourt in three-twenty-two died tonight. Can you believe it? For the first time since I've been here, there's an entire room, empty on three.' She paused and looked at him, saw the blank look on his face. 'With clean sheets on the bed and everything.'

'Hey,' Mute said, 'housecleaning don't mess around in this joint.' He flashed her a smile to show that he was only kidding around. 'What time you get your dinner? Me, I had my break already, but I don't think Smitty's gonna be reporting me if I decide to take another one.'

Diane sat on the couch before her fireplace, feeling more relaxed than she had at any time since Ben's call, last night. Why hadn't he called yet? He'd said that he might call late. Her mind was trying to race, wanting to barge in on her peace, wanting her to worry about Ben and even about the man she knew Ben would have gone to see by now, the man who'd called her at the office.

Dear God, what if it had just been a crank call after all? And Ben went out and killed some semi-innocent man who'd done nothing at all to harm them. A man like Ben would have made enemies over the years, there'd be a group of them he could look at, then decide which one was cowardly enough to make a threatening telephone call. He would base his final decision on how he felt personally about the man he'd kill. Or help to commit suicide, as he'd done one time before.

She hadn't considered the possibility that the threat might not be genuine earlier, what with her anger, her fear over what the man had said to her that morning. Then afterward, seeing Ben, learning that he was indeed truly dying, *that* had become the focus of her attention. Back at work, trying to catch up, she hadn't made time to think about it in depth. But now, in front of her fireplace, the kids in the kitchen, taking care of their chores, a library book in her lap, Diane had time to think.

The fire always relaxed her. It was like taking a tranquilizer, even more relaxing because she didn't get fuzzy-headed from fires, didn't have a hangover from them the next morning. She could sit there for hours, gazing at the burning logs, seeing the red and yellow and white and blue flames leaping up, as if seeking some personal freedom.

It was one of the reasons she had stayed in the house, after the divorce, the same house in which Ben had gone on some of his most violent rampages. It was strange how, now that he was gone, there hadn't been one wall that needed patching, and not one single door that had needed to be replaced.

Was he still like that, was he only showing her a side of him he hadn't before because he wanted her back? She could understand it if he was. When you knew you were dying, when they told you that your time was limited, it had to make a difference, had to make you rethink your ways.

And Ben's ways were evil. No matter how sorry she felt about his illness, she couldn't allow herself to forget that, the man had evil in his blood. But still, she had once loved him, and that afternoon, he hadn't said that he *used* to love her, or that he'd *once* loved her; he'd said that he *did* love her, her and the boys.

Was he capable of it, could he ever love another person? After a fashion, she decided, he could. In a way that she herself could never understand.

She'd been raised nearby herself, very close to where she now lived. Hegewisch had been her home for her entire life, and she had not yet even thought about where she'd go when they bought her out and tore down her house to put in their lousy airport.

During the big snow of '67, while shoveling after the blizzard, she'd stood in her front yard and watched in horror as her father had died of a heart attack. She'd been too paralyzed by fright to move, Diane just having turned fourteen, thinking about a boy named Bobby, wondering if he liked her too, shoveling snow with her dad, her biggest problem being acne, then suddenly she was standing there, watching her father die.

She couldn't even run into the house, couldn't go in and call an ambulance. After a while of standing there, paralyzed and crying, she'd been able to go over to him, to lie down on his rapidly freezing body. Which was where her mother had found her, Mom pulling her off and tossing her aside, shrieking, screaming her husband's name. Mom in her housecoat, the one with the flowered pattern, with fuzzy slippers on her feet and her hair still in curlers. An hour ago Mom had been in the kitchen, feeding her husband and daughter bacon and eggs, pouring coffee for her husband, a Kent cigarette dangling out of the side of her mouth, her father's Camels on the kitchen table, ready, for when he was done eating. He would smoke after every meal, put his ashes on the plate, talking to his daughter as she cleaned the kitchen, wanting to know about her life, how she felt about things that were happening at school or in the world.

How her mother had blamed her! Their relationship, never strong, had deteriorated after that terrible day. In January of every year, throughout the entire month, Diane would be depressed, her father always on her mind. Dead, at thirty-eight, from a fucking heart attack.

It had to be better to go that way than to die slowly and in pain, the way Ben was slated to depart.

Diane sat on her couch, her book on her lap, staring into the fire and wondering about such things. She was three years older now than her father had been when he'd died, and she didn't miss the contrast between what she had once thought, and what she now knew.

Back then she'd seen her father as omnipotent, knowing all, seeing all, there to fulfill her needs. He'd worshipped her, he'd been her shoulder to cry on, never looking down on her, never laughing at her problems. Mom was the disciplinarian, the mean parent in her life, the one who shooed away Diane's emergencies, who saw things in practical terms, who did not have time to indulge her daughter's flights of fancy.

But Daddy, he'd always listened, nodding his head, his brow furrowed, paying attention to her and then dispensing his wonderful, helpful advice. God, how she'd loved him. It had taken her almost thirty years to realize that he hadn't been some god, that he hadn't known everything. She'd seen him the same way her kids would see her now, having it all together, a wise person who could fix all the problems in life without even half trying. The difference being that kids were more cynical today, they seemed to grow up more quickly than they had when she'd been just a girl. At least that's how it seemed.

She knew now, that her father hadn't been such a person. No one was, not really. Every individual was beset with insecurities and emotional problems, all families were dysfunctional now and again.

Yet she could not remember hearing her parents ever having a terrible fight, could not even picture her dad punching a hole in any of the walls of their home. My God, you had to take your shoes off before they'd let you come into the house, and there was always a small, hand-printed piece of paper taped to the inside of the front window, requesting that you go around to the back door. Punch holes in the walls and doors? Good luck. If someone had so much as even tried it in their house, her father would have killed them.

Her father, who'd died clutching his chest in the snow, a look of agony and disbelief on his thirty-eight-year-old face.

In one cold January afternoon, Diane had gone from viewing herself as a relatively carefree, awkward but happy young girl, to the bitch who'd let her father die; it was the way she'd seen herself for years after that terrible day, and a belief that her mother would never let die. The woman had gone to her grave thinking that Diane's inaction had caused her father's death.

Ben had been her attempt at replacing him. She knew that now, at forty-one, could look back dispassionately and see what she had been trying to do when she'd married him. He was so strong, so protective, so kind, and he had money. So many of her friends had gotten pregnant during their college years, had dropped out and married relative strangers, boys who had to drop out themselves, who were barely even old enough to go and get jobs in the mill to support their sudden families. Most of them had eventually gotten drafted, leaving their wives alone, to think and look at what they'd given up, and invariably, to cheat.

It hadn't happened to Diane, she'd set her sights a little higher, although she'd always been on the lookout, dating older boys, mostly, but only those with plans for the future, boys who would someday be something more than a mill worker. Boys who planned on using their college educations to become something greater than their fathers had been.

And there Ben had come, with a plan that had already seemed to be working, sweeping her off her feet with his charm and good looks, his pocketful of money, driving her off into the sunset in his brand-new Oldsmobile.

Well, the sun had gone down on their marriage, that was for sure, and it hadn't taken very long for it to happen. And now he was dying. She felt terrible about that.

No matter what else he might have been, he was, without a doubt, the most *alive* person she had ever known. Always on the move, always thinking, talking fast and always ready for a fight, Ben taking nothing from anyone, expecting and giving no mercy or forgiveness.

He'd had so much life that it had overwhelmed her own.

Diane pulled herself out of the past, and saw that her older son, Benny, was standing in front of her. He had snuck up on her, caught her staring into the fire, lost in a time almost twenty years gone. Benny had his head half-turned, reading the title off the spine of the book in her lap. He had a quizzical expression on his face, Benny standing there, wondering why his mother was reading a book titled *On Death and Dying*. Then – she could see when it happened by the look on his face – Benny made up his mind as to why she'd been reading the book.

'Mom, are you all right?' His expression told her his feelings, Benny anxious now, frightened. 'Mom, tell me, what's wrong!'

Diane smiled, her heart filled at his concern. Ben on his

best day would never understand this, the bond that could be forged between a parent and a child. The concept would be foreign to him. It was one of the things about him that caused her to feel so much pity for him.

'I'm fine,' Diane said, calmly, but Benny wasn't so sure.

'I saw your face, the way you were looking into the fire! You're sick, aren't you? You looked so sad . . .'

He appeared to be near terror, her oldest son, the one who probably styled himself to be the man in the family these past five years. Making connections that no kid his age should ever have to worry about. But she understood his fears, his apprehension and his misreading of the way she'd been looking at the dancing flames, about the book that she was reading. It was called separation anxiety, her analyst had told her all about it. It struck at kids who'd suffered grave losses early in their lives.

'I'm not sick, Benny, I'd tell you if I was.'

'Like hell.' Benny didn't notice that he had cursed in front of her. 'Like hell you would, you wouldn't want us worrying about you, wouldn't want us to know until it was too late.'

'Benny, I promise you, there's nothing wrong with me.' Diane paused.

'It's your father who's sick. Benny, your dad is dying. Now go get your brother and come on in here and sit down, and the three of us will talk about it. I need to know how you feel about it, what you want to do.'

She looked at them, her two sons, sitting with solemn faces as they waited for her to explain things to them. God, how proud they made her! A man they hadn't seen in five years, a man who'd left them with memories that must sometimes haunt their nightmares, was dying, and there were no juvenile tirades, not even the ones that she half-expected. She'd mentioned it to Benny and she knew that he would have told John, gone into the kitchen and told him that their father was dying, and John hadn't done any dancing, he'd come in here to listen to his mother. Which didn't overly shock her.

They'd been carrying responsibility for a long time,

together, two young men who didn't bicker the way most young brothers did, who had respect for each other, and for their mother. They would follow her lead, she knew. What they *didn't* know was that she would listen to them, hear what they had to say, and take her own lead from what these two kids had said to her.

Because there was one fact in this entire deal of which she had no doubt: these two kids came first in her life. First and always. Diane had walked away from more than one serious contender for her heart, men who'd otherwise been fine and successful, who'd said things she hadn't cared to hear about her kids. And if she had to turn her back on Ben, then by God, she would. If they wanted her to, if they felt that strongly about it.

She would do everything in her power to convince them otherwise, to allow him to come over and to have them treat him at least with minimal respect, but if they didn't want to see him, she would understand. And Ben would just have to understand, too, no matter what she'd said to him earlier, when she hadn't been thinking clearly; if these boys did not want to see him, then Diane would not allow him to come around.

She could only pray that it would not come to that.

Diane did not beat around the bush with them, did not try to sugarcoat things or to lead them into it gently.

She said, 'I found out today that your father's dying of lung cancer.' She looked at them separately, saw the quick hurt that passed over Benny's face, the shock then angry nonchalance that passed over John's.

'He doesn't have long to live. Four or five months at the most.' She would not tell them what she suspected Ben would do when the pain became too intense for him to bear.

She went on, 'He's lost weight, and his hair is very gray. I saw him today, went to the hospital with him, and had a Pepsi with him later, in a restaurant on the East Side. He's calmer, older, more relaxed than I remember him.

'What I want you boys to realize is, what was wrong with me *was not his fault*. He played a part in it, and he didn't try to help me, but *I'm* the only one responsible for what happened to my life. I took the pills, and I ate the food. And by God, it was *me* who beat both addictions, with your help, yes, but I did it. Now, I couldn't have done it if he'd still been living here, but we can't blame him for what I was back then.'

'Can we blame him for the nightmares, for the way I used to pee the bed?' John was being sarcastic, disagreeing with her without calling her a liar.

'Yes, we sure can. I was an adult when I met him, I knew what I was getting into. I made choices and lived to regret them. You two didn't have any choice, neither of you asked to be born.

Benny had watched their exchange with sadness, looking slightly confused. He lowered his head for a minute, then looked up at her, pleadingly, wanting to be shown the way.

'He's *young* still.'

'He's gotta be fifty,' John said.

'He's forty-eight years old.'

Benny hadn't bothered to look over at his brother. He stared into the fireplace briefly, and Diane could see that he was crying.

'You know what I always thought about?' Benny didn't look back at her, stayed staring at the flames. 'I always thought that one day, you two, you'd get back together.' Benny spoke in a soft, wan, wistful voice. 'That he'd come and watch me play football, see Johnny playing baseball in the summer. That I could sit on the bench when the offense was on the field and look over and see him loo – loo – looking at me, and he'd be so proud of me, no matter what I did on the field, and then he'd w-w-wink at m-m-me . . .'

Benny lost it, began to sob, his head down, the tears flowing freely. Anguished sounds were coming out of his mouth, and Diane was about to get up off the couch to go to him to comfort him when his little brother beat her to it.

She sat there, crying herself now, watching John put his arm around Benny, hugging him close.

'Don't cry, Benny, come on,' John said. 'He ain't worth it, what did he ever do for you?'

Benny pushed his brother away, hard, knocked him right over on his ass, John's back hitting the couch. The violent reaction startled Diane, but she stayed where she was, did not move. She would only intervene if they came to blows.

Benny shouted, 'What do *you* know? You were only *nine* when he left! You don't want to remember the good stuff, you always hated him, even when he lived here.' Benny looked at his mother with pleading eyes, and Diane nodded her head, not wanting to interrupt.

'He doesn't remember him taking us to Sox park, doesn't want to remember Dad taking us down to meet Carlton Fisk. He doesn't want to remember the piggy back rides and the long car rides on Sundays. Daddy never hit us, never beat any of us up. I went to grade school with a *bunch* of kids who had worse fathers than we did.'

Diane nodded again, hiding a slight slender thread of resentment that was trying to creep into her blood, wanted it to boil. A slight jealousy at Benny's vehement defense of his father. Had she hurt them by keeping him away? Dear God, let them someday understand.

Benny turned to his brother now, wiping at his face with the sleeve of his shirt.

'You talk about pissing the bed, blaming him for it.' He turned to his mom. 'And you said we didn't have any choice about being born. But what choice did *he* have? Did he *ask* to be an orphan? Did he *ask* to be given up by his mother? How was *he* raised? He never hit us, but you know what happened to him, he'd tell us when we asked, the way he used to get beat – beat – *beaten up by all those foster people*!' He got the words out, then broke down again. Spoke around the tears and the sobs, shouted out at John.

'He didn't ask for that, did he, Johnny?!'

John was looking at the floor, but Diane could see that his lip was trembling. He didn't look up at his brother, but slid over, slowly, until he was close to him, right next to Benny. He reached his arms out, John half-afraid, and Benny took him into his own, held him close and tight, and cried on his brother's shoulder.

'He's still my father, and I still want him at my ballgames!' Benny cried.

'I'm sorry, Ben, I'm sorry,' John said.

Her two sons, man enough to do this. It made Diane cry, too, the sight of them down there, holding on to one another.

Diane got down on her knees and held her boys to her breast, comforted them as best she could, rocking back and forth. Both of them were already taller than she was, but it felt the same to her as it had when she had done this to them as babies. Her heart was filled with love for them, at the desire to make them safe.

John wiped angrily at his tears and got himself together, sat back on his haunches and looked at her, but, thankfully, he no longer seemed angry. Benny cried for a while longer, then pulled away slightly, wiped at his eyes and raised his eyebrows.

'So what does he want us to do? Does he want to move back in?'

'Oh, my God. Nothing that dramatic. Benny, you're the oldest.' Diane tried to smile, but it was hard. 'Besides me. Now you go first: do you want to see your father, do you want the chance to say goodbye?'

'Yes.'

Diane looked at her younger son.

'John?'

'Yeah, I guess so. If Ben wants me to.'

'That's not good enough. Remember, John, I was there. I understand if you don't forgive him. If we let him into our house, though, we have to be united on the way we're going to act. I'd rather not have him here at all than to have him come in and hear you yell at him or to have you ignore him. That would only hurt him worse, and you have to remember, he's dying. He's not coming in here and trying to pretend that nothing happened. He knows what he did, and he knows why we wanted him out.'

'Then why's he want to see us, Mom? Why doesn't he just leave us alone?'

'I'm not really sure,' Diane said, honestly, 'but I think he wants to apologize. He's not afraid of dying, he's not worried about heaven or hell. But he's never had anything in his life, really, besides us. No one to love him, at least. And he blew that, he knows it.' Diane looked at John and said the only thing she could.

'I think he only wants us to forgive him, John, I think he just wants us to remember him well after he's dead.'

'Then let him come, Mom. I'll be nice to him, but I can't say I'll forgive him, you can't make me say that.'

The defiance on his face saddened Diane. He was too young already to be going through that kind of rebellion.

She said, 'I'd never ask you to do that, darling. If he gets it, he'll have to earn it, all right?'

'All right,' her son said, then moved over to her and hugged her hard, and she didn't let on that she could feel his body shaking as John cried in her arms and tried his best not to show it.

At the same time that Mute was punching out his time card – his mind on Denise and what she'd done to him in 322, instead of thinking about MaryAnn for once that night – Ben Morer was walking into the He Ain't Here sports bar. He had no pistol on him tonight, there was more than a small chance that cops would be in this place. Cops that might want to talk to him, once they learned that he was part of the equation. Cops were lazy, and not only the ones who were on the take. They always looked for the quickest solution to any crime, the most obvious answer, rather than having to work hard at deducing shit. So tonight, Ben had no gun with him. What he did have with him were two men in business suits, wearing long topcoats, both of them older guys, men he'd learned he could trust. The two men walked in ahead of Ben and took up strategic positions at the crowded bar, while Ben looked around for Tony.

He couldn't stay in here long, not without putting his foot through the jukebox. Some loud and wild bullshit was screeching out of the speakers, turned up louder than even the basketball and footballs games usually were.

Ben spotted Tony sitting at a booth in the back, the fat sleazy greasy bastard sitting there and starting to shake as soon as he spotted Ben. There were three people at the table with Tony, men that Ben did not recognize. But they knew who he was, and looked up at him as he approached, two of them appearing afraid while one of them seemed angry.

Ben walked up to the booth and told the three of them to get lost. He never took his eyes off Tony, but he knew which man it was who decided to speak up just as soon as he heard the voice, knew that it would be the angry one, a man who was dumb enough to think that the dead Lino actually had the capacity to be anyone's friend.

'You got a lot of nerve coming in this fucking joint.'

One of the others, emboldened by the tough talk, joined in.

'You better get your ass out of here, pal, the cops are looking for you. You went too fucking far, this time.'

'I said get lost, I don't say anything three times to punks.'

Ben heard the rustle as the guy who thought he was tough began to rise quickly, then he saw Tony put a hand out, fast, stop the man with his hand on the guy's forearm, as Ben knew that he would have to. The last thing Tony wanted was a shooting in his most profitable bar, and he would sincerely believe that Ben was packing, after what had happened last night.

Tony said, 'Go over by the bar, let me talk to him for a minute.'

Ben stepped back, his hands in his overcoat pockets, watching Tony but ready to move, if he had to. No one touched him, no one said anything, but he felt their eyes burning into the side of his face, staring their hatred at him as they walked away from the booth. Ben stood standing, even after Tony asked him to sit down. He crouched down and looked under the table, felt around the edges, then stood and leaned over, one hand on the table, and patted Tony down, looking for a wire. If it wasn't on his body and it wasn't on the table, then he could say anything he wanted to and not have to worry. The music was playing so loud tonight that the people in the next booth couldn't hear what he was saying; there was no way that a wire anywhere else in the place would be able to pick up the sound of his voice.

'Where's my money?' Ben said, and watched Tony's face fall, saw the look of shock that replaced his trepidation. When Tony spoke his voice was soft and filled with wonder, amazed at what he'd just heard coming out of Ben's mouth.

'You got a nerve, you know that? Like a crazy man got it.'

'I told you this morning that I'd be here at eleven, and you said you'd tell your partner. He ain't even here, and I don't see a bag with my money anywhere.'

'You bastard.'

'Call me a name again, I'll do to you what I did to Lino last night, right here, right in front of everybody. I'll do it to him some more, too, the second I see his lying ass. Worse this time, though, because he had two chances and fucked them both up.'

Ben scooted into the booth, right over so their thighs were touching. He put his face inches away from Tony's and gave him a glare that made him push himself away from Ben.

'You say *I* got nerve? You say *I'm* a bastard? I told your girlfriend Lino last night, I wanted my money, or you were both dead. Where is it, Tony, where's my fucking money, or do I got to work on *you* this time?'

Tony was growing more and more confused with every word that Ben spoke. Ben could see it on his face, Tony's doubt, his lack of belief in what he was hearing. He knew what would be going through a man like Tony's mind.

Ben was known throughout the city as a man who carried himself well, everybody knew he was a man who did what was right. If Ben had killed Lino, he would have taken the money and called it quits, knowing that Tony didn't have what it took to come down on him for taking Lino out. If Ben had killed Lino, he wouldn't be here right now, looking for his money. If Ben had killed Lino, he'd have had his money, would be spending it by now, instead of walking right into the very heart and soul of the beast that he'd killed, into Lino's joint, challenging Lino's partner and threatening him in front of people who'd been Lino's friends.

Tony would be thinking exactly what Ben Morer wanted him to be thinking, he could see it on his face, hear it in his voice now when Tony moved back even further from Ben and spoke.

'Lino's dead.'

Ben let surprise show, then covered it up quickly, he couldn't overplay his hand. He shook his head slightly, grunted once at Tony.

'That's what it was about, why you were dumb enough to curse me. What that punk of yours was saying, about the cops being out looking for me. Lino's dead.' Said thoughtfully.

'Ben, he got shot this afternoon. He had your money with him.'

'He didn't have *shit* with him that belonged to me; what he had was his money, or yours and his – not mine. It wouldn't have become mine until it changed from his hand into my pocket, so don't say that shit, I don't buy it. I want my fifty grand, and I want it tonight.

Ben could see Tony looking over at the bar, as if for moral support. He knew Tony, and had known, in the course of his life, hundreds more guys who were exactly like him. Guys who liked to play on the wild side, but who folded when the strong heat came down, guys who melted right away in that heat, if they didn't have someone heavy to protect them. It was time to rattle him, to show him what he was.

Ben said, 'I want my money, Tony, tonight, you hear me, you motherfucker? Tonight, right now, I'm through listening to excuses.'

Tony said, 'I ain't got it.'

'Come on. Get out of the booth.'

'Where we going?'

Ben shook his head and smiled.

'What've you got in here, a hundred, hundred and fifty people? Maybe ten percent of them are players, or punks who wished they were. Every one of those fifteen, twenty guys would know what happened last night, right in here. They also know maybe a hundred people apiece, would have been on the phones all day, talking about what went down.'

'Ben, please.'

'Shut up. These guys, their friends, they're waiting to see what happens tonight, see what I do, now that Lino's dead and I still ain't got my money. I walk out of here now, and it's over for me in this town. You wouldn't understand that because you never did anything in your life but hide behind Lino's shadow. But the people in power, they know, and if I let you bullshit me, they'll take me out. Everybody in this city will know that Fat Tony the asshole put Ben Morer in his place. Do you really think I can afford to let that happen? And you ask me where we're *going*?'

Tony's bottom lip was wobbling, Christ, this weakling, he was about to break down, even sooner than Ben had anticipated.

'Tony, don't you *get* it? *I want my fucking money*!' Ben hadn't raised his voice, but he'd put a strong, hissing emphasis on every single word, and Tony had flinched at each one of them, pulling back into himself, trying to find a corner to hide in in a booth that was rounded off. There was no place for him to go. He had to sit there and look at Ben.

'And you got to pay for it, I got to take it out of you, if Lino's really gone. You know what'll happen then? After you're both dead? The Man'll split up your action, and I'll get the fifty off the street, same as I should have last night, when I was *supposed* to get it. The Man'll pay me, the Man has *always* looked out for people, done what was right to keep wars from starting.'

'The Man told Lino that it was okay with him if he killed you, told Lino that if he wanted to kill you, that he wouldn't seek revenge.' Tony was talking rapid-fire now, going on and on, with his mind racing, trying to talk his way out of it without having to resort to begging.

This wasn't good enough. Ben had to make him beg.

'Lino went to the Man instead of getting me my money? And what was the game plan, Tony, he was going to kill me tonight? You stupid asshole. The Man told me the same thing! It's the way it works when you ain't officially one of them. He'd let us battle it out and give the winner what the loser used to have.'

Now, Tony was getting it. Ben saw his eyes widen, saw what a deadly game it really was. For Tony, it would no longer be collect the money and pay everyone off. Now, in his mind, it would have gone from *The Godfather* to *The Texas Chainsaw Massacre* in one quick beat of his heart. When he spoke this time, it was almost as if he considered he and Ben to be partners, working against the Man.

'For his twenty points every month.'

Ben laughed, acted surprised.

'He told you if you killed me you had to give him twenty *points*? Shit, he told me if I killed *you*, I only had to pay him ten. What does that tell you, Tony? What does that say about what happened to Lino?'

'My God, the Man had him killed.'

'Took his money, too. Now he knows that you either pay me tonight, or you got to go, too. He can't lose. He's got me running your action, and paying him the same as you, and he knows that I'm better at the hard work than Lino could ever be. Now come on, there's some guys at the bar that want to have a little talk with you.'

'Ben, please, don't kill me, give me a chance.'

'I gave you a chance already, Tony. I gave you *two* chances.' Ben's voice was calm; now, it was just a business deal. 'You blew them both, last night, and then again tonight. What do you want from me, mercy? Mercy's for priests and fixed judges.'

'I'll get your money, I'll get it soon, I promise.'

'Soon my ass, hey, asshole, I told you to have it tonight!'

'Listen, out of respect for Lino – wait! I know you don't respect him, but just let me talk for a second, all right?' Tony was next to tears, frantically trying to find a way out of his situation.

He went on, 'You wait, and we say it's out of respect for Lino's passing. Then, the day after the funeral, I give you your money. That'll give me time to get it together.'

'What do you *mean*, get it together? You didn't have to wait for me to get it together when you came to me.'

'Ben, I got expenses, things even Lino didn't know about. But I can get your money, I promise, I can get it no later than Friday.'

'I can kill you now and get it from the Man before then.'

'*Fuck* the Man!' Tony realized that he'd raised his voice, and now he looked around, terrified, before saying it again, in a harsh, hate-filled whisper.

'*Fuck* the Man! What'd he ever do for you, but push you around and take your money? You give me the money in good faith, and I used it, put it on the street for you. Lino was the one wanted to go to the Man, I told him up front, just pay you off and forget about it. I gave him twenty-five today, in fact, my end of what we owed you. Whoever killed him took it off him, and if you want good odds, I'd go even money that it's in the Man's pocket right now, that fifty grand. You want to go to him? Why? He'd tell you to kill me, then he'll say he'll pay you off. But he's a wild one, he's crazy, and he's always fucking thinking. He might have you kill me, then kill *you*, Ben, and stick one of his own people into my places, give them all my action, and you'd be just as dead as I am. You know he'd do it, Ben, that he's capable of that. Fifty grand's a lot of money, why would he pay it if he didn't have to?'

Tony was humiliating himself, begging for his life. Ben looked at him coldly, but he'd let the glare drop down a few degrees, had pretended to be thinking about what Tony was saying to him.

Now Tony said, 'Ben, *please* . . .' and tears were running down his cheeks. He lifted his hands in supplication, his belly jiggling up and down, Tony's soft womanish breasts bouncing around under his disco shirt.

'*Please*, Ben, I'm begging you, I'll do anything. I never been a tough guy, I always counted on Lino to handle that end of things, please, Ben, don't kill me, I'll do anything you say.'

Tony reached out both hands, like a baby that had fallen

down, reaching for its mother for understanding and love. Ben batted his hands away.

'Get the fuck away from me.'

'Ben, I'm begging you,' Tony said, and Ben smiled.

Ben looked around the bar, saw that everyone was watching them, some with avid interest. Most of the people watching had disgusted looks on their faces. No matter what this pig told them later, they would never believe it. They'd been witness to his cowardice, had seen him cry and beg. Even the three men who'd been sitting there in the booth with him were now staring in shock at the way that Tony was disgracing himself. There was no way that Ben could lose face now, for allowing Tony to live. The fat man would never know it, but his cowardice had saved his life.

That, and the promise that he'd pay Ben his fifty grand.

Ben rose out of the booth, and looked down at Tony, shaking his head.

'Friday, fat boy, and if you go to the Man, I'll know about it, and I'll kill you.'

He turned and walked out of the bar, and the two men who'd come in with him walked out backward, covering Ben's back as he sauntered out of the place.

Mute sat on the shitty little couch in the parlor, with the light on and the door to his bedroom closed. He was breaking the house rules by drinking beer in his room, but everyone who lived here broke that particular house rule; he believed it had been instituted more to get the rummies out of their rooms than because Mrs Calloway was worrying about what they'd do if they got drunk. Shit, they were always drunk up here. If she didn't have that rule, these guys would head out here once a month when their checks came in, load up on Spam and whiskey, and wouldn't leave their rooms for weeks on end. He imagined that after a year or two of that, the place would start to smell almost as bad as Stateville Penitentiary.

The rule that Mute hated was the one that said they couldn't smoke. It was bad enough that he worked in a hospital where you had to go outside to sneak a cigarette, but now, in the privacy of his own apartment, he wasn't supposed to smoke, and Mrs Calloway enforced that one to the max with everyone else. Mute had seen her throw men out in the street for breaking that rule. She didn't want some drunk passing out with a lit butt in his hand, burning down the house that she'd spent most of her life living in. And Mute couldn't say that he blamed her, so they'd struck up a compromise.

He'd only smoke in the parlor, with both feet on the ground and the window open. And he had, for some reason, to keep his bedroom door closed. The outer door to the hallway was always closed and locked when he was home anyway, so that didn't matter to him. What pissed him off, though, was the way the rummies constantly bitched about it.

It was okay to keep the window open for seven months of the year, but the other five, when it was cold, the rummies always complained. Personally, Mute liked the cold, enjoyed the feel of it on his skin. But those other guys, those drunkards, man, they whined and bitched all winter. The cold filled the little room and escaped through the cracks at the top and bottom of the door, creating a draft in the hallway. If those guys owned bedroom slippers and bathrobes, they wouldn't even feel it. But they had a habit of walking to the toilet at night either naked or in their shorts.

Mute had never met a drunk yet who could handle the real cold weather. They'd argue with Mrs Calloway, tell her that she couldn't make them live by one set of rules and allow Mute to live by another, and she'd tell them that if they had parlors, she'd have let them smoke upstairs, too. Mute had the only apartment that was a two-room suite, and if they didn't like it, well then, they could always move. He never argued with them, himself. There was no percentage or profit in whipping up on winos, and besides, his heart went out to them sometimes. For all Mute knew, one of them might even turn out to be his old man.

Mute was thumbing through a magazine, smoking and drinking one beer after another, the cold wind whipping in through the window, Mute in a white sleeveless undershirt and jeans, wearing bedroom slippers, looking for the solution to his problem. He thought that he could solve it easily enough, but if he did, he might be jumping from the fireplace into the fire. He tried to sort it out in his mind in a logical, thoughtful manner. This was the way to do it, because every time he jumped right into something lately, he wound up taking it hard up his ass. Like with MaryAnn – he couldn't bring himself to call her his Mare anymore – he hadn't gone into that with his eyes open, and look at the kind of shit he was in because he hadn't thought it through.

He was thinking about hiring a mercenary to kill her. They were in there, in *Soldier of Fortune*, guys looking for adventure if the price was right. Domestic or foreign adventure, which was a fancy way of saying they'd be willing to fight either here in the United States or they were willing to go overseas.

How many of them would be set-ups? Either law enforcement plants, or guys who'd ask for their airfare to town, sent by Money Order, then who'd never show up. Scams and coppers, they could both put him in a world of hurt. Then again, cops couldn't get away with it. Even if they planted advertisements, that would be entrapment, and Mute knew that even as tough as the country was about cracking down on crime, the First Amendment was still in effect, and *Soldier of Fortune* would have told them all about it if the cops had nabbed one of their loyal subscribers.

So he would forget about the cops. All he needed to worry about was somebody ripping him off.

Or doing what he wanted after secretly taperecording their conversation, then blackmailing Mute for the rest of his life. Or coming to meet with him, and killing him in his room, taking all his money after slitting Mute's throat.

Kee-rist, it could get involved, when you knew something about human nature. About how cold people could be. Mute had learned that early on, from the other children back in kindergarten.

Besides, he just couldn't do it. He was a lot of things, but he knew that he wasn't a killer.

Mute dropped the magazine beside the chair, then tossed his cigarette out the window, then jumped as somebody pounded on his outside door. For a second he panicked, thinking that it was MaryAnn, come to make him perform for her. Then he heard a male voice, high-pitched and raspy.

'Close that fuckin' window, pal!' The guy sounded threatening. He also sounded drunk. Mute obliged, slammed the window shut hard enough so the guy could hear him do it.

'That's better!' Oh, was the rummy proud of himself. Mute didn't recognize his voice. It was probably the new guy. After he'd moved in, suddenly someone had started pissing in the bathtub. But there was no use in hurting the man, or even telling him off. Mute believed in trying to live in harmony with his neighbors. And, too, he'd learned long ago that it wasn't a real good practice to be shitting where you ate.

He heard a door slam down the hall, and he pushed the window open again and smiled, secretly. Damn drunk, he'd go to bed happy, thinking that he'd told off the big ugly guy with the best room in the house. What did Mute care? Let him think what he wanted, if it would make him feel like more of a man.

What Mute cared about was his predicament, and finding some way out of it. He leaned down and picked up the Xerox he'd made for himself, the Xerox of that guy's medical files, of the doctor's prognosis, the reports from the lab and the final diagnosis. Man, was this guy screwed.

There was an address and a phone number, right down there on the front of the man's outpatient record. Mute had to fight the urge to go out and call the guy on the phone, warn him that the mob was coming after him, that some outfit son of a bitch named Walter Ceterra would be paying him a visit soon. Walter, or someone that Walter sent. Didn't this poor sap have enough problems without the mob trying to rip him off?

Mute had always had a soft spot in his heart for most people, for the underdog especially, for sick little kids and for abandoned dogs – for people dying of cancer. Which was why he'd quit stealing and had decided to deal drugs. He just could not imagine how his victims felt, coming home from a hard day's work and finding out that everything they'd busted their asses to get had been stolen out from under them.

As a kid, it had been fun, and there'd been a great sense of getting over on the world, paying back everyone who'd ever made fun of him, everyone who'd ever hurt him. And he could tell himself that all that shit was insured, that an Allstate homeowners would get them everything back, brand new. But as the years passed, Mute had grown increasingly reflective. He'd seen what he'd been doing as wrong, and he'd adjusted his life, although he hadn't gone straight.

Drugs hurt nobody, except the people who went out and bought them. You shoot that shit in your veins and you snort it, hell, you know up front that sooner or later you'll get addicted. He saw it as being no more harmful than cigarettes, which could kill you, too, and you could buy a pack of smokes out there at any tavern in Hegewisch. And what else could you buy in taverns? All the whiskey your heart desired.

What had turned Mute off from selling drugs was the stiffer terms that had come into law in the last couple of years. You got caught turning over the volume that Mute had been playing with, and you were looking at fifteen years federal, the same at the State level now, if you were dealing. The government had the better penitentiaries, but you had to serve eighty percent of your time in them. The State joints were shitholes, but you got a day off your sentence for every one where the hacks didn't catch you doing anything bad.

Fifteen years was too much for Mute. And he wouldn't get any breaks, not when he was selling dope. He'd had over a dozen arrests for fighting, and had beaten all of them except for one; he'd gone down for the attempted murder. Every other time the judge had taken pity on him, looked down at him as Mute told his story, told the judge how the other guy had made fun of the way he looked. The judges always sided with Mute, some even chewing out the people who'd had him arrested, talking to them about sensitivity, about how even the judge couldn't blame Mute for what he'd done.

Even the big one, the one he'd gone away for, Mute bet he would have beaten the rap if he hadn't hurt a bunch of cops.

Still, there was violence on his sheet, and lots of it. He could say with total honesty that he'd never started a fight, that he'd always responded, exploded in violence over someone's insults about the face that God had given him. Those arrests, though, after a drug bust, would guarantee him a stiff sentence.

Which was why Mute now stuck pretty much to insurance fraud. He believed that he'd be facing, at the worst, small-time charges from the federal government. Using the mails to defraud, what could you get from that?

If he ever did get caught, Mute would demand a trial by jury, tell them what he'd done and why, and in particular, tell them how. He could see them, howling in laughter as he broke them up with tale after tale of smashing into the sides of Volvos and Audis and BMWs. Tell them that the drivers had run red lights, what choice did he have but to broadside them? Many of them would have had much the same experiences with those dolts themselves. He did not believe that any jury would convict him.

And besides, who was he hurting? Insurance companies and stupid people; nobody he'd ever hit had ever been really hurt.

Things had been going pretty damn well for him, these days, until last night, when his luck had drastically changed. He faced some money shortages, sure, now and then, everybody did. But he had a job, he was on good terms with his probation officer, he had a roof over his head and no one was out to get him. He didn't make enemies anymore, and he could walk away from bigmouth dolts who felt the need to make fun of him when he was minding his own business, having a few at the South Shore Inn.

Up until now, his post-prison life had been pretty good. He didn't even hate the cops who'd arrested him, or the judge who'd sent him away, or even the bullshit country asshole hacks who'd ordered him around every day. He'd gotten help for his face, had received several operations. Although he'd never be mistaken for Tom Selleck, he no longer felt like a freak all the time, he looked much better than he had since the day that he'd been born.

So what should he do? Mute had no idea. If he spoke to the guy, if he helped him out, he'd be adding to his problems, but maybe saving him from getting ripped off, too. A guy with cancer, shit, this was wrong to do.

He had an idea what MaryAnn and Walter were planning on doing, too, now that he'd had some time to think over what she'd said to him in the car. He knew in his heart that they were finding some way to rob the houses right out from under the dying people before the city bought them up. The Ceterras would do something, convince them to take a low amount for their property, then sit back and wait for the city to make their bid, wait for them to up the ante, after too many people bitched.

What had she said to him, back in her car? If they sell, something like that, then Mute would get paid. She and her old man were robbing the dead. Not billionaire insurance companies, like him. They weren't only hurting arrogant assholes who thought that they were so important that they could run through intersections against the light. They were hurting and stealing from people who were dying.

How many others were there like him, in area hospitals, giving MaryAnn her information? He couldn't be the only one; the city had decided on putting the airport in Hegewisch months and months ago. How many dying people were out there, being visited by the mob? Not to get murdered for double their insurance, as he'd thought before, but to get their homes away from them, all nice and legal.

The home in which Mute had been raised was less than a half mile from where he now sat. Nuns lived in it now, it had been turned into a convent. When the city started evicting people to tear down the houses and put up that airport, those nuns would be out on their asses, too, like thousands of other people who'd spent their entire lives in Hegewisch. A lot of them were elderly, people who'd remember when this place had been a pretty damned good place to live. Before the mills had all closed down, before the mayor had betrayed them. Good people, old religious people. People like Mute's grandma, who'd always loved him, taken him in and raised him after his own mother had taken one look at him and had turned her back on him forever.

Shit.

What should he do? Mute wasn't sure. But he knew one thing: he was feeling pretty low. This entire deal with MaryAnn was making him feel something he hadn't felt since before he'd gone away to the penitentiary.

Mute felt ugly, and he didn't much care for that.

Last night, he had prayed, and his prayers, man, they'd been answered, just like *that*! He remembered that he'd said something about giving up the gambling, laying off the married women, if God would only let Sabi's Skipper win.

Was God punishing him, was that what it was? Mute had immediately broken his promise with MaryAnn, and look what God had laid on him, look how He'd made Mute suffer.

Well, it had worked once.

Mute got out of the chair and slowly went down on his knees. He looked up quickly, and shut the windows, pulled the blinds. He would have to remember to pray almost silently. If any of the rummies heard him talking, they'd go running downstairs to tell Mrs Calloway that he had company in his room, and there was a strictly enforced house policy against that. Even Mute couldn't get away with that. As much as Mrs Calloway loved him, it was the one thing that she wouldn't abide.

Mute folded his hands, pointed his fingertips straight up at heaven, and began to move his lips.

'God? You listening?'

Mute immediately felt foolish. It was one thing to lock

yourself into a toilet stall, praying at the track when you were almost broke. It was another thing altogether to do so in your own apartment. Still, Mute had to give it a try. If his prayers weren't heard on this occasion, he'd never waste his time again.

He closed his eyes, and stopped feeling foolish, felt a sense of calm come over him. For the moment, he was twelve again, believing that God could take away his ugliness. The feeling frightened him, made Mute think about things that he'd rather put off for another thirty or forty years, but he didn't open his eyes, didn't let the fear overcome him. He felt too good right now to want this feeling to go away.

'God,' Mute whispered, 'please listen to me. I screwed up last night and broke my promise to you. I said I wouldn't do some things, and I right away went out and did them, and I don't blame you if you're piss – if you're mad at me.

'But listen, God, this woman, man, what this woman wants is wrong. She wants me to work with her, robbing the dead. I don't want to do that, I want to help that guy out.'

Mute heard the outside door slam shut, then heavy footsteps on the wooden stairway. He moved his lips without making a sound. He'd raise his voice level after the guy got into his room.

'But I'm scared. I'm so scared of those outfit people. Give me a sign, God, give me a sign. Let me know what I can do, what you *want* me to do about this shit. If you want me to call the guy, Lord, give me a sign and I'll do it.'

Mute opened his eyes and looked at the window, not knowing what to expect. Maybe a bright flash of light, a burning bush, some damn thing that told him there was a God and that God wanted him to call this dying guy up on the phone and clue him in.

Mute saw nothing, heard nothing, except for the heavy footsteps on the stairs, now hitting the second-floor landing, the footsteps stopping right outside his door.

There was a knock at the door, and Mute leaped to his feet. Walked over to the door and pulled it open, wide.

Mrs Calloway stood there, a red babushka on her head,

breathing heavily from the exertion of climbing the stairs, smiling at him. She was wearing a gaily colored red coat; her cheeks were flushed red. It was almost midnight, what could possibly be wrong?

'I closed the window, Mrs Calloway. If one of those drunks woke you up, I'll – '

'You think I sleep in my coat? Mr Calloway didn't leave me much, but there's always enough to pay the gas bill, thank the Lord for small favors.'

She was holding a thick envelope in her hand. She didn't make a move to give it to him, but he recognized the style and the letterhead, knew what it probably was.

'I was at Sophie Granowski's wake, God rest her. We closed up Opyt's and went across the street for a glass of wine.'

She thrust the envelope toward him now, and he reached out and took it, held it in his hand and looked at her. He'd never seen her drunk before, and she was looking at him funny, and Mute had a moment of sudden, acute panic. If this was God's sign, if Mrs Calloway had designs on him, Mute would never get on his knees to that God ever again. *He* might have a sense of humor, but Mute didn't think that this shit was very funny.

'This came for you in the mail. The envelope was too thick to fit under your door, and you'd locked it, and I didn't want to leave it on the railing post. It's a good building and I'm careful about who I let in, but still, you never know these days, and you do work nights, and some of the other men do like their beer, I'll tell you.'

'Well, thank you, Mrs Calloway, I surely appreciate it.'

She was looking at the envelope, as if expecting him to explain it to her.

'Just legal stuff, like usual, Mrs Calloway. They need me to give them a lot of information for my lawsuit against the State.'

She thought that he was suing them for damages that had occurred when they'd operated on him while he'd been doing time. A simple enough lie, and only partially false. He *was* in the process of a lawsuit, usually more than one at any given time. Whenever you sued an insurance company, you had to fill out a zillion forms, in triplicate, before they'd even consider your claim.

'Well, good night!' Mute said, cheerfully. 'Thanks for delivering the letter!'

'You're not going to invite me in? I could drink one of those beers, what with just leaving poor Sophie.' She sniffed, then smiled at him, shrewdly.

'And you've been smoking in here again, Michael. I hope you know how to keep both feet on the floor when you're sucking on those things!' She gave him a lewd wink. 'If you catch my drift.'

'Uh, good night, Mrs Calloway.' Shit, if he'd asked her in, the woman would *hate* herself in the morning.

She turned in a huff and walked away, and he closed the door behind her, feeling bad for her.

If she had any sense, she'd go right down the hall. She could make the entire year for the guy who pissed in the bathtub.

Mute sat back down on the couch, popped open the window, and lit another cigarette, squinting at the envelope, sent to a phony name that he'd used, but care of him to this address. He used so many phony names that he sometimes forgot which one had been involved in which accident, and where that accident had been. And he had to dump each license after the case was resolved, and he could only use each lawyer once. Not because any of them had any fucking ethics, but because if his scam was ever found out, they could go down the tubes, right along with him, if it ever came out that they knew about the scam and had done nothing to stop it from continuing on.

The legal stuff would be in the inside letter, and Mute had to tear the envelope from the mail-forwarding place open before he got to it.

Mute slit the second envelope open and turned it upside down, expecting more of the never-ending legal forms to fall out on to his lap. Instead, a bunch of thick legal-sized papers fell out, and Mute picked them up, opened them, saw that they were blank. He shook them, and an oversized check fell out, floating gently to his lap like a leaf on to an autumn lawn. Mute dropped the papers picked up the check, saw the number typed on to it, and did a double take.

Twenty-two thousand, two hundred dollars. Made out to his name, pay to the order of. Mute dropped the check back into his lap, sat staring at it, numb. He riffled through the papers, found one that had a little typing on it.

'Mikey, thought there were more fucking forms in here, eh? No, just the check from Farmer's, who decided to settle. Took our piece, the rest is yours.

'Let me know when the next one's due, I'll refer you to someone you can trust.'

His main lawyer had jotted down his initials under the message: JR. There was nothing there in the letter that could tie it to the man.

Twenty-two grand, and change.

His sign from heaven.

Suddenly, he didn't feel so ugly anymore. As a matter of fact, he felt downright handsome. Strong and ready to do battle for the Lord. One time, but righteously, to make up for the life that he'd been leading.

Mute squeezed his eyes shut tight and whispered a heartfelt 'Thank you', then got up off the couch, and put on his shirt and shoes. He had a phone call to make. He'd made a deal with God again, and this time he planned on living up to his end of it.

They sat in the unmarked police car, the two of them making plans, Midler and Slinski wanting a piece of him, of that son of a bitch Ben Morer, but afraid to go barging in and kicking his door down with a warning. If they did, they had decided, he might blow both of them out of their shoes.

Midler said, 'I don't see his car.'

Slinski said, 'He always leaves that piece of shit sitting out here, too, right in front. Like he's driving a new Mercedes, he's got the alarm on it and everything.'

'You think he did Lino?' Midler laid it right out in the open.

'I heard, the word was, Lino had the Man's protection.'

'Maybe Morer ain't too worried about the Man,' Midler said, then thought for a minute, staring up at the apartment house, even though Ben's apartment was in the back and he wouldn't be able to tell if a light was on from where they were sitting, out at the front curb.

'Slin, you figure he's that crazy?'

'Maybe, years ago, he was,' Slinski said. 'There was a time when nothing this guy did would'a surprised me one whole hell of a lot.' Slinski sighed, nearly in awe. 'He used to be the craziest motherfucker I ever met in my life. Now, who knows. Things ain't been the same for him, he ain't been his old self, since he got out of the joint the last time. Hell, what was he, forty-one, forty-two? You got to calm down by then, you got to start taking it easy. Until today, I figured we had him pretty much figured out. Now, I ain't so sure.'

'This guy, he ain't the type to ever take things easy.'

'He's still scary, I'll give you that. I mean, we go in, scare the shit out of people every day of our fucking lives. What happens last night? This guy, he looks down the barrel of my gun like it's loaded with caps and he's back on the Clay School playground. He didn't even get mad at us, and I was expecting that, him getting pissed off.'

Slinski shrugged. 'I'd bet the pension he was lying on the side of the bed with the gun pointed at the door when we started beating on it. Old habits die hard. And talk about getting mad, shit, he's a professional. He knows he ain't what he used to be, and he ain't gonna hold it against us, our taking a little more for ourselves from him now. He held back enough back then, back when he was hot shit.'

'That's what I'm saying. I'm saying that he still might *be* hot shit, and we're the only ones that don't know it.'

'Driving that car? That ten-year-old hunk of shit? Living here? Don't kid yourself, he's cold as ice. Old man dying by inches and he just don't know it.'

'Lino's the one dead, and Morer's still here.'

'You wanna find out how hot he is? Let's find out. There's only one way.'

Slinski opened his door and stepped out into the record-breaking November cold. He shivered, walked around the car as his partner got out, then the two of them ran to the side of the house and mounted the wooden outside stairs rapidly, their hands deep in their pockets to protect them from the cold.

They went into the upstairs apartment hallway quickly, Slinski going to the right of the door and Midler to the left, their hands no longer in their coats, now in front of them, holding weapons.

'I'll take it down, and you get to the left,' Midler said.

They walked together down the hall, until they came to Ben's door. Slinski stood to the left of it, his gun up high, held close to his cheek, while Midler held his pistol straight out in front of him, pointing it at the door and holding it there as he lifted his booted foot up and kicked at the door, right near the lock. As it flew open, he ran in toward the right, with Slinski right beside him, jumping through and racing to the left.

'Morer!' Midler shouted, running toward the bedroom. A light clicked on and he turned, his weapon aiming, found himself pointing it at Slinski, who was standing in the kitchen by the shattered door, his finger still on the light switch. Midler turned back to the bedroom, trying to hide his fear.

'Come on, Ben, it's us, we told you we'd be back. Don't make this hard on yourself. You're holding a weapon in your hand and we got no choice but to kill your ass, and nobody wants that, not you, not us.'

No answer. Slinski had slithered up to the other side of the door, and they looked at each other, the two of them afraid, both of them nodding at each other before they moved.

They went into the room high and low, left and right, knowing Ben could only kill one of them. They shouted as they went into the bedroom, knowing it would distract Ben if he was trying to aim. Slinski threw himself across the rumpled bed, pointed his gun at the floor on the other side. Nothing.

They tossed the apartment in a matter of seconds, found that Ben wasn't there. Found little else of interest, until they got to the closet.

It was mostly empty, Ben's suits and jackets and shirts all missing.

'He always dresses pretty good. But there isn't much here. Just shortsleeve stuff, summer clothes. What do you think?'

Slinski checked the dresser, found that all the underwear and socks were missing. He sighed and put his pistol away.

'He left the VCR, the TV . . .'

Midler said, 'Like he left in a hurry, running from the Man.'

'Or from us, don't forget that. He might not have gotten any money from Lino before he killed him, and he knew we were expecting five grand tonight.'

The phone rang and Midler strolled over to it, looked down at it for a second, then looked over at his partner.

'What do you think?'

'Would you quit saying that? I hate it when you say that. Shit, answer it, what do we got to lose?'

Midler said, 'Hello?' then listened for a second. He said, 'Wait a minute, wait a minute, what do you mean, I don't know you, who're you calling?' He paused. 'Yeah, yeah, this is Ben Morer.' He pronounced it More-er, so Slinski would know that whoever was calling didn't know how to pronounce Ben's name properly, then he winked at Slinski and nodded his head, his eyes wide, clowning.

He said, 'What? I can't hear you, why are you mumbling?' Then, 'Come on, what's your name. All right, don't tell me, do what you want. But tell me this, buddy, what's so important that you call and want to talk to me at this time of night?'

Midnight found Ben looking up at his wife's bedroom window, wondering if she were awake up there, lying in bed, thinking of him. It was too late to call, and he wouldn't go up and bother her, he just wanted to sit there for a while, close to where his family was, before he took off, found some other place to live.

He'd decided to leave, maybe even leave the city altogether. The cops would be looking for him, and maybe other people, too, friends of Lino's, and he didn't have time for that. Didn't have time at all.

The car was running, the heater on high, Chicago in the midst of a brutal cold snap. The houses on the street were dark, but odds were good that someone had spotted him. It wouldn't be smart for him to sit out there much longer, as this was, for the most part, a pretty tight community. One where people still looked out for other people on the block. And a single woman with a couple of kids would get more than her share of protection in Hegewisch. He had the guns in the car, and some pretty hot stuff in the trunk, under all of the clothing in there, but still, not hard to find if you were looking. He couldn't afford a roust. He'd just sit here for a little while longer, feeling the connection between them.

Ben was smoking, looking at the house, wondering if she'd gotten a fire going tonight. Diane had loved those things, and he'd make one for every time it got cold. Once he'd even turned the air conditioner up all the way in the summer and made a fire for her as a surprise, while she'd been out shopping, while he'd been alone with the boys.

He'd paid cash for this house, back in the days before the drug smugglers hadn't wrecked things for everybody and you could still lay out cold cash for big ticket items and it didn't have to be reported to the IRS. The house was in Diane's name, though, and that had been important. When he'd gotten convicted, there'd been heavy fines involved. If his name had been on anything of value, the government would have confiscated it and sold it to lessen what they'd thought to be his bill. As it was, he'd filed for pauper status, and gotten out of it. They still hadn't found a way to squeeze blood out of a stone.

How many times had he and Diane had sex in front of that

fire? Had to be a hundred, easy, and not only when the house was new to them. Hell, there had been times that they'd done it there after both the kids were born; he could never get enough of her, she was so young and beautiful and mostly upbeat, and he had needed that, or thought that he did.

Need. There weren't many things that Ben really did need. He'd learned that you could live without most things if you really had to, if you had no choice.

But dear God, had he needed her.

He never thought that he'd wind up divorced, never knew that there was a major problem, really, right up until the day that Diane had asked him to leave. He always thought that they'd been pretty happy, that they got along real good.

He'd always tried to make up for the things he did when he got mad in ways that he thought Diane would truly appreciate. After a blow-up, he'd bring her a fur coat, feeling bad, maybe a diamond ring. She'd take them and smile, hug him and laugh, always acting as if she'd forgiven him.

What would he have done if she'd told him abut her problems? If Diane had come to him, asked him to sit down, told him that their marriage was in trouble? Looking back, he knew, he wouldn't have taken it seriously. Long, heartfelt discussions were for characters on TV shows, not for real life.

She'd learned early on not to tell him that she loved him. Not if she was expecting a similar response, not if she wanted a reply. Ben had always believed that such talk was merely that. Believed that if you loved somebody, you didn't have to tell them, they'd know how you felt by the way you treated them, by the things you did for them.

By the things you bought them.

It was the only way he really knew how to show affection. Sure, he'd come up behind her and hug her sometimes, when he wasn't looking to get laid. And the kids, he couldn't get enough of them when they were babies, he was proud to walk down the street, pushing their buggies, smoking cigars. He was always kissing their cheeks, holding them in his arms and singing little songs to them.

But mostly, he bought things for them. For them and for Diane.

Was it that bad, doing that? Was he that out of step with the rest of the world? What about that Volvo commercial, the one that Sunny wouldn't even watch, said it was too fucking much yuppie commercialism for her?

Those little kids, sitting around a table, coloring, the one says that his daddy loved him so much, he bought him a baseball glove. Then all the other kids had to top that kid, telling him what their daddies had bought *them*, each of them topping what the previous kid had said. Then, the last one, a little girl, she tells all those kids that *her* daddy loved *her* so much, he'd bought her a Volvo.

It made sense to Ben.

But now, he wasn't so sure. There was nothing like being told that you were going to die to change the way you looked at things, to change the way you saw your life. And the way you'd lived it.

Ben wasn't that mad about dying. He just figured it was another beating he had to take, another bad fucking break. He'd been so prepared for it for so many years that to hear that it was imminent had nearly been an anti-climax. Still, there were things he'd miss, things that he was sorry about.

He'd never felt anything besides anger at getting dragged awake early on Christmas morning. He'd never said anything, didn't want to screw things up for the kids, but still, he'd always wondered why they couldn't have waited a few more hours, until the sun was well into the sky, before they came charging into the bedroom. He'd never had a Christmas to look forward to, not once when he'd been a kid. And he was impatient, he knew, didn't have time to read bedtime stories, mostly because he had trouble reading anything more complicated than the Daily Racing Form.

He'd change all of that, he knew, if he had another chance. And a hell of a lot of other things. Would change them in a minute. But he wouldn't get another chance. He'd had all of the chances that any human being ever gets, and he hadn't taken advantage of them, hadn't capitalized on a one. And there'd been opportunities, all along the way, people who'd offered him jobs, security chief to industry big shots, things like that that he'd turned down with disdain.

He would make no apologies for the life he'd led, but he felt he had some to make to his kids, he owed them a couple of things. One of the things he owed them was still in his trunk, in a vinyl bag from a bank, a present to them from Lino.

He saw the window shade pull back, saw Diane looking out at the car, squinting. Should he leave, take off right away? She wouldn't know the car. Then again, yes she would; she'd seen it just that morning, after she'd met him at the hospital. What was she doing, talking on the phone? There seemed to be a phone at her ear. That, or she might be holding a gun up high, close to the side of her head.

She waved at him, a beckoning gesture, and Ben felt trapped, surprised that the gesture frightened him. He shut the car off and got out, went over to the trunk and popped it. He searched under his clothes and got the money bag out and then started to jog toward the house, stopping when the cold air knifed hard into his diseased lungs. By the time he hit the front porch, Diane was waiting by the open door.

Diane told the woman down the street, Mrs Bjaginski, that it was a friend of hers that was sitting out there. Mrs Bjaginski had been so concerned that she'd called Diane to tell her that some man was parked outside, staring at Diane's house, and did Diane want her to call the police?

Not hardly. But she didn't tell Mrs Bjaginski that. Nor did she tell her about the terror she felt at the sound of the woman's words, either. The first thing Diane thought was that the man who had called her that morning had learned where she lived, had found out where her kids were, and was now coming to kill them.

What she did, after that initial terror, was to look out the window and see Ben's car at the curb, and she was so relieved that she waved at him, told him to come on in. Then Diane said, into the phone, 'Mrs Bjaginski, it's all right. It's a friend of mine.' This last, she knew, was weak, but she had to tell the woman something. She hung up before Mrs Bjaginski could pry any further, and she went to the door and opened it for Ben.

He came in looking sheepish, the same look on his face that her sons would have, years ago, when caught doing something that they knew was wrong. His head was down, his expression grim, and he looked up, trying to smile.

'I was just sitting out there, I didn't mean to wake you up.' She saw him look over at the fire burning in the fireplace, and an expression of sadness mingled with joy passed across his usually impassive face.

'I was awake,' Diane said, then led him toward the couch, near the fireplace. He sat in the chair that was positioned to face the fire, not sitting next to her on the couch, although she'd thought by the way she'd sat down on it that she'd made it clear that he was welcome to if he so chose. Ben gazed into the flames, shaking his head slightly. He had dropped his coat on the floor, something wrapped up in it. Was it a gun that he was hiding? Dear God, she hoped not.

'It's good to feel warm,' Ben said. 'Believe it or not, I missed a fireplace.'

'You've been out in the cold your entire life, Ben. On the outside looking in.'

She hadn't meant to say it that way, did not want to say anything that would hurt him. She wasn't even sure that her words weren't harmless, until she saw the pain sneak into his expression, there then instantly gone. Ben always could keep that under control. It was anger that he always just had to express, never sadness, never insecurity. Rage being about the only emotion he could successfully articulate. But now she saw the sadness, his understanding of what she'd said.

'I spent my lifetime trying to get inside, to get close to the fire, where everyone else was.' His voice was soft and introspective, Ben opening up to her.

Diane knew that she had to be careful here, had to watch what she said and how she said it. She wanted more than anything to understand this man, what drove him, why he had done all the things that he had.

'There's so much good in you, Ben, so much intelligence . . .' A soft start, calculated to draw him out. She got an unexpected response however. Ben laughed.

'You know how many times people have said things like that to me? Not about being good, that, I never heard. But about being smart, how I could have done anything I wanted if I put my mind to it? Sometimes I'd even have to sit there and eat it, shrinks in the pen telling me what I was capable of.' He made a disgusted sound, and she had to look to make sure that he hadn't spit upon the carpet.

'I spent most of my adult life busting my ass twelve, sixteen hours a day, just to stay ahead. Sometimes I'd do real good, other times not so good. I'd spend weeks and months on burglaries, setting them up just right, putting the right people together, making sure that nothing was left to chance. If I'd put that energy into a job, they said, I'd have wound up running the company.'

'So why *didn't* you, Ben?' Diane asked, and he didn't even need a second to think about his response.

"'Cause I'd have spent half my life kissing ass, climbing ladders, making friends with the hypocritical fuckers who can do you some good in the business world. Can you see it, me, joining a country club? And what was I supposed to do, go back to school at thirty, learn how to read and write good enough? Who'd have hired *me*, Diane? Even at eighteen, I already had a record.'

'You could have sold insurance, *any* kind of sales job, you could have made a fortune.'

'Not me. Not me, Diane. It's a cute thing for someone to say, that's all it is. "You could have done anything with your life." You act like I had a choice in what happened.'

'And what do *you* think happened? Do you think it just happened to you accidentally? That you were sitting around minding your own business and fate made you a criminal?'

'It would never have worked. I tried to get jobs, don't you remember, back then? When we first got married?'

'You can't start a job and be the boss in two weeks.'

'But doing what I do, I *am* the boss. I'm always my own boss. I keep all the profits and I take all the losses, just me, no one else.'

There were arguments that she could make about that. For example, that hatred had always really been his boss, had always ruled his life. And there were other, less metaphysical things that she could point out to him. Such as who'd been the boss in the penitentiary, where he'd had to take orders from barely literate, bullying guards?

She could have said these things, but she didn't. She did not want to draw him into an argument, nor did she wish to insult him. Diane was, in fact, being extremely careful not to let her personal feelings toward him come into play. She was trying to find out what he really was; not how *she* saw him, but how he truly saw himself.

And so she said, 'And you don't regret it now, you don't wish you'd done things differently.'

'Diane, what was there for me to do? Go into the mills? The mills closed. I'd be on welfare. Tend bar somewhere, begging for tips? What else could I have been than what I was? Nobody told me what to do, nobody ever pushed me around. I'll go to my grave knowing that I never took any shit from anyone.'

'I'll put that on your headstone.'

'I already have that covered.'

He smiled, then looked away from her, as if not trusting himself to look into her eyes for too long. She saw him look down at the books on the floor, the open Kubler-Ross book, *On Death and Dying*, right on top. He flipped it a few inches with his foot, turned his head and tried to read the spines of the books stacked under it. The word CANCER was in all the titles. Diane watched the corners of his lips turn downward, in distaste.

'Looking for cures for me?'

'It's the strangest thing,' Diane said. 'There are men in the Philippines who actually believe that they can rub the cancer right out of the body. There's a man in India who claims to have duplicated all of the miracles that Jesus Christ performed, including healing the dying and raising the dead.' She sat forward now, her forearms on her knees. She waited until he looked up at her, then she nailed him with a glare that she hoped conveyed all the intensity of his own famous scowl.

'And there are doctors across the United States who are utterly experienced in battling the exact type of cancer you have. Ben, they can perform, if not miracles, then damn near the real thing. You know what those books taught me? That you didn't get a death sentence today; what you got was a diagnosis from a doctor who isn't even an oncologist. He's only an intern, on the ward.'

'He got guys he consulted with, older guys who know their stuff. I don't even have insurance, who can I expect to see, the Surgeon General?'

'You're missing the point, this thing can be fought, and sometimes it can be won! I've been reading through these books all night, and even *I* can understand that.'

'The doctor said – '

'*Fuck* what the doctor said!' Diane realized that she had raised her voice, and shook her head in anger. She wasn't the least concerned about how he might respond to her anger – the woman she'd once been, the one who'd lived in fear of him, had been dead for quite some time – her concern was that she'd awaken the kids.

She forced herself to calm down. He *would* listen to what she had to say, even if she had to knock him out with a fireplace poker and tie him up, then wait for him to come to. He was looking at her strangely, as if seeing her for the first time. But he didn't look mad. Too goddamned bad if he was.

Diane said, 'You haven't been listening to me.' She thought of an analogy that he might understand.

'Say someone down the street, he's in his twenties, he's a wiseass, he's stealing for a living, doing all right for himself. Now, would you let him tell *you* about the criminal life? Would you take his word for it for whatever it was he told you? Like hell you would, because you forgot more about stealing than he'll ever know. It's the same thing with lung cancer, Ben. This guy, this doctor, what was he going to do, what was his battle plan? Stick you in the VA hospital and let them take care of you. That's not good enough. There are plenty of doctors, with experience and unquestioned expertise, who might be able to help you. I've been reading about them all night.'

He was giving her a blank look, neither cold nor angry, just looking at her. Was he really listening to her? Was he just sitting there looking for someone to care about him because he was dying, or did he respect what she had to say? There was only one way to find out.

'What I'm saying to you is, open your damn mind, Ben. Just because one doctor in one hospital in one of the most depressed areas of the city says something, doesn't mean that it's absolutely true. It doesn't mean that God has spoken. This guy might push through fifty cancer patients a week to the VA. Does he know anything about interferon, about the other drugs, about the experimental therapies? You can't take one man's word for it. You have to get it out of your head that they're God, that any single doctor can tell you whether you're going to live or die. You have to see a specialist, at least, get the opinion of someone who knows lung cancer the same way you know stealing.'

Diane stopped and looked at him, sitting there, the son of a bitch, now smiling at her. She felt rage fill her.

'Don't you dare sit there like that, looking at me as if I don't know what I'm talking about. What are you, better than me? Because you're a crook and I work for a living? Guess what, big shot, my business grossed more last year than you've earned in your career! Look around you any time you think differently, Ben. Who put this together, who built a life for us? Not you. I'm telling you your options and you're putting up with it? Don't do me any favors, guy, I don't need that bullshit.'

'Who, who, hold on,' Ben said. He had lifted his hands to shoulder height, palms out, sat there, still half-smiling, the bastard.

'I wasn't laughing at you, or making fun of you. I was just – surprised at what you were saying. I didn't know you cared.'

'You're going to sit there making *jokes*? Are you *crazy*?'

'You're the second person today to ask me that,' Ben said, and now he was no longer smiling.

'I remember when you used to be a fighter. The thought of you quitting without a punch being thrown, Ben, I can't believe it's happening, I just can't believe you'd give up.'

'You're forgetting something, Diane. All that stuff, those specialists, those older guys who deal with this for a living, they ain't free.'

She was ready for that one.

'You said earlier that you would try it if you had the money.'

'I'd go to the moon, too, just to see it, if I could afford the trip.'

'What if we could come up with the money?'

'Who, you and me?'

'That's right. What if we could come up with the money? Would you go? And think about it, don't just blurt out an answer. We're not talking space flight, here. We're talking about life and death. Yours. Then think about this, Ben, think about this long and hard.' Diane got to her knees and walked over to him on them, put her hands on his knees, then leaned forward and looked him right in the face.

She saw shock there, at what she'd done, Ben sitting far back and looking at her, quizzically. She pushed herself up until she was kneeling as tall as she could, looking him right in the eye now, face to face. If he decided to speak, she'd know if he was lying.

'Say there's an answer, Ben. Say it's through the special cancer doctors. Say these doctors can fix you up, can save your life for you. Even if they *couldn't*, even if they can only give you another two or three years, what would you do with that time? Would you still think that you had no choice? Would you still believe that stealing and doing whatever else you do is all that you possibly *can* do?' Diane took a deep breath, let her words rush out with her breath.

'Would you still be the man you are, do the same sort of things you've always done?'

Diane squeezed his legs now, hard. When she spoke her voice was silken steel, low and quiet, but challenging.

'Or would you change. I don't mean *try* and change. I mean actually change.'

'Jesus . . .'

'He's not the topic of discussion here, Ben, *you* are.' She let him go and rose to her feet, stood looking down at him, and put her hands on her hips. When she spoke now, her voice sounded almost drained.

'You think about that, Ben, and take your time. I'll put a log on the fire and leave you alone, if you want. But I need an honest answer, and without any rationalizing or any justifications. You've done it your way for forty-eight years. Now I really need to know if you're willing to try it my way.'

Ben was looking up at her, his mouth open wide, moving fractionally. Open an inch, shut an inch, Ben trying to say something but not knowing how to go about it.

'Don't say anything now, don't kneejerk some tough guy answer out at me. I could be offering you another chance, Ben, some hope for once in your entire goddamned life. Don't blow it by being macho, because the offer won't be open for long.'

She watched him shut his mouth and then look over into the fire, Ben seeing for the first time that there might be alternatives for him that didn't include dying before next May. Diane looked away from him, went and grabbed a piece of wood, tossed it on the fire then pushed it in there good with the poker, put the screen back in place. She picked up her books and then walked out of the room without looking back at him to see what he was doing.

MaryAnn knew that she might be in for another very late night. Things were looking good on three of her potential clients, people whose files she'd gotten from a male nurse who had worked the oncology ward at St Margaret's hospital in Hammond, Indiana. She'd miss him. He'd been so good, so open to suggestion. Unlike Mute, who just seemed to resent her.

She thought that she might have pushed her luck too far with Mute already. Lying to him about all those things, about Walter being a big man in the outfit. He was dumb enough to believe it, stupid enough and afraid enough to be intimidated into doing what she wanted, but in the cold light of reality, she knew that he wouldn't last.

Who'd have thought that he had a conscience? He hadn't acted like a particularly responsible individual last night. The major mistake, the single error that had seriously damaged their future, had been his coming to her house. If he hadn't done that, if he hadn't felt the urge to show her how slick and smart he was, they might have worked something out, their relationship could have lasted until the city started laying out fair market value bucks to the people who lived in the homes that the city planned to destroy. Could have lasted until then, or until the dumb bastard got himself caught and fired, just like the nurse over at St Margaret's Hospital.

What a thrill it had been, though, making him bend to her will. Although she knew that that was not the way to do it. The work had to be done voluntarily, the bait dropped to the man slowly, over a period of a week or two. Mute would have snatched at it, jumped in with both feet. What had he told her earlier today? He thought that he was falling in love with her. And a man in love could be led around by the balls for as long as she felt he was needed. Then, hell, you cut them off. Threw them away and went about your business.

But Mute had come to her house, and that had been the end of any chance that they might have had to do significant business together. It might have been fun, particularly knowing that he was totally in her control. But he'd be too risky now, she couldn't chance it with him anymore. She'd just let him sit there, jumping every time the phone rang, the big ugly harelip bastard thinking that it would be her calling.

Then, after a week, a month, she *would* call him, just to screw around with him. She'd wasted time and trouble on him and she hated to be proven wrong.

MaryAnn sat behind a table in a small cold office that was on the fourth floor of a near South Side building. Close enough to the loop to be considered decent office space, and far enough away that she could get the office for a fraction of what the same space would cost her if she was in the loop itself, or, God forbid, even a little further north.

Four-fifty a month, and the landlord paid the bills. Anywhere in the downtown area, that could be considered a steal. She'd furnished the place lightly, the main piece of furniture being a fold-up pressed wood banquet table, the type you pulled out when you had company for Thanksgiving. She also had a large locking steel file cabinet, which had cost several times more than the table. There was a phone on the desk, and a recording machine hooked up to it. She'd had an alarm installed that had cost her more than three months' rent: MaryAnn was taking no chances, what she had in here was valuable. What she had in here was her freedom. The best part about the place was that she paid cash, the first of every month. No lease had been signed, the landlord held no paper on her that proved she rented here. She could pack up and be gone, be out of there in a matter of an hour if she had to.

There was a motel a block-and-a-half away, on 13th and Michigan, that had underground parking with an armed security guard. The price was seventy a month. Worth it, even if she couldn't use it as a tax write-off. She wouldn't have to worry about leaving the car out there at night, on Wabash, next to a parking meter, an invitation for a joyride. So when she was in here she was safe, virtually anonymous. The only trouble she ever had was with some of the punks upstairs at the South Loop Youth Center, which owned the top two floors, fighting in the hallway and cursing loudly on their way down the stairs. MaryAnn stuck to the elevator, and never answered her door when someone knocked on it at night. Another problem, more immediate, was the fact that the old radiator under the pulley-wheeled window was ice cold.

She was looking over a file, checking out this guy, Morer, her coat on against the chill, waiting for a phone call that could change his life for him, maybe give him hope.

Next to the checked box that said he was divorced, was another little box, a next of kin thing, asking for the name and address of your closest living relative. Morer had written down the name and address of a woman named Diane Morer, and in the area where you described your relationship, he'd written in WIFE.

All she could deduce was that he'd made a mistake, checked the wrong box at the start, DIVORCED instead of MARRIED. The home address was different, too, his in South Chicago instead of in Hegewisch, where his WIFE lived. Other than that, he seemed perfect, and you could expect a man to make some mistakes, Christ, when he had lung cancer. There'd been a time when she'd seen forty-eight to be ancient. Now it was about fifteen years younger than she defined ancient to be. Too young to die, certainly. She thought that she herself would live forever.

She knew the area where Ben's wife was living, knew the area well. Knew, too, that there were no apartments on that block. The woman would own the house, or else she might be renting it.

She wondered now if she was wasting her time with this customer. If they were separated, or if they were in the process of divorce, the woman might well not want to sell the house. She might be so bitter that she'd die before selling the property.

Then again, to get her piece of it, all she had to do was get the dying man to sign a quitclaim deed, assigning MaryAnn whatever rights he might have in the house. If the wife didn't want to sell, then the widow and MaryAnn would own the house, jointly. After the man passed away. When the city camc calling, handing money out all over the Hegewisch neighborhood.

That would be fine, if it had to happen, she could live with that. But she'd prefer not to let it happen, would prefer to own all the rights to the house all by herself. Or, rather, her trust would own it, over at the bank.

There were fifty-three properties in there already, sitting patiently, waiting for the city to make its move. They'd start buying those houses up within the next two months, and MaryAnn would sell them all of the property that she'd acquired, making a tremendous profit, profits so large that she could walk away forever. *After* she liquidated the real estate business. She'd let Walter keep his precious money, the divorce wouldn't cost him a cent. But she'd insist on keeping everything from the liquidation of the corporation; that was her baby, she'd created it, mothered it, strengthened it into a powerhouse.

One year from today MaryAnn could drive away from Chicago with a million dollars free and clear, to use to start over somewhere, anywhere else. If that bastard Walter wasn't in the office every day, she could do this work during office hours. God, she couldn't wait until she could walk out of his life forever.

The phone rang, and MaryAnn jumped, in her little straight-back chair. She reached out for it before it could ring again, as if it were liable to wake somebody in the building up.

'Yes.'

'MaryAnn.' It was her computer wizard and party partner, Alfredo.

'Yes, Alfredo, what did you come up with?'

'Hall of Records has nothing on him. No property ever bought or sold, zilch.'

'Shit!'

'*But* . . .'

'What, Alfredo, don't fool around with me.'

'If I gave you some good news, how grateful would you be?'

She could picture him, his tie and suspenders still on, large round frameless glasses pushed up well into his full head of black, slicked-back hair. At twenty-seven Alfredo

Garcia had more money than Walter had ever dreamed of, and he knew what to do with it, too. Which was to use it to make even more. He could get into anything, any file on computer record. He'd shown her that was true by giving her a glimpse one night of the Pentagon top-secret security file on Oliver North.

But he had the habit of fooling around too much – a rich young man who had the philosophy that it wasn't worth doing if you couldn't have fun doing it.

'Come on, tell me.' He was wheedling, acting like a child.

MaryAnn sighed. There was no use in arguing with him when he got like this; you had to play along or he'd hang up the phone and make you beg, later, when curiosity overwhelmed you.

She said, in a seductive voice, 'Well, it all depends on what you have . . . I could be talked into a lot of things if the information was good enough.'

'Oh, it's good. You'd want this real bad.'

'Is it about this Morer guy?'

'You're getting warm.'

'If you found out he has a secret bank account somewhere, with millions in it, it'll do me no good.'

'He has no bank account, no credit rating, he only filed income taxes once in his entire life. The guy seems to be a complete bum. Probably a drunk or a junkie. I can run an FBI records check, if you want me to. There's a seven-year-old Cadillac registered in his name, it's all that he seems to own in the world. He didn't even get a social security card until he was thirty.'

'Then what good is he to me?' She wasn't kidding around now.

'Ah, the bitch is back. Wait, I'll give you a hint. Someone very close to him owns some property.'

'The *wife*.'

'Ex-wife. She filed for and received a divorce five years ago.'

'Still does me no good.'

'Maybe not. Did you ever think that they still might love

each other? That she still might look out for him, and vice versa?'

'Alfredo, I don't have time to waste on ifs or maybes, all right? You want a blow job? Run on down here, it'll be good to see you again. You want telephone sex, call a one-nine-hundred number and get it from Jessica Hahn. I'm too busy to play around with your speculation.'

'Well, now, wait a minute, don't go getting all excited. I *told* you there's good news. Let me give you another hint. The wife? Diane Morer? She has more than one property in your target area.'

'Really?' MaryAnn was interested again.

'*And*,' Alfredo said, 'she's had an insurance policy on his life for eighteen years. Ten grand, enough to bury him. With herself as the beneficiary. Paid up for a full year again just last week.'

'She's divorced and she's paying for his life insurance?'

'Enough to bury him, like I said.'

'He's a veteran, right?'

'Dishonorable discharge in sixty-eight. He'd have no benefits from them, no hospitalization, no burial funds.'

'And she keeps the policy paid up.'

'Doesn't sound like a bitter woman who wants the bastard dead, does it?'

'Well, it's worth a shot . . .'

'And remember, she's doing all right. I can tell you all about her, what she does for a living, how much she makes.'

'And how much property she owns.'

'Third and last hint. She obviously doesn't believe in banks. Likes real estate, like Bob Hope.'

'And me. How much property does she own?'

'How grateful would you be to hear it? What would you do if I made your day?'

MaryAnn hid her impatience, and began talking into the phone, telling this greaser son of a bitch just what exactly she'd be willing to do to him if he gave her information that would be of use to her.

Diane sat in her bedroom, trying to read, giving him time to make up his mind. In the back of her mind was half an idea, almost a hope that he'd come in here, into the bedroom they'd once shared.

She might even be able to handle him now. She had his respect, his affection, maybe even his love. The things she'd wanted so desperately back then, and which were now coming her way due to the fact that she'd kicked him out.

Was she the crazy one, wanting to sleep with him? It had been a long time for her between encounters, sure, what with the diseases and all, and the quality of men out there in the world. But she had a nearly full box of Trojans hidden on her closet shelf. Even though the doctor had said nothing about Ben carrying any viruses, she'd still make him wear one, if he came in here, if he wanted her.

She'd spent thirteen years intimidated by him, then another two nearly hating him. The past three years had been mostly neutral; when she thought about him at all, it was with sadness at the way that he had destroyed his life, destroyed what they could have had.

But now things were different. Now he was a lonely man who had nothing, who had no one. No one to love. No one who loved him.

The same as her.

The thought popped into her mind unbidden, with the force of a hard slap in the face. Was that the way she saw herself, was that the way she was? She had the kids, damnit. They loved her with all their hearts.

But they were still kids, would go out into the world too soon as it was. In four short years they'd both be in college, and after that, who knew? Marriage, perhaps, or even if they stayed single, they'd want to be out on their own. They certainly wouldn't want to come back home and live with their mother.

My God, was she that miserable in her life, was she that lonely, that she could even compare herself to him? Yet what did she have, who loved her and needed her? The men who'd passed through her life had been, for the most part, arrogant and pushy. Gentlemen in the beginning, until they thought that they knew her well enough. Then the orders would begin, get me this, hand me that, sometimes they'd even try to tell the kids what to do. Men today, in her age bracket, seemed to have an expertise at seeking your vulnerable spots, then trying to exploit them.

Then, inevitably, after the first or second date, they'd call and want to talk about their 'relationship'. How they really believed that adults today should be physically involved early on in a relationship. Trying to talk her into the sack before she even knew when their birthdays were.

None of those people could carry Ben's jockstrap, when it came to being a man. Which he was, through and through, once you got past the violence.

There was a goodness about him, that sense of right and wrong. Ben never spent time staring at walls, angst wasn't in his vocabulary. He'd been so *alive*, so full of life, that if he had only toned it down a little, only stopped destroying things in the house – including her mind – she would have stayed with him forever, just hoping that some of it would rub off on her.

He always smelled of tobacco, and although she'd never smoked, she'd been attracted to it, to that scent. The smell was somehow manly, in the wool of his coat or on his sport jacket, mingled with the smell of his cologne. And when he stepped into a room – a bar or a restaurant – filled with strangers, other men would look at him with barely concealed jealousy. He was so solid, so handsome, so totally sure of himself. His sense of self radiated off him, attracted people to him. He had a way of making everyone around him feel safe, as long as they did nothing to anger him, which nearly everyone usually did, sooner or later.

If only he hadn't been so physically savage, didn't equate manhood with brutal acts of violence.

But he didn't, not anymore. Now he was dying and he had to be afraid. And he was alone, just like her.

She'd read in a book once that people with missing parts always recognized each other. Thought now that that might indeed be true. The man she'd been with that morning, the man downstairs right now, was the man that she'd thought she'd married eighteen long years ago.

But was that true, was he really that man? She'd just been thinking about phonies, about men who said one thing and did another. She had evidence of Ben's shortcomings, memories that still hurt her. As John had said, there were still the nightmares. Things that had to be worked through somehow.

Could they work them out? Diane didn't know. But she was willing to find out, if Ben was, too. And it would be as equals this time, the two of them starting afresh. She could sell those damn houses before the city government gave her half of what they were worth for them. She could dump them and take the money and get Ben the help he needed.

But only if he was willing to change, only if he'd change his life. Which he seemed to have made a start on already, by even being willing to think about changing.

Twenty years ago, ten, even five years back, it would have been a joke to him, being asked to change his life.

But that had been before he'd learned that his life was about to end. It had to change you, facing sure extinction. She thought that no human being who didn't have a terminal illness could completely understand how it felt. But there were small hints that he had given her, glimpses into his soul. If she couldn't ever really know what it was truly like, she might somehow be able to come close, if he'd show her more. Wouldn't it be nice if everyone got their Biblical allotment, three score and ten? Then you could plan ahead, then you could truly put your affairs in order.

Or maybe not. If humans knew the date of their deaths, she thought, a great many of them would do as they pleased right up until the very last minute, then they'd be on their knees, begging for forgiveness. If there was a God, not knowing when you were going to die might be the only edge He had over the seductions of the devil. And it was an edge that didn't seem to be holding up much anymore.

She had seen the pain in his eyes as she spoke, Ben the realist, hearing about miracles and no longer having the freedom to reject them out of hand as the dreams and wishes of children and the weak. He needed one and she could help to give that miracle to him, if he was willing to try and do something positive with what would be left of his life.

Because she was definite about one thing. There was a lot of uncertainty in her mind right now, plenty of self-doubt as to what she was doing with him, but there was indeed one thing that she intended to be absolutely rigid about: he could change his ways and have hope for a few more years, or he could die in six months; the choice would be up to him.

She looked down at the Kubler-Ross book in her lap and shook her head in sadness, thinking that Ben was unique, so different from the pack. There were stages to terminal illnesses, Kubler-Ross believed, that patients went through during their journey from diagnosis to death.

Denial and Isolation was the first one. Ben had never denied anything in his life, in fact, he had thought that he'd die much sooner than he had. Death, to Ben, had been a part of the game, and she couldn't count the times that he'd told her that the things he was doing, he was doing for her. For her and the kids, for when he wasn't there anymore. Back then she had thought that he was just being overly dramatic, but now she thought differently, now she believed that he'd been prepared for his death for a very long time, maybe even since he'd been a little kid.

And she'd sat in the doctor's office with him, had watched him as the man gave Ben the bad news. Ben hadn't denied a damn thing. Even now, the only thing he seemed willing to deny was the fact that the doctor might have been wrong in his prognosis. He had looked at it realistically, had suspected it and had really only had his suspicions fulfilled by Doctor Evan.

As for Isolation, what was the first thing Ben had done? He'd near begged her to go out with him, so he wouldn't be alone. And there he'd been that evening, sitting outside the house they'd once lived in together, as if drawing strength from the brick. Ben wasn't the type to hide, not from anything besides the law.

The second stage was Anger, and, until she'd read it, that had thrown her off. He lived with anger as his best friend, Ben's anger being perhaps the driving force behind his life. But that was anger at life, and the book discussed Anger at the disease. The patient felt angry because his body had failed him, wanted someone else to have it; why *me*?

Ben wouldn't consider that. If he wanted someone to die, there were other ways for him to achieve that goal.

The third stage was Bargaining, and Ben would never do that. She'd asked him once if he'd ever talked to God, ever turned to Him during a prison sentence, wanting freedom in exchange for a promise to lead a different life. Ben had looked at her and laughed at her for even bringing up such silliness. He was the type of man who had refused even to go before the parole board. He said that he'd rather stay inside than have to kiss anyone's ass.

He was not the type to make private deals with God; in fact, it was *Diane* who was trying to make a deal. Change your life and I'll help you. Don't and I'll let you die. Playing God and offering him a deal. She thought he might know enough about plea bargaining to cut a good deal when he saw one.

But not with God, and not with any doctor. Diane had read in the paper a few years ago about a local boy, who'd been dying of cancer, whose only wish had been to graduate with his high school class. He'd made it, against all possible medical explanation, accepted his diploma, then had gone home and died that night.

There was nothing that Ben would want to do that badly. Nothing on heaven or earth that could make him seek such a deal. Diane's only prayer was that he'd been so lonely that he'd bargain with her, maybe being smart enough to know that her love and understanding came along with the deal.

The fourth stage was Depression, and that, to Ben, was a joke. He didn't believe in it, had always lived for the second, saw depression as the whining of the lazy middle class. His favorite expression, years ago, had been 'Life is too short', and she'd never seen him actively throw away a second.

Even prison hadn't depressed Ben; he'd spent his time working out and writing short letters to the boys. 'One day at a time', the letters had always ended, just above his signature, Ben signing off with the only way that he could ever do time and come out of it with his sanity.

He wouldn't be depressed about this, either. How depressed could you be when your game plan was already laid out in your mind? She'd never known him to show self-pity, ever. There was a time when she'd thought that that was due to his lack of character, but now she wasn't so sure, now she might even be seeing him as some sort of twisted champion.

Was his complete lack of depression due to his limited imagination, to the fact that he couldn't see beyond the nose on his face?

Dear God, Diane was the one who was getting depressed. But not Ben, he'd learned the news and gone right to the final stage, something he'd been practicing since the day that they'd first met.

Acceptance.

He accepted everything, Ben did. Usually after beating himself over the head with a hammer until he figured out that he couldn't break it, that it was harder than his skull.

Ben would pound someone into the ground, thinking that would change them. Do it again and again, and twice that she'd known about, he'd even committed murder. Maybe three times, if the person who'd called her that morning had suddenly committed 'suicide'. Sooner or later, though, no matter what he was raging at, Ben would shrug his shoulders and walk away, and she'd hear him mutter, 'Fuck it.'

As good an example of acceptance as you were ever liable to get. There was another explanation, though, one that frightened Diane to consider.

Maybe he *wanted* to die. Maybe Ben was looking forward to it. He didn't believe in God, or in heaven or hell or any other kind of afterlife. Death to Ben would simply be an absence of life, a sleep that never ended. And when you were sleeping, there was no pain. If you were lucky. Was he suffering that badly. Was his emotional make-up so warped that he could view death as being preferable to life? That would explain his sudden gentleness. That would explain a lot of things, perhaps even the way he'd lived his life. He might have spent all these years seeing death, and now he was just getting his wish. That might be the answer, Diane thought, because otherwise, without doubt, the famous Morer rage would have been exhibited by now.

This cancer, what had happened, he hadn't raged at it from the start, unless he'd done it at home, somewhere away from Diane. Maybe because he'd been expecting it, because he'd always seen his life as having very little value. Diane didn't know, but she did know that he was now, suddenly, relatively calm. Wanting only to make amends with her and the kids before he went on to whatever there was after life.

Would he accept her bargain? Would he decide to take a chance at life? She'd know soon enough, it sounded as if he had made up his mind.

She could hear his footfalls on the staircase, Ben coming up softly, trying not to make any noise, not wanting to wake up the kids.

MaryAnn looked at her watch, and was shocked to see that it was a quarter past midnight. She'd seemed to have been speaking on the phone much longer than that. That damned Alfredo. He would lapse into Spanish when he got sexually excited, forget his flawless English and spoil all the fun for her. Well, half the fun. MaryAnn had to admit, she liked hearing the curse words, they really turned her on. But they didn't do much for her if she couldn't understand them.

She had another call to make, though, before she could head home to her loving husband Walter. And the guy she called was going to be angry. He was close to Alfredo, almost as close to him as MaryAnn was, but in temperament they were as far apart as two people could possibly be.

James would have been in bed since nine, so he could be up before dawn to run his five miles along the lakefront. Then he'd catch a quick weight workout at his health club, and a steam sauna before he'd go and have breakfast somewhere to fuel him through his power morning – attending closings and accepting checks from people who would be incredibly grateful for the little things he'd spotted, the changes he'd make in contracts that would save them thousands of dollars down the road. His practice wasn't restricted to real estate – plenty of money came his way through lawsuits against insurance companies – but it was quickly becoming the bulk of his income.

James was a lawyer, and it was MaryAnn's belief that if he had decided to specialize in criminal defense he could have been a multimillionaire before he'd turned thirty. He had those looks, that full head of thick, gleaming brown hair, those straight white teeth, those high, insolent cheekbones. James had innocent eyes; more often than not they'd be wide open, guileless. Juries would fall in love with him, with his innocent appearance, with his quick self-deprecating smile. He'd surprise you, when you learned what a cold and cruel man he could be. Enjoyed being, in fact.

She couldn't get him into bed. He was the one man she'd ever met who seemed totally uninterested in her, and that fact made her insecure around him. He had a girlfriend who lived somewhere on the North Side, also an attorney, who didn't want to move in with him, who liked having her independence. He'd mentioned that they had a monogamous, intense relationship, which had made MaryAnn set her sights on him with increased vigor, but to no avail; the man simply wasn't interested.

Which was why she had an anxiety attack about picking up the phone and calling him. She could call Alfredo, Mute, even Walter, among others, and not feel the least concern about waking them up in the middle of the night. But James, you never knew how he was going to act. She'd never had him in bed. She'd never had any control over him.

She dialed his number before she changed her mind and decided to wait until morning. She did not want to call him from the real estate office, ever. And also, if he didn't get mad at her, he could have the information she needed before MaryAnn even got into the office tomorrow.

He picked it up on the first ring, the way he always did at night, and when he said hello he sounded awake, clear-headed and alert, which didn't mean anything; James was more alert in his sleep than most men were at their daytime peak.

She said, 'James?'

'Yes, MaryAnn.'

'Uh – did I wake you?'

'What do you want?'

'I've got a subject with four properties, all supposedly completely unencumbered. At least there're no liens or second mortgages on them.'

'Give me the owner's name and the address, I'll double-check first thing in the morning.'

She did, wondering why his voice had no inflection. You could never tell how he felt about anything until he blew up at you. She didn't think he would, though. He hadn't yet, and he was so very smart he'd see the importance of this call, how much MaryAnn stood to make.

He said, 'That's all four. You ran this by Alfredo, of course.'

'Naturally.'

'I can't be too sure. You two mix business with pleasure so much, who could tell when you're going to let it interfere? You get mad at him, he gets mad at you . . .'

'We're both professionals.'

'If you were professionals you wouldn't be fucking each other. I'll have the title searches done by noon. You thinking quitclaim?'

'If she'll go for it.'

'We can get a warranty deed, if the deal's cash, and close by tomorrow night if the seller's ready.'

'You can do all four *that* fast?' He did not respond, and she knew she'd made a mistake, questioning his proficiency.

In order to cover her error, she said, quickly, 'Maybe we'll close the day after, I'm not sure, with this client. She's not even a client yet, and won't be until I'm sure of her resources.'

'Let me know,' James said, and then she heard the soft click as he disconnected the line.

'Jeez.' MaryAnn sat in silence for a moment, thinking, then got up quickly and took the Morer file over to the drawer, locked it up inside, pulled on the drawer to make sure that she'd locked it properly. She set the alarm and walked out the door, pulling it shut behind her.

Ben tapped lightly on the doorframe and looked in, saw her lying there, her eyes on the book now, illuminated by the glow from the bedside lamp. Diane looked up at him, her face betraying her hope. The second she saw him, though, she knew that her bargain had been rejected. He was wearing his overcoat now, and there was a large bulge in the right-hand pocket.

'Come on in,' Diane whispered. 'Close the door behind you.'

'You want to just come downstairs?' Ben seemed uncomfortable. Good. She did not want him in his element right now, it would be one more thing she had going in her favor.

'No, come on in,' Diane said, sadness evident in her voice.

Ben did so, his face unreadable. He walked over to the side of the bed and sat down on the edge, lowering himself gently. He acted as if a hand grenade would go off if he sat his full weight down upon it. Ben smiled, almost as if he was embarrassed.

'I feel like I would walking into a church.'

'That ain't no altar you're sitting on, and it *sure* ain't no virgin on it.'

He looked at her, shocked, then realized it was a joke, and his smile grew slightly broader. To hell with him, with his simple-minded morality. She'd bet this house that he'd been thinking that that wasn't the sort of thing that a lady would say.

Ben said, 'Diane, I want you to know that I didn't take what you said lightly. Downstairs, when you were talking, you thought I was making fun of you when I was smiling, but

I wasn't. I was smiling because I was so happy that you still cared that much about me.

'I figured, right from the beginning, that you might be decent to me, just out of kindness. You always were sweet, sweeter than anyone *I* ever knew. And, I don't know, maybe because I always sent a little something for the kids. But I didn't expect you to offer something like this, wanting to do that much for me.'

'For *us*, Ben. For you and the kids, but for me, too.' She hated the way she sounded, as if she was begging, god*damn*it! But she couldn't help herself, she could just not watch him waste away and die without doing anything about it.

She said, 'Ben, they deserve the chance to get to know their father, as he really is, instead of just the mask you always showed everybody.'

'That mask was *me*, Diane. Yeah, I was a lot of bad things, but I was never a mooch, never a leach. You know what I was feeling down there, you want to know my *feelings*?'

He had raised his voice slightly, Ben upset, his temper getting the best of him. He looked toward the door and compressed his lips tightly, shook his head in frustration at his own loss of composure. She imagined he had sworn to himself that he wouldn't cause them any more grief, that the kids would never again awaken to the sound of his voice, shouting.

Ben said, 'All I could feel was *depressed*, Diane. Sad because I had you and didn't know, didn't even *look* at what you were. All I could see you as back then was my wife, there to protect, to take care of.'

'So? You did that, when you weren't in jail.'

She hadn't said it in an accusatory manner, but Ben had to look up quickly, to assure himself that she wasn't making fun of him. When he spoke now his voice was tinged with awe, as if he had just this second understood that he'd been wrong all these years.

'I left, and you went on, built up what you have, shit, I sat down there thinking about that, wondering what you did, how you could have possibly put that much money together.

I never looked into anything, I didn't pry. I knew you had a cleaning business, but I didn't know what it *did*. I thought the five hundred every week would help you make ends meet.'

'I put it into an account every week for the boys. For their college.'

'Diane, I left you with nothing, no skills, just this house. I always believed that if you ever really needed anything, you or the boys, that you'd come to me. And I would have helped you. Now here you are, after I've been gone five years, going to do that for me, willing to give up everything you've worked for, just so I can have a year or two more.'

'I've built it up once, I can build it up again.'

'I won't let you do that.'

Diane found herself slamming her fists into the mattress. *'You can't fucking stop me, Ben!'*

Diane paused, shocked at herself, surprised that she'd spoken so forcefully, with such anger. But it was true, he *couldn't* stop her anymore, from doing anything that she chose to do. And he had to learn that, had to realize that she was no longer under his power.

'I can't stop you from doing what you want, you're right. But I can stop you from doing anything for me. I won't accept your help. I won't let you destroy the kids' future, and yours. If I'd been here, if we'd been married, Diane, I'd *expect* it from you. It's what people who love each other do for each other. But I won't take what you have, because I was never here for you.'

'What would *you* do, Ben, if it was *me* who had the disease?'

'Heaven and earth, I'd move,' Ben said, without even pausing to consider it. There was a sincerity in his voice that was impossible to disbelieve.

'But there's a difference, Diane, between you and me.'

Diane glared at him. How *dare* he! She spat out the word: 'What?'

Ben's eyes softened, and he looked, as he spoke, ineffably sad.

He said, 'You were always there for me, always. Right from the beginning, Diane, and right up until the day you couldn't take it anymore. Until the day I almost killed you. You said it yourself, I remember it like it was yesterday. "You're killing me!" is what you said, and I knew you were right. I knew I had to get out. You were always there for me, and I wasn't smart enough to figure it out, wasn't smart enough to be there for you.' Ben grunted.

'If you got cancer, hell, even now, I'd find the best surgeon in the world, stick a gun in his face and drive him here in the trunk of my car.' He smiled. 'Set up a surgery in your basement, and if he didn't fix you, I'd shoot his mother.'

'That's the way you operate, Ben. And this is the way I operate. The only way I can. I can help. Let me help you.'

'I don't deserve your help. I haven't earned anything from you but your hate.

'I don't hate you, Ben, I love you.'

'Don't say that!' It was as if she'd slapped him. Ben's face twisted and he turned it away from her.

'Don't say that to me!'

'Why, because nobody is allowed, Ben, my God, what's *wrong* with you? You're *dying*, you have *cancer*, Ben, and you're telling me that I'm not allowed to love you?'

'Diane, please, stop.'

'Give me a reason to.'

'You want a reason? I'll give you a reason. These past five years, Diane, what do you think I've done? I've got that second jolt behind me, I lost a lot of ground while I was inside. I'd do things, sometimes, make a major score, but I'd lost some of the respect, the *fear* that I used to command. Other people moved in, Diane, guys who'd put your fingers over a stove and hold them there while you screamed, then eat them.'

'I don't want to hear this . . .'

'You're gonna hear it, you asked for a reason.'

'I didn't ask to hear about the psychotics out there.'

'Because you don't want to believe they're there doesn't make you safe! They're out there, Diane, and I had to live with them. I had to deal with them and if I was going to survive, I had to be just as bad as them, I had to be even worse.'

'Ben, please.'

'Ben, please, my ass. You want to know what I thought about, to take that away? Those thoughts of what I'd done, some of the things I'd seen? I'd drink, Diane, and I'd lay in bed, and I'd imagine you saying those words to me. Lay there and pretend that you forgave me and I had a job and things were different and I never scared you, never hurt you. My girlfriend came in once and looked at me, and she thought I was on dope, she said I looked too happy to be straight.' Ben looked away, remembering.

'She interrupted me, and I'd been thinking of you, and then I looked at her. It was the closest I've ever come to hitting a woman in my life.'

Diane felt the tears behind her eyes, and she fought them. Emotion would not work with Ben, he would not even be aware that he was expressing emotion himself right now. Logic could win him over, logic and profit, and there was a profit in this for him, if he'd ever just open his eyes.

'Ben, I love you.'

'Don't!' He shook his head, looked down at the bed, away from her.

Diane reached over and slapped him hard, across the side of his face, and it hurt her hand. He turned his head to her, quickly, unbelieving at first, and then he transformed, his face changed, and Diane saw what she imagined an exorcist might upon entering the rooms of the possessed.

She watched him battle with himself as he stood there, staring down at her. His hands were fists, and he was breathing hard, his tongue between his teeth, Ben biting it, trying hard not to hit her. She glared right back at him, got out of the bed, standing right up to him.

She slapped him again, on the other cheek.

'Jesus *Christ*!' He didn't say it loud, but he said it with meaning.

Then he did something she never thought she'd see Ben

Morer do. He backed up, away from her, opening his hands, forcing them down to his sides.

'You want to hit me? Go ahead.' He sounded defeated, totally exhausted. 'Go ahead, Diane, I got it coming.' He lowered his head and shook it, slowly, back and forth, twice.

'I'm so fucking tired of fighting,' Ben said, in a voice so soft she had to lean forward to hear him.

'I don't want to fight you, Ben.' Diane walked slowly over to him, grabbed his arms, held him there, looking up at him. 'I want to love you. And you can't stop me. I know you love me, too, and that you've already changed, or you'd have killed me just then when I slapped you. I could see that you wanted to.'

'No – '

'Yes, you did.'

She looked into Ben's eyes and saw despair inside them, deep. Stood looking into the eyes of a man who had absolutely no doubt that he'd burn in hell forever.

'I love you, Ben, and I want to help you. I *can* help you, and you're going to have to let me help you.'

'*Why*, Diane, what in the name of Christ would make you want to help me?'

'Because you weren't the only one who lay in bed, imagining things,' Diane said. She squeezed his arms a little, and he shook his head again, he didn't understand.

'I spent years adoring you, Ben, wanting to please you, wanting to serve you, wanting to make you happy. I got lost inside of you, got too wrapped up in there, in what you were. But after a while away from you, I'd think about us, together, you coming back and seeing what I was, finding out what I really was as a person.' She laughed a little, without mirth.

'I'd see you slap yourself in the head, and realize what a fool you'd been. See you leave that foolish life, and come live with us again, working with me, not for me. I pictured the four of us at Bears games, at Bulls games, baseball in the summer.

'We can *have* that, Ben, at least for a while.'

'All I wanted was to say goodbye right, to see the kids, to have you guys not hate me.'

'Well, I guess you got the bonus plan, buddy, because that's not the way we are. People who love each other look out for each other, Ben, you said it yourself. You told me about the past, how you knew you messed it up, but did you ever think of a future? Did you ever see a future for yourself? You can't have what you wanted, not without hard work.'

Diane let go of him, but stood looking right at him. Her gaze was unwavering, Diane standing tall.

'Now, I'll ask you again, and I have to have the truth; I can't take any more of this, at least not tonight. Will you let me help you? Will you give up what you are and try and live what you have left in some kind of goddamned peace?'

Ben said, 'There aren't a lot of opportunities, in my line of work, for guys with one lung, Diane.'

'What are you saying?'

He took a deep breath, reached up and wiped at his eyes. She knew what he'd been saying, but she had to hear the words, had to listen to him speak them. Because if he did, she'd hold him to them, from now until the day that he died. But it wouldn't be easy for him, asking for help. He was hesitating already, looking at her, torn between walking out and taking her into his arms. When he opened his mouth to speak, Diane had to restrain herself from stopping him, from putting her hand over his mouth. It seemed obvious to her that he was going to turn her down.

Ben said, 'I want you to help me. I want to try and live.'

'Thank God.'

Diane moved in close and hugged him, held him to her, felt his arms go around her back, those strong arms squeezing her. Christ, it had been so long. She had the urge to break the moment by saying something flippant, something he'd respond to, and then they could go to bed. But she didn't, couldn't bring herself to do it. This moment was so special, so beautiful, that she'd wait.

Instead, Diane said, 'Let's go down by the fire now, Ben.

You smoke your last cigarette while the log burns down.'

'My what?'

'You heard me, you have to quit. And tomorrow, I'll look into where we can get you, what treatment center will be best suited for what you have. And we get you on the vitamins right away, the beta carotene, massive doses of C. Niacin and the others, they were in the books. Until you leave for the hospital, you eat right, you live right, and you're through with tobacco.'

'What if the doctors say it's too late, what if they can't do anything for me?'

'Then we get you into a hospice, where you can be allowed to live in dignity.'

'You'll be with me, you and the boys?'

Diane pushed back and looked up at him, saw the longing there on his face, Ben Morer finally admitting that he needed someone other than himself.

'You bet your ass we'll be there for you, Ben, all the way.'

And wasn't it amazing, what you could learn about people you'd known most of your life? Ben stepped into her, hugged her close, and she literally *felt* the burden lifting from him, his past flying off his shoulders.

'Thank you,' Ben whispered. 'Thank you, Diane.' She held him, felt his body shaking, heaving violently. Ben was crying.

'Wha – what the hell have I *done*?'

Diane shushed him, rubbing his back, her head up against his powerful chest. She could hear the wheeze in there, a freight train running inside him.

'Don't think about what you've done, Ben, think about what you're going to do. What *we're* going to do, you and me and Benny and John.'

After a minute, he could pull away, his face looking so relieved, so *normal* for once – Ben looking like a regular man for the first time since she'd known him. A man with weaknesses as well as strength, with as many doubts as certainties. A man who could cry as well as laugh, and love as well as hate.

Ben sniffed, reached into his pocket, and Diane's heart leaped into her throat; was he going to shoot her?

He pulled out a vinyl bag with a zipper across the top. She could see a bank's name stenciled in fading ink across the side.

'I almost forgot.' He held the bag out to her, sniffed in hard, standing there with dignity. 'For the kids,' Ben said. 'This is for the kids.'

MaryAnn walked into the house as quietly as she could, through the front door, and stopped trying for stealth as soon as she saw that the kitchen light was on. For some reason she felt a shiver of fear. What was she afraid of? Hell, she had Walter figured out. Still, she did not want a confrontation, not this late at night, at least. She had to get some sleep, she hadn't been sleeping well at all these last few months.

'MaryAnn?' He was standing in the kitchen doorway, looking in at her. At least, thank God, he didn't appear to be drunk.

She kept walking toward the staircase, said, over her shoulder, 'Give it to me tomorrow, Walter, I'm too tired tonight.'

'I'll give it to you right now, MaryAnn. You come in here or you'll spend the rest of your life wishing that you had.' She was halfway up the staircase, in no mood for his threats. 'If you don't,' Walter said, 'there might not *be* any tomorrow for you.'

That stopped her. Was he threatening her life? No, he wasn't capable of that. Even though he had defended enough subhumans probably to qualify as one, he had never acquired their attitudes, as some defense lawyers had done. He hadn't assumed that because he defended tough guys, he automatically became one himself. Walter simply wasn't man enough to kill another human being. Still, what could he mean by a crack like that?

MaryAnn was hit with a quick second of panic. He'd found out about the other houses. That had to be it.

She was standing on a stair, one foot on the step above, frozen there, knowing that she'd have to move, one way or the other. Otherwise Walter would see her acting weak. She instinctively turned, fighting the panic, and sneered down at him.

'Are you *threatening* me, Walter?'

'You bet your ass I'm threatening you.' Walter turned around and walked back into the kitchen, certain that she was going to come back down and follow him.

That act alone gave her the incentive she needed to go on up to her bedroom; who the hell did he think he was? Still, Walter was a lot of things, but she didn't think he was a bluffer, at least not anymore. His criminal conviction seemed to have taken that out of him, made him meek, not a player anymore, as he'd once been. He had something, or he wouldn't dare try to pull a power play like this.

MaryAnn walked slowly down the stairs, and swaggered into the kitchen, the sneer still curling her lips. She leaned against the door jamb, her body language, her facial expression, everything about her telling him that to her he was nothing more than a joke.

'What.'

Walter was stone-cold sober, she could tell. There was a cup of tea in front of him on the table, beside a mountain of legal papers. Had someone told him about the stranger at the house that day? One of the neighbors with binoculars, a busybody looking through the kitchen window and seeing that big ugly mutt drinking coffee at her table? Or was it something else? He was sure taking his time answering her.

At last, Walter said, 'We made a pot of money this year, MaryAnn, at Ceterra Realty.'

'*I* made a pot of money. You sat on your ass and collected your percentage.'

'I put up one hundred percent of the money, my percentage's more than fair.'

'What's your point, Walter? I'm tired.'

'Late *showing* tonight? Or were you out *listing*?' The way he spoke the words left little doubt as to what he thought she'd been out doing. He took the most common words in the real estate profession and somehow twisted them until they sounded obscene.

Walter said. 'You know, it's amazing, the reputation you have, after such a short time in the business. The things people say!'

'Walter, fuck them. They're jealous little shits. Who's telling you things, your ex-colleagues? Your *male* ex-colleagues? There's no successful woman in business today who doesn't get accused of blowing her way to the top. Give me a break.'

'Oh, the rumors aren't from *outside* the company, the rumors are within, coming from your own hand-picked staff.'

'Bullshit.'

'I don't think it is.'

'Walter, think what you want.'

MaryAnn began to walk out of the room, when Walter slammed his hand down on the table. She turned, shocked, smiling at him, making fun of him. Was he weaker than she'd expected, was Walter secretly insecure? Wouldn't *that* be a surprise. She might have given him more credit than he deserved, might have misjudged him. Oh, did she hope that she had. She wanted to own him more than any man she'd ever met.

'Oh, we have a temper, do we? Mr anal retentive himself, losing control over whispered rumors or things he read while locked in a shithouse stall. You've had too much tea, Walter. You're overdosing on caffeine.'

He was staring at her harshly, hatefully.

'And I'm tired of your snide little comments, your attempts at emasculating me.'

'Not a possibility. First, you'd have to have balls.'

'You *bitch*.'

'Why, thank you, Walter, good night.'

'Stay right there.' For some reason, maybe the tone of his voice, MaryAnn took what he said seriously, and stood her ground, looking at him. He had something, Walter did, or he wouldn't be so imperious.

'Where's the money?'

'What money?'

'I'm legally entitled to half of everything that company brings in, half of all your profits. I've got a contract that spells that out in black and white.' Walter slapped his hand down on the pile of papers on the table.

'There's eleven million worth of deals closed this year. You want to come over here and look at the net profits for the company?'

'Walter, I don't have to. That's seven-hundred and seventy thou, gross. Don't forget that half of that goes to the agents who closed the sales. The business would have made three-eight-five.'

'One-fifty that I can account for.'

'Walter, there's salaries, there's lights, there's phone, rent and all sorts of other expenses. Not to mention that most of the houses we sold weren't listed by Ceterra agents. You have a problem with the books, talk to the accountants. I draw a salary.'

'*And* bonuses, *and* your own percentages from sales and listings.'

'Which are usually three and a half percent, figure it out. I don't generally sell my own listings, and I sell houses other agents listed. I don't do the goddamned books, either.'

'But that three-and-a-half should stay in the company, if the other agents from Ceterra sold it, right?'

'One seventy-five of it, Walter. Don't forget the salesperson's commission.'

'What I'm looking at here are seven-seventy in commissions going our way. You've been juggling this, and there's two-thirty-five that I can't find. Where is it, MaryAnn?'

'*I'm* not the one who's been convicted for juggling books, Walter. I can only assume that if there's a discrepancy, *you're* the one who would know where the money is.' That got him, she could see she'd struck a nerve.

'Why would I bring it up with you, why would I point it out to you, if I were robbing the company?'

'Who knows? Maybe the IRS is on to you, maybe the feds are auditing you again. If you're expecting me to break down and admit to embezzlement, if you're wearing a wire, you're out of your mind. I don't pay the salaries, I don't do the books. We have people to do that, and they're in the office all day, sitting on their asses, just like you. I draw my salary, and everything else I plow right back into the company.'

'That's a good thing, MaryAnn, because I'm going to talk to the accountants tomorrow. I'm going to find out where the money went. And I'm going to find out where it's been going since I started this business.'

'*I* started this business.'

'With my money, don't you ever forget that. And it looks as if some of my money is going somewhere other than in my pocket.'

It was time for some controlled outrage; she could see that he was wavering. Walter grasping at straws, looking for a reason to communicate with her, no matter how low he had to sink to do so. She could smell the fear coming off him, and she felt a surge of power. Fear could always be used. MaryAnn walked over to the table and leaned down over it, put her knuckles down on the wood and near shouted at Walter.

'I'm fucking well entitled to my commissions and my salary. My profit-sharing. If anything's missing, Walter, I'll find out. And if you're draining this company to try and scare me, for some kind of bullshit blackmail deal, then I'll end it all for you, Walter, this time you'll go to jail. And guess what, babycakes? If you do, *everything's* mine.'

She watched him closely as she spoke, and knew that she'd been wrong before; Walter *had* been bluffing. But something had made him think that she was doing outside business. He wouldn't dream up a stunt like this without some sort of prod, some hint that she was doing something that he didn't know about. What he had here before him was a first strike. He'd have some evidence from someone that would have made him suspicious, made him stick his neck out like this. She had to find out what that was, who had told him something, and what that person had known. But how could she do that? She'd have to play it be ear.

Walter had leaned back as she spoke to him, her forceful words slapping at him. Now he leaned forward again, breathing heavily, Walter disgusted.

'I have friends, you know. Not everyone abandoned me. Friends in the profession, friends on the police force. I know what you're doing, and I think I know how. Cuckolding me to get information on people.'

'*What*?'

'That's right. Using your fucking body to get what you want from people.'

MaryAnn grinned at him, immorally. She said, 'Cuckold you? Walter, you're a joke! Get it through your head, little man: I married you to use you. I never loved you, I never gave a shit about you one way or another. You were nothing more than a means to an end, and I was getting kind of old for what I was doing at the time. I took care of you and you took care of me, it was a marriage of convenience both ways, that's all it ever was.'

She saw him getting mad, the great, always composed Walter sitting there losing his cool. MaryAnn loved it. She leaned over even further, her face less than a foot from his now.

She said, 'You just hate it that I'm successful at something, don't you, Walter? All you wanted me to do was to lay on my back or be down on my knees. Those days are over now and you just can't stand to see that happen, can you? So you dig through papers, looking for evidence of my committing some crime you can hold over my head.'

MaryAnn reached out one hand and slapped the papers off the table, but Walter didn't grab at them as she'd expected, just kept glaring at her, maliciously.

'What would you do if you found one? You wouldn't even go to the police, I'd bet.' She was hissing at him now, telling him his secrets, letting Walter know that he wasn't nearly as smart as he thought he was, nor anywhere near as unique. MaryAnn was smirking at him, mocking him, watching him get more and more angry, getting excited at the sight of his loss of control.

'You'd use it to control me, to get me back into bed and down on my knees. Well I have news for you, Walter, that day won't ever come, not in this life! You want to know if I'm fucking other men? *You're goddamned right I am!* How do you like that, Walter? And let me tell you something else. Every damn one of them's better than you ever were. When I'm in bed with them, Walter, we talk about you, about what an uptight asshole you are –'

He hit her. Walter hadn't projected it, she'd barely seen it coming. One second she was leaning over, taunting him, enjoying herself, and the next second she saw his fist coming at her face with a speed she didn't think he was capable of.

The fist bounded off MaryAnn's cheek and she lost her hold on the table, fell face first down on to it, smacking her nose hard. She could smell Walter's spilled tea, trickling close to her face.

She felt hard, sudden dullness on her ears, the top of her head, and realized that he was hitting her, slapping her head down on to the table. MaryAnn reared up in rage and threw herself across the table at him, shrieking, but she wasn't strong enough, she'd misjudged him. He grabbed her and pulled her to the floor, held her down on the tiles, his left knee on her chest, his trunk turned away from her, so she couldn't grab his balls.

Walter was breathing in great heaves, his hands shaking, the tip of his tongue out of his mouth, his teeth clamped down on it. His eyes were wide and wild, his sparse hair disheveled. He brought both fists up, over his head, and MaryAnn looked up at him, and spat as hard as she could.

It hit him in the cheek, and he looked down at her beneath him, slowly reached one hand over and wiped at the spittle on his cheek, pulled his hand away and looked at it, strangely. In slow motion Walter moved his head downward, looked from his hand to his wife, then wiped the spit on his shirt. He fell off her, on to his ass, sat on the tiled floor and began to cry.

MaryAnn pushed herself away from him, scooting backwards on her ass, until her back hit the cabinets. She got to her feet, leaned against the counter. When her breathing and her fury were both under control, she looked over at him, down at her husband Walter.

He was sitting there whining and crying, his shoulders shaking, looking down at his hands.

'I – I – I'm sor – sor – '

'Save it, motherfucker,' MaryAnn said. 'Save your whining for your divorce lawyer.'

'No!' Walter looked up in terror, a totally broken man. She'd seen him before, had created more than a few. She looked down at him, at what was left of him, and knew that she had at long last won.

'No, don't leave. I'll do anything, MaryAnn, anything to keep you. I love you. I love you. You're all I have in this world.'

She laughed, wanting him to keep it up, not wanting this to stop. For the first time since she'd met him, she had him totally, completely in her power. And God, did it feel *good*.

'You want me to stay? Let's make a deal, Walter. I don't want any of your money, your house, nothing. What I want from you, Walter, is to be left the fuck alone.'

He was sitting there, surrounded by his precious papers, nodding his head up and down, agreeing with every word she spoke. She could push him further than Mute, she knew, and she'd pushed Mute pretty damn far. Good thing that Mute wasn't here right now. MaryAnn had told him that this sniveling, shattered, sorry excuse for a man was an outfit big shot. Fat chance of that.

She said, 'You stay out of that office, away from my real estate company. At the end of the year, we pull your investment, and the entire company goes into my name, everything in there. I'll pay you interest, but after the first of January, you're out, you got it?'

He was nodding his head up and down rapidly, his eyes wide, eager to please. It was getting better and better. She would not even have to leave Chicago.

'I want that in writing, Walter. You do that tomorrow, on your first day away from the company. Get a contract to that effect, and then we'll talk about other things.'

MaryAnn could barely see out of her left eye. The bastard, he'd tagged her a good one. Her ears were ringing where he'd slapped them. The top of her head felt sore. Still, she smiled. It was a small price to pay.

She said, 'Give me that, Walter, stay out of my business, make it mine, and I'll stay. I'll even sign a prenuptial agreement, what's yours is yours, what's mine is mine. Starting on the first of the year, neither of us can ever take what belongs to the other, how's that? I give up any interest in your assets, and the real estate company is totally mine.'

'That's fine with me, I'll do that, MaryAnn – '

'Tomorrow, you'll do that.'

Walter was mostly through crying now, just jerking every so often as a sob ripped through his body, making little hiccupping sounds. He was grinning like a puppy dog whose master was petting him behind his ears. MaryAnn was soaking wet down below.

'You do that, Walter, and there's even a reward in it for you.'

'You'll stay, that's all I'll ever need. MaryAnn, I need you, I always have – '

Magic to her ears. How could she not have seen it earlier? Jesus, she'd thought that he'd hated her. It just went to show how much anyone knew about anyone else. There'd be time to gloat later, after she cut him in two. For the moment, she had to get what she wanted, talk this man into doing her bidding.

'Another time, Walter. Don't you want to hear about your prize?'

'Yes, what's that?'

'You sign those contracts up, get them written, and Walter, twice a week, minimum, you can come into my bedroom.'

She saw his face light up, Walter so very appreciative, getting far more than he could ever have expected.

'But we play by *my* rules from now on, Walter. You'll do what you're told in there or you can get your ass out.'

'MaryAnn, I don't know what came over me. I don't believe I hit you.'

She would never tell him how much his hitting her had meant to her.

Instead, she started to walk out of the room, smiling broadly, the victor finally, after a decade-long battle. She wanted to scream, wanted to shout with joy, but she couldn't. She had him where she wanted him, and now she had to keep him guessing.

Over her shoulder, MaryAnn said, 'Make it up to me by getting those agreements together.'

'And you won't divorce me, you won't leave me?' The hope in his voice disgusted her.

'No, I won't, Walter,' MaryAnn said, and turned the corner, out of the kitchen.

Why would she ever have to divorce him now? It would be like divorcing a car, or a horse. You didn't divorce personal property, you got rid of it when it no longer suited your needs – that, or you had to put it to sleep.

She didn't tell Walter that, though, just went up the stairs to her bedroom, wanting to take a shower and wash the day off her.

She believed that he was smart enough to figure that out for himself. Then he'd do everything he possibly could to ensure that the day never came when she'd want to trade him in. Glowing, elated, MaryAnn stepped through the door of her bedroom and locked it firmly behind her. He'd get none of what she had to offer until the contracts were signed, and even then, she could withdraw her favors any time he displeased her. This was wonderful. Her life was now complete. The only thing that could make it better was to learn that this Morer woman was willing to sell her homes.

Ben awoke with a moment of horror, unsure of where he was. There were sounds and unconscious smells he'd always awaken to, things that made him realize that he was in his apartment, that he'd made it through another night: the woman down the hall cooking beans for her husband's lunch, car horns honking outside – things that were missing now. It was like this the first few weeks in the penitentiary, Ben jumpy, waking up with dread. It took a while to get used to things, to assimilate yourself to your new home.

This wasn't prison, though, this was Diane's house. *His* house, the house he'd paid for. Bought for them years ago, and look how well she'd kept it up.

Ben rolled out of bed silently, knowing that he was alone, noticing that the bedroom door was shut. Thank God. He didn't want the kids to see him, would be ashamed if he were caught in their mother's bed. He hadn't spoken to them in five years, and he didn't want that sort of awkwardness to screw things up right away.

Ben felt a spasm in his stomach and ran for the private bathroom, barely made it to the toilet. He fell to his knees and retched up only bitter bile and blood, bright red, little floating octopuses, their tentacles trailing underneath them. He fell back against the tub, eyes shut tight, panting hard. The pain in his chest must be what had awakened him, he felt it now, that familiar burning in his lungs. Just running into the bathroom had left him exhausted. How had he found the strength to do what he'd done to Lino?

Ben waited until he felt stronger, then flushed the toilet and went back into the bedroom, found his pants and T-shirt and threw them on. He slowly opened the bedroom door, stepped out into the hall. He could smell fried food, perhaps bacon, hours old. The house felt empty. Good. He stepped back into the bedroom and looked around until he saw the clock on the nightstand, red digital numbers telling him that it was a little after ten.

After ten? He'd slept around eight hours. He couldn't remember the last time he'd managed to pull that off without having first drunk a fifth of Royal Salute. Usually, four or five hours after he'd passed out he'd be up, looking for something to do, some other scam to pull off.

Speaking of scams, what was he doing here? Was he

scamming her, or was she somehow scamming him? Ben stripped his clothing again and went into the bathroom, ran water in the tub. As it ran, he searched through his clothes for his cigarettes, then muttered a curse, remembering last night's ritual.

Diane had taken them from him, thrown the entire pack on to the embers of the fire. They'd watched as the package had curled up, as the cigarettes had smoldered and the paper of the pack had flamed, briefly. Soon there was just the blackened aluminum, curling up, turning into ashes.

Well, if he had to, he could get another pack anywhere in the city. Ben shut off the water and slowly lowered himself into the hot water of the tub, then lay there thinking about what had happened last night, and how he felt about it now, in the morning, in the cold light of day.

He loved her, he still felt that. That knowledge had lifted something inside him, some burden he'd been carrying. The snakes in his head had suddenly fallen asleep. He could only hope that they were dead.

In spite of what was wrong with him, he felt better right now than he had in years. He had slightly resented it when Diane had insisted that he wear a rubber when they'd gone to bed together, but he hadn't said anything, he was still feeling his way around what they had. And doing it with Diane with a rubber just once was sweeter than the entire sexual relationship had been with Sunny, or any of her predecessors, or all of them wrapped together.

But it was more than the sex, more than his sense of being wanted, needed and loved. Whatever the hell it was, it had started downstairs, after she'd left him, as he'd been looking into the fire, mesmerized by the flames. He hadn't lied to her, he had indeed thought about the things that he'd told her, but there'd been more there, feelings more than thoughts, things he was unable to articulate last night, and wasn't sure he could even now, maybe not ever.

There was a sense of belonging, of being on the inside. It was far stronger than it had ever been when they'd lived in this house together as man and wife. It might have had something to do with the years they'd been apart, or with the way he'd expected Diane to treat him when he called, which had made it such a shock for him when he'd realized that she could still somehow feel kindness toward him.

What kind of woman could feel that, after all these years? After all the hurt and pain and suffering. What sort of woman could put that heartache on the shelf and rally around you when she found out that you had a fatal disease? She had gone out and gotten books on the subject, studied them all in one day, had found out that maybe the doctor had been wrong, that there might be something, someone out there who could do Ben some good. And she was offering more than support, she was offering to foot the bill.

Which he'd take care of, later, after he got this thing inside him under control, if that was possible. There were a few things he'd been eyeing, scores he could take down that would make him that kind of money. He'd pay her back, as soon as he was well enough to go out and do what he had to do.

She wouldn't even have to know, there was no way he could tell her. His deal was to change for her, to change his ways, and he would. But there was no way he could let someone pay his bills without making every effort to cover them for it later. With interest.

But she'd hate him if she found out, and he didn't think that that was something he could take again. Maybe she was right, maybe he could work with her, do it the right way for a change, and cover his debt to her that way. Christ, it would sure be different, making honest money.

He'd always laughed at working stiffs, seen them as fools, suckers to be taken for everything that you could get. What were they if not robots, puppets on somebody's string? Get up every day, go to work for some son of a bitch, get yelled at, told what to do, when you could eat and go to the toilet, and then come home and take the same kind of shit from some woman who probably pushed you around as bad as your boss did. And who could blame her? Guys like that, they'd already proven that they didn't have any balls. If they did, they'd be on their own, making money, taking down scores.

He soaked, the steam floating around his face, rising from the water, Ben's face and toes the only parts of him that weren't totally submerged. He felt relaxed. He lay there wondering if he'd really believed that about guys who held jobs, or if it was just some more of his bullshit, believed in order to justify what he'd done with his life.

He'd spent his entire life pushing away the sort of intimacy that he'd yearned for so terribly last night. When was the last time that he'd cried? When he'd been ten, eleven years old? He knew that he hadn't shed a tear after he'd turned twelve. That was something he was certain of, he'd remember that, if he had. He'd always thought that if you cried, someone, somewhere would smell the tears on you, would know that you were weak and would capitalize on it, maybe even kill you.

But it had felt so good. So rewarding, so fulfilling. He'd felt himself lose fifty pounds, no, a hundred, as he'd cried. With Diane holding on to him, that was the best part.

What was wrong with him? Had learning that he was going to die somehow made him soft? He couldn't deny the fear he'd felt, sitting downstairs, looking into the fire. After the doctor had told him that he was going off the count, Ben had been busy, what with Diane being with him, then having to straighten things out with Lino. She hadn't even asked about that last night. She'd learned a lot, had done a lot, during the five years that they'd been apart.

After Lino, Ben had had to plot against the law and Fat Tony, thinking, his mind racing, having no time to dwell on what the doctor had told him. He remembered, vaguely, doing a little thinking about it, but only to assure himself that he wasn't frightened, that he was in fact relieved.

But sitting in front of the fire, he hadn't felt so relieved. There'd been an incredible sense of loss, not over the passing of his life, but over what he'd done with it, how he'd squandered it. He sat there thinking that on the day he died, others would still be living, his passing would hardly be noticed. A couple of guys would feel bad, guys he'd known for many years and who knew that Ben would stand up. But they'd go out and get drunk and tell stories about him, and the next day Ben would be nothing but a rapidly diminishing memory. He wasn't the sort of man whose friends felt deep emotional attachments.

And for every man who mourned him, there'd be ten who'd celebrate, dance on his grave. That was something to think about, something he'd pondered in front of the fire.

He would die, and nobody would notice. The people he'd passed through with, they'd be drinking, partying, snorting coke and gambling. Others would be going to the show, watching television, catching the news and hearing about that violent maniac Morer whom justice had finally caught up with. Life would go on for everyone else, his death would mean nothing to anyone. Which meant, when he thought about it, that his life had had no meaning.

Who would shed a tear at his passing? Would anyone think of him fondly, after he was gone? His sons certainly wouldn't, their memories of him would be branded into their minds, visions of him destroying things, yelling himself hoarse. He wasn't looking forward to having to face them later today.

And what about Diane, would she grieve for him, after he was gone? There had been something about her ultimatum that made him think that she wouldn't. If he had turned it down, he knew in his heart, she would have turned him away and not given him another thought. He understood that, too, it made all the sense in the world to him. If you held a branch out to a man who was sinking in the lake, how could you feel badly if he pushed it away, preferring to drown rather than let you pull him out?

Diane had offered him that branch, and the name of that branch was hope. He'd sat there thinking about it, about what he could do with two more years, and the need for that hope overwhelmed him.

He could set things right for those kids, let them see that

he truly loved them. Be strong for them instead of for strangers, for people he hardly knew. Ben had spent a lifetime doing things designed to make total strangers view him with high regard. With a year, two, maybe even three, he could win that respect from his children. And his wife. The people who mattered in life.

Diane, his wife. The words were so important to him.

She'd held him last night, snuggled up close to him, naked, after they'd done it, her head in his chest, Ben feeling her breath separating and tickling the gray hairs on his chest. 'You can fight this,' she had told him, 'I knew you weren't a quitter.'

What had she said in the restaurant yesterday? Amends, that was the word she'd used. She'd told him that was what he was doing, trying to make amends. He had plenty of them to make.

Ben took a deep breath, felt no pain in his lungs. Thank God for small favors. So all right, he'd been afraid. Terrified, in fact, at dying with no one by his side, no one to hold his hand and, later, after he died, mourn him. He'd sought solitude from the time he was old enough to comprehend the meaning of the word, and once he'd found it he realized how terrible a thing it was. Loneliness, which had always been his friend, was now his mortal enemy. Time was no longer on his side. Last night, he'd been alone.

He'd been offered a choice: remain alone, or come and stand with us. If you come with us we can help you, we can love you and support you. If you stay alone, you die in misery, at your own hand, alone. What choice was there in that? What choice did he possibly have?

Whatever kind of cleaning business Diane had, she was obviously raking in the dough if she could go to the bank and take out a couple of hundred grand. Hell, he should have stayed with her, should have stuck around and learned how to do things legally. She didn't have to pay the Man, didn't have to take any shit from any miserable, swindling cops. That kind of money, put together in five years. It made him realize how pitiably he'd lived his life.

He'd pay it back, though, every dime, with interest. Let her know that she hadn't backed some loser, some leech who was only looking to save his own ass. He'd show her what he was, the kind of man he could be. He'd make her proud of him, he'd earn the love she'd offered him. What a shame, what a terrible shame that it had taken forty-eight years and a fatal disease to make him realize what he truly wanted out of life.

But maybe he should be grateful to the cancer. It had brought them back together. Had made him realize how much he loved her, how much he needed her in his life, Diane, and the kids, too.

Ben didn't give Lino's death a second thought. It wasn't the sort of thing he'd dwell on, or feel any guilt over. Nor did he think of the other terrible crimes he'd committed, the lies and deceptions, or of the men who were no longer walking the earth because of his actions, overt or covert. All he could think of was Diane, the one person alive who could validate him, who could love him and make him whole.

He would never fully be able to understand why her love and support meant so much to him, nor would he ever feel anything but shame at experiencing the normal human emotions of fear and terror when confronted face to his face with his rapidly approaching death.

Ben lifted his foot out of the water, turned the hot water on with his toe. He let the tub fill some more, get as hot as he could stand it, then he kicked the hot water off, lay back, and closed his eyes. The only thing causing him any discomfort was his urge for a cigarette, but that, he knew, would pass.

There was no understanding of the concept that when one lived a life of unrelenting pain, its absence was clearly realized. Ben lay there soaking, with absolutely no idea that there was a smile on his face.

MaryAnn sat in her office, behind the wall of glass, wearing large round sunglasses that obscured her swollen eye. The punch had made the flesh around her eye multi-colored, a rainbow with a slit of blue that was her eye peaking out from the center. The glasses looked like a car windshield, and they were heavy, she wasn't used to wearing them. But it was better than not wearing them. Her looks had at one time been everything to her; it was painful for MaryAnn to look in to a mirror and see that cheek, that eye. But two things kept her from taking it too hard. She'd been beaten far worse, albeit long ago; and look what it had gained her – one punch had made her see Walter in a light that had never been cast his way before.

As she left the house he'd been hard at work, in his study, drafting the contracts. He'd looked up at her hopefully and she'd given him a quick, professional smile, then he'd looked right down at his papers, a sign of submission that she'd loved to see. MaryAnn didn't know how long she could keep her spell over him, suspecting he had too much pride to put up with it for long. As long as he signed the contracts, though, she didn't care if he lasted much longer than that.

And then again, maybe he had no pride left, maybe she could run him forever. He was getting up there in years, his looks had failed, he was a convicted felon now, and his name wasn't in the newspaper columns twice a month anymore. Maybe it could last. It would, at the very least, be a good excuse to keep suitors at bay. She could tell them that she was still married, that she was trapped in a loveless marriage. It would hold them off until they'd served their purpose, until MaryAnn had gotten whatever she'd needed from them.

Now she sat shuffling through papers, waving her employees off when they wanted to come in and commiserate with her. From what Walter had said last night, at least one of them was a dishy, bitchy, gossiping son of a bitch. She would not lean on any of them, not that she ever had. But from this day forward, she would never discuss even little snippets of her private life. If someone had an inquiry into her private affairs, she would ask them if they were taking a fucking survey.

The papers on her desk were computer printouts and hand-written analyses – Alfredo's reports and the things he'd hacked out of the many files he'd located with his computer on this Diane Morer person. MaryAnn went through them, reveling in her newfound glory, able for the first time to do this sort of work in the office, to be able to take phone calls there, unafraid that her husband might be listening in through the thin wall that separated their offices. Walter wouldn't be in the attached office anymore. He'd never be there again. Maybe she'd turn it into a private bathroom, put a shower in there, for when she was working late hours.

And she would be working many of them, locked in here after everyone else was gone. With Alfredo and James, going over their game plan. She'd already spoken to both of them today, and had even seen Alfredo, to collect a package she needed from him and James. She'd told James over the phone that the man he'd recommended, this Mute person, was totally unacceptable. She advised him to dump this clown, he was unreliable and he talked too much. She'd been smiling when she said it, paying the musclebound oaf back for the grief he'd caused her, the loss of her time and effort. She hated to waste what she knew was a dynamite lay on someone who couldn't do her any possible good.

A crook with a conscience. How quaint. But Mute wouldn't be a problem, not anymore. James would dump him and they'd move on. James trusted her, so much so that there were two packets in her purse, which Alfredo had handed over. Both packets were filled with cash, hundred dollar bills that she'd put to good use this morning, hopefully buying more houses.

When the city began buying property, they'd clean up. Work their asses off in the process, but before the first ceremonial shovel of dirt was turned, MaryAnn intended to have a million dollars that was all hers, free and clear, even after Alfredo and James had gotten their piece of the pie.

The city had announced their plan to buy up all the property in Hegewisch late last January. Public domain, all legal and above board. Eleven thousand homes would be bought up, some that had been in family ownership almost as long as the city of Chicago had been incorporated. There was a tavern out there, the South Shore Inn, that had once been a speakeasy during the prohibition years, was still owned by the same family who'd run it back in the days when big Al himself would come in, sit down, and order a pitcher of his own beer. All those homes, all those people, dislocated, moved away, their homes to be torn down.

MaryAnn loved it, ate it up with a spoon. Their suffering, their anguish, would make her a rich woman.

She'd already made more than a few dollars off the neighborhood. She'd shown her concern for them before the city had even been officially chosen, back when people were still denying it was going to happen, when you could still list a house down there and sell it if you worked at it. MaryAnn had sent out a mass mailing, a laser-printed form letter that had been individualized, telling the Hegewisch residents how sorry she was that the city seemed ready to betray them. Telling them too that if they should find themselves in the need of a real estate agent from the community, she would be happy to serve them, to see them through their time of crisis.

Some business had come her way through that letter, and some hate mail too, but she didn't worry about that sort of thing. She had to be pragmatic, put her feelings under a heavy coat of emotional armor, forget the slings and arrows and just help the people who'd accept it from her.

And boy, there had been plenty of those, the second the search committee had made its announcement. Instant buyouts, most of them, the only way to fly. Her fellow brokers had made that easy for her to do, coming in with their bullshit, their polyester suits, too cheap to take a real risk and gamble their money away. *They* wanted to market the houses, leverage them, find mortgages for buyers, forgetting one of the major problems in any such maneuver. Even if they *could* find financing for those houses at a decent rate, who the hell wanted to move into and out of a house within a year? These weren't renters they were dealing with, here. Any people looking to buy in that neighborhood were looking to be true homeowners, most of them first-time buyers, looking for the American dream that the real estate industry had convinced them had to involve home ownership as a part of the complete package. They wouldn't want to pack, move in, unpack, then start packing again when the city came around, taking their houses away. And, too, they'd be terrified that they'd lose money on the deal. They were so used to the city of Chicago fucking them around that they'd only expect it to happen again.

MaryAnn, though, knew that that wasn't going to happen. The city would not be fucking them. Would not even come close. Right now, as she sat looking through Diane Morer's stolen files, there wasn't a single For Sale sign up on a lawn in Hegewisch. No one could list them at what they'd been worth two years ago, the town was a salesman's pariah, a ghost town, because nobody trusted the city.

James, however, trusted the city. Or, rather, trusted his lover, who worked for the city's corporation counsel. And she'd told James the inside scoop, what the houses would be selling for, to keep the furor down to a minimum, to keep the people from rioting. The city had learned its lesson from all the bad publicity it had attracted when it had bought up all the houses around what was to become the new Comiskey Park.

Houses in Hegewisch, which had sold for fifty thousand two years ago, would soon be bought from their owners for from eight-five to a hundred. *And* there'd be a twenty-two five relocation payment.

Big money to anyone, tremendous money if you owned a lot of that property – if you'd moved in and bought it out when people were sick, when people were frightened, put cash in the hands of people who hadn't seen any for a while, not since the mills had closed down and they'd been forced out of their jobs. Couples who'd been forced to work three and four jobs between them just to make the same money that the husband had once made at Republic or the US Steel plant would look at forty thousand as a fortune, would jump all over offers.

She had insider information, the ability to ingratiate herself into the hearts of many of the Hegewisch residents, and she had people in place to tell her who was dying, who was going under, who was behind in their mortgage payments. She at one time had had two hospital workers and three savings and loan officers working for her, providing her with information, so she could move in and provide a helping hand. Now she'd lost both hospital workers, and one of the savings and loan officers was himself in the MCC, awaiting trial on embezzlement charges. Just when she needed them all the most, half of them were gone. The information they'd provided her with had been invaluable, had allowed MaryAnn to walk up to a house and ring the doorbell, enter and within minutes be seen as an angel sent down from heaven, one who had the answers to all of the owners' problems.

She had all these things going for her, yet MaryAnn's greatest assets were the age of the average resident of Hegewisch, and the number of years that they'd owned the home. People who'd paid fifteen or twenty thousand dollars for a house thought they'd hit the grand prize when you offered them forty grand cash to sign the papers. She'd already gotten plenty of them to do it; she'd make her fortune off this airport.

As would a great many other people, some of whom her friend James was even now working on, digging up information, things that could be used against them. If one of them should discover what she was doing and decide that they were going to bring it to light, well, James would be right there, with his little documents, shaking them in their faces and asking if they really wanted to go public with their findings.

It was the best of both worlds, and now she'd even gotten Walter off her back. She felt so optimistic this morning, that she knew, without even speaking to the woman yet, that Diane Morer would sell her property to her.

What was there to stop her? Her love of the community? The poor woman had obviously seen real estate as the only safe investment, had bought up three properties, just in the last five years. If they hadn't decided to put the airport in that town, this woman would have owned most of it before the end of the century, the way she was going.

And she was a smart cookie, too, had obviously learned valuable lessons from the mistakes of the overleveraged eighties real estate magnates, some of whom today could not get a pawn on their watches. This Morer woman didn't play around, she paid off every house as soon as she could, came up with huge down payments, tripled and quadrupled the monthly principal payments, sent in thousands to add to that, every month that she could.

MaryAnn had the papers right in front of her, what the woman had done with those houses. She also had the woman's MasterCard and Visa histories, her records of payment, which was monthly, in full. She had Diane's TransUnion and TRW credit reports, which gave her their highest ratings. She'd never been late with a utility payment in her life, and she had life insurance policies on her own life valued at more than a half-million dollars. She seemed, by all appearances, to be a wonderful, major opportunity for MaryAnn to exploit. There were only a couple of things that would stop her from approaching the woman.

First, there was the little matter of the dying husband having a different address than she did; what could that mean? Still, that wasn't enough to keep MaryAnn from trying, not on its own, particularly in light of the fact that Diane had paid a life insurance policy on this Ben guy, her husband or ex-husband or whatever the hell he was. If anything were going to keep MaryAnn from going to it with all her guns blazing, it would be the fact that Diane seemed to have such good business acumen. A prosperous business, the intelligence to pay off her property, to buy it one house at a time, paying that one off in a year or eighteen months before moving on to the next one.

Still, how good could she be doing? She didn't have any liquid assets to speak of. There was no insurance for Ben, not from the company, at least. Forty-some employees and the man she kept an insurance policy on wasn't covered? It could scare you off, if you let it.

MaryAnn wasn't going to let it. She'd spent her life struggling, backing away from things out of fear and insecurity. But the Street had taught her one thing: if you wanted something, you couldn't wait around for someone to come and give it to you. That had happened to her once in her entire life, with Walter. He'd given her respectability, a name and the confidence to look into herself and see what was there, without any bullshit. She didn't expect it ever to happen again.

No, if she were going to get those houses, she couldn't sit back and wait. Every dime she made went into her project, the Hegewisch project. James and Alfredo bankrolled most of it, too, but even on the deals that they were in on, MaryAnn would get the lion's share of the proceeds. She was the one who went into the street and fought and begged and made the deals happen. That was worth more than someone with a fistful of ready cash money, any day.If she were going to have those houses, she'd have to go out and fight for them. Diane wasn't going to come to her, looking to bargain, she'd wait for the city's offer.

But she might be in a money pinch now, if she loved that man, Ben.

MaryAnn had two stops to make in Hegewisch this morning already. There were four people she had to talk to: one older couple who were all ready to go for her deal – she thought that she could do it today, when they saw the money in one of the packets – and another that was on the fence, a younger couple who were looking for more money than MaryAnn was willing to pay. They somehow thought that she needed them more than they needed her. Which was their mistake.

She'd show them what she had to offer, and if they still balked, she'd tell them to save his unemployment check, they were going to need it. Then she'd walk out of their front door, acting as if she felt sorry for them. If they stopped her, if they called her back, fine, she'd have them where she wanted them. If they didn't, screw them. Either way, she'd be in the perfect frame of mind to approach Diane Morer.

She would have just asserted her independence, shown a couple of know-it-all kids that she had more on the ball than they could ever dream of having.

And after last night, after the way that Walter had caved in on her, MaryAnn believed that there was no way on earth that she could ever lose again, no matter what happened with the young couple from Hegewisch. She'd save all her charm, use it – and her wit, her feminine instincts, the simpatico attitude that she always extended toward single mothers that she was trying to talk into doing business – on this Diane Morer. And she'd get those houses, she knew that she would. Because she wanted them. And, for the last thirty-six hours, nobody had been her equal when it came to getting what she wanted.

Walter sat behind the desk in his den, working on the contracts that MaryAnn wanted prepared, and he jumped when the telephone rang, looked down at it with distaste. Should he answer it? He had a pretty good idea of who it would be. Men he didn't want to talk to, cops with bad attitudes.

There had been a time when dirty cops had been his bread and butter, when buying them off to change their testimony had been the second most important thing that caused clients to flock to his doorstep. The first being his knowledge of which judges would take the money. Greylord had destroyed his business; even judges who had been so discreet that no one could ever get a real line on them had gotten terrified when Dan Webb and his troops had started unsealing indictments.

Greylord had only caught the ones who'd stolen without caution, who'd become so brazen and arrogant in their positions of authority that they thought no one could ever harm them. Had *they* ever been proven wrong.

When the cops had come knocking on his door that day, long ago, Walter had thought that they were coming to collect some forgotten debt. When they'd arrested him, Christ, what a shock it had been.

He let the phone ring, looking down at it, not about to answer it no matter how long the bastard on the other end let it ring. MaryAnn wouldn't allow him to put an answering machine on the line, said that her people needed instant access to her. He would have to buy one now, to screen calls when she was gone. There were other things he would have more time to do now, now that he'd be home more often, and MaryAnn would be at work.

He was indulging one of those hobbies even now, sitting at his desk; he had gone and changed as soon as MaryAnn had left the house.

Walter was wearing pantyhose and one of MaryAnn's bras. He had a skirt on, pulled to the waist, but none of her blouses had been large enough to fit him and he couldn't buy any that would; if she'd found out about them, these last few years, she'd have used his predilection against him, to destroy what was left of his reputation in a courtroom, going after the money he'd earned through a lifetime of hard work.

There had been a time when he hadn't had to hide his desires, when MaryAnn would do anything he wanted, enjoying it, no matter what he came up with. He'd whisper something into her ear and he'd see her eyes light up, and he knew that he'd found the woman he'd been searching for, one who had no hang-ups in the sexual arena.

What had happened to them? She'd changed so much, these last few years. He'd paid for her schooling and he'd put the money up for her business, and she never did anything but try and hurt him, broke his heart at every turn.

That damned phone! How could he get any work done when it wouldn't stop ringing? He shook his head at his own stupidity, then pushed the ringer button over to off. There, that had shut it up. He could still hear it ringing in the kitchen and the living room, but his door was closed and the sound was muted; it wouldn't distract him, wouldn't keep him from his work.

Whoever it was calling, they really wanted to talk to him. It couldn't be someone after MaryAnn. Everyone she'd ever met knew how to reach her. They'd either call her at work or on her beeper, her car phone or, after hours, here at the house. No, this call was for him. Probably Midler or that sleazy Pollack he had for a partner, wanting to see if what they'd told Walter last night was worth any money.

Not a dime. It wasn't worth a dime. Because Walter was no longer looking for something he could use against her in a court of law. Now, sitting there, thinking of MaryAnn, he wasn't at all certain that that was what he'd been trying to do in the first place. What he'd wanted, most of all, was for her to pay attention to him. And the more of a bitch that she became, the colder he acted, the less of himself he'd shown her. He'd thought that he'd known her, that ignoring her would drive her crazy. That the insecure little sex toy he'd married would fold as soon as she truly thought that he didn't care about her anymore.

Had he ever been wrong about that. The less attention he'd paid her, the more she'd found in other arenas.

Walter had no doubt that she was sleeping with other men; he could see her doing it, if only to hurt him, to drive him out of the house. When he'd at last realized that she didn't need him anymore, that she didn't love him, he had died a little inside. And a little more with each passing week.

Last night, he would have committed suicide. He could not have hurt her, punched her, and lived with himself. Even as he cursed himself, he knew that it was more than likely what she'd been wanting for years, the sort of act that she'd been soliciting, on some level, since she'd gone to real estate school.

Whoever attacked first was the loser.

Walter knew enough about psychology to understand it, that the one who was being punished truly held the power. He'd felt the urge to be punished often enough, lately, although he hadn't acted on it, at least not with another person. Only in his fantasies, only when he was alone.

Walter would dress up in women's clothing, imagine himself tied to a chair in the bedroom, forced to watch as MaryAnn fucked another man, the both of them cursing Walter, telling him he wasn't man enough to do anything but look. Maybe, if he was good, they'd untie his hands and make him masturbate. Since losing his license to practice law, he'd been having incredibly complex fantasies, touching himself with his eyes closed, seeing MaryAnn in his mind, making him up, doing his eyes and cheeks, shaving the hair off his body. He'd do the chores around the house in drag, MaryAnn walking around behind him, either ignoring him or punishing him.

The orgasms were so intense that he sometimes thought he was dying.

Now Walter heard the phone at last cease to ring. He sat back in the chair, thinking of MaryAnn, knowing that his fantasies were no longer out of the realm of reality. That they'd probably come true in the very near future. He knew her well enough to know that she'd want to humble him, hurt him sexually now, and that was all right with him.

Although he wouldn't show her that. He'd play hard to get, secretly exploring his inner female side, forcing her to demand that he do what she wanted. MaryAnn would never know that it was what he wanted, too.

So who'd won last night?

Walter pushed himself out of the chair and walked lightly to the door of his den, stepping with exaggerated care. He had plenty of time to draw up contracts, all the time in the world. There was nothing else for him to do anymore.

Before too long, he'd be able to buy all the blouses he wanted to buy, and MaryAnn would even encourage it. He was free now. He had his money, he had his home, and now he had his wife. If she insisted on sharing her body with other men, there was nothing he could do to stop her.

That thought excited him further, seeing in his mind MaryAnn with another male, naked, rutting. He stepped out of the den and walked to the bathroom, looking for Vaseline, was in the hallway when the phone in the living room began to ring again.

Diane sat on the couch in her office, the long telephone cord reaching there from where the base sat on her desk. She was arguing with a banker, some idiot from the same bank she had used to finance three of her houses. Her legs were crossed and her toes were bouncing up and down, Diane unconsciously moving with nervous energy.

She said, 'Listen, do you understand the volume of business I do with your bank?'

'Mrs Morer, we understand fully.'

'I don't think so.' Diane's voice was cold. 'Check your records. I run a couple of hundred thousand dollars through there every year. I have my business accounts and my personal accounts with your bank. I've financed three *homes* through your bank. And now you're telling me that I can't get a mortgage on my fully paid off *property*?'

'Mrs Morer, please – '

'Please, my ass. You juggle your numbers one more time, sonny, and come up with what I need, or by God I'm going to be there before the end of the business day and close out every goddamned account I have.'

'It's not just us, ma'am, it's *everywhere*. Believe me, there's a moratorium on loans in that neighborhood, what with the risk involved, what's going on with the airport.'

'You'd think you'd jump all over that! The government'll be buying those houses up, you know you'll get your money back. Put that in as a codicil, for Christ's sake, that the money from any sale to the city goes straight to you.'

'We can't do that, and besides, what if they come in lowball? Mrs Morer, we don't want to lose your business, but you have to understand, you're asking the impossible this time.'

'This time. *This* time? What other times have I ever asked you for anything?'

'Uh, Mrs Morer, please. It's right here in front of me. You've financed three houses with us – '

'And paid every one of them off within two years – '

'And there are more than a few thirty, sixty, and ninety day loans . . .'

'Which I paid back with interest! You never *gave* me anything!'

'Mrs Morer, *please*, it's a business decision, a company policy now. We can work things out once we know what the offers are that the government's coming in with, but until that time – '

'Until that time I'm taking my banking business down the road.'

Diane cut him off in mid-plea.

That son of a bitch. That arrogant son of a *bitch*! He had actually believed that *he'd* done things for *her*? What? Loaning money out at usury rates, rates her husband risked a prison sentence for when he loaned money out at the same rate on the street?

She caught herself then, realized what she'd just thought.

She'd thought of Ben as her husband, and even as angry as she was, Diane smiled. This afternoon, they'd face the kids. Ben and Diane together. She wouldn't actually say anything, but she'd make it clear that she was on Ben's side. Touch him, maybe even hold his hand. Sit next to him on the couch, they could even have a fire. It certainly was cold enough for one. Maybe the fire would stir fond memories for the boys, remind them of other times that they'd sat in front of the fireplace as a family.

Wouldn't that be beautiful, if that was a possibility? With Christmas coming up, around the fireplace together. She wouldn't expect Ben to sing carols, but he could be there, with them, happy together, as one.

He could begin his treatment as soon as she could get him into the hospital. It had surprised her that a hospital so close, Weiss Memorial, could have top-shelf cancer treatment. He wouldn't have to go to Mayo, wouldn't have to fly out to Maryland. She'd get him in there, this afternoon if she could. Put her houses up as guarantee of payment, the hospital would accept them.

Or would they? They weren't in the real estate business, after all. Nor were they in the business of charity. Her assistant, Marie, was looking into that right now for her. The best ways to pay them off, what she would have to do. Diane was smart enough to know that promises wouldn't go very far. If she were going to get her husband the best treatment possible, it would be cash up front that would get him in. Especially seeing that they were divorced. The hospital and the doctors could make no claim on her business.

Those with the money got to live, and those without it had to die. It was the way things had been since the first time the doctors decided that the Hippocratic oath meant that they had to be hypocrites. But she had the money, the property, at least. And now it looked as if she couldn't get that liquidated, couldn't translate it into cash. No bank in Chicago was going to give her a mortgage on her properties? My God!

Diane felt a stirring of panic, then fought it down. She had to stay in control. She was thinking about all the time it had taken to buy her houses, from the first day she'd looked at them until the time that they had closed. It had to have averaged out to three months, minimum. Even if she could get mortgages on all three properties, it would take three months to close on them, to get the cash. And then she'd have to pay points. And taxes, and escrow. And now, it seemed, real estate fees. A connected realtor could find her financing from out of state, but that would take time, something she didn't have. In three months, Ben's disease would be too far gone for any kind of treatment. He'd be halfway through the six months that the doctor, Evan, had allotted him.

Where could she get cash, fast?

It was Ben who lived down the street from the church. Diane smiled ruefully, thinking of what they'd talked about last night. He hadn't even known that the Our Lady of Guadalupe church housed the national shrine to St Jude, the patron saint of hopeless and difficult cases. She'd asked him why he hadn't gone in there, gone up to the shrine and prayed. A miracle might even prove to him that there was indeed a God. He had only looked at her as if she were insane.

So be it. And on this one, for a change, she agreed with him. Diane couldn't sit around and wait on miracles. She'd have to go out and make one herself.

She buzzed her assistant.

'Marie?'

'Still trying, their collections department must be out to lunch.'

'Lunchtime?' Good Lord, where had the morning gone? 'Go ahead, Marie, try back later. I've got LaVonna coming in at one to cover for me, I'll be taking most of the afternoon off.'

'*You*?'

'Ha-ha.'

'Then you want me to go to lunch now?'

'Go ahead, Marie, and I'm taking lunch too, today.'

'Two days in a row, Diane. You're going to get spoiled.'

'I'll be making up for it. You always pay for your sins.'

Diane cut off the connection and rose, put on her coat and buttoned it up, deep in thought.

There were places, she knew, where you could get cash for your property quickly and without a lot of questions asked. She was reluctant to go to a loan company, where she would be stuck with interest rates and payments that she couldn't possibly handle without going into bankruptcy. She would if she had to, but first she had to see if she could find a legitimate or semi-legitimate source that would buy her houses and pay her in a cashier's check that very day. Not three months from now, not even two months from now. She wanted a piece of paper that she could take to the hospital cashier, show them that she had the money coming, that Ben could be treated. Even then, that might not be good enough. Still, she had to try, and she had to try right away.

She'd seen such places advertised in the newspapers, back in the real estate sections, the ads generally worded to catch the eye of veterans who'd lost their jobs. She could try one of them. She'd do that right now, go look up their numbers and see how serious they were. She'd have to take a loss, sure, but she knew that these places weren't in the business of charity.

The important thing was that Ben never be allowed to find out what it was that she was doing. He needed to think that she had the money in the bank, that she would just make a phone call and transfer the cash to the hospital. That charade had to be kept up, because she knew Ben, and even now, with the way he'd changed, he had too much pride to let her lose all that she had just so she could help him. He wouldn't see himself as being worth it. Would never understand that to her, he truly was.

So she would have to watch what she said, the way she answered his questions. They had a deal, and she would stick to her end of it. She had to make sure that he did, too.

The sound of someone beating on his door woke Mute up. He heard the heavy knocking on his outside parlor door and he stirred, then leaped from his bed in fear. He'd learned how to be a sound sleeper in the pen, where there was complete chaos, around the clock. Inside, the hollering didn't stop when the lights went out.

Now he stood, trembling in his undershorts, by the side of his bed, wondering if he should pretend that he wasn't home. Then he shook his head. Why the hell would he have to hide?

Mute hollered, 'Who *is* it?'

'It's me, Mrs Calloway, come on, open up, Michael.'

Mrs Calloway? Was she still looking to get laid? Mute threw on a pair of pants and shot a look at his watch, saw that it was eleven. He'd had a few too many beers last night, in a hillbilly bar down the street where the pseudo-cowboys mostly left you alone, no matter how you looked or what kind of clothes you wore. He'd smoked and drunk and now he had a hangover and a raw feeling in his throat, and a soreness in his bicep from arm wrestling for beers until two in the morning, and now Mrs Calloway was out there, yelling shit at him.

Mute went to the door and opened it, stuck a sleep-ravaged face into the crack.

'What's the matter, Mrs Calloway?' Even half-asleep, he could see that she was kind of pissed off, the old woman standing there with her arms crossed, glaring at him.

'You have a phone call.'

'A *what*?'

'You heard me, Michael.' She turned and walked away from him, waddling down the hall. Mute followed her.

'Mrs Calloway, I ain't never given out your number to anyone, the only people who got it is work, in case of emergency only . . .'

He was wasting his breath, she wasn't paying any attention to him. Pounding down those stairs like she was still a young woman. She'd get to the phone first and stand there listening to his conversation. Who the hell could be calling?

MaryAnn, it had to be. The thought filled Mute with fear. Had she done some detecting of her own, learned where Mute lived, what his landlady's phone number was? Dear God.

Mute walked into Mrs Calloway's apartment, bare-chested, squinting, cats roaming around his feet, rubbing themselves against his legs as he walked toward the little phone stand. He picked the phone out of Mrs Calloway's hand – she was offering it to him, staring at him in a way that told him she wanted to speak to him as soon as he got off the phone.

'Hello?' Mute said, and heard a high, Indian voice speak his name, a voice he recognized immediately. 'Doctor Raimas, is that you?'

'Michael, I have some bad news for you.' The doctor's voice was filled with his disappointment. Had Mute been caught? Had somebody seen him making copies of the report last night?

'What's wrong, Doctor?'

'Mr Smithers has filed a complaint against you for insubordination. You have been suspended for two days on that charge. I had no choice but to report it to your probation officer.'

'You *what*?'

'But I smoothed it over for you, I think. I explained to him that Mr Smithers has – shall we say an overinflated opinion of himself.'

'You bet your fucking life – ' Mute saw Mrs Calloway's expression turn to one of pure outrage, and he lifted his free hand to her, shook it back and forth in apology.

'He sure does, Doctor. He had me suspended for two days? I didn't *do* nothin'.'

'Well, you certainly have the right to file a grievance through the union.'

'I will, too, I'll go out to a pay phone and call the rep right now.'

'Uh, Michael, that's not the bad news.'

'What? Doctor, what are you saying to me?'

'We could overlook that, I might have, too, if this other thing hadn't come up.' The doctor was obviously uncomfortable now, but Mute didn't have time to listen while the guy beat around the bush.

'What is it now, Doctor Raimas?'

'Well, the head nurse on three reported a certain, er, sexual transgression between yourself and one nurse Denise Weaver.'

'She *what*?'

'I understand that she has evidence, that she'd been trying to catch you doing something like this for some time now, Michael.'

'She ain't got *shit* on me.'

'Well, we have begun an internal investigation. If it's proven that you and Nurse Weaver were – uh – so engaged during company time, on hospital property, Michael, we'll have to be letting you go, and there's no union representative in the world who would back you on such a charge. Now, Michael, did you engage in such conduct during your tour last night?'

'Hell, no, I didn't.'

'You see, I have to ask you that, Michael, as Nurse Weaver is married, and this could get rather embarrassing for everyone involved.'

What he meant was that it could get uncomfortable for his precious hospital. Mute wasn't about to let him off the hook that easily.

'I'm physically handicapped, that's why she hates me. That's Burge, right, Nurse Burge on three? She always had it in for me, said I scared her patients. I'll sue if I get fired.'

'Now, Michael, no one has been fired yet.'

'Ex-con trying to run his life straight, and what do I get? How you think the reporters will go for that? They show me, then a picture of Denise, with her happy little hubby and kids, you think anyone'll believe Burge's story?'

'Well, Michael, I hate to say this, but Nurse Burge claims to have a full confession from Nurse Weaver.'

'It's a set-up, the two of them are out to get me!'

'Michael, calm down – '

'*You* calm down, don't tell me to calm down! You ain't the one being told you're getting fired over something you didn't do!'

Mute felt the moral indignity that the guilty always felt when denying their fault. He was warming up to it, having seen enough politicians on bar-room newscasts to know how to play it without going too far.

He was at least winning Mrs Calloway over, he could see that much. She was looking at him with compassion now. He wished he could cry at will, that would make her forget all about his getting a phone call on her private line.

He said to Doctor Raimas, 'I'll calm down when I get a full apology! When someone convinces me she ain't just doing this because of the way I look!'

'Michael,' the doctor's voice was small and frightened. He was a little man, very short and slender. Mute's size alone intimidated him, even when Mute was in a pretty good mood. He would catch Doctor Raimas staring at him, longingly, when the doctor thought that Mute wasn't looking.

'There's really no cause for such anger just yet.'

'It ain't you been accused.'

'You'll be given a chance to tell your side – '

'My lawyer will tell it. His name's James Richmond. And he's connected to the city, all the way to the mayor's office.' Mute hung up and looked at Mrs Calloway, a stricken look on his face.

'They're saying they're going to fire me. They're going to fire me because I'm ugly, Mrs Calloway!'

It did the trick, Mrs Calloway was on his side. The look of compassion and understanding she gave him was the same look he'd seen on her face when she was out on the sidewalk, where she'd take in every stray cat that walked up to her.

Mrs Calloway said, 'Go put a shirt on, then come down here. You call your lawyer from my phone, it's better than standing outside in the cold, trying to think straight while you're freezing.'

Mute went up the stairway quickly, into his rooms, and locked the parlor door behind him, threw open the window and sat on the ratty couch. He got up, walked into his bedroom, got a cigarette going and came back out and sat down again, confused. If that head nurse had a confession from Denise, then the threat of a lawsuit would be a joke to the hospital administrators. They'd can him, make him the scapegoat, and Denise would probably even keep her job, a reward for not fighting it when that dyke Burge had approached her.

What could he do? Was there any way out? If he lost his job, he would be in trouble with the law. But he didn't think that they'd put him back in jail. Hell, people got fired, it wasn't like any formal charges were being brought against him, he hadn't been caught stealing, just fucking.

And talking back to a little man with a big mouth. Damn. There were ways to deal with dolts like Smithers; he'd had no idea what he was getting himself into here. Mute tossed his cigarette out the window and got up, went into his bedroom and rolled on some deodorant and put on a shirt. He pulled on his shoes and grabbed his shaving kit.

He'd go down and call his lawyer before he took this morning shower, see what James could do for him about this business. Hell, James would probably be glad to hear it. This meant more commission money for him, sending Mute to his lawyer buddies who would handle cases for him and keep their mouths shut.

But he wouldn't go downstairs again until he brushed his teeth. There were some things a man just had to do before he could be expected to act like a human being this early in the morning.

MaryAnn had an oversized purse hanging off her shoulder, one with compartments, her version of a briefcase. There were different forms in each separate compartment, forms she could pull out and hand over without even looking at the purse – she'd learned from experience where everything was. The innermost pocket held a messenger envelope, only one; the other had been handed over just a short time ago.

Forty thou in cash, spilled out on to a table, had proved to be more than the older couple were able to refuse. She had a signed quitclaim deed in her purse, assigning her all the rights that each party had to the house. She'd already known from Alfredo that they owned all of the place. There were no liens or back taxes owed, no bank notes or second mortgages, the house hadn't been used as collateral for anything. His databases were worth twice what he got for them, which would be twenty percent of all the profits after the city bought their properties. Including the one that she'd just bought.

It was hers, now, free and clear. Would be soon, at least, in the eyes of the law. As soon as she had the quitclaim recorded and paid for the tax stamps, the house would, legally, belong to her trust.

It was stealing without a gun, racking up these houses. Everyone had it in their minds that they knew so much about real estate, and it was a mindset that MaryAnn never tried to disabuse them of. She'd let them go on, nodding her head, her eyes wide at what they would see as her respect for their expertise, while all the time she was safe in the knowledge that she had them, that their asses belonged to her.

A little knowledge was a dangerous thing. And she had a lot of knowledge, one hell of a lot more than some dullard who'd years ago taken an eight-week real estate course in order to meet the conditions of some sort of degree. She'd listen to them, walk them in, then watch the trap door open as they signed away their rights, these people in near awe at how fast MaryAnn could move.

She could make you an offer in the morning, and close in the afternoon. Tell you she trusted you, that you looked like honest people. Hand over a packet of hundred dollar bills and smile as she did so, showing you where to sign, right there, where'd she'd marked the X. The people who accepted the money were flattered at her faith and trust, never knowing how deeply and thoroughly they'd been investigated by Alfredo. Any other tax paperwork could be sent on later, by certified mail, for them to sign. All there really was left to sign were the tax papers, and they were a breeze. Most of these people wouldn't understand the tax situation, would not know that if they were under a certain age they would have to plow the money right back into another home or wind up paying capital gains taxes on any profits they'd made. But that wasn't MaryAnn's problem; as long as she had the quitclaim deed, the house was legally hers, and that was all she cared about, that and covering her ass.

This couple this morning, she'd even let them cut a deal that seemed to them to be working to their own great advantage. She would let them stay there, in her house, until the first of the year, by a contract that all parties had signed, without paying a dime in rent. They'd keep the house up, would pay all utilities, and had promised to paint every room in the bungalow, including the ceilings, before December 1st. By the fifteenth every carpet in the place had to be shampooed. They would be laying out a minimum of a thousand dollars, taking care of and upgrading MaryAnn's investment. And they thought they were cutting one hell of a deal. MaryAnn would let them keep right on thinking so, especially seeing that the taxes had already been paid in advance.

Forty thou cash for a house that should have sold for sixty-five, easy. And they'd be putting a thou into it, saving MaryAnn that money. It would upwardly adjust the estimate, when the government regulators came calling early next year. A layout of thirty-nine for a house that would go for eighty-five, without question, and she could add on another twenty-two five for moving expenses, even though she wouldn't be moving anywhere. It was too good to be true, the money to be made in real estate. Before the end of next year, she might even produce her own late-night cable TV show, telling You, Too, How To Become A Millionaire Selling Real Estate!

The other couple, however, the younger couple, hadn't seen things quite as reasonably. They'd clearly been impressed by the sight of all the money, but hadn't bitten, the greedy bastards, they'd still wanted more. They wouldn't, they told her, take a loss on their house. They'd paid more than forty. MaryAnn had wished them luck and had become coldly professional, flashing them a wintry smile that told them just how sorry she'd been that they'd wasted her precious time. They hadn't tried to stop her, but she could see by the looks on their faces that they were in doubt about their actions.

She'd hear from them, she'd bet, and the money would still be green. The quitclaim could still be signed, any time between now and the day that the government came out and started handing out city checks. After that day, all bets were off.

MaryAnn drove with the comfortable feel of a .25 caliber pistol resting on her thigh, aware of it through the fabric of her winter coat, the weapon in her right-hand pocket, the safety off and a round in the pipe. There was no way on earth that she would allow anyone to take that money out of her purse, or to take that purse off her shoulder. That money represented a piece of her future, and that couldn't be stolen from her, not by anyone, not ever. She was willing to kill for it, and willing to risk her life for it. The weapon guaranteed her that no random act of violence would cause her to lose that money. And that James wouldn't have her robbed and still charge her for the cash; she wouldn't put it past that filthy son of a bitch.

Not that she'd be needing the pistol here in Hegewisch. The place looked like a ghost town, this late November morning. She saw old women pulling fold-up market carts behind them, heading from the store, with babushkas on their heads. Easier marks for muggers than MaryAnn could ever be, and they seemed perfectly confident, unaware that they were indeed targets.

It was a good community, Hegewisch. She would always remember it fondly, after it was destroyed, and she was a rich woman. Whenever a plane came in over South Chicago, heading for a landing at Runway One, she'd smile, she knew.

MaryAnn didn't need to consult her map or her folder full of information on Diane Morer in order to find the house. She had the address committed to memory, knew exactly where it was, and she glided to the curb. Leaving the Morer file on the front seat, she bounced out of the car and then locked it and set the alarm with a touch of her remote control button. She got out and took a deep breath, adjusted her sunglasses and stood looking at the house, nodding her head. It was a good one.

It was black and brown brick, with a second story, and it had a detached garage with a basketball hoop attached above the large door. A chain-link fence surrounded the back yard. The lawn was well tended, and there wasn't a leaf on the ground. The gutters looked new, the eaves freshly painted. The windows were leaded, and she would see that expensive heavy drapes had been hung on the picture window.

Eighty, ninety thou, easy. She'd offer fifty, see what happened. If this woman needed money – and MaryAnn had evidence that she might – she might go for that, if fifty was offered for each house. Two hundred thou, cash, right in Diane Morer's palms. She would look at it and swoon, MaryAnn bet.

She loved dealing with people from this community, they were so damn naive, so impressed with money. A maid was what Diane Morer really was, up against a shrewd and aggressive seller of real estate, a trained professional.

It would be like taking candy from a baby.

Knowing in her heart that the house would be hers within a matter of hours, MaryAnn began to walk up the sidewalk quickly, in control.

'You what?' Mute said. 'I don't believe I heard you clearly, James. First I got to wait a half hour for you to return my call, now I got to listen to threats? Is everybody in my life going crazy, today?'

He was coming on strong, not about to take a lot of shit from some yuppie, suspender-wearing son-of-a-bitch North Side lawyer, not after he'd been suspended from his job. Not after it looked like he might be fired.

He should have gone over to the Tavern and made the call from the back-room booth, though. He knew now that it had been a mistake to call from Mrs Calloway's house, what with the woman standing there, listening to every word he was saying. He couldn't curse this lawyer out the way he wanted to, or make the kind of threats he'd've liked to, not with Mrs Calloway listening.

'Mute, I am not in the habit of listening to such garbage in my life, you understand me? Now I am telling you this for the last time. I gave you plenty of opportunities to make money, threw a lot of action your way. If it hadn't been for my actions, you'd have been caught up in some federal sting by now. Your limited intelligence and lack of imagination would have landed you behind bars. You don't *think*, Mute, all you do is *act*, and I can't have people like that around me anymore.'

'Who ain't thinking now, talking over a telephone like this?'

'You're making my point for me, Mute. I've paid five hundred dollars a week for the last two years to have the latest equipment planted and monitored on my telephones. Your little Radio Shack recorder would only get a bunch of garbled messages, believe me, so don't even try taping this conversation. The National Security Agency couldn't descramble my lines.'

'I'll descramble more than your lines – '

'Mute, don't dare ever threaten me again. I've covered myself and my associates every single step of the way. I've got copies of your licenses, of every paper filed in your behalf under all your various aliases. None of it can be linked to me. All I have to do is drop this in the state attorney's lap, Mute, and what do you think happens? I walk away, the conscientious attorney who found out he'd been defrauded by the ex-con. You go back to jail, and I get swept into an alderman's seat due to my honesty, what I did for society.'

'You can't do that, I got confidentiality rights from you!'

'For your first case, Mute, that's the only one I handled. You can't even prove that I referred you to other attorneys. You don't have a leg to stand on, and now, Mute, you're on your own.'

'What the fuck is this all about?'

Mute didn't care anymore about Mrs Calloway, didn't even see her mouth fly open, her hand fly up to cover it. He was seeing the bulk of his income flying out the window, and he needed to know why, had to understand what he'd done to get James so mad at him. He was no longer angry. Now, Mute was frightened.

'About? What's it about? How about alienating one of the most profit-making women I know? How about talking too much in front of her? You blew it, Mute, with your big mouth. I was good to you and you blew it.'

What the hell was he talking about?

All Mute could think to say was, 'I was good to you, too.'

'Let it go now, Mute, now we just call it a day. I wasted this much time with you just so you'd know what I have on you, what I could do to you if you forced my hand. But now, it's over. I won't take another call from you. You leave me alone and I'll leave you alone. You're just wasted fat to me from this day on.'

Mute, panicked, said, 'What about the other lawyers?'

'You do what you want with them, but I won't vouch for you anymore.'

'And the money, what I got coming?'

'It's washed through me, as always. I'll resolve what's left for you, anything still on the burner. But after today, Mute, I can't help you anymore.'

The phone went dead in Mute's ear, and he took it away from his ear and looked at it for a minute. Had the guy really hung up on him? Was James that arrogant? Didn't he know that Mute could catch him after work and break both of his filthy, yuppie, marathon-running legs.

Mrs Calloway said, 'Michael? Is something *else* wrong?'

'You bet there is. You just bet there is,' Mute told her, then dropped the phone and ran out of her apartment, heading for his room, going after his car keys.

Diane pulled her car to the curb and saw the blonde-haired woman looking up at her house, and wondered what the hell she wanted, what she was doing there. The last thing she needed today was some saleslady, trying to push something on her that Diane didn't need.

Still, with all that was on her mind, Diane, after a moment's reflection, knew that she wouldn't be rude. This was the exact same way that she had begun her own cleaning business, going from door to door and asking people if they wanted a maid, on the cheap.

She'd be polite, but firm, and get rid of the woman quickly. Besides, the woman's financial condition couldn't be too dire – she'd gotten out of a new sports car, it was parked right where Ben's had been. Where was Ben's car? Had he taken off somewhere? Dear God, don't let him have changed his mind.

Diane got out of the car and hurried up her walkway, catching up with the woman at the cement staircase.

'Excuse me, can I help you?' Diane said, and the woman jumped.

'My God!' The woman spread the tips of the fingers of her left hand across her chest. She had to take the hand off the strap of a heavy purse to do so. Her right hand was in her jacket pocket, deep in there when Diane had walked up, but now Diane caught a glimpse of the wrist, then the hand disappeared back into the coat.

'You gave me a scare!' The woman was smiling sheepishly at Diane, and Diane found herself apologizing.

'I *am* sorry, but I saw you walking up my sidewalk . . .'

'Oh, this is *your* house?' The woman smiled brightly, all professional now, hiding her embarrassment well, no longer sheepish. She stuck her right hand out.

'My name's MaryAnn Ceterra,' the woman said.

'Diane Morer.' There was something about her, something about her face. Diane was squinting at it, seeing the discoloration under the glasses.

The woman put her hand to her face, as if ashamed of it.

'It's so mortifying.' She lifted the glasses up briefly, and Diane saw the injury, the bruised, battered cheek.

'My husband . . .'

'You've called the police, haven't you?' Diane was instantly one with her sister. 'He can't be allowed to continue such behavior. It only gets worse, you know.'

The woman hung her head, and when she looked up her face was bright again.

'May I have two minutes of your time? I'd like to speak with you about what the city is planning on doing to your home, and what I can do to help you before the bastards do it.'

Ben left his car in the church parking lot and walked slowly up the side stairs that led to his apartment. He held the bannister tightly, putting both feet on each step before lifting his right off and putting it on the next one. There was something about the cold weather, it was tearing into his chest, knifing at his lungs, Christ, suddenly he could barely breathe.

He felt a little better the second he got out of the bitter cold, in the vestibule of his apartment building, surrounded by familiar smells and sounds. Crying babies, frying beans. Radiant warmth.

Was he that sick already, or was it just in his head? It had been cold yesterday, too, and he hadn't had this kind of trouble. He hadn't smoked all day, you'd think that would help him out, do some good, shit, it was killing him, not smoking.

He saw that his apartment door was open, hanging by the top hinge, the bottom hinge gone, and the first thing he thought was that he'd been burglarized. The second thing he thought was that he'd better get downstairs and get one of the guns out of the car. He passed his door quickly, as if moving on to another apartment, glanced in and had his third thought, knew that the cops had been there.

The TV and VCR set-up was in plain view from the doorway, the back of Ben's chair, too. Someone could even be sitting in it, waiting for him, with a pistol. Should he go downstairs and get something, one of the guns out of the trunk?

It was so damn cold and his lungs hurt so bad.

If someone wanted to kill him, fuck it, Ben thought, let them. He was no longer in Diane's house, smelling the remnants of his children's breakfast. No longer in her bed, making slow love. Not in her tub or in front of her fireplace, thinking that he could be like everyone else for a change.

Now he was back out in the real world, and it had descended upon him with the weight it had always carried.

The pain was back, the snakes dancing, rattling their tails.

Ben entered his apartment with both hands in his pockets, looked around quickly, and saw that he was alone. The neighbors knew him, what he was. They wouldn't have stolen his property. And if someone from the neighborhood who didn't know him had done this, they wouldn't have left a thing in here that hadn't been nailed down. So it had to be the cops.

The question was, had they set him up? Put a dirty gun or some drugs somewhere in here? He'd only come back for the TV and VCR, wanting them as a peace gesture, a way perhaps to mollify his kids, break the ice with them. Two minutes ago his biggest problem had been how he was going to carry the stuff out in his condition, now he had to wonder if the cops had the place under surveillance.

There were things they'd do, if they were going to pull it

off legally. In order for this to stand up in court, the warrant would be on the table, out somewhere in plain view. He didn't see it anywhere. Why hadn't they left it?

Ben was backing out of the apartment, his mind racing, leaving the TV and VCR to whichever neighborhood junkie came across it, when the phone rang and he stopped, had a flash of anger as he listened to it.

Who did they think they were? Did they think their bullshit scared him? A mind game that kids would pull, calling you up to give you some shit. Ben walked over to the phone and yanked it up, shoved it at his ear.

'Yeah?'

'Ben? Is that you, Ben? Jesus Christ, where you been all day?' He didn't recognize the voice.

'Yes, this is Ben, who's this?'

'This is Mike, we talked last night?'

The guy sounded as if he were at least half in the bag. And Ben hadn't spoken to anyone last night, only Fat Tony, and this wasn't Tony.

'Where'd we talk last night?'

'Right there, on your phone.'

Ben was about to hang up, when he looked at his broken door. Someone had been in here last night, and that someone might have talked to this guy. In the background, Ben could hear country music playing – whoever it was calling was in a bar somewhere. It wasn't the way the cops would do it. Still, you never knew.

'Look, pal, we got a problem here, it's called credibility, if you know what I mean. You say we talked last night, I was out of here at ten.'

'No sir, it was midnight, I asked for you and some guy said he was you. But you don't sound like that guy.'

'Someone broke in here last night.'

'Oh my God.'

That was real fear in the man's voice. That sort of terror couldn't be faked.

'God, I knew it, it was *them*.'

'Who?'

'Forget it mister, forget I ever called.'

'Look, this is important, I need to know what you talked about.'

'If this is Ben Morer, if that's what your name is, then what's your problem, why were you in the hospital yesterday?'

Hospital? What did this guy know? It could be someone checking up on him for the Man. But he'd been terrified a moment ago. The Man wouldn't deal with people who understood fear, unless it was in the way they could make others feel it.

Ben said, 'Lung cancer, I got it, that's why I was there.'

'All right.' Then, 'No, I might have said that to the guy last night. What was your doctor's name?'

'Evan. He's young, with brown, wavy hair. Tall, muscular, looks like a weightlifter.'

Ben heard the guy expel his breath, in disgust.

'He ain't no fucking weightlifter. Nautilus, maybe, that's about it.'

'Listen, I answered your questions, now you've got to answer mine. What did you want last night?'

'You know where the StarLight Lounge is in Hegewisch? Across from the train station? Come on over here. I know how old you are, I know a lot about you, mister. And you don't know shit about me. I see you walk in, I think you're you, I'll approach you, how's that. Better yet, put a *Tribune* under your arm, with Bob Greene's column facing out, just in case.'

'You know how much time I have to waste?'

'Oh, I won't waste your time,' the man said. 'Not even one second of it, Ben. You come to the StarLight and I'll know you right away. Just don't wear a cowboy hat, it'll be easier to cull you out of the crowd that way.'

She was falling for it. It would be MaryAnn's biggest deal yet, four houses in one day. Had she ever played her cards right on this one? Her instinct had never failed her yet. She had to be cautious, though, this woman was no dummy.

Friendly and looking for a friend, yes, but still, her eyes radiated with intelligence, and there was a way about her, the way she moved, that made MaryAnn feel just a twine of envy.

So graceful, so reserved, so dignified, this woman was. All throughout her childhood, people had told MaryAnn how awkward she was, how ugly and clumsy. She'd grown tall early, and those first years of high school, God, what she'd done to try and win a boyfriend. After her second year she'd dropped out, knowing there were other ways to get ahead in this world.

She'd bet that this one here had never had to do that. This Diane would have had the boys all eating out of her hand. And she was probably too tightass ever to sell what she used to give away, as MaryAnn had.

She'd take her right to the cleaners, the bitch. With her high-class manners and her phony concern over MaryAnn's face. But she couldn't let her contempt show. She had this woman eating out of the palm of her hand, and she couldn't blow it, had to keep it up. It was only a good scam if they never knew they'd been taken.

Diane poured her another cup of coffee and said, 'It's as if you were sent by heaven, you're just what I've been looking for!'

'Heaven, I don't know about that, Diane. But I can make you a heavenly deal.'

'De-*als*,' Diane said to her. 'Plural. I have four houses, three others including this one.'

'My God, is that right?' MaryAnn acted surprised. 'Well, I've got an answer to that, too, cash money, Diane, you won't have to wait.' As soon as Diane sat down MaryAnn reached over and patted the back of her hand.

'I know how difficult it can be at times like this. What with your husband and all.'

'Oh, MaryAnn, I didn't know *how* I was going to pay for that operation! I figured I could always make more money, but how many lives would I be able to save?'

'Now *you* sound like the one who was sent from heaven,

Diane. How many people care about others anymore? Especially ex-husbands!'

'It's not that big a thing. More importantly, MaryAnn, is getting you away from a man who beats you.'

'It's only the first time.'

'I've got a lawyer, a woman, who eats men like your husband alive. I should call her and get her over here.'

'Later, after we're through. Lawyers always complicate things, I don't work with them, not ever. I've walked away from profitable deals when those people get involved.' There. Establish some ground rules right away, let her know that her feminist lawyer friend wasn't going to be a part of this deal.

Diane didn't seem to mind, though, she was too eager to get her hands on those greenbacks.

She said, 'I know what I paid for the other houses, but I have no idea what this one's worth. What the city would give me for it.'

'I'll tell you what *I* can give you for it, today, cash, no waiting, closing in four hours.'

'And how much is that?'

The woman was looking at her now, and not in a sisterly fashion. She seemed slightly afraid, as if aware that she'd said too much. Diane was suddenly realizing that she shouldn't have spilled her guts about her need for money, her ex-husband's disease, the expenses of fighting it.

She also had absolutely no idea that it wouldn't have mattered if she'd never said a word. Diane would never discover that MaryAnn had known all those things before they'd ever shaken hands. She smiled to take the sting out of what she was about to say – the price she would quote her – and reached out and took one of Diane's hands into both of her own.

'The city will kill you, make you wait six months before you see a dime. I can offer you fifty thou apiece for all four houses, a total of two hundred thou, in your hand before the end of the business day. We can close here or at my office.'

She spoke and the woman squeezed her hand, Diane's

expression never changing. MaryAnn knew in her heart that she had her cold when the woman smiled and told her that it wasn't nearly enough.

Ben walked into the StarLight Lounge and stood in the doorway, letting his eyes adjust, making a conscious effort not to breathe too heavily. These hillbillies wouldn't know the difference between lung disease and fear, would think that he was afraid of them if he began to breathe too hard.

It was the kind of place that you locked up at night, then sat at the bar, all by yourself, listening to Willie Nelson records, drinking Jack Daniels and knowing that it was okay to cry.

Ben could see these cowboys doing it, too, looking at the large set of horns over the bar, at the smoky mirror, at the huge autographed picture of Hank Williams on one wall. Some crying music was coming out of the jukebox, with violins and sliding guitars, some nasal-voiced whiner talk-singing about his breaking heart. One of the cowpokes around the pool table was mouthing the words to the song; the other three standing over there had looked at Ben curiously when he'd first walked in, dismissed him, then gone back to watching the game.

Ben spotted the guy he was looking for, one of the half-dozen sitting at the bar. He was a huge man with a deformed face that would match the mushmouth he'd spoken to on the phone. The guy was looking at Ben's arms, trying to see if he had a folded *Tribune* under one of them. An amateur, but that was good. Ben had had enough dealings with professionals lately to last him. He walked directly over to the man, sat down and put a ten on the bar.

'Give my friend one, I'm not ready yet,' Ben told the bartender, then looked at the guy next to him. 'My name's Ben, you called me a little while ago.'

'Well, Je-zus, how'd you figure that out?'

The guy didn't look scared, just curious. His biceps were the size of Ben's thighs, and he wasn't the type of man who'd fear anyone smaller than himself. If Ben pulled Lino's .44

snub out of his pocket, there'd be an equalizing factor real quick, he knew. But the man didn't have to know that, at least not yet.

He said, 'You made fun of Doctor Evan, said he wasn't a weightlifter. That proved that you were, so I just looked for the biggest guy in the joint.'

'I'll be damned, I'd better watch my mouth.'

'Not yet, don't watch it yet. Tell me what you were calling about, and then worry about keeping secrets.'

'Mister, I know you're dying. I know you ain't got long.' The guy had lowered his voice, so nobody could hear him. 'By the way, my name's Mute.'

'Mute?' Ben shook his hand.

'Short for mutant. They laid it on me in the joint.'

So he was bragging on himself, letting Ben know he was a man of the world.

Ben said, 'All they ever laid on me in the joint was trouble. And I don't intend to ever go back, Mute. You understand that right up front.'

'The butchers they got inside? They'd change your odds from six months to six *days*, shit, I know what they're like. *I* got preferential treatment, outside doctors who saw me as a challenge.'

'So what are we talking about here, what did you tell that guy last night, and who do you think it was?'

'I ain't got to think nothin'; I *know* who it was.' Mute took a drink of his beer and put his bottle down, looked around carefully and spoke out of the side of his mouth.

'It was the outfit, in your apartment. Walter sent them.'

Ben kept his face blank, sat staring at Mute, giving him the glare. Then he called the bartender over and asked for change, told him to give him enough for the cigarette machine over there in the corner.

Mute did not know how to act in front of this guy. First, the guy had known who he was without a whole lot of thought, which proved that he was smart. Second, he was no slouch in the staredown department; Mute had seen guys like this in the pen, who could ward off trouble just by looking at you. There was something in that stare that told you that you were dead if you crossed his path, if you thought you could turn him out or otherwise cause him grief and suffering.

Mute had never gone in for any of that stuff, not inside and not on the outside. He was big enough, mean enough, and ugly enough to head it off right away, even though from time to time some pervert would want to get engaged to him. After you kicked enough ass they left you alone. There were too many young guys inside who would give in without a problem.

Which didn't mean that Mute hadn't had his share of trouble. He thought about those times as the man with the bad eye went and got himself some smokes.

There was a long thin scar on Mute's belly, the reminder of a battle inside, when he'd been poked with a home-made ice pick, a sharpened piece of bedspring that had been hidden up a guy's sleeve. The scar wasn't from the poke he'd taken, but rather from the operation later, when the butchers had decided that he had peritonitis and had to operate right away to repair what was torn inside him.

Mute had almost died that time.

He'd been under the knife more times than even sickly men twice his age, an entire series of operations that had changed his appearance, improved it, made him less ugly than he'd been before. This guy Ben had looked at him and not blinked an eye, a man with inoperable lung cancer who was now pulling the lever on the cigarette machine, ignoring the pool game, ignoring the stares of the cowboys in the joint, over there in the corner waiting their turn to play.

He seemed to know and understand danger, to be aware that there wasn't much in this place for him to fear, just as long as he kept to himself and didn't start any shit. It was in the way he carried himself, the attitude that told you that he wanted to be left alone and that you'd have your hands full if you didn't agree with his simple, single demand.

Should Mute tell him the truth? He didn't know how far he should go with the man. He didn't seem the type who'd understand divine intervention. But he had to talk to *some*body, this torment, this conflict, it was tearing him up.

Mute would pray, and then a miracle would happen, and then, the next day, he'd wind up getting fucked. Was there a price to pay for miracles? Or was he paying for the misdeeds of his past? The thing with MaryAnn was terrifying enough, what with her outfit husband probably going to put a contract out on Mute as soon as they found out that he'd lost his job at the hospital. But still, how had he found her? He'd prayed for a miracle and it had been granted, at the racetrack. That same night he'd found MaryAnn, and look at what had happened then. It was as if temptation was being laid down in his path, God testing him, to see if Mute was worthy of future miracles.

But last night, what had he done wrong? Nothing. He'd said a prayer and then gotten a check, and then he'd called this guy Ben, but hadn't talked to him, he'd talked to some outfit guy. Shit. What had been the thing he'd done wrong, what had offended God? He'd called from this very same tavern, from the private phone booth with the closing door in the back, and he'd felt so good after making the call that he'd stayed in here, shooting pool and drinking beer and telling lies until the place closed down at two a.m.

Was that it? Was he not supposed to drink, either? If that was it, then God sure had some strange restrictions, some pretty peculiar restraints that He'd lay on you. He'd granted Mute two miracles, but then expected Mute to do things that were contrary to his nature.

Mute looked at the beer in front of him, wondered if he should push it away, not drink anymore. Or smoke, either. If he was a conduit, if he actually had a pipeline to Jesus, then the implications could be unimaginable. But it was obvious to Mute now that there were things that God expected in return.

Ben sat down next to him again, pounding his cigarettes on the bar in order to settle the tobacco, tearing off the cellophane and pulling one out of the pack. Non-filtered, but what the hell, the guy wasn't going to last too long either way.

Or maybe he could. Maybe Mute could pray for him. What was it his grandma used to say? The Lord worked in mysterious ways, His wonders to perform. Wouldn't it be something, wouldn't it be a gas, if God had chosen Mute Buffo to work through? If he'd been wrong all these years about doing things for yourself? What had that thinking gotten him besides a record, and maybe even a mob contract with his name stamped on it? Had Jesus shown him the way? Was God working in his life?

There was gooseflesh on his arms, and Mute was wearing a tight T-shirt. He had to stop thinking like this or Ben would think that he was afraid of him.

Mute pushed his beer away from him, offered his lighter to the man, who took it out of his hands and used it to light his cigarette by himself.

'Thanks,' Ben said, and pushed the lighter across the bar.

'Keep it,' Mute told him. He pushed his cigarettes away from him, too, put them over by the bottle of beer. The record on the jukebox changed, and Patsy Cline was now singing 'Crazy'. Mute could relate to that.

'Mute, if you would, tell me everything you know. Start with whatever you told that guy last night, then tell me how you're so sure that he's mobbed up.'

Mute looked at him, saw what was on his face, in his eyes. Compared to himself Ben was a little guy, but suddenly Mute felt just a slight shiver of fear. This guy wasn't fucking around. Someone could get hurt here.

Mute reached over and grabbed his bottle of beer right out of the bartender's hand. The bartender looked at him – he'd been about to pour it out – but he didn't say anything. Mute put the beer back in front of him, grabbed his lighter back off of Ben's pack, used it to light one of his own cigarettes. God would just have to forgive him. Then, slowly, trying to put everything in order, he began to talk to Ben, who was glaring at him in a way that made Mute know that he had to tell this man the entire truth, right from the very beginning.

Diane sat behind the desk in her office, waiting for LaVonna, not knowing exactly what she should do. Her initial instinct was to reach out to Melissa, seek her help and guidance, but she knew that that would blow the deal. If there even was one.

MaryAnn would not deal with lawyers, and she was offering Diane a way out. Maybe. Diane felt that she could get more money if she held out, but how long could she wait? Ben's disease would be progressing. And a loan company, even if they did give her the money she needed, would charge her double-digit interest, nineteen or twenty percent. And she'd still have to pay them, even after the city bought her property. With MaryAnn it was cash, this very afternoon. It seemed an incredibly short amount of time to do this kind of transaction, but she seemed to know her business, and she *was* offering cash.

Could she trust this MaryAnn? She seemed like such a nice person. And besides the cash that she was offering, she was also offering Diane and the boys seven weeks to get out of the house, if Diane chose to move. If not, MaryAnn would offer her a rental agreement, and offer the same agreement to the people who rented from Diane, allowing them to stay in the houses on a month by month basis. They could all stay right in their homes until the government came in and began to plow them under. It seemed like a good deal all around.

But in spite of what MaryAnn told her, about how the city would rape the homeowners of Hegewisch, Diane just couldn't sell the houses for less than she had paid for them. Even though the offer of fifty thousand apiece would go a long way toward Ben's hospitalization. Two hundred on top of the fifty he'd handed her last night. Which brought up another thing that troubled her, but she couldn't think about that now, about where he'd gotten the money. As far as her counter-offer to MaryAnn was concerned, she could only hope that the woman would see her point of view. Even though MaryAnn hadn't seemed happy when Diane made the counter-offer. In fact, she'd looked downright steamed.

Diane wasn't a woman who indulged herself much, nor one who even thought a great deal about her own needs.

She'd spent most of her life looking out for someone else, first Ben, whom she'd wanted to please, and always, always, her children. Diane did not care to dwell on the days before Benny was born. It was as if she'd first begun to live on the day that he'd been conceived, when she knew that she was responsible for a growing human being.

As soon as she'd gotten the results, she'd quit smoking, and did not take a drink throughout the next nine months. Ben was solicitous, even going overboard with it, bringing home carryout food constantly, handing her gobs of money for maternity clothing and to decorate one of the extra bedrooms for the baby. She couldn't remember exactly what he'd been doing back then, but it was during her pregnancy that he'd bought the house for them, laid out thirty-two cash for what was still Diane's home.

She'd often thought, over the course of the past five years, that if she'd just remained constantly pregnant, their marriage could have survived.

Had Ben even hollered once during either of her pregnancies? She couldn't remember him doing so. He'd seemed so gentle, but she knew when he was mad. The veins in his neck would bulge and his lips would turn down, as if he were making an extraordinary effort not to upset her. He'd leave the house and come back hours later, with whiskey on his breath and his fists marked up, sometimes his face would be banged up, too. She'd known where he'd been, what he'd been doing. Taking out on somebody else what he'd wanted to do to her.

Which was why she didn't like to think about the past, what he was, how he'd acted, how he'd nearly destroyed her life. And those of their children. Good Lord, what would they have been, if he'd stayed around, if he'd lived with them all these years?

And now she was risking everything to give him a little more life.

She didn't owe him anything, did not feel as if she did. Diane's greatest sense of obligation was to her sons, first and always. Her loyalty to her workers and to her friends was, however, unquestioned. She was known as the woman to come to when you needed more than a shoulder to cry on. Diane could fix things, could take care of things, could find ways to get you out of your messes, even the ones you'd created yourself.

Was that what she was doing now, taking control of Ben's problems? Making him her pet project, nursing him back to health in order to have some claim on him? He'd said he'd change, and she had believed him, had felt his hot tears on her cheek as Ben had cried. Later, too, after they'd made love, he'd cried, although she was sure that he hadn't known that he was crying.

She'd looked at him, though, Ben lying on his back, his breathing so terribly heavy, so heavy that it frightened her, and she'd seen a tear fall from his eye, go past his ear and wind up in his hair. What had he been thinking of? Had he been thinking of what might have been? She certainly had, as she'd bucked beneath him, letting go, knowing she was with Ben and she didn't have to hide her passion.

No matter what else had been happening in their lives, he'd always had some way about him that made her feel safe. And he was the only man who had ever evoked such an absolute sense of safety within her. Lying beside him, even after one of his episodes, she'd always been able to go to sleep with the knowledge that he would protect her, no matter what happened in the dark of the night.

With Ben there had been no middle ground; she'd either felt totally safe and secure, or completely frightened and vulnerable. The bad times had been the worst of her entire life, and the good times – she could look back and see – were the best that she'd ever known. He had made her feel complete.

Today, she didn't need that from a man, not from him or anyone else. She was herself, had her own life, was relatively happy even though she was alone.

But God, had she felt safe last night. Not once had she gotten up to recheck a door or to make sure that the embers had died out in the fireplace. She hadn't slept long, they'd been up until after two, but it had been the deepest sleep she'd had since the day she'd thrown him out. She'd slept well in the knowledge that Ben was there, knowing that, even dying, he would protect them from all harm.

Her mother had never married again, after the death of Diane's father. Had never even dated, although she was attractive, remained so until she herself had died. Her philosophy had been that you were married for all eternity, that you lived together and after you died you were reunited in heaven forever.

Some of that had obviously rubbed off on Diane. It was perhaps the only belief her mother had that she had taken with her into adulthood. She loved Ben, she knew now. Had never really stopped loving him. And he loved her, too. Diane didn't know about heaven or hell, how she felt about an afterlife, about reunification with loved ones. But she knew how she felt about having one grand love in this life.

Ben had been that love, the sort of love that she'd never have with anyone else again. She could give him what he needed, hopefully, and that was a little more time. Time to heal the wound with the boys, time to get his affairs in order. Time to repair the damage he'd done to his life, maybe even to wipe away the blots that were on his soul.

She wanted, more than anything, for Ben to live for a while longer. Long enough to realize how much they truly loved each other. Long enough for him to know that it hadn't been her fault. Long enough for them to make what could have been into what was.

Although Diane was not the type to overindulge herself, she found herself feeling grateful when LaVonna came in. She hugged the woman and thanked her for coming in early on such short notice.

LaVonna looked at her strangely.

'Diane? Are you all right?'

'I'm fine, I just have some things on my mind, that's all. I'll take care of them this afternoon, and be back tomorrow morning.'

LaVonna said, 'Well, don't worry about anything here. I can handle things for one day alone.'

'And if Melissa calls,' Diane said, 'don't tell her I took the day off, just take the message and call me at the house. If a woman named MaryAnn calls, tell her to call me at the house, immediately.'

'Are you sure you're all right?' LaVonna said. 'I've never seen you look so nervous.'

'I'm just waiting for an answer from MaryAnn about something, a telephone call that could change things for somebody I care about.'

Diane threw on her coat and grabbed her purse, looked over at LaVonna and gave her a quick smile.

'See you tomorrow.'

LaVonna said, 'I hope someday I find some man who cares about me the way you care about this man of yours.'

Diane did not know how to respond. How did LaVonna know that her concern was for a man? Instead of speaking, Diane flashed her another smile, and went home to wait for the phone call that could change things for all of them, the call that might even save her husband's life.

MaryAnn, too, was in her office, sitting behind her own desk, which was made of teak rather than of steel, as was that piece of shit desk that was in Diane's office. MaryAnn convinced herself: she was in an office that was larger than Diane's, sitting in a better chair than Diane's. She had more of a business than Diane, would make more money this year and from here on out than Diane would ever see in a lifetime of cleaning fucking factory toilets.

MaryAnn had to tell herself these things, because it was the only way that she was able to think of the woman and not scream out loud.

Who did that bitch think she was? Throwing a counter-offer her way, as if she had some power, some control over this deal. She'd been offered a good price for four pieces of property that she'd said she just had to get rid of, and as soon as MaryAnn showed her any compassion, any sort of understanding, the bitch had to go and decide right away that they were having a negotiation.

Which wasn't what it was supposed to be. It was supposed to be an offer, take it or leave it. Diane had left it, had been adamant about getting sixty thou for each home. With the money Diane made, she could recoup any losses in a matter of months, but still, she had to break MaryAnn's chops, had to act as if she knew her way around a deal.

MaryAnn's battered face hadn't worked in her favor, except for right at the beginning, when it had drawn them together as females and given them a common bond. But after that, Diane had seemed to use MaryAnn's face against her. If she'd allow her husband to beat her, why shouldn't Diane take a shot, too? It was another thing she owed Walter. Something he'd be paying for, and real soon.

MaryAnn could not believe the sense of control she had over Walter, who'd always been so powerful, so in charge of everything around him. Now she had him where she wanted him, and she knew that she had to get her mind off him, had to exercise some discipline, or else she'd take the afternoon off, go home right now and start showing him who was boss. She had plans for him, now that he was broken. There were things she would do to him that he could not imagine right now. Rent him out to her girlfriends, even. Make him watch her with other men. The possibilities were endless.

But she couldn't think about that now. At the moment, she had to think about what she would do about Diane.

The thing that bothered her the most was, she wanted those houses, badly. Even at sixty thou per, she would be making out better than she had ever expected for one day's work. She'd bought the house that morning from the older couple, and now she could make it five in one day, and the worst thing she could imagine about it was not being able to brag about what she'd done.

MaryAnn took out a calculator, and tapped in some numbers. She'd get, as a bare minimum, eighty-five thou from the city for each house. Plus the twenty-two-five each for moving expenses. That was four-thirty, minus her cash layout. One-ninety would go into her pocket. Not as good as the two-thirty that would have been hers if Diane had been hot for her deal, but still, nothing to sneeze at, either.

She had to make a call.

MaryAnn reached out and dialed a number, got Alfredo's answering machine and immediately hung up. Which meant that she'd have to go to James. He'd have the cash on hand, and his company drew up all the leases for the rentals. She never tried to hide anything from him, he was too smart for that. He was in on everything, knew exactly what she'd been doing all along. James had even set up the trusts that she put the properties into. But he became totally unreasonable when she needed to borrow money.

Alfredo, on the other hand, would ship it over via bonded messenger, tell her to get it back to him when she could, and sometimes he'd just take it out in trade. Her cash flow was down to a drip; every dime she had in pay and bonuses, all of her commissions, went into buying more of the Hegewisch houses. She'd borrowed most of the money from Alfredo for that morning's action, and still had forty left in her purse. She'd need another two hundred thou, and she'd need it right away. She wanted to close these deals, have the houses in her possession before the close of business hours this afternoon.

Should she demand the money from Walter? No, she couldn't do that. She owned his soul, not his checkbook. Right now his will was broken, but they'd made a deal, and MaryAnn couldn't break it. She would leave his money alone and he would stay away from her business; she was having him draw up contracts to that effect even now, as she worked. In a month, maybe two, she could begin to drain him financially, she'd have to wait and see how deep Walter was in her trap. He was no slouch, either, when it came to the brain department. The last thing she could give him was leverage to use against her, somewhere down the road, if her spell should wear off.

But for now, she'd have to leave him alone. She'd learned her lesson about rushing men into things with that monster, Mute. Thank God she had been able to handle him. Thank God that she had the gift of being able to think on her feet.

So it was James, or nothing, and she had to decide, fast. If she didn't, MaryAnn knew, Diane would go to a loan company. And no one was more aware than she of the fact that they would help her. Sixty grand apiece? They'd either buy the houses outright or else they'd loan her the money with the houses as collateral, charge her twenty percent interest and clean up just on the vig. And Diane might even be able to pull herself out of the debt; her business made good money, and, like MaryAnn, she'd sunk all of her cash into real estate. Without house payments to make to some bank, Diane would be swimming in cash. She'd be able to get out of a loan in just a few short years. And then, of course, the city would come sniffing around. MaryAnn had to close this deal before Diane got some professional advice, found out that the right move for her would be to wait.

She had to decide, and right now. Get the two hundred thou from James, or let the deal expire.

She reached for the phone and tapped out James's number, then had to wait five more minutes while his secretary beeped him, before he got back to her.

'Yes, MaryAnn,' James said, as usual cutting out the preliminaries. She wondered if he believed in foreplay, or just started right in on the humping. He was on his cellular, she could tell. There was a hollow sound to his voice, and she could hear traffic in the background. James was walking somewhere, downtown.

She said, 'We're on, but she wants sixty apiece.'

'Alfredo's database appraised the home she lives in at one-fifteen, the other three all come in over ninety. Those are minimum numbers, MaryAnn. He told us she's got good title, and my connection at Metro backed that up. Fuck waiting for the letter of commitment, and we won't waste time or money buying title insurance on something we're sure of. Take the deal, MaryAnn.'

'I'm short on cash.'

'How short.'

'Two hundred.'

'I'll have it there in an hour, at ten points to you.'

'James, come on, give me a break. Take twenty points of my piece of the final sale from the city.'

'And you take that offer to the bank, if that's what you're looking for. You want two hundred grand of my money, you're going to have to put it to work for me. I'm taking it out of commission for you.'

'James – '

'You want it or not, MaryAnn, I'm busy.'

'You talked to Alfredo today?'

'He's given you all that he's ever going to.'

'James! You stay out of our relationship!'

'I'll stay in for my percentage, and I'll cover my ass, and I want my money working for me, today, tomorrow, and until you pay me back.'

'Have it here in an hour. I'll put it to work for you.'

'Count your blessings. I'm juggling accounts to do this for you.'

'Taking it out of what, accounts paying you seven, seven and a half? Then charging me ten.'

'You don't like it, go to Commercial Credit, pay them nineteen.'

She had to be careful not to let her resentment show. James could tell her now, could back out of the deal. MaryAnn had tried her best, and she'd failed, and now she had to eat whatever James decided to feed her. But if he'd queered her deal with Alfredo, she swore, as soon as the trust was sold, she'd kill the son of a bitch.

Before he could hang up she said, 'James?'

'Yes.'

'For that amount, I think it'll be better with a certified check – '

'Forget about it. I don't do that.'

'This isn't forty, fifty thou here, James – '

'You want certified checks? Go to the bank. I bring you cash or I bring you nothing. The only thing that's certified is the man that delivers it.'

'James, this woman would balk at that kind of money.'

'Then let her go elsewhere. MaryAnn, come on, I'm in the

middle of something. You want me to call you back, give you time to decide?'

Big of him, but she couldn't wait. He was inflexible. He was a man. He was a bastard. And he would pay, dear God, someday he would pay.

'No, send it over to the house.'

'I'll enclose all the tax forms and have the deed prepared, in the trust's name. Does she know where her tax statements are?'

'This is an organized woman, James. She's still got the receipt from her wedding gown.'

'We'll get a warranty deed signed by six. The clock doesn't start ticking against you on my money until tomorrow morning.'

MaryAnn looked out of her window, at the horde of real estate hustlers she'd trained.

She said, 'James, send it to my house, don't send the courier here. Even with Walter gone, I couldn't count that much money here, not with this fucking wall made of glass.'

'Where did you count Alfredo's eighty this morning?'

'At – at his place.'

'Jesus Christ, MaryAnn, the two of you are starting to scare me. Walter's gone, right? Use *his* office.'

Damnit, he'd out-thought her. She hated when she acted poorly.

She said, 'Too many people walking around, too many eyes watching and ears hearing. Have him at my house, I'll count it in my bedroom. Bonded messenger, before five, right?'

'And count it out in front of him, don't sign the receipt until you do.'

'I'll send the quitclaim deed from a morning sale back with him, James. It has to be recorded and the tax stamps paid for.'

'Right.'

There was an electronic beep and then his cellular went off the air.

Two hundred thou, at ten points, with compounded

monthly interest. By the time the city closed on the houses, she'd be in the hole, if she had to borrow much more from him. James would not collect on the money until the deals were closed, until the city owned all the property, but then he'd want his cash back, right to the penny, and it would all come out of MaryAnn's piece. She'd end up clearing less than twenty thou on each one of these four goddamned houses.

She sighed, sat back, lit a cigarette, and waved off one of the agents who'd been patiently waiting outside her door for her to get off the phone. She didn't have time for that right now. At the moment, she had other things to think about.

James would already be on the phone, ordering transfers of funds, getting her the two hundred, having the deed prepared for Diane's signature. Even if Diane didn't want to go ahead with the deal, he'd demand twenty thou on top of the two hundred before he'd even let MaryAnn return it.

And what had he done to Alfredo, what could he have said to that man? James did not believe in mixing sex with business – not that he had any morals; it was just that he thought it complicated things. She should have asked him if he'd taken care of Mute. Then again, she was glad that she hadn't. He would have been offended. Mute would have been dealt with, and if he hadn't, he would be soon. It seemed, unfortunately, that Alfredo had been taken care of, too. Goddamn that fucking lawyer.

MaryAnn took a deep drag of her cigarette and smashed it out in the crystal ashtray on her desk, reached for the phone and dialed Diane's number. She'd probably have to go over there and search through boxes of the woman's belongings in order to find the tax papers that Diane would need in order for the deal to close properly, but then again, maybe she wouldn't. The woman seemed organized enough, she might know where everything was. And if she didn't, then screw her. All MaryAnn needed was her signature on a deed, one that would be recorded first thing in the morning. After that, as far as she was concerned, the woman could drop dead. She'd be James's problem, James and whoever he had taking care of the rental leases. She would lay that part of it on him tomorrow, after she had the deal done, the warranty deed right there in her hand.

There was no way on earth that MaryAnn could lose.

Diane answered the phone on the first ring, and suddenly MaryAnn's voice was cheerful, professional, filled with her joy – as she explained to Diane – that, in spite of their misgivings, she had talked her male partners into accepting Diane's higher counter-offer.

Midler and Slinski met at the Purple Steer restaurant, in a booth by the window, away from the rest of the early dinner crowd. They were both tired, having gotten little sleep. They were assigned to the midnight shift this month, and had awakened early, to decide a course of action now that Morer had flown the coop.

'I still think the broad's the one we want to muscle,' Slinski said.

Midler disagreed. 'She's got steel balls, I've known her since she was on the street.'

'I called that son of a bitch Walter ten times today, he never bothered to answer the phone. The real estate company said he didn't work there anymore.'

'See? And you want to go to the broad. Walter's already hiding. She won't back down, but he will.'

'We go to her and she does what we want, or else we go to the press,' Slinski said.

'Wait a minute, wait a second, that's bullshit, that defeats our whole purpose. We go to the press and what happens?'

Slinski had to think about that a second.

'She gets busted.'

'For what?'

'For fraud, for ethics shit, who knows? She gets busted.'

'What she's doing may not be illegal, Slin, and even if it is, what's in it for us for turning her in?'

'We still got Morer.'

'We got shit. Morer's *bread* is what we got, if we play our cards right.'

Slinski tore into his steak and eggs, sopped some of the egg yolk up with a forkful of rib eye. Chewing, he said, 'Can you believe that son of a bitch? That guy last night said he had a house in Hegewisch.'

'Makes you wonder what else he got that we don't know about.'

'We know about the cancer. Ain't you gonna eat nothin'?'

'I'll stick with coffee, Slin,' Midler said. 'So we got to stay away from the broad, this Ceterra. Walter's weak, he's always been weak. Can you believe he got that kid believing he's the head of the outfit?'

Slinski nearly choked. 'Walter?' He swallowed another bite of his meal, still chuckling. 'That tightass son of a bitch! The outfit guys made fun of him to his face, he'd get them off and want to kiss them, like he's Bruce Cutler and they're Gotti, and they'd push him away, tell him to go find some other motherfucker to suck spit with.'

'We go to Walter,' Midler said, 'and we talk to him the way we talked to Morer. Tell him how it is, how we know what it is he's doing. Then we let him know that we're in for a piece, that he can't cut us out or we go to the Man, tell him that Walter's using his name without permission.'

Midler sipped his coffee and made a face. It had grown cold.

He said, 'The broad's not gonna shake. If I know Walter, she's just waiting for a chance to dump him, for an opportunity like this to come along. We go to her and tell her we're going to the Man, she shrugs, tells us to go ahead. The Man whacks Walter, we got what? We got shit.'

'And Morer still ain't paid us.'

'He will, one way or another.'

'We going to the old lady?'

'You bet that's where the fifty grand is at.'

'You think he took it off Lino?'

Midler said, 'He's the only one that could have it. Lino didn't take chances. Who else could have killed him; Tony? Tony ain't got the stones. And the fat man, he ain't good enough to lie to me and get away with it. He was scared to death when I went and saw him, while *you* were still sleeping.'

'I was calling Walter,' Slinski said.

'And I was out busting my balls.'

'So what do you want to do? You want to find out where Walter lives tonight, go pay him a visit tomorrow?'

'I didn't drag you in here six hours before work just to tell you we're gonna do something tomorrow. I already *know* where he lives. And we go there tonight. Talk to the man before we go to work. We got other plans for tomorrow.'

'Which are?' Slinski said. He was rubbing his toast in the dregs of the steak sauce, the steak juices, what was left of the egg yolk. He popped the toast into his mouth and looked up at his partner, rubbing his hands together to get rid of the toast crumbs, his eyebrows raised.

'Tomorrow, we go and find Ben's old lady. We find her, we find him, and we find the fifty grand.'

'Five of which is ours.'

'Like hell,' Midler said, and waved for the waitress. He wanted some hot coffee. '*All* of it's ours, Slin. Every last dime. And if Morer don't like it, we can hasten his departure from this earth.'

'"Hasten his departure", I like that, that was good,' Slinski said.

Walter Ceterra, the head of the outfit? Ben listened carefully, not showing any emotion. He did not want Mute to know that he'd ever heard the name. Yet he had, many times; he'd known Walter since he'd been twenty-five years old. And he knew damned well who and what Walter was. Knew that Walter used to defend some outfit guys, but hadn't in a while, not in four or five years, since he'd gotten pinched for trying to steal from them.

So Walter's wife was lying to this kid, had used him to steal some files and then lied about her husband in order to keep him from coming over to her house.

Should he tell Mute? Maybe later, he'd see about that. The kid wasn't too tightly wrapped, going on and on about

Jesus having suddenly changed his life.

'You're dying, Ben. Do you think about it? Do you want to turn to the Lord?'

'Mute, let it go.' Even if Ben were entertaining the idea, he wouldn't be converted by a harelip drunk in a hillbilly bar.

Mute's face was serious, and Ben could read it like a book. This was not a man who would walk away winners from any poker table in the country. Mute was playing it as if they were equals, but not knowing exactly how to go about it, just imitating whatever hardasses he'd run across in prison. The way they looked, the way they spoke. If Ben ever wanted to do a small dope deal, this was his man. But for anything heavy, for what he might have to do today, the kid would be out, although Ben could use some back-up.

Who could he get ahold of, and still maintain the illusion of health in front of them? What man could he call and ask to risk his freedom and even his life, then tell that he'd have to do it for nothing, do it just to help Ben?

No one. Not a soul. He wouldn't do that to anyone he trusted or respected.

Ben had no doubt as to what was going on. He'd been around con men and hustlers his entire life, knew about switches and pigeon drops and Michigan rolls and small and big cons. How con men weren't even close to the lovable rogues that Hollywood portrayed them as being. This wasn't Newman and Redford, this was real life. Elderly widows had been robbed of their entire life savings while trying to rid their homes of cancer of the bricks. People like this would milk you dry and then laugh at your gullibility, laugh even harder at your weakness after you wound up killing yourself.

Ben knew too that Diane would fall for a scam, that she was naive enough and enough in love to give everything away just to save his sorry life. She always did think with her heart. It was what had driven them apart.

Ben had to work to keep his face straight, had to remember where he was and who he was with. The thought of Diane, of what she was doing for him, was enough to break his heart if he should somehow convince himself that he still had one.

Mute said, 'You want a drink?'

'No, but let me buy you another.'

Mute nodded, trying to keep his face as blank as Ben's.

'I want to think about this a little bit, about what you told me.'

'Okay.'

'You stay here, Mute, and watch my back. Have a couple of beers and relax while I think. Do that for me and I promise you, Walter Ceterra will never bother you again.'

The kid's face lit up brightly, he was nowhere near good enough to hide his pleasure at what he'd heard. Then it got dark again, and he looked a little suspicious.

'You can't do that. Who can fix something like that?'

'*I* can, Mute. If I want to. Walter owes me big.'

'Jeez.'

Mute fell silent, sucking on his beer and thinking about it. That was a good thing, it gave Ben the time to do some thinking of his own.

He'd been wrong, he knew that now. Thinking he could change after a lifetime of being a crook. What would he do, call the Man up on the phone and tell him he was retiring? Gonna take care of the little woman and she's gonna take care of me. The Man would hang up, laugh for a little while, then put the hit order out on Ben and Diane and the kids, too, just for good measure. To end the line, once and for all.

There were too many miles of bad road already crossed to try and pretend that it could ever be made straight and narrow. At least for him. For Ben, it was over. The kids, they could have their shot, and he had to make sure that Diane had hers. It had been a pipedream, living a few more years. He didn't have the right to look for miracles, not at this stage of the game. His plan to get things right, to straighten things out, shit, it felt good when he was thinking about it, but it wasn't the way he was built. He'd lived his life like an out-of-control animal, and now he would have to die the same way. There could be no more big plans. He'd had his chance, long ago, and he'd blown it. The day he'd walked out of Diane's life, he'd blown it.

So his problem now was what he could do here. How could he straighten this out? If he didn't find a way, Diane would lose everything she'd worked for, these players would take it all away from her, and Ben would just wind up dying anyway.

Ben's initial reaction was to hunt down Walter and this MaryAnn, put a single bullet through the back of each of their heads. Walter was obviously in on it, had sent his wife out to seduce this kid, this dummy sitting next to him. Worse than a pimp, Christ, what kind of man could do that to his own wife? Ben would have no compunction about killing them, but there was another problem he had to address first: what this kid had told the cops last night.

Ben knew that was who Mute had talked to. He would not have spoken to anyone from the mob. If the Man had sent someone to kill Ben, they'd have done more than kick down his door. There'd have been a surprise package somewhere in the apartment, a pressure switch somewhere, under a throw rug maybe, right inside the door. Ben would have walked in and it would have blown the top floor of the building down on to 92nd Street. Those guys wouldn't have cared about the children in the building; if the Man had ordered them to hit Ben, Ben would have been hit by now. The Man wasn't offering Ben any help, but he also wasn't going to hurt him.

There would be nothing in it for him, the Man would make no profit off Ben's death. Ben had cleared up a problem for the Man, had gotten rid of Lino, and that act had effectively neutralized the cowardly Fat Tony. Now the Man could move in and take over their operation, knowing that Ben wouldn't try and muscle in, he'd somehow known that Ben was dying of cancer.

So what did the cops know, besides what Mute had told them? Would they have known about Ben's cancer be*fore* Mute had told them? The Man obviously had. The question was, did he share it with them, would there be a profit in it for the Man to tell the cops about Ben's problem? None that he could see, but the Man had better eyes.

Had they been there to get their percentage, as they'd said the night before? Or had they come to kill him, to take it all for themselves? Ben had to figure that out. It would make an important difference in the way that he conducted himself. Because if they were going to try and take the money that Ben had given to his wife, if Diane or the kids were in jeopardy from them, then Ben would have no choice but to kill them both.

Christ, had it been the *cops* who'd called Diane at her office? Lino, about to die, had sworn that it hadn't been him. He could see Midler doing it, trying to scare a woman. But no, that wouldn't have been them – they would not have known that Ben had moved out yet, would have expected that their piece was coming to them that night.

Ben did know for certain that the cops knew about MaryAnn Ceterra: Mute had told them about her, thinking that he was warning Ben. And he'd told them that Ben had cancer, too, if they hadn't learned it from the Man. But that might not be a bad thing. They were smart enough to realize that now, Ben had absolutely nothing to lose. They might leave him alone with the knowledge that he would kill them without hesitation, knowing that the threat of prison or death would no longer be much of a deterrent in his life.

Fuck it. It didn't matter. Nothing mattered but stopping Diane from giving everything away in order to save his life. So he'd go with his initial plan. Walter and his wife, they'd both have to go.

Ben's head was starting to hurt. What the hell could he do? First thing, right off, he had to cover his wife and kids. It wasn't their fault that he was dying, and he wouldn't let them carry the weight for his life's mistakes. Diane would just have to go on without him, she'd done all right without his ass for the past five years. The rest of her life would be a cinch.

So he had to stop thinking about the cops, about the Man, about himself, about anything else but her and his sons.

In order to save her, he'd have to destroy her. Again. For Ben, it would be easy. Then move on to Walter and his wife. And he'd save a bullet for himself. He'd at least go out with some decency.

He took his change off the bar and walked to the back, closed himself into the phone booth. Dropped in some change and dialed his wife's number.

'MaryAnn!'

See? She was easier to read than Mute.

Ben said, 'It's me.'

'My God, Ben, where are you?'

'I'm in a ginmill in Hegewisch, I changed my mind about the deal.'

It was harder to do than he'd thought it would be. There was a pain that ran from his heart down into his stomach that made the cancer seem nearly mild by comparison. He heard her draw in her breath, and when she spoke her tone was soft, but there was an underlying edge of hysteria in her words.

'Ben, come home, right now. The boys are here and they need to see you. They need you, and so do I, all right, do you understand that? I *need* you, Ben.'

'I don't need you. I don't need anyone or anything. Not in this fucking life, and not in the next.'

Outside the booth, the jukebox went silent, and Ben knew that was a good thing because one of the cowboy pool players was loudly calling one of his friends a cocksucker. He opened the door to the booth so that Diane could hear the discussion.

'Ben, I've got a way to help you, we discussed it last night, *you gave me your word*!'

'I gave you the pipe, that's all I gave you.'

'Ben!' She was crying now.

'Forget about it, Diane. I don't want your help, and I don't want to see the kids. Forget about me, and forget about that bitch Ceterra. Keep the money I gave you for the kids, it's yours. Ceterra's a con artist. She'll rip you off. Whatever she's offering you, the city will give you double.'

'Ben, don't you do this to me, don't you do this to me again!'

'You shouldn't trust people, Diane. They'll use you every time.'

Ben hung up the phone and walked out of the booth, his face grim and angry. One of the cowboys looked over at him and smiled drunkenly, sarcastically, about to say something cute to him, Ben could tell. He reached into his pocket and stood his ground, the barrel of the .44 snub pointed at the man. He waited, and the guy saw what he was doing and looked away. Ben walked back toward Mute.

'Let's go,' Ben said, then walked out of the bar without bothering to check and see if Mute was following behind him.

Diane sat in the living room, on the couch, wondering if she should start a fire. She had MaryAnn's office number, and she had her beeper number, and she sat there wondering now if she should pick up the phone and call her. It was easier to think about than her boys – about their feelings, how they were upstairs rushing through their homework, expecting to see their father. What she could tell them now?

They'd be devastated if he didn't show up, or if he showed up drunk, dear God, as he had all their lives. If he came there drunk, she wouldn't let him in, would explain to the boys that the stress he was under had made him do something stupid. Again. To break their hearts. That miserable, rotten, no good son of a bitch.

He *would* be under stress, would want to revert back to what he'd been, to how he'd lived most of his life. But still, he'd made a deal, and he'd always prided himself on being something of a man of honor. He'd lived by his word for his entire life.

And now he'd broken it, smashed her trust again. What had he said to her? He'd laid the pipe last night. Taking their lovemaking and turning it into something dirty, something obscene. So he could be able to relate to it, the bastard.

She'd allowed herself to be manipulated again, let herself

be used. It was the price you paid for trusting people, for wanting to help them out. No, not people, just him. She would not stop trusting everyone because a man like Ben had hurt her.

She realized what a fool she'd been, how she'd wasted the past five years, pining over a man who was less than a man, was nothing more than a tough guy, a punk, with a lot of heart. He could fight all night and gamble all day and still get drunk and want to make love, but that didn't make him a man. That didn't even come close.

All right, so she'd go up and tell the boys, let their hearts be broken again, she'd watch them cry once more. And then it would be over. She'd apologize from the bottom of her heart, and assure them that it would never happen again. They'd wait for six months and after that there'd be nothing he could do ever to hurt them again.

Because he'd be dead. And good riddance.

Diane looked at her watch, saw that it was closing in on five. MaryAnn had said that the money would be in her hands by five, had made it clear, too, that the money had been hard to get. She wanted to do the deal right there in Diane's house, and Diane had thought that to be a good idea, had thought that Ben would be there, and he would know how to protect such a huge sum of cash. Now, having the thought of so much money around frightened her, made her shiver. Diane rubbed her arms.

Should she take the deal anyway? Take the cash and get out while she could? If MaryAnn was right the city would take her to the cleaners. But if she didn't take the deal, she could talk things over with Melissa, see what she might know about what the city had to offer. She should have called Melissa anyway, just to get advice. How stupid could she have been? If it hadn't been for her concern for Ben, she would have called Melissa, just to see what she thought of the deal.

But she hadn't, because MaryAnn had said that she didn't trust lawyers. Well, all of a sudden, out of a clear blue sky, Diane wasn't feeling so filled with trust herself.

She'd talk to the boys first, though, before she called MaryAnn. And when she did she would be polite but firm; the deal was off, and she could keep her damned money.

Ben drove quickly down the expressway, following Mute's instructions, asking the kid questions because it was the only way to shut him up about God. It was all the kid wanted to talk about, Jesus this, Jesus that. And he was supposed to be a hustler? But Ben wasn't too surprised, he'd seen enough conversions in the joint. Weak-minded people went one of two ways after life had kicked their ass hard enough to make them want to die: they either turned to dope, or they turned to the Lord. Sometimes they did both. Mute had picked on God.

Which made Ben feel less guilty over what he was laying on the guy, telling him that he was going to straighten out Walter, when in reality he was going out to kill Walter and his wife. And then himself. He didn't plan on coming out of this one alive, would not spend his last few months in the County, awaiting trial. For these murders or for the murder of Lino, one way or the other, the cops would take him down. Now that they knew he was dying, they'd go all out to put him away for his disrespect. It would be easier to die by his own hand than to die in a shootout with a couple of crooked cops who would come out of the thing as heroes.

His decision made, Ben was able to relax. He'd be saving Diane from a royal scam, even though she'd never know it, even though she'd always hate him. Saving a hell of a lot of other people, too, if Ben was right, because Walter and his wife wouldn't just be picking on Diane. There'd be dozens of people in this predicament that they might know about. People like that would be seeing themselves as doing those folks a favor.

Ben knew better. Knew that it was he who would be doing the world a favor tonight.

Mute would be as responsible for the murders as Ben himself, and if he didn't haul ass when he heard the gunshots, he'd do time for a couple of murders. Which was all right with Ben. Mute could practice what he'd been preaching in Stateville or Pontiac prison, saving the souls of men who needed it, rather than fucking with him.

'You want to be saved, Ben? I really think I got the power.'

'Mute . . .' Ben didn't know him well enough to tell him to shut up, and if he waved the gun the kid might grab at it, they'd be wrestling in the car, and the kid, he was big.

'I know, I know what you're trying to say,' Mute said. 'You're a skeptic, and I understand that, I used to be that way myself. But I'm telling you, from my heart, Ben, I believe I have the power.'

'Then use it to ask God to give you the strength to be quiet.'

That got to him, he took Ben's advice. Ben didn't hear another word from him until he said, sulking, 'You want to exit right here.'

MaryAnn had come home and sent Walter to his den, telling him to stay there until she came and told him it was all right to come out. He went, almost eagerly, and she watched him go, thinking. Had he enjoyed being ordered around? There were real possibilities, here. Look at him, in his silk robe, she could imagine that he had a hard-on as he was ordered to his den.

But there was no time for that, not right now. Later tonight, after the deal was done, she might come back home and test her theory. Ride him like a fucking bronco, pinch his nipples hard as she came. MaryAnn sat down on the sofa and waited for her delivery, letting her mind wander, letting the juices flow.

At five sharp, the doorbell rang, dragging her out of her fantasy.

'Who's that?' Mute wanted to know, and Ben told him that he wasn't sure. To wait a couple of minutes, maybe they'd find out. They sat and watched the man with the briefcase cuffed to his wrist as the guy stood on Walter's doorstep, rang the bell and looked around.

'You think he spotted us?'

'Fuck him if he did. He's a delivery boy. All he wants to do is get inside.'

'But he might tell Walter.'

'Walter's not going to be a problem.'

The guy looked past them, not paying much attention, but if he was a pro, he wouldn't have. Would have just kept in his mind the fact that they were there.

A woman answered the door and the man stepped inside without giving them another look. Good.

'That's her,' Mute said. 'What are we gonna do?'

Ben got out of the car and walked around to the passenger side. He said, 'Scoot over, get behind the wheel.'

'What do you want me to do?'

'If there's trouble, if I come out running, you drive.'

'Ben, I can't do that.'

'Look, you had to come along because I'd never have found the house. You told me that yourself. Now you fucking well shut that Jesus freak bullshit up and do what you're told, you got me?'

Mute began to get out of the car, and Ben took the pistol out of his pocket, pointed it at him.

'I've got your name. I'll find you if you run out on me. I'll stay alive long enough to hunt you down and kill everything you love.'

'God*damn*it,' Mute said. He sat back down, slid over behind the wheel. He pounded his fist on the steering wheel as Ben got into the car. 'See what I get, for trying to help?'

'Pray for strength, Mute,' Ben said, 'but don't do it so I can hear you.'

MaryAnn took the courier up to her bedroom, had him lay the briefcase down on the bed and uncuff himself while she watched. She counted the money out, every single bill, then signed his receipt and refused his offer to help her repack it in the briefcase, did it all herself and added her forty to the pile. He slid the cuffs on to the back of his belt, and

MaryAnn got to keep the briefcase. She walked him to the door and let him out, did not say good night as she closed it behind him. She was wearing her coat, with the pistol in the pocket, and her hand was on the trigger as she bolted the door behind the courier.

'You can come out now, Walter,' she hollered, and waited for him. He slunk out of his den, his eyes cast downward. Well, he couldn't hardly make it any more obvious.

She laughed at him.

'This is what you wanted all along, isn't it?'

'Whatever *you* want.'

'All these years.' MaryAnn's voice was distant. She was speaking more to herself than she was to her husband.

'You really had me fooled, Walter. If anything, I thought you'd want to swing the other way, from what you used to want to do to me before we got married, the things you made me do for the first few years after. Son of a bitch, you never know, do you?'

'I was wearing your clothing this afternoon!' It came out all in a rush, Walter getting it out before he changed his mind and didn't say anything about it.

'You want to wear my clothes, you worm?'

'Oh, God,' Walter said.

'You want to be humiliated?'

'Oh, dear God.'

'*Answer* me!'

'Yes!'

'Yes, *what*?'

'Yes, mistress.' His voice was low, breaking, Walter disgraced and loving it.

'You wait here for me. I have to go out for a while. When I get back, I'll show you what happens to bad boys.'

MaryAnn didn't hear his mumbled reply, she was already walking up the stairs. She had to go, and right now. If she toyed with Walter any longer she would get too far into it, would not be able to leave until she'd gotten off on his subservience. And she couldn't do that, she had a deal to close.

She hurried up the stairs and grabbed the briefcase off the bed, was walking to the bedroom door when the phone rang, startling her.

'I've got it, Walter!' she hollered out, then went over to the bedstand, grabbed the Princess out of its base.

'Yes?'

'MaryAnn?' It was Diane. MaryAnn smiled.

'I was just walking out the door to come see you. I've got your money, all right here in my hand.'

'I'm glad I caught you then, that was what I wanted to talk to you about.' MaryAnn did not care for the tone of Diane's voice, and she knew that she'd have to calm herself down. She couldn't allow the freedom she had with Walter to intrude on her business life; there were other ways to gain power over sellers, you couldn't just order them around.

MaryAnn said, 'I know what you're thinking. It's common, it happens all the time, Diane. Minutes before the deal closes, the seller gets cold feet, wants to back out. You're not the first one it's happened to, believe me.'

'Then you understand?'

'I understand that we have a deal. I understand that I moved heaven and hell to get you the money *you* asked for. I understand that if you back out, you'll get nothing from the city. I understand that if you go back on our oral agreement, I can sue you for damages. Now, Diane, do *you* understand?'

'MaryAnn, I didn't make any oral agreement.'

'Of course you did, when you agreed to the deal,' MaryAnn said, and the woman surprised her with the strength in her voice when she replied.

'Prove it,' Diane said. 'You don't come here, I don't want your money. If you come here I'll have you arrested –'

'Listen to *me*, lady, we had a deal!' MaryAnn screamed the words, thinking about the charges that James would want from her for the money, thinking about all the thousands that wouldn't go into her pocket. She realized that she was screaming into a dead phone, and she yelled even louder.

'You *bitch*!' MaryAnn slammed the phone down, hard. 'Nobody backs out of deals with me!'

She had been screaming so loudly that she didn't even hear the doorbell ring.

'Hello, Walter,' Ben said, and shoved the gun up under his nose, pushed him into the house. Ben kicked the door shut behind himself, and smiled.

'Long time no see.'

Walter was wearing a maroon silk robe, standing there with his skinny legs sticking out, horror-stricken.

'The little woman home, you thieving son of a bitch? Let's go say hello real quick, I've got something to say to the both of you. I want to tell you what happens to people who try to steal from my family.'

Mute sat in the car, his lips moving and his eyes shut tight, his knuckles white around where he gripped the steering wheel. His head was bowed down on it, Mute praying hard to the Lord Jesus Christ, needing another miracle, bad.

'Lord, let him come out of there without having done something stupid, *please*!' Mute didn't feel any warmth now, just the cold fear that had been gripping his spine since the second he'd seen the gun in Ben's hand. Ben was a good man, Mute could tell. A good man dying, who was only confused, who needed help.

'God, please, I'm begging you, this ain't like the track, this ain't like last night. You give me this, you let me get out of this without getting pinched, and I swear to you, God, I'll do your will the rest of my life.'

There was a wee, slight sense of warmth, beginning to loosen the ice on his spine.

'Praise Jesus,' Mute said, meaning it, and began to pray even harder. 'God, this is it, just one more night. I get away from this maniac, and I stay out of trouble forever. I don't steal, I don't gamble, I dedicate myself to Thee.'

The warmth was spreading even further, Mute felt himself relaxing.

'I'll do what's right, I swear to Thee. Find a good Christian woman and settle down, give whatever comes in from the lawyer to charity, and no more scams, ever, I'm through.'

The warmth filled him now; Mute felt the presence of the Lord, felt Jesus touching his shoulder. He began to cry, softly at first, then let them flow freely, feeling the power of God.

'Thank you, Jesus!' Mute shouted out.

He knew in his heart that he'd be a preacher, become born again, that he'd travel the country, singing the praises of the Lord. He'd get out of this, he felt it, there was no way he'd get busted. Ben would talk to Walter and Mute would get about the business of the Lord.

Mute looked up, through the windshield and out to the street, seeing the quiet neighborhood through streaks of tears.

He felt the cold fear come over him again as he saw the unmarked squad car pull to the curb, as he watched two fat cops get out and walk quickly up MaryAnn's sidewalk.

Ben pushed Walter up the stairs quickly, wanting to get him up there while the man was still in shock. He could use Walter's fear to his advantage, but he didn't know how long it would last, before Walter would scream out and give his wife a chance to lock herself in a room somewhere and call the cops on the phone.

'Get up there.' Ben said it savagely, kicking Walter from behind. Walter whimpered.

'You motherfucker, you fucking thief.' Ben was working himself up, for what he had to do.

They got to the top of the stairs just as a door opened, and a blonde woman began to walk out, carrying a brief case in one hand. She had a look of determination on her face until she spotted them, then the look turned to one of terror, and Ben pointed the pistol at her.

'Don't you move, lady, don't you move an inch.' He pushed Walter toward her, held them both in his sights.

'Listen, whatever this is, we can work it out. James sent you, didn't he, to rob this?' MaryAnn shook the briefcase. 'I knew he'd try it someday, he's no good, you have to understand that. He'll kill you as soon as he can, but *I* can make you happy.'

What the hell was she talking about? Ben didn't have time for this.

'In the bedroom, slowly. *Slowly*, lady, I ain't playing around with you!'

She backed into the bedroom, one hand holding the briefcase, the other at her side. Walter got in front of her, blubbering, and Ben couldn't see her right side anymore.

'We can make a deal, I can do things you never dreamed a woman could do for you.'

'You're a player, are you?' Ben walked through the bedroom door, saw that the woman's hand was in her pocket. 'Freeze!' He shouted it as he felt something burning at his side, saw the woman's coat pocket start on fire at the same time that he heard the boom of the pistol, saw her patting at the fire as Ben fell against the doorframe.

The fire saved his life. The woman saw it, began slapping at it with her hand, pulling her other hand out of her coat before it got burned, the gun still in it, pointed down as Ben shot her twice through the chest. He stood straight up as she was propelled backward by the two heavy shots, the gun booming in Ben's hand, trying to jump out of his fingers. He only had to shoot Walter once.

Ben ran to her and stumbled across the bed. There was something of value in the briefcase, something she thought some guy named James had sent him to steal. He had to see what it was. If it was money, the kids could use it.

Which meant he couldn't die here, he had to get away.

Ben grabbed the briefcase and got to his feet, ran for the bedroom door, was through it and on the staircase when the downstairs door came crashing in. He lifted the gun and fired twice more before he recognized who it was, saw Slinski fall to the floor, dead, and Midler behind him, staring down at his partner.

Ben wavered and pulled the trigger one more time, saw the window next to Midler explode and then he heard a click and knew that the gun was empty.

'You son of a bitch!' Midler said, as he began to point his gun at Ben. Ben tossed the briefcase down the stairway at Midler just as the gun blasted and the bullet hit him in the chest.

Ben propelled himself down the stairs, slamming into Midler, his momentum taking them both through the door, tumbling head over heels down the concrete steps. Ben felt faint, could feel nothing in his upper left chest; he used his right arm to punch at Midler, hitting him hard, as the two of them landed on the sidewalk.

Ben's forehead hit the concrete and he was stunned, seeing stars, his vision swimming as he fought to a sitting position, looked down and saw Midler lying there, his eyes wide open. He'd landed on top of Midler, had somehow broken his neck. The son of a bitch was dead. Good.

Now Ben could die in peace.

Ben sat there, breathing hard, spitting up gobs of blood, shaking his head, the briefcase beside him, upset only at the fact that he wouldn't be able to get it to his wife. Mute would have taken off when he heard the gunshots, he couldn't count on a guy like Mute. The cops would come, somebody would call them, but he wouldn't make it that long, he could feel the life slipping out of him.

Ben sat there, awaiting death, when the pain came into his chest.

He hollered, loud, as he felt himself being pulled to his feet.

Mute. Mute. The son of a bitch, he was still here.

'Get the briefcase!' Mute didn't seem to hear him, was pulling Ben toward the car, which was idling at the curb. Ben struggled, tried to pull free. 'I need that fucking briefcase!'

He felt Mute shove him, then felt a cold material on his cheek. Ben was facedown on his back seat, smelling eight-year-old Cadillac leather. He felt something solid land on his back, then heard the car pull from the curb in a long loud shriek of rubber. He struggled to sit up, made it, saw that the briefcase was on the floor.

It hurt like hell to lean down and pick it up, Ben's chest was on fire, he could hardly breathe. He felt thick blood running down his chin. He popped the snaps on the briefcase.

Sat looking down at a case filled with hundreds, Ben Franklin looking up at him, wise Ben smiling. Dumb Ben, dying Ben, had a smile left to return.

'Mute.' Ben didn't know if he'd said it loud enough to be heard. He tried again. 'Mute!'

'What, Ben, relax back there!'

'Mute, it's important, Mute, I need your help.' The words were hard to come by, Ben could barely get them out.

'I believe I've helped you all that I'm likely to.' The kid was shaken up, scared to death.

Ben wanted to tell Mute that he'd been a thief all his life, wanted to tell him that he'd been one, but he'd changed. Mute couldn't steal anymore, Mute couldn't take this money. This money was for his kids! Mute had to understand that. God would not want him to steal it!

Ben wanted to tell Mute these things, but he couldn't, he didn't have the strength.

Ben shouted out an address, and heard Mute ask what he'd said. He shouted it out again, said to give the briefcase to his wife. Said something else that was important to him before his voice gave out on him. Ben managed to close the briefcase then fell back, Ben in agony, waiting for the end.

He felt the car stop and wondered if the cops had found them, if this kid Mute would do time for having helped him out. He hoped not, Mute had shown that he was a stand-up guy. Even if he stole the money, Mute was still a stand-up guy.

It was the highest form of praise that Ben Morer was capable of giving.

He heard Mute's voice, closer now, from above him. The kid sounded like he was crying, near-hysterical, his voice filled with panic.

Mute said, 'Ben, do you accept Jesus Christ as your Saviour?'

What the fuck?

'Ben, are you sorry for all the sins of your life?'

Ben hadn't realized that he'd slipped to the floor until he opened his eyes. He looked up, saw Mute's face, that ugly mug above him, all twisted up in his suffering. Mute's lips were curled back and trembling; Ben could feel Mute's saliva dripping down on to his forehead.

Then he got it, what the kid was doing. If he'd had the strength, he would have laughed.

'Ben, can you hear me? Do you accept Jesus as your Saviour?!'

'I do,' Ben said. The words came out with a burst of blood.

'*Are you sorry, Ben*!' Mute was shouting down at him. The kid panicked, trying to save Ben's soul. Or maybe something else. Maybe if Ben gave in the kid would take the money to his wife.

Ben started to say the address again, and felt Mute slap him hard.

'Fuck that, I heard the address! Are you sorry for all the sins of your life!'

'I'm sorry,' Ben said, and felt the pain going away. He felt almost good, knew that death was near.

'All right.'

Ben felt the car take off again, and lay there looking at the velour that covered the inside roof of his car. He felt his blood slowing in his veins, felt his heart slowing down. He wasn't afraid; it was better than he'd thought it could be. At least it didn't hurt anymore. At least he'd be through suffering. He'd never been much of a player, had lost the heart for it somewhere down the road. The only regret he had was that he hadn't seen his kids. Maybe they'd understand someday, maybe they'd remember him well.

With a sigh of relief Ben Morer turned his head to the back of the seat and died, smiling as the rattlesnakes finally, forever fell silent.

It was more money than Mute had ever seen in his life.

He left Ben's car in the South Shore Station parking lot,

knowing that the body would be found before morning. He walked quickly away from it, needing to get home, to walk the two blocks to his apartment before someone noticed him. As it was he might have been spotted through the South Shore Inn's window, or by someone waiting for a train, hell, it wasn't even six yet, there were plenty of people out.

'God, don't let me get caught.'

It became his mantra as he walked, Mute feeling the blood drying on his arms, Ben's blood that had spilled there as he'd lifted the man off the sidewalk. He should have left him there, should have taken off. If he had, he wouldn't be an accomplice to murder. If he had, he could be at the bar right now, having a cold one and trying to forget what he'd seen that night.

But if he had, he wouldn't have had all this money, now would he?

Mute made it to his apartment door without passing anyone he knew, not even Mrs Calloway, thank God. That was all he'd need; the woman would put it together as sure as he was born. The blood on Mute, the body a few blocks away. She'd have to call the cops and tell them, too, she'd had trouble with a killer once before. With that Thom Geere guy that she was always going on about.

Mute didn't even bother to lock the door to his room, just grabbed a clean pair of pants and a shirt, some underwear and his toilet kit, and headed for the bathroom.

He stripped quickly, with the door locked, the briefcase underneath the claw-foot bathtub. Thank God there'd been no piss in the tub tonight. Mute lowered himself into the tub, feeling a little better as the warm water encased his body. He had the check, back in his room, hidden between the pages of the bottom copy of the stack of *Soldier of Fortunes*. He'd take it with him, cash it from out of town.

He couldn't stick around now, as cops had been killed. And he knew that even after all the surgery, he had a pretty recognizable face. If there had been any witnesses, if anyone had peeked out their windows, they'd look through the mug shot book and Mute would go down for life. Might even get the chair, seeing as cops had died.

Mute could almost feel the money underneath him, burning through the bottom of the tub. What he could do with that kind of cash – there had to be a hundred grand there, maybe more.

It was a pattern now, and he recognized it. He prayed, and he got something good, then he fucked up again and got punished. There would have to be a hell of a lot of punishment to make up for this kind of money. God must be planning something seriously bad for him tomorrow. Tomorrow, when Mute would be history, would take his fake driver's licenses and his money and be gone.

Quickly, urgently, Mute began to scrub his massive body.

Diane sat in the kitchen, at the table, with her sons. Their disappointment was evident on their faces, but they were being strong for her. It had been Diane who had broken down, who'd cried like a baby as she'd explained things to them, and they'd comforted their mother, come to her and held her, told her that they hadn't really expected their father to show up in the first place.

He was a bum, John had told her, and Benny hadn't argued.

They were playing Parcheesi now, the three of them pretending that everything was all right. It was the only way that they could handle it right now. There'd be time enough to talk tomorrow, and the next day, and for however long that they needed. Tonight was for acting normal, to pretend that nothing had happened.

Although she knew that something had; for a moment, she'd felt love again.

Which told her that she was still capable of it. And it was time to open herself up to it.

Diane reached up and wiped at a tear, sniffled, and the boys ignored it, did not make a big thing out of it, sensing her need for normalcy.

'It's your roll, Benny, come on, what are you doing?' John

was angry, taking his anger out on his brother, who seemed to understand. He didn't start to argue, didn't assert his status as the elder.

The doorbell rang and the three of them jumped, then Diane composed herself and got to her feet.

'I'll see who it is,' she said. 'You two stay right here.'

She walked to the door, knowing it was Ben, knowing that he was drunk, knowing what she would say and do. She was capable of loving again, but not him, not with him. He would have to die as he had lived, alone, all by himself. And if she was wrong, if it was that MaryAnn Ceterra, well, there were a few things that Diane could say to her, too.

She had either speech prepared as she threw open the door.

Stood looking at the ugliest man she'd ever seen, perhaps the most muscular, too, standing there staring at her, holding a briefcase in his hand.

'You Ben's wife?' His voice was soft, non-threatening. The sound of it slightly eased the terror she felt at the sight of him on her doorstep.

'Don't worry about it, ma'am,' he said. 'Everyone looks like that when they see me the first time.'

She realized she'd been gaping, and she swallowed hard.

'I'm sorry.'

'Ben said to give this to you. Said it was for the kids.'

'What?'

'Ben, he's your husband, right? I got the right address?'

'Yes, yes, I'm sorry, you startled me.'

He held the briefcase out toward her, and she reached for it tentatively, their hands touching as it changed hands.

'This is for the kids,' the man said, then turned his back and began to walk away.

'Wait!' Diane hollered, then lowered her voice. 'Please, wait.' He turned to her, his eyebrows raised, that ugly face looking at her, eyes blazing into hers. She could smell his cologne, mixed with something, some sort of soap.

'What?'

'Where's, where's Ben? Is he coming here later?'

'No ma'am,' the man said. 'He won't be coming here no more.'

Then his face softened and Diane somehow knew that behind that horrible face he was doing the very best that he could to look at her with compassion.

'But he died in a state of grace, I think you ought to know that.'

Then he turned again and walked away, and Diane closed the door, reached up quickly and turned the deadbolt.

She went over to the couch and heard Benny calling from the kitchen.

'Mom? Mom, was that *him*?'

'No,' Diane said, then popped the latches on the briefcase, slowly opened the lid.

She immediately slammed it shut, sat staring at the wall, both hands on top of the case, as if what was inside would bite her. She took a couple of deep breaths, and shook her head to clear it. Then lifted the lid a few inches again, saw that the briefcase was still filled with money.

'For the kids,' the man had told her. Ben had left it for the kids.

'Mom? Is everything all right?' It was John this time, speaking in fear, from the kitchen doorway. 'You okay?'

Diane snapped the lid shut, closed the latches with her thumbs.

'Everything's just fine, boys,' she said. She put the briefcase down beside the couch, between the couch and the wall. She would deal with it later. He'd left it for the kids. And to the kids it would go. But not right now, she couldn't think about it now.

Now, Diane said, 'Come on, boys, let's finish the game, all right?' Forcing herself to smile, she put an arm around either son and walked back toward the table, almost collapsing halfway there, needing her sons to keep her from falling.

'Mom!' Benny was terrified.

'I'll be all right, I'll be all right.' Diane took a second, tried to compose herself, let the boys walk her to the chair and felt them easing her down.

She buried her head in her hands and she cried, for Ben, who had died in a state of grace, the man had said.

'Mom?!' John's voice was tinged with panic, she had to control herself.

'It's your turn, Mom,' Benny said, his voice strong, and Diane was grateful.

She nodded her head and wiped her eyes and sniffed. Then she sat up straight and picked up her small round cup, shook the dice inside then let them roll out on to the table.

Also by Eugene Izzi in Arrow

BULLETIN FROM THE STREET

The murder count has been high for a Chicago winter, and when a black woman is elected mayor it looks set to increase.

A fanatical preacher, The Reverend Afrikaan, is stirring the black population into a racist frenzy while a group of vicious white supremacists seize the opportunity to get even. A race war of apocalyptic proportions is about to explode.

Barry Henry, Denise Durkin and her homeless friend, Booker, are struggling to survive the rising heat of violence. No laws can protect them now, and Henry should know, he's about to get kicked off the vice squad for using the only laws that work – his own. If they stay off the streets they might pull through. But it isn't that simple. An insane doctor has moved from euthanasing AIDS victims to spearing hobos, and now he's zeroed in on Booker.

'Eugene Izzi is a pro, one of the very best in the crime field.'
Elmore Leonard

SAFE HARBOUR

Tommy Torrelli, a New York wiseguy and right-hand man to the boss of bosses, goes for the score of his career, the one that will get him out of crime and into a normal life for him and his son. But he gets busted and when the mob threaten the life of his son he talks, and enters the witness protection programme.

Now, fifteen years later, he has escaped the Programme with a new identity thanks to a sympathetic fed. Tommy has become Mark Torrence, with a wife, three kids, a home in Chicago, a job helping reform young offenders – and a new character. He thinks he has left the past behind. But knows he is fooling himself.

The people he shopped years ago have not forgotten him. Photos of his new home have started to appear on someone's desk in New York, and the most ruthless hitman in America, a killer who doesn't even consider himself human, smells revenge . . .

TRIBAL SECRETS

To his millions of fans, Babe Hill is the rich, reclusive star of his own television series, a man who defied Hollywood and made it on his own. But to the few who know his past, he is something else: part of a violent criminal family, the part that got away . . .

Or did he? Here on Chicago's rage-filled streets, no one can outrun their past – and Babe knows it. He knows even before he hears of his father's lethal mob debts, before his depraved younger brother embarks on a murderous rampage, and before an obsessed fan starts stalking him.

He hasn't escaped. He has to go back. Back to the bloody streets where he grew up. And back to fight the most intimate enemies a man can have – enemies tied to him by blood and history, who have the power to destroy him . . .

'A brilliant bouquet . . . of lush orchids and razor tipped thorns. Crime master Eugene Izzi takes us deep into that ultimate underworld . . . the human heart.'
Andrew Vachss, author of *Sacrifice and Flood*

Acclaimed crime fiction by James Ellroy in Arrow

THE BLACK DAHLIA

A chilling novel based on Hollywood's most notorious murder case.

Los Angeles, 10th January 1947: a beautiful young woman walked into the night and met her horrific destiny.

Five days later, her tortured body was found drained of blood and cut in half. The newspapers called her 'The Black Dahlia'. Two cops are caught up in the investigation and embark on a hellish journey that takes them to the core of the dead girl's twisted life . . .

'One of those rare, brilliantly written books you want to press on other people' – ***Time Out***

'A wonderful tale of ambition, insanity, passion and deceit' – ***Publishers Weekly***

THE BIG NOWHERE

1950s Los Angeles: The City of Angels has become the city of the Angel of Death.

Communist witch-hunts and insanely violent killings are terrorising the community. Three men are plunged into a maelstrom of violence and deceit when their lives become inextricably linked as each one confronts his own personal darkness . . .

'Ellroy is a unique voice in American fiction'
– **Jonathan Kellerman**

'Epic, obsessively imagined history.' – ***The Face***

'Like Hammett and Chandler, but Ellroy adds layers they never dared. One of the most compelling crime novels in a long time' – ***Philadelphia Enquirer***

WHITE JAZZ

Los Angeles, 1958: a city on the make. A boom town at the edge of a new era ripe for plunder.

Lieutenant Dave Klein: in turn a lawyer, bagman, slum landlord, mob killer. Klein stands at the centre of a complex web of plots where violence and death will intersect.

'A vivid enthralling read . . . James Ellroy is the outstanding American crime-writer of his generation'
– **Peter Gutteridge, *Independent***

'At last, the final part of James Ellroy's LA Quartet is available.' With it, he has completed a climb to the very pinnacle of crime writing. Names like Robert B Parker, George V Higgins and Elmore Leonard certainly don't pale into significance, but they don't shine so brightly any more. *White Jazz* is without doubt his best yet'
– **Marcin Miller, *City Limits***

'Recent novels by the likes of Carl Hiaasen, Andrew Vachss and George V Higgins . . . James Ellroy . . . may be the exception. He seems in less danger of burnout than of going supernova' – **John Williams, *New Statesman and Society***

DICK CONTINO'S AND OTHER STORIES

Dick Contino – 50s accordion player, a star in the making, is destroyed by a draft-dodging scandal. His life is on the skids until he comes up with the idea of resurrecting his career with a fake kidnapping scam.

Meanwhile a serial killer is on the loose in Los Angeles . . . a killer who is closer to Contino than he suspects – a killer who wants in on the kidnap, *for real* . . .

Plus five previously unpublished short stories.

'The outstanding American crime-writer of his generation' – **Peter Gutteridge, *Independent***

'James Ellroy writes like a man possessed about men possessed' – **David Pascoe, *Modern Review***

'Not since the days of Hammett and Chandler has the crime novel been so eloquent or seductive' – ***Vox***

BROWN'S REQUIEM

Los Angeles – Fritz Brown, ex-alcoholic private eye with a stained past, makes do with car repossessions and classical music. Then he is offered a case by Freddy 'Fat Dog' Baker, an eccentric golf caddy whose sister has made off with a much older man.

This is the beginning of the nightmare: the underworld of golf caddies, arson and incest played against the backdrop of an LA surreal by night and bad by day; of long hidden secrets that will drive Brown back to the bottle and to the gun: all conspire to make this one of the most hypnotic crime novels ever written.

Brown's Requiem was James Ellroy's first novel and was the first in which his obsession with Los Angeles and its criminal underworld was realised.

'An undeniably artful frenzy of violence, guilt and unappeased self-loathing, Ellroy's crime fiction represents a high mark in the genre' – ***New York Newsday***

'Ellroy is a master at juggling plot lines, using a stripped spare *noir* style that hits like a cleaver but is honed like a scalpel'
– ***Chicago Tribune***

AMERICAN TABLOID

1958 – America is about to emerge into a bright new age – an age that will last until the 1000 days of John F. Kennedy's presidency.

Three men move beneath the glossy surface of power; men allied to the makers and shakers of the era. Pete Bondurant – Howard Hughes's right-hand man, Jimmy Hoffa's hitman. Kemper Boyd – employed by J. Edgar Hoover to infiltrate the Kennedy clan. Ward Littell, a man seeking redemption in Bobby Kennedy's drive against organised crime.

The festering discontent of the age that burns brightly in these men's hearts will go into supernova as the Bay of Pigs ends in calamity, the Mob clamours for payback and the 1000 days ends in brutal quietus in 1963.

'Intense and flamboyant . . . excellent. The plot runs on high-octane violence . . . a powerful book . . . one emerges breathless, shaken and ready to change one's view of recent American history' – **Savkar Altinel, *Sunday Telegraph***

'Brilliant and appalling. It is deeply repelling portraiture, yet mesmerising' – **Marcel Berlins, *Times***

'Laconic violence, terse, slang-driven sentences, and a gleeful blurring of the moral line between good guys and bad guys . . . Seven hundred pages of this stuff left me feeling punch-drunk and dizzy, but then it sure beats the hell out of Anita Brookner' – **Jonathan Coe, *Mail on Sunday***

'A frenetic and explosive thriller . . . Ellroy is said to document the "underbelly" of America, but underbelly, my foot. This is the backside, the inside, the blood and the guts' – **Sabine Durrant, *Sunday Times***